The
Rainbow

BOOKS BY CARLY SCHABOWSKI

CARLY SCHABOWSKI

The
Rainbow

Bookouture

Published by Bookouture in 2021

An imprint of Storyfire Ltd.
Carmelite House
50 Victoria Embankment
London EC4Y 0DZ

www.bookouture.com

ISBN: 978-1-80019-810-4
eBook ISBN: 978-1-80019-809-8

*To Grandad, and to all the Polish men who found themselves
forced into the wrong army.*

PROLOGUE

This is Poland.

I sit on the bank of the river, my feet in the cold water, watching the ripples they make against the flow. There is a field behind the river that holds the ruins of an ancient gypsy caravan and a rusting tractor. The paint is almost gone now from the rotting wood, but flecks of it hold on, showing that it was once painted in bright blues, reds and greens. Its wind chime still hangs from the roof, tinkling and singing in the almost still evening air.

It is getting late in the day now; the last rays of sun dance upon the water and a breeze blows through the trees, making the leaves whisper to each other. I wrap my scarf around my neck – a scarf made of the thinnest, finest silk; stripy, like the colours of the rainbow. It was my grandfather's scarf, once, here, long ago.

There is a diary beside me, and it is falling apart. The binding has let go of the pages, so the insides spill messily. There's a sudden breeze which lifts the edges of the pages and they begin to flap like a baby bird's wings – testing to see if they can take flight. On top sits a medal, dull and uncared for, but it weighs down the cover, keeping the stories inside.

The diary's curling yellowed pages are filled with neat lines of the writing of a young man who is keen not to forget, and careful drawings of people, of cities – Kraków, London, Paris; then of men with guns, of barbed wire, of trenches. Then the diary stops. The young man disappears from the pages never to return, never to explain who he once was or who he would become.

Yet, there are stories that I sit here and remember, told to me as a child by my grandfather, of horses, caravans, and a man wearing a scarf, whose hair is blown by the wind; of a boy who spent a childhood running through green fields, stealing apples from orchards and swinging from branches of trees with his friends. And I sit and wonder if this boy could truly grow up to be the man in these diaries, the man with this dull medal for bravery, a medal that is the wrong type, coming from the wrong side.

It's hard to know where the story truly begins. But then, of course, the only place to start is at the very beginning, when the past intruded into my life on a cold January day, finally taking me back here, to the banks of this very river, in this very field, to meet someone I had always thought I knew.

CHAPTER ONE

Isla

England, 2015

Sheep-freckled fields greeted me as I drove through the narrow village lanes towards my grandparents' house, lifting my spirits from the drabness of London, the endless grey buildings and exhaust fumes. I opened the window, letting the icy bite of January air into the car, breathing it in and welcoming the cool catch of it at the back of my throat. In almost every village, church spires grasped their way towards the heavens, and gravestones leaned into sunken soil; the engraved tributes to their dead, covered with moss and smoothed from years of unpredictable English weather. It was quieter here. No swish, swish of tyres like the city, no honking from irate drivers, only the sweet trill of birds as they flew, landed, then hopped from branch to branch, their eyes keenly scouting the cold ground for food.

The sun peeked out from behind powder-puff clouds as I turned into their driveway, where their house sat back, alone, old and frail as the two of them. Once a stone farmhouse with tended gardens and fields that travelled in every direction, it was now crumbling with the ivy that grew through the cracks in the brick cement, the garden overgrown and encroaching upon the house, the fields empty and barren, with thick, muddy tracks where hikers clomped through them on their way to the Thames.

I waited a moment before knocking on the door, feeling guilty as I looked at the faded, peeling cornflower-blue paint on the windowsills and the few tiles on the roof that were promising to fall away with the next strong gust of wind. We needed to help more. Me, Dad and Mum. We had to get the house in better shape for them.

Suddenly, the door flew open, revealing Gran with her hair in hot-pink rollers.

'Isla!' She grabbed me and drew me close. 'Happy birthday!'

I kissed her papery cheek, smelling her rose-scented face cream. 'It was last week,' I said. 'I got your card and the bottle of wine, though.'

She ushered me in, closing the door against the chill, which, quite frankly was pointless as the house felt colder and damper than the outside.

'Doesn't matter. We're celebrating it today. I made a cake and put my hair in these things so it would be all special for you.' She patted the rollers, which were threatening to come loose at any moment.

'Thanks, Gran.' I wrapped my arm around her tiny frame. 'You're the best, you know that?'

'Oh, I know! Of course I am.' She shuffled away from me into the kitchen where a pot bubbled furiously on the stove. 'Don't touch that!' she yelled at me as my hand hovered over the pot lid, ready to let the air escape.

'It's going to boil over,' I said.

'No, it won't.' She pushed me aside towards the rocking chair she kept close to the oven. 'Sit down and warm yourself up.'

I did as I was told, thankful for the heat. 'Why isn't the heating on?'

'No need for it in here. I've got the fire on in the living room for your grandad. That's enough. You young people have no tolerance. When I was young, we didn't have central heating, just put a cardigan on and that was that. Besides' – she eyed me closely – 'didn't you know that there's global warming? I heard about it on the news,' she said conspiratorially.

'I had heard, yes.' I grinned at her.

'So you see then, I'm just doing my part.' She walked to the kettle, pulling at the rollers, finally freeing her wiry hair.

'How is he?' I asked, nodding towards the closed living room door.

'Not bad. He knew what day it was and remembered what he had for breakfast, so I think today is a good day.' She turned and winked at me.

'I'm just going to go and say hello,' I told her.

'Good, good, ask him if he wants a cup of tea. I'll bring the cake in, in a minute.'

The living room was stuffed with antique bookshelves that threatened to spill their contents out onto the thick blue carpet. Grandad was sitting next to one, a book on his blanketed lap, but his eyes were not focused on it. Instead, he stared at the fire as the flames leaped and licked at the burning logs.

For a moment he didn't notice I was there, and it gave me a second or two to see how he had aged again in only a month. Once tall and proud with a crop of snow-white hair, he was shrunken, his hair thinning and his skin sunken into his cheeks. Even his hands seemed to have changed again, thinner, bonier, as if he were morphing into someone else, or rather, disappearing altogether.

'Ah! Birthday girl!' He finally saw me and, grinning, held his arms out for me to give him a hug. 'You see, I remember,' he whispered into my ear as we embraced. 'I say to your gran that I can still remember things, but she thinks maybe not.'

I pulled away; a small lump had caught in my throat after feeling how frail he was in my arms. 'Yes, Grandad, you remembered,' I told him, sitting across from him on the purple sofa.

'I remember all sorts of things, you know. Just this morning I say to your gran, "Look outside, Jack Frost has been!" His English was still muddled after all these years, his Polish accent still thick on his tongue.

'It's just frost, Grandad, there's no Jack Frost!'

He shook his head. 'I tell you, one time I look in the garden, many, many years ago, and I see a little man, looking cold and blue and running around making the frost on the ground. I know it was him, Jack Frost.'

I nodded, indulging him in his make-believe, remembering how he always told me he used to be friends with a magician, a man who could make a rainbow appear in the sky.

'It's your birthday next,' I told him, as Gran carefully made her way into the room, her hands holding a tray filled with a pot of tea and slices of cake.

I stood and took it from her, placing it on the large walnut coffee table that dominated the centre of the room.

'Not for six months,' Gran said, handing him some cake, then sitting down next to me. 'His ninety-fifth.'

'We ought to do something special, Grandad. Something big,' I said.

He was concentrating on the piece of strawberry cake, shovelling it into his mouth and spilling crumbs all over himself. He looked at me, confusion in his eyes for a moment, then asked, 'Isla, when is your birthday?'

'It's today, love.' Gran spoke for me. 'It's today.'

'Ah, happy birthday!' he said, then returned to his cake.

I looked at Gran; she had said that today was a good day. Of course I knew that even on a good day his dementia could take him away from us for moments, minutes, even hours at a time, but it still caught me off guard.

She patted my hand. 'No point telling him it already happened,' she said quietly. 'Keep things current, it's easier for him.'

'What have the doctors said?' I asked.

'He's all right for now.' She looked at the plate on her own lap and picked up a small piece of cake between her fingers, squishing it. 'He's all right for now.'

Grandad had leaned back in his chair, the cake gone. He was ready for a nap, and his lids drooped heavily over his eyes.

'So, a big birthday for him, you said?' Gran bustled about, taking the plate from him, pulling the blanket over his lap and dusting away the crumbs. 'I like that idea.'

'You don't think it will be too much for him?'

'No,' she said quietly, as she tucked a piece of stray hair behind his ear. 'It might be his last one.'

As soon as she said that, I was in tears. She ushered me out of the living room and back into the kitchen, soothing me as if I were a baby again.

'Shhh, it's all right,' she said, rubbing my shoulder. 'You must have thought it too.'

I nodded. I had thought it might be his last birthday with us, but I had put it into a dusty corner of my mind.

'Come on. Hush now. Let's think about what we can do for him for his birthday. That'll give us both something to concentrate on.'

I wiped my eyes with the back of my sleeve, feeling foolish that at thirty-six I still needed my gran to make me feel better.

'What about his brother?' I finally asked when I had composed myself, remembering the birthday and Christmas cards that came from Poland like clockwork, always signed 'Andrzej'.

'What, you want him to come here?' she asked, sitting down at the kitchen table. 'I doubt he will.'

'Why not?'

'Oh gosh, Isla, they've barely spoken in decades, you know that. Some falling out over something or other.'

'I know, I know,' I said. 'But what if this is their last chance to see each other? Does Andrzej even know how sick he is?'

Gran shook her head. 'You can let him know if you want to, but I doubt you'll hear from him.'

'I can try,' I said. 'It might help him, you know, seeing his brother, remembering his past – he might be able to remember more.'

'Like I said, you can try, but don't expect much. His cards are in a box somewhere. Probably in the attic with all the Christmas stuff. I'm sure there was a return address on it. Go and have a look, and I'll make us some more tea.' She pushed herself up to standing, then waited a moment before moving.

'Are you OK?'

'Fine, fine. Just got to get the blood moving before I set off,' she said, ignoring my concern and made her way to the kettle.

I was halfway up the attic stairs when she shouted to me, 'Isla, see if you can find the photo albums too. They're in there somewhere. Get them out, would you?'

'Yes, Gran.'

'Oh, and if you do see it – but only if you see it, mind you – I had a big winter coat up there, black, woollen. I can't find it for the life of me.'

'Yep, anything else?' I shouted back.

'I'll let you know.'

I finished my ascent into the dusty attic space, which was jammed with boxes, old clothes, suitcases and furniture. The bare bulb that hung in the middle of the room did little to illuminate the space. *In boxes, she said – which box?* There were dozens of them, each spilling out their contents; here was a shoe with a heel that their dog had chewed when I was little. I picked it up. *Why would she keep this?* Then, another box half ripped with old bills spilling out, some of them nibbled at by the attic's inhabitants. I shuddered. *Mice.*

The thought of the rodents made me move quicker, inspecting each box briefly, not daring to shove in my hand in case a furry friend was sleeping at the bottom.

I soon found the coat she was talking about. The buttons were missing, hence its banishment into the attic. I placed it to one side and stepped over two brown leather suitcases that had fading tickets on them – Egypt, America, France.

The next box yielded some treasure. First, Christmas cards from family and friends over the years – again, why had she kept them all? Then, in amongst them, a few from my great-uncle, a man who I had never met, and who had never wanted to meet me.

The most recent card came in an envelope from five years ago. I scrabbled about trying to find one from last year, or the year before, but couldn't. His address was written on the reverse in neat cursive, an address in a place that I recognised the name of – Zakopane. That was where Grandad had said he'd spent a summer holiday, at a lake house his uncle owned. I shoved the card into my jeans pocket and began to search for the elusive photo albums.

A box revealed one photo album, its cover a faded green; inside were photos of my grandparents at their wedding, summer holidays at the beach, and a few pictures of my dad in his pram. I smiled at each picture as I flicked through them, wondering if I could maybe scan them into the computer and do a slideshow or something on Grandad's birthday.

Just as I decided my search was complete, something at the bottom of the box caught my eye. A red, green, yellow and blue material was neatly folded as if it contained a present within. I picked it up and as I did, it unfolded, revealing itself to be a silk scarf. I ran it through my fingers, noticing as I did a few dark splotches staining it, and a few tiny holes from years of use. I couldn't remember Gran or Grandad wearing it. Perhaps Dad?

I wrapped it around my neck and placed my palm on the dusty floorboards to push myself up. When I did, I felt something under my hand; a piece of paper, again neatly folded. Had it fallen from the scarf when it unravelled?

I opened it to reveal a newspaper article written in German, a faded picture of two men in German army uniforms staring at the camera. It meant little to me, and I was about to fold it up and place it back in the box of forgotten things when a name jumped out at me in the text: Tomasz Jasieński.

I knew that name.

It was Grandad's.

Suddenly, my mind could not focus properly. Grandad in a picture wearing a German uniform, in a German newspaper. But Grandad was Polish. He had fought for the British when he came here; I had seen his medals and photographs. Why was he in this picture? What did it mean? Was Grandad a Nazi?

It wasn't him. It couldn't be him, I decided. It was just another man with the same name. But why had he kept it?

'Isla!' Gran's voice rang out. 'Are you still up there? Are you OK? Did you find the coat?'

I nodded as if she could see me, then realising she couldn't, shouted back, 'I'll be there in a minute.'

I stood, putting the newspaper clipping in my pocket, collected the photo album and coat and headed back downstairs.

'You all right, love?' Gran asked as I walked into the kitchen. 'You look a bit pale. Did you see a mouse? They won't hurt you, you know, tiny little things they are. More scared of you than you are of them.'

I sat in the rocking chair, the picture in my pocket begging to be let out and looked at again.

'Where'd you get that?' Gran was looking at my neck.

'This?' I'd forgotten I even had it. 'I found it in a box.'

She stepped towards me and reached out her hand as if she were going to touch the scarf, then suddenly drew her hand back as if it had scolded her.

'What is it?' I asked. 'Should I put it back?'

'No, no. It's fine.' She opened a cupboard door. 'Now, what shall I make for dinner?'

'Gran, what is it?' I pushed. 'Whose scarf is it?'

'Oh, I don't know,' she said, but she wouldn't look at me. 'It's fine. Keep it.'

'Gran,' I said, pulling the newspaper clipping from my pocket. 'There's something else I found.'

Again, she would not look at me, and concentrated on taking tins of beans and soup out of the cupboard.

'Gosh, this cupboard is a mess. Needs sorting. How am I supposed to know what to cook if I can't find what I need?'

'Gran, please.' I stood and showed her the picture. 'Is this Grandad? What does it mean?'

Her eyes barely glanced at the picture. 'Oh, don't be daft. That's not your grandfather.'

'But it's his name.'

'Lots of people have that name.' She now took a tin of tomato soup and inspected the label. 'Look here, it says three hundred calories. That can't be good, can it?'

'Gran!' I exclaimed, desperate for her attention.

'What, Isla?' She turned now to look at me, her eyes narrowed behind her thick glasses. 'What? I've told you that's not him. I don't know why it was up there. Perhaps your grandad thought it was funny that there was another man with the same name. What do I know? And no, before you ask, you *cannot* ask him.'

Her voice had taken on an edge to it that I had never heard before, and for a moment, I didn't recognise her. Then, as if nothing had happened, she grabbed the tea caddy and asked, 'Cup of tea then, before you get going?' her voice sweet and innocent, confusing me, silencing me and making me wish I had never said a thing.

CHAPTER TWO

The weather turned that evening. The rain splotched against the windows like thick tears, whilst birch trees clattered their empty branches against one another in the wind. My second-floor flat looked out onto a communal garden where tarnished winter leaves gathered in clumps, rotting away into the flower beds. I was sitting with my legs folded under me, a blanket on my lap, watching one of the raindrops tracking its way down the pane, distorting the wintery image outside, when the phone rang, then immediately went to voicemail.

'*It isn't him.*' Gran's voice filled my flat. There was a pause as her raspy voice caught on the words – she wanted to cry. '*Please don't say any more about it…*' She stopped, then a slight cough as if she was readying herself to say more. Instead, she hung up.

I felt guilty that I had pushed her on the picture I had found, but her reaction to it, and the scarf, was so strange, so uncomfortable, that I knew she was hiding something. But whatever it was, she wasn't going to tell me.

I looked again at the picture. Grainy black and white, two German soldiers standing side by side; one smiling, the other not. I knew one of the men, no matter what Gran said – that dimple in his cheek, that deep crease in his forehead. It was Tomasz Jasieński – my grandfather.

With the help of the internet, I managed to translate most of the article, which told the story of a brave Polish man who had joined the German army in the fight for the Fatherland, and upon doing so, earned himself the golden German Cross for acts of bravery which had involved the killing of partisans in the Ukraine.

Tomasz Jasieński. Tomasz Jasieński who I knew as my lovable grandfather, who taught me to ride a bike, who told me stories as I sat on his lap, who talked to his plants and saved bumblebees when they were baffled in the summer's heat. But he was also a man who had killed people. A man who had fought for the German army. A man I did not know at all.

I stood and poured myself a large gin and tonic, the ice rattling in the glass as I sat back into the sofa. I drank deeply and quickly, the gin disappearing within seconds. I poured myself another, then another, feeling the warmth of the alcohol numb my lips, my face and finally my brain, sending me into a fitful sleep where I dreamed that my grandfather was chasing me, a rainbow-coloured scarf around his neck, a gun in his hands.

The following morning, I walked through the park to try and clear my muggy head. I rarely walked to work and rarely walked in the park either, so that morning I stopped a few times to look around me. It felt as if I had never seen winter before – the sky was unusually clear and planes flew low, streaking the sky with a criss-cross of white lines; the air was crisp and squirrels darted through, over and up branches, rustling the papery leaves so that they crackled above me. The trees had shed their rust and red costumes, and the fallen rotting leaves were scattered over pathways and settled on the muddy banks of the lake.

I took a few wrong turns, forgetting that I was meant to be on my way to work, and walked over the jewelled grass, smiling as I watched packs of dogs play and chase balls, whilst their owners shouted their names.

At another turn, I found myself at a part of the lake that seemed cut off from the rest. Bare branches of weeping willows

skimmed the water and thick winter pines filled out the banks.
I made my way towards a bench that overlooked the scene, but
before I sat, I noticed a plaque affixed to the wood. I brushed
away the thin coating of iciness that clung onto the brass and
read: *To my Mary – in memory of memories.*

My hand stroked the tassels of the silky rainbow-striped scarf,
and I thought again of Grandad. I couldn't forget what I had
learned about him. He was stuck in the limbo of dementia, so I
couldn't ask him what had happened – it would be too cruel. I
didn't know what to do, how to move forward, how to understand.

A name suddenly popped into my head. Andrzej. Of course,
his brother. He could tell me what my grandparents could not.
He would tell me that I was wrong, that it was all a mistake,
that I could still love the man I had always loved because he was
exactly who I thought he was.

As soon as I reached my office, I wrote to Andrzej at the address
from the envelope and asked my legal secretary to send it, marked
urgent. Then, I spent an uncomfortable week with nerves frayed,
and strange dreams until he finally replied.

I noticed the letter on the door mat in the morning before I left
for work. It was hidden beneath a pile of bills and cheap pizza
menus, which I threw onto the kitchen table before buttoning
my coat. I grabbed my keys and looked at the letter more closely,
noticing the stamp on the corner of the neatly handwritten
envelope. I placed it into my pocket and decided to walk once
more through the park.

I found the bench by the lake and pulled the letter from my
pocket, pressing on the stamp with my thumb, breathing a little
heavier. Did I really want to know what was inside?

I looked across the water, took a deep breath and ripped open
the envelope.

If you want to know, you'll have to come and see me.
I am old.

Yours,
Andrzej

Smoothing it out with the palm of my hand, I read the words
again. Suddenly, I grew irritated – *come and see me*. Where had
he been all these years? Why hadn't *he* visited his brother?

Could it be because the man I thought of as my sweet
grandfather was, in fact, a Nazi? Was Andrzej ashamed of him?
Or could Andrzej have been a Nazi too?

I read and re-read the letter. *Come and see me. Come and see
me.* That was all there was. I crammed the letter back in my bag.
Come and see me. He must be mad.

Yet, despite my irritation, I searched for flights to Poland when I
got to work. The stacks of contracts to be reviewed were banished
to the corner of my desk as I searched for Andrzej's address – a
retirement home in Zakopane a place I knew the name of, a place
where Grandad had said he'd spent summer holidays. A quick
internet search told me that this was a town at the foot of the
Tatra Mountains, just over sixty miles from Kraków. The next
search was for flights to Kraków, which were cheap – too cheap
and too frequent. I could be there and back in a day. I chewed at
a ragged thumbnail and tore it decisively away. It was one day.
Just one. Then I'd know the truth.

CHAPTER THREE

The bus from Kraków airport to Zakopane was cramped, and I sat next to a backpacker who held her bag tightly against her chest, as if at any moment someone would try to steal it. She was no more than twenty, I guessed. I smiled at her when I sat down, but she did not return it.

I stared down the aisle at the large windscreen, watching as we wound our way out of the city. The bus turned sharply, and I bumped into the girl. I could feel the nausea rising – motion sickness – and I stared hard at the window, focusing on the road ahead as it stretched on to the motorway. After an hour or so, it gave way to winding mountain roads. Soon, I saw snow-tipped mountains, the dusting of white reminding me of icing sugar, and my nausea seemed to disappear as my brain took in the beauty of the scenery. Pint-sized wooden houses on stilts dotted the landscape. Down below in the valley, the houses were more densely packed, surrounding a lake that looked made of glass.

As I stepped off the bus, I stood for a moment taking in the stunning view of the snowy peaks of the Tatra Mountains. Around me, Polish families and tourists with their backpacks bustled about. I waited a few moments for the last remnants of nausea to pass, then headed off, following the directions on my phone.

After thirty minutes of wandering, I finally made my way down a rutted track to a large grey stone house set against the backdrop of the mountains. The dullness of the house made everything around it seem much brighter. Rose bushes which were waiting to bloom come spring edged the drive, and a small pond sat at the end of the wide lawn, with two old men huddled together on a bench in thick coats and woollen scarfs, watching the fish beneath the murky water.

I expected that there would be security of some sort, but the door was wide open, leading into a cool marbled entrance hall, an empty reception desk and a curved staircase dominating the echoing space. It wasn't the kind of retirement home I was expecting; it did not smell of day-old cabbage soup, nor was there the feeling of utter sadness usually associated with the last home people will ever have. Instead, it felt like a stately home. I half expected to see a woman in a ball gown sweep down the staircase, whilst a man in a tuxedo awaited her at the bottom.

'Isla.' A voice echoed around the hall, breaking my train of thought.

I turned and saw a thin old man at the front door who leaned so heavily on his walking stick that it made him look shorter than he was. He did not smile at me. 'Andrzej?' I asked.

He nodded. 'You're late.'

'The bus took a little longer than expected.'

He nodded. 'We will sit outside. Come.' He straightened up now, showing his full height, towering over me. He walked out of the front door with no hesitation in his step, and I wondered why he had the cane at all.

I followed him back outside and down towards the fishpond. As the two old men saw Andrzej approaching, they quickly stood and hustled away.

'It's cold out,' I said, noticing my breath hanging in the air. 'Wouldn't it be better if we talked inside?'

Andrzej shook his head. 'I like the cold. It keeps me awake.'

'I'm sorry for bothering you,' I said, sitting next to him on the bench, feeling the iciness through my jeans. 'But it's about Grandad. It's important.'

'No matter.' He waved my apology away. 'You are here now. What is it which you want?'

His English was good, but his accent and his small grammatical errors reminded me so much of Grandad.

'I don't know much about his life before he came to England…'

'And you want me to tell you?' he asked.

I nodded. 'Why did you never come and see him?'

'That is the past,' he said. 'No need to drag it up. We were young, and he made a mistake. I was angry about it for a long time.'

'And now?' I asked.

'And now I am old, and it doesn't really matter so much anymore.'

I slowly pulled out the newspaper article from my bag and handed it to him. 'I'm trying to understand what this is about.'

Andrzej squinted, held the paper away from him, and then drew it close. He looked a little like Grandad – the same large, pointed nose, high cheekbones. But I missed the warmth Grandad had in his face: his rosy cheeks; twinkling, laughing eyes. Andrzej's eyes were dark and brooding, his face like chalk. Finally, he handed it back. 'And?' he asked.

'And, he is in a German uniform. In an article about the German army.'

'So?'

'Well, why was he in the uniform?' I asked, incredulous that he was being this difficult.

Andrzej lifted his eyes from staring at the murky fishpond and turned to look at me, his hands resting one on top of the other on his cane. 'Where did you get that scarf?' he asked.

My hand went to my neck, feeling the scarf I had found in the attic. 'I found it.' A drop of water fell on my nose as I spoke.

'It will rain,' he said. 'Come inside. Quickly.'

As we walked back, the rain fell heavily. I followed a drenched Andrzej up the stairs to his room: a single bed, a desk and a small TV was his home.

Andrzej handed me a striped blue-and-white towel to wipe away the rain on my face. 'Dry yourself, then I shall get you some tea.'

I nodded.

'I am going to the bathroom to change. I cannot stay in wet clothes at my age. I could die from this, you know?'

'I'm sorry,' I said, then felt foolish for apologising; it wasn't my fault it had rained.

He went out of the room, and I dried my hair with the towel, then stood up to put it on the radiator next to his desk to dry.

As I did, I saw an open box underneath the desk, filled with a stack of red leather-bound notebooks. It looked like there were about six or seven of them; also some letters and postcards. I reached under the desk and took out one, peeking inside; it was a diary – Andrzej's. The next, though... the next one said 'Tomasz' on the first page.

Footsteps were coming down the hallway, the tip-tap of the cane altering me to Andrzej. As I placed the diary back into the box, Andrzej was in the room. He watched as I straightened up and said, 'Some of his diaries from when he was a child and some letters he sent during the war. Some of mine too.'

'Sorry. I shouldn't have looked.'

He walked over to me, bent down and picked up a few of the notebooks, and handed them to me. 'There isn't much more, but maybe it's better that you know,' he said.

I took them gently, feeling his warm fingers touch mine. He sat down on the end of his bed, looking suddenly exhausted. 'There are only stories after this. Some memories, perhaps, not just mine, not just his. Others'.'

'Whose memories?' I asked.

Andrzej shook his head, slowly, sadly, as if those that once held some stories had long since departed.

'I'll read these. Thank you. I'll get them translated.'

He nodded. 'I tell you, there's not much there, but maybe it will tell you something, give you a different way of looking at him.'

'Will you come to his birthday?'

He shook his head. 'I'm too old to travel.'

I nodded and placed the diaries into my bag.

'Will you at least call him? I think it would help.'

He sighed and rubbed his palm over his chin. 'You asked me why we haven't spoken, why I haven't been in his life. It was that picture – and what he did after that. As I said – he made a mistake, and it cost lives.'

'What mistake?' I asked.

'I still loved him, you know. I still looked out for him and made sure he was safe. He was my brother after all.'

'I don't understand what you mean.'

'It doesn't matter anymore, we are too old.' He shook his head, then lowered his eyes.

I waited a few seconds to see if the silence between us would make him speak again. But he didn't. Only the pitter-patter of rain on the window filled the room.

Finally, I spoke. 'Thank you, Uncle Andrzej.' I kissed his cheek and made my way to the door. Then, turning, I asked him – I had to. 'Do you know the whole story? Can you not just tell me?'

'It is not just my story to tell. And you cannot trust me, my memory is bad too now, I dream so much I don't know which is which anymore. I'm sorry. But I am old, just like him. Those diaries, they may tell you something. But then maybe they won't.'

I nodded at him, feeling a little bereft. I didn't want to leave him there, lost in memories that I had evoked, yet I couldn't stay any longer. Dejected, I left him sitting on the end of his bed, his cane in his hands, staring at nothing.

*

Back in London I had the diaries translated by a student I found online, eager to earn some extra money. She was quick and efficient, and within a few weeks she sent me the first translations. It was mid-winter when I came home to find a brown paper package on my doorstep. I picked it up, took it inside and placed it squarely on the kitchen table.

I let my hands unwrap the paper slowly, cautious of what was inside. Finally, I allowed my eyes to take in the words on the typed pages in front of me. I don't know when I sat down, I don't remember standing to turn on the light when the night crept into the kitchen, but I must have. I sat all night reading the start of a story of a child, fragmented and unusual. There were large gaps between months: unwritten, invisible memories that could never be told. But there was enough to understand, to trace his journey across those early years, allowing me a glimpse into who my grandfather used to be, allowing me to imagine it all, as if I were there, watching him play as a child, watching him meet the man he had spoken about when I was a child. The magical man who could conjure rainbows.

CHAPTER FOUR

Tomasz

Poland, Summer 1930

Tomasz Jasieński sat on the edge of the riverbank kicking his small feet in the cold water, watching the ripples ebb against the flow. He looked east towards the dense Czarownica woods and beyond to the village church tower, which peeked over the treetops like a prying neighbour. Behind him, fields stretched between apple orchards, and in one stood a small colourful wooden caravan with an American McCormick tractor parked nearby.

Tomasz's feet were cold. He took them out of the water and, drying them on the long grass, he pulled on his brown socks and shoes and walked towards the field.

The tractor gleamed red and chrome; Tomasz had never seen anything like it before. It belonged to the farmer, Kowalski, who owned the land that stretched from the edge of the woods to the first bend in the Warta river.

He was scared of Kowalski, who always smelled of the tangy *bimber* that he brewed himself, but the tractor was too new, too wonderful, and Tomasz needed to overcome his fear if he were ever to see it up close. He was tired of being called chicken, tired of sitting at home with Bruno the dog, whilst his brother sneaked into Kowalski's field with his friends to smoke cigarettes rolled with tobacco stolen from their father. He wanted to sit on the tractor like they did, and play on it until it became dark, proving that he was no baby and no chicken. At ten, Tomasz was almost a man – at least that's what his mama told him – and men, he thought, sat on tractors and ploughed fields.

Tomasz looked about him once more, checking that Kowalski was not in sight, and leaned on the fence ready to begin his climb over into the field. He needed to be quick if he was going to do this; today the fair was in town and Tomasz desperately wanted to go, but he wanted to see the tractor too so that he could tell his friends. It was then that he thought about the caravan – had it been there when he had come to the field before? He couldn't remember seeing it. No, it was new too. Maybe Kowalski was inside, protecting his tractor with his shotgun. Tomasz leaped away from the fence as though it had scalded him. He watched the small square windows of the caravan for any sign of its owner as the chimes hanging from its roof played a haphazard song.

He chewed on his bottom lip as he made his decision. He looked towards the woods that led to home, then back to the tractor; shiny red like the apples Kowalski grew, and just as irresistible. He would be quick. He started to climb over the fence, feeling a rough splinter of wood press into his palm. He could hear his heartbeat in his ears as he climbed.

Suddenly, a large black-and-white horse appeared from behind the caravan and lazily walked towards him. Tomasz swung his leg over the side of the fence, jumping down to land in a crouched position. The horse raised its head at the intruder and whinnied. Tomasz looked behind him to the river then to the tractor – it wouldn't take him long, a few minutes at most. He ran towards it.

The gleaming American metal begged to be touched. Tomasz stroked the paintwork as he made his way around it. He pulled himself up and sat in the seat, turning the wheel left and right, imagining himself driving through town with everyone's eyes on him. In this tractor, he could plough the whole of Poland.

He would take Bruno with him, and together they would travel from town to town, ploughing fields till sunset. Then at night they would camp together, eating shiny sweet apples until their bellies hurt.

Glancing at the caravan, he saw the horse had moved, and next to it, stroking and patting its neck, stood a naked man.

Tomasz leaped down from the seat of the tractor, scraping his knee as he stumbled onto the ground. On all fours, he crawled to the rear, poking his head around to see the man patting the horse.

The man was not Kowalski. It was someone else. Who was it? And why was he naked?

'Hello, my lovely,' the naked man said, interrupting Tomasz's thoughts.

The horse whinnied in reply and walked away from him. The man laughed and stretched.

Tomasz, realising that he had been holding his breath, exhaled heavily, as the man walked away from him into the centre of the field. He saw that the man wasn't entirely naked – a rainbow-coloured scarf was draped around his neck, its long tails fluttering behind him as he walked. Why would he wear a scarf and be naked at the same time?

He watched as the man turned to face the woods, his back to the tractor, and Tomasz looked towards the fence. It wouldn't take him long to get there. If he was quick, the man might not turn around in time to see him. Taking a deep breath, he slowly stood up, preparing himself to run.

It was quiet; only the rhythmic swish-swish of the horse's tail could be heard. He took a step, and the crunching of the long grass made him wince. It was too loud; surely the man would hear him?

He took another step, and as he was about to run, a deep noise pierced the air. Scared, Tomasz plunged behind the tractor. The sound became deeper and louder, a strange chant in a language

Tomasz did not understand. Tomasz watched as the man stretched out his arms, just like the Christ on the cross that hung above the altar in church, and tilted his head to the sky. The chant became louder and faster, and the man spun in circles, his long black hair fanned by the air as he turned, his lithe body moving elegantly as a dancer as his muscles pushed against his taut skin.

Tomasz wiped his face where a small drop of water had landed and looked to the sky, to see that the clouds had merged into a bulk of grey and rain was falling. The man stopped his mantra, and slowed his spinning. With his head still tilted towards the sky, he laughed as the water soaked him. Tomasz crouched closer into the tractor to try and shield himself from the downpour. He didn't like this man, he thought. He didn't like that he could make it rain and he didn't like that he was naked. He had never seen anyone naked before, apart from himself, and this man dancing as if he were fully clothed gave him a funny feeling in his stomach.

He looked at the orchards and wondered whether if he ran into them, he would be able to find a way out without bumping into Kowalski and his gun. He had never been in the orchards before and wasn't sure if he could find his way out of the maze of trees.

He wiped at the blood on his scraped knee and remembered the story Andrzej once told him of the gypsy Filip, and his travelling circus who turned young boys into animals. Tomasz felt the small hairs on the back of his neck stand on end, and he started to sweat. Was this man like Filip? Would he turn him into an animal?

He knew he would have to run to get away, and he was nowhere near as fast as his brother. But he could make it if he tried, he thought, if he really, really tried.

Back on all fours, he crawled over to the rear of the tractor and poked his head around once more. The man had stopped chanting, and the rain was lessening. Tomasz could hear the gentle swish-swish of the horse's tail again.

He watched as the man walked back towards his caravan. Tomasz sat on his haunches and took a deep breath. Then, without warning, he sneezed.

The man turned and saw his secret watcher. He smiled and strode towards him, his long legs advancing quickly through the long grass. Tomasz leaped up but his right arm did not follow, and he was jerked back towards the wheel of the tractor – his brown jumper was snagged on a small piece of metal jutting from underneath the chassis. He pulled at it until he felt tears prick his eyes. Tomasz clumsily began to remove his jumper, wriggling backwards out of it until his head and one arm were free. He looked up; the man was there.

'Hello, boy,' the man said, smiling, his colourful scarf so bright that Tomasz thought it could not possibly be real. Despite the fear, he felt a desire to reach out and touch the scarf. Suddenly, the man's arm shot out towards him, and Tomasz screamed in panic, making the man stand back.

Tomasz quickly pulled his other arm out of his jumper, leaving it dangling from the tractor, and sprinted through the long grass. His lungs burned and his breath came in quick, raspy gulps. He reached the fence; the river; safety. He looked back. The man stood watching him, holding his jumper up in the air.

'Boy!' he shouted. 'Boy, you forgot your jumper! Won't your mama be mad? Here, boy, come and get your jumper!'

Tomasz ran into the wood, his feet crunching the leaves and snapping twigs underfoot, the sound of the man's laughter ringing in the air. He ran all the way without stopping, without looking back, his legs almost falling over themselves in their haste to get home.

CHAPTER FIVE

Only when he could see the farm in front of him and his mother hanging out washing on the line in their garden did Tomasz stop running.

'Tomasz!' his mother shouted. 'Tomasz, come now, hurry, get ready.'

Tomasz walked towards her, trying to calm his breathing, checking over his shoulder every few steps just in case the naked man had followed him.

'What have you been up to?' his mother asked him as he walked past her. 'Get inside and get cleaned up.'

He went straight to his bedroom that he shared with his brother, sat on the edge of his bed, and pulled off his shoes and socks. Then he undressed until he was just in his vest and underwear. He sat for a moment and thought of the man – he hadn't followed him, so he was safe, wasn't he? The man couldn't find him here.

Then he thought of what his friends would say; they would be impressed, he realised. He could tell them how the gypsy tried to turn him into a frog, but Tomasz had fought him, and in the fray had left his jumper behind. He stood and smiled. Yes, he could be the brave Tomasz, the Tomasz that everyone would talk about; the boy who fought a magical gypsy and won!

He clumsily washed his hands and face in the small bowl of warm water his mother had left him on his dresser. Then he changed into a new crisply ironed shirt and brown trousers.

He walked into the kitchen-come-living room of the farmhouse where his father was sitting in his favourite rocking chair in front of the cold fireplace. Tomasz watched as his father polished his shoes, a cigarette hanging out of the corner of his mouth as he worked.

'Bring your jumper with you.' Tomasz's mother was fixing her hair in front of the mirror that hung near the front door. 'Your brown one,' she said. 'It gets cold in the evening. Go and get it.'

Tomasz watched his mother, feeling a funny flutter in his stomach that made him cold all over, then want to vomit – he didn't have the jumper, the naked man did.

'Go on,' she said. She stopped fussing with her hair to look at him.

'I lost it,' he said.

'Where?'

'I was in Kowalski's field.'

'Go back to get it then.'

'Now?' he asked, looking quickly out of the window as the sun was finishing its descent, the sky already turning its night-time blue.

'Tomorrow,' she said. 'You can get it tomorrow. But you will get it, Tomasz. You cannot throw money away. Your father does not work this land for you to leave jumpers in fields.'

He watched as she slicked lipstick onto her thin lips, and he chewed at the bottom of his own, wondering how he would go back, how he would ask the strange, naked man for his jumper.

'You look nice in your new clothes.' His mother turned and walked towards him and fussed with his hair now, trying to straighten a tuft that stubbornly stuck upwards. 'Doesn't he look nice?' she asked his father.

His tata looked up. 'Fine,' he said. 'Not sure why we all need to dress up so much.'

'Oh, Piotr! Such a grumbler. We can't turn up to the fair with the whole village there, looking like poor farmers!'

'We are,' his father said. He beckoned Tomasz to come over to him.

'Well, at least we don't have to look it,' she said.

His father ignored her and handed Tomasz a shoe. 'Help me finish these,' he whispered to him. 'She'll not let me go until they're shining like the sun!'

Tomasz shared a secret laugh with his tata, and sat on the floor, polishing the old, crumpled leather until it started to shine.

'Where's Andrzej?' Tomasz asked his parents, as they left the farmhouse behind and walked to the nearby village of Mściszewo.

'He'll meet us there,' his mother answered. 'He's been at Szymon's all day.'

Tomasz heard his father grumble.

'Let him be young,' his mother scolded his father. 'There's plenty of time for him to work.'

Tomasz looked at his father who shook his head.

It did not take the three of them long to reach the fair. It normally only visited the city of Poznań, almost thirty kilometres away from the village, but it had found them that summer and everyone, it seemed to Tomasz, had flocked there that Saturday night. Burning lanterns lit the way into the fairground, which covered two fields. Stalls sold large pots of steaming stews filled with cabbage, sauerkraut and thick hunks of pork; *kiełbasa* sausage hung from ropes over frying onions and garlic, and there were pots of *pierogi* dumplings, some stuffed with meat and potatoes, others with fruit and covered in cream.

Other stalls decorated with paper bunting sold fudge and chocolates filled with marzipan. A *karuzele* with bright lights and white horses boasting gold-and-red saddles revolved to folk music; for older riders, the new German Waltzer sped around, twisting and turning the people so quickly that Tomasz could not make out their faces. Tomasz walked with his parents, and twice his mother had to drag him forward as he stopped and stared at the large red-and-white striped tent that stood in the middle of the field, then again at a clown with a monkey sitting on his shoulder.

A fire-eater appeared in front of them, blowing flames into the night sky, and a man wearing a black top hat and stripy blue trousers walked around the crowds on stilts that sent him almost to the moon. From his height, he dropped down sugared bonbons, small wooden dolls and miniature bears for the little children who followed in his wake.

The smell of sweet spun sugar filled Tomasz's nostrils as the family walked amongst the chattering crowds. A roasting pig turned on a spit, the hot fat and juices hissing and popping; a man with an accordion played a happy tune while a young girl with wild black hair sat and read palms.

Tomasz's parents saw some friends at a stall selling cider, and his father handed two five-grosz coins to Tomasz and to his brother, Andrzej, who had appeared at just the right time.

'That's all you get,' his father warned them. 'Spend it wisely.'

'Don't be too long,' their mother added. 'You spend it, then come straight back here.'

The boys promised to be quick and to stay together. As they walked from stall to stall, Tomasz could not decide whether to tell Andrzej about the naked gypsy in Kowalski's field. Would he think he was chicken because he ran away?

'You going to buy anything?' Andrzej asked him.

Tomasz shrugged. 'In a bit. Maybe I'll get some sweets or go to the show with the bearded ladies.'

'You're acting strange. I thought you wanted to come here?'

'I do. Andrzej, I have something to tell you—' Tomasz began.

'Ah, look! There's Szymon. Listen, don't go too far, spend your money, then go back to Mama and Tata, all right?' Andrzej said, already walking away from him.

'Why? Where are you going?' Tomasz asked him.

'To see my friends. We're going on the rides.'

'I'll come with you.'

'You're too little. Go get some sweets, then go back to Mama.'

Tomasz stood in the crowded fairground and watched his brother run out of sight to his friends, feeling much smaller and younger than he actually was.

Soon, he was almost back near his parents, and the money was still in his pocket. Looking around, he tried to decide what to spend his money on before it was too late. It was then that he saw him – the rainbow-coloured scarf bright even under the cheap lanterns – the gypsy man from Kowalski's field, playing cards on a low table with a girl wearing a blue dress.

Tomasz turned quickly before the gypsy saw him and tried to weave and dodge between the people that stood in his way, heading back towards his parents.

'You win!' Tomasz heard him cry. Then, Tomasz heard the girl. She laughed loudly and in such a sing-song way that immediately Tomasz wanted to laugh too. He stopped and turned around. She stretched out her hand and took her prize; a blue ribbon that matched the blue of her dress. Why wasn't she scared?

Tomasz watched the girl as she ran the ribbon through her fingers, testing the feel of the material.

'My favourite colour!' she cried. 'How did you know?'

'I am magic.' The gypsy shrugged.

'Tomasz, come!' Suddenly, his mother's voice broke through the chatter of the fair.

Tomasz turned and saw his mother beckoning him.

'One minute,' he shouted back, disappearing quickly into the crowd so she could not get hold of him.

Tomasz felt the cold metal of the coins in his pocket. He could do this. He could be brave. The man couldn't hurt him here, could he? He walked towards the gypsy and the girl in the blue dress.

'You want to play?' The gypsy noticed him immediately.

Tomasz nodded, swallowing hard, remembering how this man had danced naked in the field only a few hours before.

The man smiled at him and Tomasz tried to smile back, all the while telling his heart to slow down its beat; it was all right, he was safe, it was all right.

'It's easy.' The girl looked at him, and he saw that her eyes were bluer than her dress.

He nodded at her.

'Really, it is,' she said. 'Here, give me the money.'

Tomasz clumsily handed the coins over to her.

'You just have to find the queen.' She nodded to the cards spread out, face down in front of him on a small table.

The gypsy flicked a card over, showing the Queen of Hearts. 'Follow her,' he told Tomasz, placing the card face down once more.

Tomasz watched as the gypsy moved the cards about on the table and tried to follow where he thought the queen was. Finally, the cards were still.

'Which one do you think it is?' the girl asked him.

Tomasz bit his bottom lip – he didn't know.

'Come on,' the girl said. 'Take a guess. It's just a game.'

'That one.' Tomasz pointed to the middle card.

'Are you sure?' the gypsy asked.

Tomasz looked at the girl to see if she agreed with his choice.

'I think it's this one.' The girl pointed at a card nearer to her.

'So, which will it be?' the gypsy asked. 'Will you choose, or will you let this lovely girl decide for you?'

Tomasz looked at the man – the strange man living in a caravan on Kowalski's land. 'I'll let her decide.'

The gypsy nodded and flipped the card over to reveal the Queen of Hearts. The girl squealed with delight.

Tomasz smiled at her, and she grinned back.

'I'm Zofia,' she said.

'Tomasz.'

'And now your prize,' the man said. 'But to whom does it belong?' The gypsy held in his hand a small heart-shaped piece of wood that had been polished and shined so it looked almost like a gem.

Zofia reached out to touch it. 'It feels so smooth,' she said.

'A heart for the Queen of Hearts,' he said, winking at Tomasz.

'Take it,' Tomasz said.

'But it's your prize,' she answered. 'It was your money.'

'That's all right. You chose for me. You take it.'

Zofia clasped her hand around the carving and smiled.

'Tomasz!' he heard his mother shout once more.

'I have to go,' Tomasz said.

'I'll see you again,' Zofia replied as he walked away.

As he made his way back to his mother, he heard the gypsy's voice. 'Come and see me again. Tomorrow in the field. I shall give you your jumper back!'

Tomasz looked back at the gypsy who smiled at him, the colours of his scarf glowing against the black backdrop of the sky.

CHAPTER SIX

Kapaldi

Poland, Summer 1930

He knew the boy was there, waiting. He threw another log on the fire and warmed his hands. Within minutes, he saw the small shadow approach, eventually standing in front of him, his eyes wide with fear.

'I knew you would come,' he said to the boy.

'My jumper,' the boy said quietly.

'I will get it for you.' He walked slowly to his caravan and returned, giving the jumper to him.

'Thank you,' the boy said.

He sat back by the fire and waited. The boy did not walk away.

'Are you frightened?' he asked.

'Yes.'

'Of what?'

'I don't know.'

The fire hissed and crackled, and he drew out a large stick and prodded at a log, making sparks fly into the blackness.

'Why don't you sit for a while?' he asked.

The boy sat down, holding his jumper tightly in his hands.

'My name is Kapaldi,' he told the boy. 'And you are Tomasz.'

The boy looked at him.

'I remembered, from the fair,' he said.

Tomasz nodded.

'How is your friend, the girl with the blue eyes?'

'I haven't seen her again,' Tomasz said.

'You will.'

'How do you know?'

'I know many things, my friend. You see' – he prodded the fire again, sending more dancing sparks into the air – 'I am a magician.'

'What kind of magician?' Tomasz asked him.

'A great one, of course. I can see into the future, I can make it rain and make rainbows appear, I can even magic sweets from thin air!' Suddenly, he threw his arm up in the air as if catching something, then opened his palm to Tomasz. Inside was a small boiled sweet. 'See? Take it.'

Tomasz took the sweet and popped it hungrily into his mouth. 'Do you turn little boys into animals too?'

Kapaldi laughed, but seeing the boy jump in fright, he stopped. 'No,' he said gently. 'Why would I ever want to do a thing like that?'

'That's what my brother said gypsies do.'

'I'm no ordinary gypsy.' Kapaldi shook his head. 'I travel alone, not with a troop of circus acts. Why, just hear my name, Kapaldi, which is not a gypsy name, is it?'

Tomasz shook his head. 'It's not Polish either. Where are you from?'

'Now that, my friend, is a long story.'

'I can stay awhile,' Tomasz answered. 'Mama thinks I am asleep. I can stay and hear your story.'

Kapaldi smiled at the boy. He knew he should walk him to the woods and send him on his way, but there was something about him, something about the way he had so easily trusted him, that made him want to make the boy happy. 'All right,' Kapaldi said. Wrapping his long scarf around his neck, he began.

'I remember my mother very well, and I remember that she was beautiful. She had long black hair, and she had chestnut-coloured skin like me. She was not Polish, I do not think; she would tell me that she came from the earth, like a flower in the spring. She told me that because she came from the earth, anywhere she planted her feet was home.'

'So, she was a gypsy?' Tomasz interrupted.

'Listen first before you name what she was, or what I am. Open your mind a little, Tomasz. When you came to me, did I say, ah yes, there is a Pole? Did I comment that you look a little German?'

'No.' Tomasz shook his head and blushed.

'See, I do not name you or brand you. To me, you are Tomasz, my friend who likes tractors.' He smiled at the boy.

Tomasz smiled back. 'I am glad we are friends,' he said.

'Good. Should I continue?'

'Please.' Tomasz pulled on his jumper and sat closer to the fire, resting his elbows on his knees and his chin in his hands.

'Where was I? Oh yes, my mother, who came from the ground.' He winked at Tomasz. 'My mother and I travelled, sometimes alone and sometimes with others. Some of them were what you think of as Roma, gypsies, but my mother and I and a few others were different. We did not like to be in a circus, or dance for money or tell fortunes. We enjoyed travelling, seeing the world, and learning new things. My mother delighted in taking new jobs, learning to churn butter, shoeing a horse, digging holes. She smiled every day and was happy in every job she had – no matter how hard.

'I remember when I was about seven years old, my mother and I arrived here in Poznań. We found work on a farm much like this one, and in one of the fields was a colourful wooden caravan and black horse.

'The man who owned the caravan had also found work on the farm. He did not speak to me often and would sit on the steps of his caravan and read books. His beard was black and pointed and he wore glasses; thick, black-rimmed glasses that I had never seen on anyone before. My mother did not trust the man; she said he was Italian Roma and that his ways were not ours. But there was something about this man and his books that I could not leave alone. In those light summer nights when the sky never darkens, I would wait until my mother fell asleep and sneak out to see the man. Bit by bit, he and I became friends, and he would teach me things from his books: science, mathematics, history! The whole world and all its knowledge in books! Can you imagine, Tomasz? I had travelled with my mother from Berlin to Rome, from London to Paris, from Constantinople to the coldest depths of Moscow, but then a man sat on some steps of a caravan and showed me the world in those books; pictures and scribbles would tell me the secrets of the universe, and all I had to do was learn those strange shapes for myself.'

'He taught you to read and write?' Tomasz asked.

'Yes, he did.'

'Why didn't your mother teach you? Did you not go to school even?'

Kapaldi shrugged. 'My mother was not of this earth, of that I am sure. She had little use for books and words. She preferred to experience life for herself, I think. She must have known a few words herself if only to get us from country to country. But I liked to sit with this strange man every day. It was only when I had known him for a whole month that he told me his name, Capaldi.'

'Like yours!'

'Yes, like mine, but not quite the same spelling, his with a C, mine with a K.'

'Why the difference?'

'Just wait, Tomasz, you'll soon see.' He could see the boy wriggling with impatience, yet he didn't want the story to end so quickly, because then he would leave. 'Are you hungry, Tomasz?' he asked.

The boy nodded. He stood and fetched a plate of bread, meat and cheese from the caravan, placing it between them both on the grass.

'I'm always hungry,' Tomasz said. 'My brother, he says that one day I will be really fat and won't be able to move. But I don't think so, do you?'

'Not at all,' Kapaldi said. He popped a piece of cheese into his mouth. 'I think if you are hungry, you should eat, and when you are tired, you should sleep. I think it really is that simple.'

He watched the boy eat, reminding him of himself at that age; when legs and arms grew longer every day and when his stomach would constantly growl at him, even after he had just eaten. He wondered when that stopped. Was there a moment when he had suddenly stopped growing, stopped being hungry all the time and he had missed it? He wished he was like Tomasz now – hopeful, curious, naive. He wished he could sit as Tomasz did and eat without abandon, filling his stomach, ready to race off on the next adventure.

'You can continue with your story if you want to,' Tomasz said, breaking through his thoughts.

Kapaldi nodded. 'Ah, yes. My story. Where was I? Capaldi, with a C. He was indeed Italian, and came from Rome, but he had travelled widely with his family, who were what you would call authentic gypsies. They knew magic and could read your mind and your future in your teacup. All of this Capaldi knew too, but he said he never did it anymore; his books had far more magic in them, he told me. But like any young boy I wanted to see flowers appearing as if from nowhere, animals transformed into beautiful women. Every day I begged him to show me some real magic, but it was not until the end of summer that he finally relented.'

'What happened? Did he turn you into an animal? That's what my brother Andrzej said happened to a boy in the village – a gypsy turned him into a frog!'

'Ha-ha! Such silly stories, Tomasz! No, he did not turn me into a frog. He taught me how to make it rain.'

Kapaldi turned his head to the sky and knew that Tomasz was doing the same. 'You saw me do this already, I think?' he asked the boy quietly.

'Yes,' Tomasz answered. 'But why do you need to make it rain? It rains anyway.'

'Does it?' He looked now at Tomasz. 'How do you know that it is not only raining because someone somewhere is dancing and willing it to rain?'

'That's not how it works,' Tomasz butted in. 'My teacher said—'

'Enough!' Kapaldi said. 'If you believe your teacher, I will not tell you the rest of my story. Do you wish to listen, or do you wish to argue?'

'I want to listen,' Tomasz said quietly.

'Good.' He smiled at the boy and threw him another boiled sweet.

'So, as I said, it was at the end of summer, and the whole town had been waiting for it to end. It had not rained since May – the crops were wilting and so were the people. I remember that it was suffocating. I slept most of those hot days away and only woke in the evening to see my friend. We would sit by the riverbank with our feet in the cool water and listen to it roll over and over our feet. My mother had become sick at this time too, and the farmer had sent her to the hospital in the city. I had wanted to go with her, but she told me to stay and she would be back soon. Capaldi, naturally, offered to watch me for the time, so we sat together on those long, hot evenings and talked of books and all the stories in the world. And those stories made me forget a little of the sadness and worry for my mother, and for that, I was very grateful.

'It was now the end of September, and there had still been no rain. One morning, I woke to see Capaldi looking down at me whilst I slept.'

'"Come," was all he said to me, and held out his hand.

'I took it, and together we walked into a field very much like this one and sat in the long hot grass. From his pocket he pulled out a long multicoloured scarf.'

'Like yours!' Tomasz pointed at Kapaldi's neck excitedly.

'Yes, this was his. He wrapped the scarf around his neck and told me he was going to show me some magic, but that it would take a little time. At the end of the magic would appear the most beautiful sight, and I would then feel better and would not be afraid.'

'I don't understand,' Tomasz said.

'Neither did I, Tomasz. But I sat and listened to him talk. He said first, we needed the sun, then we needed a storm, and as the storm grew, we would need to dance, and sing, and chant strange words, willing the clouds to open and pour down the rain we needed! Oh, it would be wonderful, he promised. That cool rain soaking the roasted ground and our hot tired skin. Then with the rain would come a rainbow, a magnificent rainbow covering the sky, showing us beauty in the world, even when there is a storm! So, he showed me how to do it, how to make it rain and how to make the rainbow appear whenever I needed to see it. And for that, when I had learned, he gave me this scarf and his name, changing it slightly with a K as he said I had to be different, just a little, from him.'

'So, you are a real magician?' Tomasz smiled widely. 'I knew that you were when I saw you dancing.'

'Indeed, I am,' Kapaldi smiled back at him. 'My speciality is conjuring rainbows from dark skies, and making it rain at just the right moment. I can make something good from something bad.'

'I'd like to do magic like that,' Tomasz said, looking at the stars. 'I'd like to be able to make people smile with rainbows in the sky. Like Tata, after he has had a hard day on the farm. Or my friend Michal, he gets sad when his brother punches his arm. I'd like to make him smile.'

'I tell you what, my friend, now it is time for you to go home to your mother. But, if you come back tomorrow, I will show you how to make it rain and how to make a rainbow for yourself. But you cannot tell anyone about me, not yet anyway. Do not tell your brother or your friends that you come here, nor tell them what I am teaching you, all right? They won't understand – some don't like people like me.'

'Gypsies, you mean?'

'Exactly.'

'All right,' Tomasz answered. 'I promise.'

Kapaldi took the boy's hand and shook it, sealing their deal. Then he walked him through the woods until the lights of the farmhouse could be seen.

'Hurry now,' he whispered to the boy in the dark. 'And remember, do not tell anyone.'

'I'll remember,' Tomasz answered.

Kapaldi smiled in the dark as he watched the boy run like a sneaky fox to his bedroom window and clumsily climb through before his mother realised that he had been gone. He stood for a while watching the house, unsure of what he was waiting for.

Soon, the last light in the front room was extinguished and all was dark.

Kapaldi turned slowly and walked back through the woods, cooing in answer to the night-time call of the wood pigeons as they settled in their nests, remembering how his mother had held his hand and walked with him, teaching him the sounds of the birds around him. He would teach the boy tomorrow. Tomasz would like to learn it, he was sure.

CHAPTER SEVEN

The next day, Kapaldi sat on the steps of his caravan and looked up to the clear blue sky. He twisted a piece of long grass in his hand as he questioned whether the boy would come or not.

By midday, Tomasz still hadn't arrived, and he felt sad that Tomasz had given up on him so quickly. He walked into the caravan to make lunch when suddenly he heard shouting and laughing coming from near the woods. Venturing back outside, he watched as a group of teenagers made their way through the field and towards him.

When the group were halfway through the field, he stepped down and went to meet them.

'How are you, my friends? What can I do for you?' he asked, smiling.

A boy of around seventeen strode forward. He was large, built heavily with muscle as well as fat, and was the obvious leader of the group.

'We've come to tell you to leave. We don't like Zigeuner on our land!'

Kapaldi stepped closer to the boy until he was so close, he could smell the scent of alcohol on the boy's breath.

'I'm not on your land,' Kapaldi said.

The boy was confused for a moment and looked to his friends to help him out with the argument.

'Tell him, Harald. Tell him that it's all our land, not for untouchable gypsies like him, and not for Jews either. It's for clean people!'

'Exactly!' Harald's confidence was buoyed by his friend's narrative. 'Exactly, gypsy. It doesn't matter whose land it is. Just know it's not yours!'

Harald pushed Kapaldi so hard in the chest that he stumbled backwards. He held his hands up. 'I do not want to fight,' he said.

The boys laughed at him and suddenly, without warning, jumped on him. Falling to the ground he curled into a ball, his hands protecting his head from the kicks and punches that rained down on him. He hoped they would soon get bored of their game. But it seemed that the heat of the summer sun, combined with whatever alcohol they had drunk, was making them crazy. He realised, too late, that they would not stop until he was dead.

Trying to get away from them did not help. As he made to crawl towards his caravan, he felt a kick in his stomach, making him gasp and collapse to the ground, face in the dirt. He could hear his horse whinnying somewhere nearby, and he hoped, more than anything, they would not hurt his horse.

Soon, he felt no pain anymore and realised he was going to pass out. He was glad. It would be over in a moment. Then, just at the brink of blissful oblivion, the kicks stopped.

Suddenly, there was screaming. The boys – the boys who had kicked him had stopped and were screaming. He couldn't understand why.

Then he heard the deep roar of an engine, and more scream-ing. Yelling.

He turned his head slowly, and before he fainted, he could see a small boy riding a tractor, trying to mow down the group as they scattered themselves through the field. The tractor veered left and right, and the boys frantically tried to escape the large wheels and the roar of the engine that continued to aim itself at them. The tractor followed all the boys towards the fence, which they scrambled over. Then there was more shouting – a man – a pop of a gun, then, finally, silence.

*

Kapaldi awoke to the sound of crying. He opened one eye to see Tomasz's wet, swollen, pink face above him.

'You're alive!' Tomasz screamed, and hugged Kapaldi so hard he almost cried out in pain.

'Leave him be,' another voice boomed.

Kapaldi sat up slowly, realising he was inside his caravan. The farmer, Kowalski, who had allowed him to use his field and had given him some work, sat on the steps of the caravan looking in.

'You all right, my friend?' Kowalski asked. 'You took quite a beating,'

'Yes. I think so.' He touched his swollen lip, then felt his ribs – two broken, he thought – but other than that he only felt the pain of bruises; bad ones, but just bruises, nonetheless. Kapaldi had experienced this before.

'Right. If you're fine, I'll be going back now. No point in alerting the police – they won't do anything – but my suggestion is that it's probably better for you to move on, as soon as you can.'

Kowalski stepped inside for a moment, and awkwardly shook his hand, placing some money in it. 'For all your work,' Kowalski said.

'Thank you,' Kapaldi said.

'Tomasz. Go home now. Leave this man be!' Kowalski ordered the boy, who, Kapaldi noticed, was terrified every time Kowalski spoke.

'It's fine. He can stay awhile. I made him a promise.'

'If you're sure…' Kowalski made to leave. 'I suppose he could stay a few minutes. He did save your life, after all. Riding around on my tractor! If I hadn't heard the engine start up, I wouldn't have run down here with my shotgun, and those boys wouldn't have disappeared like they did!' Kowalski laughed, and Kapaldi saw the boy smile.

'But don't do it again, you hear me?' Kowalski pointed a finger at Tomasz. 'Don't play on that tractor again.'

'I won't, sir,' Tomasz answered meekly.

Kowalski winked at Kapaldi, tipped his hat, and left the two of them alone.

'I suppose it's time to make a rainbow then?' he asked Tomasz.

The boy grinned at him.

'No, no! Your arms need to be wider. Yes, just like that. Like a bird almost. Wider! Yes! Now sing the words I taught you. Sing them loud. Up to the sky so the heavens can hear them. Sing them, Tomasz, sing them so that you make it rain, so that the rainbow can come out, and bring us something good today!'

Kapaldi directed Tomasz from the steps of his caravan and sipped at a cup of tea he had brewed himself, knowing that the pain would soon ebb away from the potent properties of the herbs he had infused.

'Like this?' Tomasz yelled, his face red with exertion.

'Yes, like that! Exactly like that!'

He watched the boy spin and spin for a few more minutes before he collapsed in a dizzy heap in the grass.

Kapaldi looked to the sky and saw that the sun was beginning its descent, the moon already out.

'I think, Tomasz, that it is too late in the day now.'

Tomasz sat up. 'I wanted to make it rain. I wanted to make a rainbow.'

'You will one day, my friend. You will. When you truly believe that you can do it. When you truly need it, then it will happen. You have the magic now.'

'If I have the magic, then why isn't it working?' Tomasz whined.

'It is just too late, that is all. The sun needs to sleep now, and soon so do I. It is for the best. You have learned the magic now, and that is the most important part. No one can ever take that from you.'

He watched the boy think about this. Soon, he nodded and stood.

'Do you want me to walk you home?'

'Do I have to go? Can I stay a little longer?'

'A little,' Kapaldi answered. The truth was, he did not want to say goodbye to the boy yet.

Together, they walked to the river to fetch water to make more tea. Tomasz sat on the bank and dropped his feet into the water. Kapaldi did the same.

They sat side by side as the sun set, swishing their feet in the cool water, hearing the church bells chime the hour.

'You know, this place reminds me so much of my childhood,' Kapaldi said.

'What happened to your mama? You said she was sick when you were little. Did she die?'

Kapaldi nodded and watched his feet as he moved them in the water.

'Why did she die?' Tomasz asked. 'I thought today you would die. Mama says that one day we all die, but I hope not yet. You won't die yet, will you?'

Kapaldi looked to the boy and smiled. 'No. Not yet.'

'But your mama died when you were young.'

'She did. But she was sick.'

Tomasz nodded.

'I will tell you what happened, but you cannot get sad. I am not sad anymore, all right?'

'All right,' he said.

'We were in a village outside Poznań, working on the farm when my mother began to vomit blood,' Kapaldi began. 'Every morning she would hack and cough until her whole body shook, then out of her mouth would spurt crimson. One night, after I had visited my friend Capaldi in his caravan, my mother sat on the edge of the low wall, watching as I walked towards her. She held out her hand to me and she pulled me up, and together we sat side by side, watching the sunset.

"'I must leave tomorrow," she told me, keeping hold of my hand. "I am unwell, and the farmer here is kindly sending me to hospital."

"'Why are you sick?" I asked her.

"'Because some things that happened to me when I was young have made me ill. All my life I have tried to fight against it, against all those memories – my parents, your grandparents dying so young, of being alone, of always fighting against those who wished to hurt me. Then, I had you." She smiled at me. "And I believed then that you had cured me. You alone had made it all go away, my beautiful boy. But I realise now it was only a matter of time before it came for me again, and now here in this town, the town where you were born, the town where I was most happy, it has found me again."

'I had never heard my mother talk this way before. She had always smiled and made life seem easy, seem so wonderful. It shocked me to think that all this time she had been hiding... suffering.

'My mother and I sat on that wall until it began to become cool, the air taking on the feeling of freshness as the sun dipped out of sight and the moon sat in the sky. We held hands until morning. Neither of us spoke and neither of us said goodbye.'

Kapaldi stopped talking and dropped his head to his chest and closed his eyes.

'Are you all right?' the boy asked him, a tremor in his voice.

Kapaldi lifted his head and looked at him. 'I am. I am fine. Look, the sun is almost gone. You should go home.'

'I don't want to. Not yet. Finish the story. What happened next?'

Kapaldi rubbed his hand over the stubble on his cheek, feeling the bruises under his skin.

'The farmer who took my mother to hospital was a good man.'

'Like Kowalski?' Tomasz butted in.

'Yes. Exactly. Just like Kowalski. But he had a wife and a son. The son was not much younger than me and we became friends. The farmer said that I could come and live with them. But one day, I heard the farmer and his wife arguing about me. She refused to have me to stay. "That woman's son! I will not have that gypsy in my home," I heard her shout. She called my mother the most horrible of names. The next morning, I woke to see Capaldi standing over me – that was the day he taught me the rain dance and the day I left the farm and my friend behind.

'The boy from the farm, that was my half-brother. That is why his mother would not have me. My mother, you see, had brought me there because she knew she would die. I think she hoped my real father would take me, but he could not. But I had Capaldi, who taught me magic, and for me, that was enough.'

'So, you have a brother?' the boy asked him, his eyes wide.

'I do.'

'I have a brother too,' Tomasz said. 'But he annoys me. He calls me names and punches my arm.'

Kapaldi laughed. 'That is what brothers are for.'

'Where will you go now?' Tomasz asked. 'Will you go and see your brother?'

'I don't know yet. I need to think. I cannot see it yet.'

'What do you mean, you cannot see it?'

Kapaldi rubbed at his chin for a moment. 'It is another form of magic. One I cannot teach. I look into the fire in the evening, and in the flames, as they dance and intertwine themselves, I see what I must do next.'

'Like telling a fortune?'

'A bit. I cannot see everything. Just small pieces. Like a jigsaw.'

'Can I stay until you have lit the fire? Can I stay until you see something?' Tomasz asked eagerly.

Kapaldi smiled. 'Yes. Just until I see something. Then you must go.'

They walked back to the caravan, and outside, they made a small fire. Kapaldi made tea, this time with no potent ingredients, so Tomasz could have some. He also gave him some sweet biscuits to eat, and to keep him occupied whilst he wrapped the rainbow scarf around his neck and looked into the flames.

After a few minutes, Kapaldi looked away. He felt a cold shiver down his spine, and his hands felt clammy.

'What's wrong?' Tomasz asked. 'You've gone pale.'

'Nothing, I'm fine. I just need sugar – a *biszkopt* will do the trick.' Kapaldi grabbed a biscuit and ate slowly until the cold feeling had left him and he became calm again.

'You know, Tomasz, because you saved my life today, I owe you a debt.'

'What kind of debt?' Tomasz asked.

'A life debt. One day I will have to save your life.'

'So, we will see each other again?' Tomasz beamed at Kapaldi.

'Yes. We will see each other again. We shall be great friends for many years.'

'Is that what you saw when you looked into the fire?'

Kapaldi nodded.

'Did you see anything else?'

'Nothing that concerns you now. All you need to know is that one day I will save your life. And in the meantime, as your friend, I will look after you.'

'So, you will stay here?'

'No, I must leave tomorrow.'

'Then how will you look after me?' Tomasz asked.

'I will always be nearby. You will see me when you need me.'

He watched the boy screw his face up in concentration. Before Tomasz could ask any more questions, he said, 'It is time for me to walk you home.'

They walked slowly through the woods; Kapaldi was in pain with each step he took, and he could sense that Tomasz was reluctant to leave his new magical friend, falling slowly into step with him, not leaving his side.

When they reached the farmhouse, Tomasz looked up at him. 'Do you promise that one day I will make it rain?'

'I promise.' Kapaldi smiled at him.

'So, I need to wait until the sun shines, then I dance and chant as you showed me? Then a storm will come, then it will rain. Then there will be a rainbow, at the end?' Tomasz asked quickly, counting each point off on his fingers.

'Yes, exactly right.'

'But how will you know?'

'What do you mean?' Kapaldi asked.

'How will you know that the rainbow that is in the sky is made by me? How will you know?'

'I will just know.' He watched as the boy thought over this response. He saw a crease in the boy's brow. 'What is wrong?'

'I was thinking also, you said before that you will save my life. When will that happen?'

'When you are in danger, then I will come and save you, just as you saved me.'

Tomasz kicked at the dirt in the ground.

'You are not happy with my answer?' Kapaldi asked.

'I just think, if you are my friend, I would know when I will see you next. I don't want to wait until I am in danger. Maybe I never will be!' Tomasz held his arms in the air.

Kapaldi smiled at the boy. He saw that he was now near tears.

Against his better judgement, Kapaldi bent down, and with his finger tipped Tomasz's chin so that the boy was looking into his eyes. 'You will see me again. Of this I promise you. I will come to Kowalski's field once every year, just to see you, all right?'

'All right,' Tomasz said and grinned at him. 'You promise?'

'I promise. Now go on home before you get into trouble.'

Kapaldi stood and ruffled the boy's hair, and watched as Tomasz ran off towards his house, every now and then turning back to wave at him.

CHAPTER EIGHT

Isla

England, 2015

I ran the scarf through my fingers, staring at it as if by doing so I could see this man who my grandad thought was magical. Kapaldi. The man who danced naked in a field and made it rain, a man who befriended a young boy and promised to always be there for him.

I remembered the stories from my childhood, when I had slept over at my grandparents' house, where late at night, over hot chocolate, Grandad would tell me about the magical man who lived in a colourful caravan, who could perform tricks, turn naughty children into frogs, and make rainbows appear. I had, of course, dismissed them as made up, but now I understood and now I knew whose scarf it was. Yet, why had Gran been so scared of it?

I placed the scarf on the kitchen table and tapped my fingers in an irritated, impatient drum on the wood. I wanted the rest of the diaries, but the student hadn't finished translating them.

'Damn it,' I said, the words angry and lingering in the empty space.

There was one other option, one that I had put off because I was afraid to upset him, and to upset Gran – I could try to talk to my grandfather.

*

Saturday morning came with blue skies streaked with wisps of clouds that gave the illusion of spring, even though it was still a month or so away. The chill in the air made me reach for my trusty knitted scarf, but I quickly changed my mind and instead wrapped the thin silk scarf around my neck – this would help him remember something, I was sure of it. Maybe it would get him talking – it was my only option.

The brass knocker still shone on their front door, and it made me sad to think of Gran still trying to keep one thing polished, one thing right in the house and in her life.

I lifted it and knocked three times, waited and then knocked again, wondering if she had seen me through the window and perhaps did not want to open the door to me, scared I would bring up the picture once more. Finally, Gran edged open the creaking door, her grey hair wild on her head, her glasses slipping slowly down her nose.

'Isla!' She grabbed me into a strong hug, her strength belying the small frail woman she seemed. She had forgiven me.

'What on earth are you doing here?' she asked, ushering me into the house, which thankfully was warm.

'I just thought I'd pop up and see you,' I said.

'Get that coat off, you'll melt in here. I've had the heating on for hours because your dad said it was freezing – had no interest in my global warming speech.'

I removed my coat but kept the scarf around my neck. She eyed the scarf but said nothing.

'You look well,' I said, surprise in my voice. She was moving easier, not hobbling about; her movements were quicker too.

'Of course I am well,' she replied, walking in front of me to the kitchen. 'I'm making soup. Chicken soup. It's not ready yet, but you can have some if you wait.'

I sat at the kitchen table and watched as she bustled about. She was wearing a purple hoodie and leggings, something that I had never seen her in before. 'You look nice,' I ventured, nodding towards her outfit.

'Do you like them? I got them off the internet. I can tell you where if you want some. Moira from church got a lime-green set. It's for when we do our exercise class.'

I almost laughed. 'Exercise class? Since when have you done any exercise?'

She turned to me, a wooden spoon in her hand, and pointed it at me. 'It's important, Isla, to keep moving. I saw it on the telly. You have to keep the joints going or you'll just stop. Moira and I go three times a week now. I went this morning, and I tell you, I feel like I'm twenty again!'

'Good for you!'

'You should do it too, Isla. You need to look after yourself more. Do you eat? What do you eat?'

'Gran, I'm fine, really. I eat, don't worry about me.'

'I do worry, though. I do. You young people running about, not sleeping or eating. I saw it on the TV, you know, lawyers like you. They die when they get into their forties because they forgot to eat and sleep.'

I shook my head at her. What on earth was she watching on TV?

'How's Grandad?' I tried.

'Upstairs, in bed. Says that because it's the weekend, he's resting. Thinks he went to work all week.' She stirred the soup, the steam fogging up her glasses. 'Work. Can you imagine? He's not worked for twenty years, but there we are, he thinks he's been working, so I go along with it. No point telling him.'

'Can I go up?' I asked.

'In a minute you can.' She stopped fussing with the soup, sat across from me and wiped her glasses on the sleeve of her hoodie. 'I want to tell you not to mention that picture you showed me.'

'I won't, Gran. I promise.'

'It upset me, you know. You thinking that of him.'

'I know, and I'm sorry, Gran.' I reached out across the void of the kitchen table and took her hand in mine. 'You're right, it wasn't him,' I lied.

She pulled her hand away and put her glasses back on, then stared at me for a few seconds. 'It wasn't him,' she said, then stood and fussed once more with the soup. 'Go up and see him now. Tell him his lunch is almost ready.'

Climbing the staircase, I looked at the family photographs that lined the walls – of Christmases, birthdays and graduations. Then the image of my grandfather in the German uniform assaulted me once more, and I looked instead at my feet as they ascended the swirly carpeted stairs.

He was propped up in bed by a mass of pillows, and he wore his paisley-green pyjamas, which seemed too big for him. Somehow, he had shrunk yet again since the last time I had seen him. Scattered on his lap were photographs – black and whites mixed with colourful Polaroids of the seventies and eighties, then newer, shinier photographs of family celebrations. Gran had found all the photo albums, it seemed.

'Ah, Isla,' he said, his watery eyes looking up at me. 'You come see me.'

'Of course I have come to see you.'

'I look at my memories,' he said, nodding at the photographs. 'Some of them I can't find.'

'You've lost some of the photos?' I asked him.

'No. The memories. I can't find them.'

I took a photo from the pile – a black-and-white photograph of a girl playing with a puppy, one I had seen many times before. As a child I had always loved to sit and look through photographs and have Grandad tell me who everyone was. I remembered the other photos that would be in the pile – pictures of the dead taken at their funerals, some sort of strange Polish tradition, apparently.

'That's your second cousin,' my grandfather would tell me. 'Lena, she was fourteen when she died.'

'What did she die of?' I had asked.

'I don't know,' he said. 'What do people die of? Lots of things. She just died.'

A child myself, I had stared at her, lying in a coffin, a white dress stark against that black of her hair; she looked to me like she was sleeping. Every time I would ask to look at the photos, I would check hers first, just to see if she had woken up.

I shuddered at the memory and handed back the photo of the girl and the puppy, and he gave me another in return – one of an old woman, dead, in her funeral clothes.

'My mother,' he said. 'You take one of me soon.'

'No, Grandad! That's awful!'

'Take it, Isla. You take nice photos. Always nice. So, you take one of me when I am dead, all right?'

I agreed to his request, macabre as it was.

'How are you, Grandad? Gran says you have been working?' I played along.

'Working? I don't work anymore, Isla, I am retired. Your gran, she gets things muddled all the time. Don't listen to her.'

I smiled. He was here, he was lucid.

'Grandad…' I slowly took the scarf from my neck and held it in my hands towards him like an offering. 'Do you remember this?'

His watery eyes barely glanced at it. 'No.' He looked away.

'Really? I found it and I think it is yours.'

'You are as muddled as your grandmother. It isn't mine.'

I wasn't going to show him the picture – that would be too much, too cruel. I just wanted him to remember his friend, and maybe it would make him want to remember more.

But before I could ask anything else, Gran appeared at the doorway, tray in hand, with a bowl of hot soup that had spilled half of its contents during her bumpy walk up the stairs.

'Here you are, love,' she said. She eyed the scarf in my hands as she walked towards the bed. She knew what I was up to.

She settled next to him and tucked a napkin under his chin. 'Do you want me to help?' she asked, her hand already on the spoon.

'I am no child, you know. Isla here, she is a child. You go feed her!' He laughed.

She grinned at him, and for the briefest of moments, I forgot that he was ill, and I forgot about the picture. There they were, my grandparents, getting older but not yet faded away.

'Isla, stop sitting there and staring, and go and get me and yourself a bowl of soup – bring it up, would you?' she asked.

I nodded, happy to sit with them, eat lunch and forget the past, for a few hours at least.

It was almost two weeks before the rest of the translations of the diaries were sent to me, and during that time I had not thought about much else besides my grandparents, particularly the scene of the two of them as they ate soup together and talked of the garden, of the weather and of Gran's new exercise class. The love between them was fierce; it excluded all others. It had made me question the need to find out more about the past.

But then, as I read the diaries, as I tried to reimagine the past, it became clear to me that I could not stop now – I loved my grandfather, but he was not the person I knew him to be. I needed to know the truth.

CHAPTER NINE

Tomasz

Poland, Winter 1939

It had snowed for five days, blanketing the villages and towns, and quietening their inhabitants. Tomasz worked the land with his father until the sky had turned to ink, his fingers and toes so frozen that he had to spend the evening by the fire until his blood warmed once more.

One Saturday evening, Tomasz and Zofia lay in the straw in his father's barn, a mass of blankets covering them, whilst their families huddled in their beds against the freezing snow outside.

'I missed you,' she said, holding him close.

'It's been three days!' He laughed.

'I know, but I want to be with you always. Every day.'

'I am with you as much as we can be. When we are married, we can be together every day.'

'Tata has asked me when we will get married.'

'Soon, *kochanie*, soon.'

'You think?' she asked, her voice excited.

'Of course! You know I love you and soon I will go to your father and ask him if you can be my wife, then we will marry and live happily ever after!'

She laughed at him, and he pulled her closer and kissed her forehead, her eyelids, her cheeks.

'Wait! Wait!' she squealed underneath him. 'I want you to tell me more. Tell me what our lives will be like.'

'All right,' he said, lying back in the straw and folding his arms under his head as she rested her head on his chest.

'Soon, I turn twenty, and I will go and see your father. Then, I will ask you to marry me, using my grandmother's ring, which is a diamond set about with rubies. Mama has already said that she thinks you will look beautiful wearing it. When you say yes, we shall get married in town, at the church, in spring when all the flowers have just opened. Then I shall buy us a cottage to live in…'

'And you will farm?' she interrupted.

Tomasz shook his head. 'Perhaps to begin with. Perhaps. Do you remember that tractor in Kowalski's field?'

She nodded. 'It's old now.'

'I know. But I would like to learn how to fix it. How to make it work again.'

'Would that make you happy?' she asked.

'You make me happy.' He grinned at her, then kissed the tip of her nose. 'I'd like it, though. To understand how the engine works. To be able to make one myself, with my own hands. Now, you tell me. I will fix tractors and all sorts of machines, and what will you do?'

'I'd like to teach,' she said. 'The little children in the local school, I'd like to teach them. Then in the afternoons, I would tend my garden. I'd have a beautiful rose garden, like Widow Reiter had.'

'Then you shall have it,' Tomasz said.

'You think so?'

'Of course. There is nothing stopping us from having every-thing we want. We can have a house, a garden, perhaps a shed where I can repair engines. Then one day, we will have a house filled with children.'

'How many would you like?' she asked.

'Maybe four. Yes, four. Two girls and two boys.'

'And what will their names be?'

'Zofia and Irena for the girls. Tomasz and Bruno for the boys.'

'Bruno?' Zofia laughed. 'No!'

'Yes, Bruno.'

'You had a dog called Bruno. I'm not naming my son after a dog!'

'But he was the best dog!' Tomasz laughed. 'We were best friends. We were going to plough the whole of Poland on Kowalski's tractor together.'

She laughed. 'You're so silly, Tomasz.'

'All right. We won't call the other son Bruno, but the first one, he will be called Tomasz, and then we'll get a dog and call him Bruno?'

'Deal,' Zofia said, picking up his hand and holding hers against it.

'I will speak to Tata. Maybe I could go and learn about the engines, or maybe he knows someone who can teach me.'

'But the Germans…' she said.

'No matter.' Tomasz waved her comment away. 'Tata says nothing will change. We can have everything we want. Nothing will be different for us. They'll come and leave us alone, I promise.'

'I love you,' she said.

'And I you,' he replied, leaning down to kiss her. He held her to him until they fell asleep, covered with straw, their arms wrapped around each other.

On Sunday evening, Tomasz sat close to the fire and looked at the beaten red leather of the book that he held in his hands: *The Adventures of Mr. Nicholas Wisdom*. He mouthed the words of the title, then carefully turned the almost see-through pages and read the familiar story.

At some stage he heard his father enter, and he looked up briefly, wondering why he had returned home so late on a winter's night. But the book pulled him back, and he returned to the story.

It was some time before Tomasz realised that his father had not come to sit near the fire in his favourite rocking chair. He placed the book on his lap and looked to see his father at the rough wooden table in the kitchen, speaking quietly to his mother, the pair of them huddled together. In front of them, Tomasz saw, were papers, which his father occasionally pointed to, but he was too far away to see what was written on them.

There was a knock on the door and a friend of his father's, Oskar, let himself in, along with the bitter December air.

'Close it!' his mother admonished.

Oskar smiled and quickly closed the door. 'Good evening,' he addressed them, nodding at Tomasz, then walked towards his father.

Tomasz watched as Oskar sat next to his father at the table, and the two talked in hushed tones. He couldn't hear what they were saying, and assumed it would be to do with the farm, so he ignored them, as they ignored him, and he returned to the book.

'Here, take it,' Tomasz heard Oskar say a few minutes later.

He kept his head down, pretending to read, and listened to the voices that had risen.

'I cannot,' his father hissed.

'It's the only way. Piotr, you worry too much. It will all be all right, you will see. They won't do anything. This way you are protected. You and your family. Take it.'

Tomasz turned his head and saw his father take some more papers from Oskar.

'I suppose it will be as it was before,' his father said to Oskar. 'Nothing will really change that much. We have only been Polish for how long?'

'Since the last war.'

'So, it will be the same. We will go back to being Polish German again.'

'Exactly. Fill this in. Take it all tomorrow.'

'We just take it to the police station?' his mother asked.

'You are saying on the form you have German family. Piotr's mother and his grandfather. I have given Piotr some fake birth and death certificates. That's all you will need. The forms and these. They will believe you.'

'And if they don't?' his father asked.

'They will. You have land. You are telling them that you are a good German family with your own land. That is what you are saying.'

'And Andrzej?' his mother chimed in. 'He fought in the Polish army, Oskar, not the German.'

'Tell them he is dead. Tell them you have only one son now, Tomasz.'

Tomasz watched as his father shook his head. 'I don't know. I just don't know.'

'Piotr, I have risked so much just to bring these to you. I am your friend. I would not do this for just anyone. Trust me, please. Just fill in the forms, take the certificates and be done with it.'

His father nodded.

Oskar stood up. 'I must be leaving.'

'Thank you,' Tomasz's mother said to Oskar; his father kept his head low, looking at the other papers, still on the table.

Oskar strode to the front door and opened it wide. Then he turned to Tomasz. 'Be good. Do as your father asks you, all right?'

Tomasz nodded. 'Yes, sir.'

'Good.' Oskar nodded. 'Good.' He stood for a moment letting in the frosty air, as if deciding whether to stay or leave, then suddenly he stepped out into the night, slamming the door behind him.

Tomasz closed his book and waited for his father to explain. When he didn't venture a word, Tomasz coughed, making them look at him.

'It'll be fine, Tomasz,' his mother said, a fake smile on her lips. 'See, your father has it all sorted. We will register as Germans, get a German ID card – we will be safe.'

'Oskar said that you must say you only have one son,' Tomasz said.

His mother came to him and sat beside him. 'We have to pretend that Andrzej doesn't exist, just for now. If they find out that he was in the Polish army and that he is still alive, we are not safe – he is not safe – do you understand, Tomasz?'

He nodded and stared at his lap.

He felt his mother's hands on his face, gently turning him towards her. 'He'll come back. When all this is over, Andrzej will come out from wherever he is hiding. The Germans will be gone, and it will all be like before. Do you believe me, Tomasz?'

'I believe you,' he said quietly.

She kissed his forehead, leaving behind a tear that had silently fallen from her eyes.

CHAPTER TEN

Spring, 1940

Tomasz lay in Kowalski's field with Zofia by his side. Spring had finally found them, and in the warm April air, they spent their days in the field where Tomasz had spent so much time as a child. He stretched out his hand and his fingers lightly touched hers.

The tractor nearby was rusted, the bright red American metal tarnished with age; the caravan was gone. They lay silently, listening to the wind blow through the orchards and the sound of the river lapping at the banks.

He rolled over onto his side to look at her: her blue dress matched the ice blue of her eyes that watched him from under thick dark lashes. The black curls of her hair fell around her, almost perfectly – she didn't seem real.

He brushed a stray hair away from her forehead, leaned down to kiss her. She kissed him back, then pushed him gently away. He lay down again, folding his arms underneath his head, and stretched out his long legs, listening to her gently hum a tune.

'Do you see that?' she asked.

He turned his head, and she pointed to the sky. 'There – a rabbit.'

He looked at the bloated white cloud overhead. 'That's not a rabbit,' he teased. 'It's a horse.'

'Don't be silly. Anyone can see it's a rabbit.' She laughed and rolled onto her front. She frowned as she played with a blade of long grass, finally snapping it, and wrapping it around her slender fingers like a bandage.

'I need to go soon,' she said. 'I don't want to.'

'I'll take you,' he said.

'I don't want to leave you.'

'I don't want you to leave me either, but I'm scared of your father!'

'Ah, Tata is a baby!' she said, laughing. 'It's Mama you have to worry about, she's the one who kills the chickens for dinner!' She fell silent again. After a few minutes, she laid her head on his chest. 'I'm scared,' she said.

'Of whom, your mama?'

'No. Of the Germans. Of what's happening.'

'Don't be, *kochanie*.' He kissed her. 'I'm here. Nothing will happen. I promise.'

'But where do you think Kowalski has gone?' she asked.

He thought for a moment. They were lying in what they called Kowalski's field, yet Kowalski was gone – he had disappeared in February, and a German family had been given his home and land.

'I don't know,' he replied eventually. 'Don't think about it.'

There was silence for a minute before she asked, 'Do you think Zygmunt is alive?'

Her brother had gone missing whilst fighting with the Polish army as the Germans had advanced, just as Tomasz's own brother had done. The difference was, Andrzej had sent word he was alive; Zygmunt had not.

'Yes,' he said, holding her close.

After some time, they sat up together and stretched, getting ready to leave, and Tomasz looked at the river for a minute, remembering sitting on the bank as a child, dipping his small feet in the water. The wind blew through the trees, and he watched the silvery leaves of the birches catch the light as they moved.

They walked along the riverbank, holding hands. Every now and again he looked at Zofia, watching her blush under his gaze, and felt his heart and head tumble as he realised how much he loved her.

'Do we have time to go into the city?'

'Why?' Tomasz asked her.

'I just don't want to go home yet. Anyway, aren't you curious? Don't you want to see what it is like now? My cousin says that the Germans brought all different types of chocolate. She says the square is much nicer now.'

'I thought you said you were scared?' he asked her. He had heard about the cafés, the bars that were full of German soldiers. But he had heard too about the beatings and the round-ups.

'But you said there's nothing to worry about. Either I should be scared or I shouldn't.'

He looked at her and kissed the top of her nose; he knew he was not going to win the argument. 'If you're sure? But only for an hour,' he answered.

'I'm sure. It will be fine.'

The bus dropped them near Ostrów Tumski, the emerald-green domes of the cathedral glinting in the spring sunshine. They followed the river for a while, then turned into the town square, heading for the Abkewiczs' sweet shop. For a moment, they stood hand in hand, and Tomasz looked about himself, wondering if he had somehow made a wrong turn. He looked down at Zofia and saw that she too was confused.

In front of them, what had once been a family-owned sweet shop was now a café. Tables were set up outside where German soldiers and pretty women sat, talking loudly and smoking, the women's lipstick leaving red smears on the ends of the white tips of their cigarettes. They turned away and were confronted with the large black swastika on a red background which was hung from the town hall.

It was strange to see some things different and others exactly the same, as if there were only half a war, half an invasion, in Poznań.

It had been German before, in the first war, and so many Germans had stayed, made a home for themselves, just like Zofia's father had done. He had married a Polish girl, had a son, a daughter and spoke Polish most of the time. Just a year ago, Tomasz had thought of him as just like everyone else; now, whenever he dropped Zofia home, he felt uneasy, as though he were going to tell Tomasz he was not good enough for his daughter anymore.

It had been foolish to come into town, to think they could eat ice cream as if nothing had changed. Just because the buildings still stood, just because they were safe at night in their beds, did not mean that things were not different – they were.

'We can go somewhere else?' she asked, breaking into his thoughts.

'We could. If you want to?'

She nodded, taking his hand tighter now, and walked confidently through the square. They turned left towards the rear of the town hall, heading to another café that they knew. But before they reached it, Tomasz pulled Zofia quickly over the cobbles of Wroniecka Street.

'What are you doing?' she asked, tugging her arm back.

'Look.' Tomasz pointed.

There, exiting the café, were a few of their friends from school who had joined the storm brigade, Volksdeutscher Selbstschutz. Boys that Tomasz had swung from trees with, stolen apples from Kowalski's orchards with, and who had helped him celebrate his birthdays, were now violent and cruel. They had simply changed overnight and took pleasure in beating Jews and Poles in the streets for only one reason. They believed the German blood that ran through their veins was now superior to their Polish former neighbours. He had heard the stories, and now he could see it for himself.

'Come, let's go.' He tried to pull Zofia away, but she resisted.

He watched as one of them lashed out at a passer-by, knocking him to the ground, and another drew out his gun, holding it against the man's head, laughing as the others kicked and punched him until the man was still and his blood spilled over the cobbles.

The young man returned the gun to its holster. The others laughed and followed him back into the café, each giving a last kick to the heaped body on the ground.

A small boy of no more than five years old suddenly ran up towards the body, yelling, 'Tata! Tata!' and a woman wearing a green dress chased him, her sobs as loud as her son's.

'Let's go,' Zofia whispered, a tremble in her voice.

They walked quickly and silently up Wroniecka Street towards the tram, both of them keen to get home. Suddenly, Zofia stopped. 'Remember Mateusz? He used to have his shoe shop here,' she said. 'He had the nicest of shoes, all pretty ones, with bows on and shiny leather. I was obsessed with them.'

Tomasz stood next to her and looked at the shoes still displayed in the window. Mateusz was the best shoemaker in Poznań. He was quick and accurate. He sewed the soles himself, leaving his initials imprinted on the bottom, so there was no getting away from his creations. But Mateusz was gone now, and soon a German would take this shop, take his place, and charge more if you were Polish.

'Tata promised that on my twenty-first birthday he would buy me a pair of shoes from here, ones with heels and in any colour of leather that Mateusz had, even pink ones, Tata said, if he could find them.'

Tomasz thought about Mateusz, a man he had known since he was a boy. He had gone to school with his children; they had all gone to the same church.

'Are you wondering where they are?' Zofia asked.

'No.'

'I wonder. After the transit camp, where did they get sent?'

'I don't know.'

'I saw them leave. They were skinny, I remember. At first, I didn't recognise them. But it was them. Skinny and walking in a line to the train station,' Zofia said, walking away from the shop. Tomasz followed and took her hand again in his.

'Tata says they've been relocated,' Tomasz said. 'Oskar told him.'

'What does that mean? Where to?'

Tomasz shrugged. The Glowna transit camp set up on Baltyka Street was full of people he knew – their homes taken from them for resisting the German occupation, for being intellectual or rich or sometimes for no particular reason at all. They would be told that they were leaving – just like Mateusz and his family. It did not matter if you were Jewish or Polish – both were targeted.

'I heard that Mateusz had angered a German official by not saluting him in the street,' Zofia whispered as two German soldiers passed them.

Tomasz did not doubt that the rumour was true; it seemed as though the strangest of things were daily becoming a reality.

'Halt!' a voice suddenly shouted at them, waking them from their thoughts and stopping their feet on the pavement.

In front of them a troop of soldiers were busy at work, dismantling the Stawna Street synagogue, taking down the Star of David from its facade. Through the open doorway they could see a construction crew inside, turning the holy site into a swimming pool, he had heard. Beyond, Tomasz could see the tram which would take them back towards the green-domed cathedral and then a bus on to home.

'It's finished!' a tall soldier exclaimed in German. 'The last star!'

Zofia looked at Tomasz, her eyes filling with tears. 'I want to go home,' she whispered to him.

The tall soldier noticed, and he walked towards them. 'Can I see your papers?' he asked in unhurried German. He smiled at them, showing his teeth.

Tomasz quickly pulled the papers out of his pocket, and Zofia did the same.

'Zofia Schmidt, a good German name!' he said. 'Your father?'

She nodded, then looked at her feet and quickly wiped a stray tear from her cheek.

'Why are you upset?' the tall soldier asked. 'You are not upset about this building, are you? Are you sad to lose this Jew building from your city?'

'No,' she answered, raising her head to meet the soldier's eyes.

'She's lost her puppy,' Tomasz said hurriedly, his voice sounding strange to him as it spoke the rarely used German.

'Ah, *Liebling*. Don't cry.' He stepped closer and tilted her head to look at him. 'You'll find him. And if not, I will bring you a new puppy myself!'

Tomasz held his arms at his sides, his hands curled into fists.

'Thank you,' Zofia whispered.

'And you?' The tall soldier looked down at Tomasz's ID card, a vertical stripe across the middle denoting that Tomasz had signed the Volksliste and was Volksdeutsche. 'You are German?' he asked him.

Tomasz nodded.

'Your German is not wonderful. Do you not speak it at home?'

Tomasz could feel Zofia's eyes on him. 'My grandparents were German,' Tomasz said.

The soldier cocked his head to the side for a moment. 'Hm. I suppose,' he said. 'You are tall. Yes, perhaps the correct blood flows in you somewhere. Who is your father?'

'Piotr.' Tomasz looked the soldier straight in the eye. 'He is a farmer.'

'A farmer. Does he have a lot of land?'

Tomasz nodded; his throat had gone dry, and he was finding it hard to swallow.

'And he wants to stay on his land?'

Tomasz nodded again.

'It is good that he is German then, is it not?'

'Yes, it is good,' Tomasz replied, mispronouncing the German '*gut*', inflecting the 't' rather than the 'u'.

The soldier winced. 'Tell your father to speak German at home if he is German.' He handed Tomasz his papers back.

'Thank you again,' Zofia said hurriedly, grabbing Tomasz's hand. 'We must go. Our tram.'

'My pleasure.' He smiled at her again as they walked quickly away. 'If you can't find your puppy, remember, come and look for me. Ask for Franz Lieberenz. Someone will find me, and then I will go and get you a brand-new puppy!'

They could hear him laugh as he walked towards the workers who were now smashing the concrete star into a million pieces.

CHAPTER ELEVEN

They caught the tram to the cathedral, then the packed bus, which rocked over potholes on the road home. After about half an hour, Zofia finally asked: 'Why didn't you tell me that you had papers saying you were German?'

'I didn't know how to tell you. Tata said it wasn't safe to tell anyone.'

'But you let me imagine that maybe one day you would be in that transit camp. I was always worrying about it, Tomasz. You should have told me you were safe.'

'I didn't feel safe,' Tomasz replied. 'I still don't.'

They both sat in silence again, then Zofia lowered her voice. 'Who lied?' she asked.

'Tata.'

'When?'

'In winter, during the census.'

'But you said you could never become German. Never join them.'

He pressed his fingers hard into his temples to try and relieve some of the pressure and pain. 'I didn't want to. I don't want to. But what choice did I have? I believed him, I believed Tata. It was meant to be like it was before. They would come and then they would go. We would be safe.' He looked out of the window, watching the fields fly by. 'He said nothing would change.'

Neither of them spoke again on the way home, but he felt Zofia rest her head on his shoulder and he knew that she had forgiven him.

*

He walked Zofia home and said hello to her parents who asked him to stay for dinner. Zofia held on to his arm, and he knew she wanted him to stay, but he felt drained by the day and he needed to be at home, quiet, where he would not have to smile and pretend that everything was all right.

'I should go,' he said. 'Mama will have made dinner.'

Zofia walked him outside and gently closed the door. She kissed him, deeply, so he wrapped his arms around her waist.

'I don't care what you did. I am not mad at you,' she said, pulling away.

He kissed the top of her nose. 'Good. I did it so I am safe. So we can be together always.'

She kissed him again, pulling away quickly when her father shouted to ask why the door was closed.

As he walked away, he could hear her saying something to her father, something that made him laugh, then the door closed and finally there was silence.

Tomasz reached home as the sun began its slow descent. He saw that the moon was already out, an orange ring around it, and the chalk-white surface looked as though it was dotted with blood. He was sure it was supposed to mean something but couldn't remember what.

His father was sitting in the rocking chair when he walked in. Tomasz sat down across from him, watching him smoke his cigarette. His mother fussed around the kitchen; her hands fluttered across surfaces, cleaning, tidying, rearranging constantly.

'Are you hungry?' she asked, not turning around.

'No,' he said.

'You should eat,' his father said.

'I went into the city with Zofia,' he said. 'They took the last star down from the new swimming pool.'

His father looked away.

Tomasz listened to the creak of the rocking chair as his father gently moved.

'There's an orange ring round the moon,' Tomasz said, breaking the strange silence. 'I can't remember what you said it meant, Mama?'

Her face white, she walked over to Tomasz and gave him a bowl of stew.

'Nothing to worry about,' she said, 'just silly folk tales. They don't mean anything.'

'That's not what you used to say,' Tomasz said.

'Nothing to worry about,' she said again, and wiped imaginary dust from the table.

Tomasz began to eat, and his mother watched him closely. He noticed that she would not leave his side. Her eyes had started to fill with tears. 'What's going on?' he asked, looking at her, then his father.

'Nothing,' his father said.

'Mama?' Tomasz asked.

'Nothing. Everything is fine,' she said.

His father, unsettled, stubbed out his cigarette and rocked in his chair. His mother smoothed down her apron, wiped her eyes and returned to the kitchen.

Tomasz lay down on his bed and thought of the orange ring around the moon. Maybe it wasn't his mama who had told him what it meant. No, it wasn't. It was Kapaldi. He remembered now, one summer when Kapaldi, keeping his promise, had visited him in Kowalski's field. That day, Tomasz was on his way home from school when he found a small pebble near the gate post, a rainbow drawn on it. He put the pebble into his pocket and smiled – his friend was back.

He had waited until evening and sneaked out to the field. Kapaldi had the fire lit and two mugs were set aside.

'Ah, Tomasz!' Kapaldi cried. 'Look at you! So grown now.'

Tomasz gave his friend a hug, his head at the same height as Kapaldi's. 'And you look no different,' Tomasz said.

'Ah, I am getting older, look here.' Kapaldi pointed to some grey streaks in his black hair. 'You see. We are both changing.'

Tomasz sat down and Kapaldi filled his mug with some red wine. 'You are old enough. A young man. You can have a proper drink now.'

Tomasz drank, feeling the warmth fill his mouth, then slide down his throat. He gave a little cough, and Kapaldi smiled at him.

'Where have you been this year?' Tomasz asked and set the mug aside.

'This year I haven't been too far. I went to Hungary to see a friend and stayed a while. The world is not what it was anymore.'

'What do you mean?'

Kapaldi looked sad. 'It is changing. Things are happening, and it is harder for me to move about so freely. There are many, as you know, who do not like me.'

Tomasz knew what he meant. There had been a building unease with Germany's physical and political growth and with the stories he had been told about what was happening to the Jews who lived there. In fact, he had heard that some had left and gone abroad. 'Maybe you could go to England,' Tomasz suddenly said.

Kapaldi shook his head. 'This is my home. I will be all right. Besides, I have to look after you!'

'I'd rather you look after yourself.'

'I'm fine, really.' Kapaldi poured some more wine into his mug. 'Now tell me, how is that girl of yours?'

'She is well,' Tomasz said and blushed.

'Just well?'

'Yes. She is. We go to town together sometimes. We see each other after school if her father will allow it.' Tomasz could feel his face flaming once more. At fourteen, he wasn't used to talking about Zofia, and even with Kapaldi, he felt embarrassed.

'Did you notice the moon this evening?' Kapaldi asked, changing the subject.

Tomasz looked above him where the moon, partly hidden now behind a cloud, seemed to have an orange hue around the edge. 'Why does that happen?'

'I don't know,' Kapaldi said. 'I am sure there is a reason, as there is a reason for everything. But my mother, she would say that it meant something – that it meant things were going to change, quickly, suddenly and sometimes not for the best.'

Tomasz, despite himself, shuddered. He had grown out of believing in folk tales and magic, but Kapaldi always sounded like he was telling him the truth.

'But then, it can mean change in a good way,' Kapaldi said, reaching out for the bottle of wine and pouring more into Tomasz's mug. 'So don't worry, Tomasz.'

Tomasz drank and felt the wine relax him a little. He looked at Kapaldi over the flames, his face a little older, a little sadder than it had been before. This time, his words seemed fake and Tomasz worried for his friend.

Now, Tomasz got out of bed and looked out of the window at the moon. The orange glow seemed stronger than ever. He wished he could see Kapaldi and seek his reassurance. His stomach felt uneasy; his head still ached. Tomasz turned from the window, undressed, and climbed into bed, glad that sleep would take away his fears for some time at least.

CHAPTER TWELVE

'Wake up!'

Tomasz rolled over, half asleep, ignoring the loud voice intruding on his dreams.

'Wake up!' the voice insisted, this time pushing him hard in the ribs.

'What do you want?' he mumbled. 'I'm sleeping.'

'Tomasz! Get up now or I'll kick you!'

Tomasz sat up quickly. To his amazement, he saw his brother, Andrzej, standing over him. For a moment, neither spoke.

'What are you doing here?' Tomasz asked.

'Get dressed,' Andrzej said.

'Why?'

'We are leaving. You are coming with me.'

Tomasz rubbed at his eyes. 'I don't understand.'

'Can you for once, Tomasz, just do as I ask? It's important. Get dressed!' Andrzej handed him his shirt and trousers which he scrambled into, scared at Andrzej's tone. He pulled a jumper over his head and thrust his feet into his shoes.

Andrzej grabbed his arm and pulled him into the kitchen where his mother, in her nightgown with an apron tied over the top, scrubbed at an already clean pot. His father sat in a chair looking at his shoes.

'We're going,' Andrzej said.

'They might not take you,' his mother told him. 'Maybe just wait and see?' She turned to look at them. Her eyes were red, and a false smile played on her lips. 'We'll be all right!' she said. 'Please just stay. Just wait. They won't want Tomasz!'

'Hanna.' Their father stood up. 'They will. They took the Gombrowicz boys and Sendzimir's two. They will take him.'

'It's your fault!' she screamed at him. 'Why did you say to me everything would be all right? Why didn't you…' She began to sob. Tomasz watched his mother kneel on the floor and pull at her hair.

'Mama.' He walked towards her. His father blocked his way and picked his wife up from the floor, holding her close.

'We're going now,' Andrzej said again, and picked up a bag that was near the door.

'It was to keep you all safe,' his father said quietly. 'I had no choice.' Tomasz watched his father slump into the rocking chair and put his head in his hands.

Andrzej turned away from him and opened the door. 'Come, Tomasz,' he said quietly. 'It's time to go.'

'But Zofia…' His head felt as though it was stuffed with something soft and there was a strange buzzing noise in his ears. 'Where are we going? I don't understand.'

'They are coming for you,' Andrzej said. 'They are taking men, boys, to make them fight for their Führer. You are on the list. Tata is on the list – they want his farm. Do you really not understand what is happening, Tomasz? Tata said you were German. He signed to say so, to keep you safe. But it doesn't matter. Pole or German, they will take you.'

He shook his head, but he knew. He had seen what was happening, how his friends had been sent to army training, how you could not refuse, could not hide.

'You're wrong,' Tomasz said.

'Wrong? I know these things, Tomasz. Where do you think I have been? I couldn't come home after we lost, I couldn't risk that for you, so I have been fighting – we have been fighting.'

'Who is *we?*'

'Anyone who cannot bear to see our country taken from us. I got word that there was to be a round-up of young men, and I have to make sure that you are kept away from this. You cannot fight for them. You have to come with me so I can get you somewhere safe.'

'It's all right, Tomasz.' His father came to his side and placed his hand on his shoulder. 'You must go. Save yourself now. Do what I could not.'

Tomasz, his head feeling full of cotton wool, the voices around him muffled, allowed his brother to take his arm and lead him away from his home, his feet following, his legs heavy with each step. He was dreaming, he must be. This was not real.

Reality filtered in within a few hours. Tomasz's brain, still scrambling to understand what had happened, was now aware that this was all too real. The Czarownica woods were dense, filled with ancient oaks and elms. The branches drooped down, and weak moonlight filtered through onto Andrzej as Tomasz trailed behind. He had forgotten to wear his socks, so his brown lace-ups rubbed at the back of his heels, making them red and blistered. His legs were still not as fast as his brother's, whose long strides quickly covered the mossy ground. Tomasz tripped on the root of a tree and fell to the ground, losing sight of his brother for a moment. He lay on the thick spongy floor of the woods, the damp swollen moss and rotting leaves providing a mattress, and he wished he could fall asleep.

He stood up and half ran to follow Andrzej, who was heading further into territory where they had never ventured before. The usual path they had taken as boys, down to the river and into Kowalski's field, was the only way Tomasz knew, but Andrzej seemed to have gained a nose for direction.

The only noises were from the occasional broken twig or the swishing of a leafy branch being whipped back to allow them passage.

As he walked, Tomasz thought of Zofia. Of the ice-blue eyes he would not see for some time – if ever again. With each step he was further away from her, and it took all his strength not to turn around.

They walked for another hour, then suddenly Andrzej stopped. 'Can you hear it?' Andrzej whispered to him. The night had taken away his features, replacing them with the dark, but Tomasz could feel the warmth of his body close to him.

'Hear what?' he asked, but Andrzej did not answer. 'Hear what?' Tomasz asked again.

'Shhhh.' Andrzej stopped. 'Listen.'

Tomasz listened, but all he could hear was the occasional coo of a wood pigeon, its night-time call eerie in the stillness.

'They're not far now. They'll be here soon.'

'Who?' Tomasz asked. 'The Germans?'

'No. Some friends.' Andrzej sat down, his back to a tree, pulled out his lighter and lit a cigarette. 'Sit for a while,' he said. 'They'll find us here sure enough.'

'What are you talking about?'

Andrzej took a deep drag. 'I've arranged for some friends to come and get us. They'll take you somewhere safe.'

'But where will you go?'

'Back to work. Back with the underground.'

'I'll come with you,' Tomasz blurted, thinking only of seeing Zofia again.

'You can't,' he said. 'Mother can't lose both of us.'

'She won't. I don't care what you say. I'm coming with you.'

'Shhhh! Be quiet. Calm yourself. Do not worry about any of that. They will be all right; I will make sure of it. But I cannot be sure of keeping you safe if you stay.'

Suddenly, Tomasz heard the crunch of footsteps, then a call of a wood pigeon.

'They're here.' Andrzej jumped up and cupped his hands round his mouth, cooing back to the call of the bird.

Within moments a familiar face appeared, lit by a small torch. 'Zygmunt!' Tomasz cried.

'Shhh!' Zygmunt, Zofia's brother, said, and smiled. He wrapped his arm around Tomasz's shoulders. 'How's my sister? You have been keeping her safe, I hope?'

Tomasz nodded. 'I have.' Then another, larger man appeared next to Zygmunt.

'You know Kowalski, right?' Zygmunt moved the torch under Kowalski's face.

Tomasz looked at the face he had been frightened of for years. Now he was thankful to see him, and the weapon slung over his arm. Kowalski nodded at Tomasz.

'How's my farm?' Kowalski asked him.

'There's a German family there now.'

'I thought as much. Glad I left when I did. I pray every night that my apples will now rot on the branches so they cannot get their greedy German hands on them!' He spat on the ground.

Suddenly, there was a distant noise of something that did not belong in the woods, coming from where they had travelled. Tomasz looked to his brother whose face showed fear, the same fear that Tomasz felt in the pit of his stomach.

The torch went out and he heard his brother and his friends running away. Tomasz started to run, following them stumbling in the blackness. He could hear the noise of twigs snapping, boots, voices, coming closer.

'Andrzej!' he half shouted this time, panic making his voice rise. He couldn't see the shadow of his older brother anymore. The only thing he could see in front of him was his breath that hung in the air like smoke. He stopped, turned, squinted, trying to see where his brother had gone.

He fell once, twice; his palms were scratched by the bark of a tree as he pulled himself back up.

More voices. He could hear them. Not Polish. German – German voices behind him and coming closer. There was a flashlight now – a flashlight that lit a tree next to him. He dodged behind a trunk. His breathing was coming hard; his heart punched against his ribcage.

One, two, three, he counted, then ran again, zigzagging now, trying to avoid the light. Then he heard a dog bark – loud, vicious – and voices reacting to the dog. The flashlight scanned the woods closer to him now. Tomasz continued to run, scared to look over his shoulder, scared to see who was there.

He tripped again, this time losing a shoe. He scrabbled about amongst the dirt and leaves trying to find it. The dog. He could see the dog now. A German shepherd. The dog had seen him too and began to gallop towards him, barking, its mouth wide showing its teeth. Tomasz pushed himself up and ran. He looked behind him to check where the dog was. It was coming closer, the voices following it, shouting. The flashlight found him, illuminating him.

'Halt!' A voice appeared in the form of a German soldier. 'Halt!'

Tomasz looked over his shoulder and saw that the soldier had a gun pointed at him.

Tomasz stopped. The dog was behind him, barking constantly, waiting for its master to appear. Tomasz turned slowly, his hands up in submission, and as he turned the flashlight blinded him, so he could not see the features of the person walking up to him. He squinted and tried to shield his eyes with his hand. The shadow was approaching, closer and closer. But before it reached him, something hit Tomasz on the back of the head, and the last thing he remembered was falling to the ground.

CHAPTER THIRTEEN

Tomasz didn't know what time it was. Hands were under his armpits, pulling him out of the back of a truck then along the ground. He could hear the birds singing their morning song and the church bells ringing. He opened his eyes. It was daylight. Where was he? Home? Where was Andrzej? And his head, his head hurt so much, a thick throb that radiated around his skull and behind his eyes.

German voices spoke, then he was dropped to the ground. He turned his head to the side and saw shining black boots.

'Get up!' a voice commanded in Polish.

Tomasz slowly, achingly pushed himself up. Around him were five soldiers, the grey slate of their uniforms dull against the bright colours of the countryside, like rain clouds in an otherwise blue sky. His eyes were drawn to the heavy pistols that sat neatly in their belts.

'What is your name?' one of them said. Tomasz didn't answer. The owner of the voice roughly grabbed Tomasz's hair, turning him to look directly into his face. 'I said, what is your name?' Tomasz looked into the roughly shaven face of the tall soldier from in front of the swimming pool with the smashed star.

'Tomasz,' he whispered.

He released his grip. 'Tomasz who?'

'Jasieński.'

'Your father is Piotr, the farmer.'

Tomasz nodded.

'You're awake. You can walk on your own now.'

A fat soldier pushed Tomasz forward to walk, shoving him every few steps for no particular reason.

The tall soldier walked in front, a curl of smoke appearing over his head.

Tomasz could not grasp that this was real. He could still hear the birds in the trees. The sun was out in full; the grass was still green. If this was real, then surely the sun would not be here. Surely the birds would know not to sing, and the grass would have dried up and died?

His mouth was dry. He had never known such thirst, yet his body was damp with sweat. His feet tripped over themselves, keeping up with the pace of the strong soldiers who had dragged him.

It wasn't real. *Look, there, a cow.* His father's cow grazing, not even looking up at the men walking past. If it were real, the cow would surely look up?

Tomasz tried to think quicker – the farmhouse was nearby now. He tried to walk, to breathe, to find saliva for his mouth, when he was thrown to the ground once more, his head almost landing on the boots of the tall soldier.

'You remember me, don't you?' he asked Tomasz. 'My name's Hauptmann Franz Lieberenz – that's captain in Polish. You remember, don't you? You were with a pretty girl wearing a blue dress.'

Tomasz tasted dirt and blood from a split in his lip. Should he run? Could he run? Would they get their weapons out quickly enough?

'Stand when I am speaking to you, Pole!' Lieberenz yelled at him, kicking more dirt into his face.

He stood quickly, feeling his heart hammering in his chest and sweat covering his skin.

'Your father said you would be coming back soon.' He smiled at him, almost in a friendly way, and Tomasz was not sure how to respond. 'I'm glad you are here now. You know, we were worried when you weren't home.'

Tomasz watched him blow a silky stream of smoke out in front of him.

'You don't speak?' Lieberenz asked, looking at him quizzically. 'Yesterday you spoke German and now I speak to you in your language, yet you are quieter.'

'I speak.'

'Well then, talk to me, young Tomasz,' he said.

Tomasz wiped the dirt from his face and the blood from his lip, streaking his palm with crimson. 'You speak Polish well,' he ventured.

'Thank you, thank you, young Tomasz.' Lieberenz was pleased with the compliment. 'I try. You know, most of them don't bother. I tell them all the time we have to try; it helps us in the end.'

Tomasz glanced up at him. A game was being played that he didn't understand.

'How old are you?' Lieberenz asked.

'Nineteen.'

'Nineteen. My goodness. When I was nineteen, I was already fighting for the Führer. What have you been doing?'

'Helping my father,' Tomasz answered.

'Sure, sure. Farming in a way helps the fight. It feeds us, no?'

Tomasz looked towards the front door, which he had run through with Andrzej; it seemed like a lifetime had passed since then.

'They are there, your parents. Inside. Shall we see them?' the Hauptmann asked, but before Tomasz could answer, he roughly shoved Tomasz into the door, making it swing open quickly.

Sitting at the table were his mother and father. His mother had been crying. His father was smoking and did not look at him.

'And, of course, your girlfriend,' Lieberenz added. Tomasz looked at him, confused. Then he heard footsteps behind him.

'Zofia!' he said.

She was brought into the room by one of the other soldiers who sat her with his parents. Her face was pale, her blue eyes wide. As she walked past Lieberenz, he smiled at her and pinched her on the cheek.

'Ah, so pretty,' he said.

Tomasz watched as Lieberenz walked over to the rocking chair, stroking it almost affectionately before sitting down. He rocked backwards and forwards, the wood creaking under his weight.

Tomasz felt a weight on his chest and exhaled, then took in some more air. *Just breathe*, he told himself, and looked at Zofia who had not taken her eyes from him.

'You see, Piotr, I have looked at your documentation. You say your son Andrzej is dead. And Andrzej was in the Polish army. So, I cannot understand how a good German family, with ancestry such as yours, would have a son in the Polish army?'

Lieberenz leaned back in the chair and his fingertips drummed on the wood of the armrest. Tomasz could hear the crackle of his father's cigarette as he smoked. Was he ever going to answer? More sweat collected at the back of his neck, and he tried not to wipe it away.

'I'm sorry, my Hauptmann,' his father finally said. He pushed himself up from his chair, his hands shaking. 'My son Andrzej was wild, I could not contain him. That damned Polish government made him go. They could not be trusted, I told Andrzej this. I tried to make him a good German man, just like Tomasz. But he would not listen, ran away with his friends.'

'And never came back,' Lieberenz said.

'Yes. He never came back. He died a foolish boy. And now I only have Tomasz. He helps me on my farm. I have no one else to help me.'

'The way you talk is weak for such a German family.' Lieberenz looked at his father.

'I am sorry, *mein* Hauptmann. After my parents died and my grandparents, we did not hear the language anymore.'

'Perhaps I could send you away to work with your German brothers then? We are sending people every day to farms in the Reich, to factories and such. I think you would like it there. Hard work. Back-breaking, you could say.'

'I'm sure I would like that.' His father's voice was as shaky as his hands now. 'But I would like to do my part, to provide food for our soldiers as they fight.'

Lieberenz looked at the armrest for a moment, as if trying to decide. 'Fine. Good. That is a good idea. But Tomasz will come with us. I think it is the least you can do for your Führer. It will make up for what your other son did.'

His father looked at Tomasz and Zofia. 'But his help on the farm?' he pleaded. 'I need him here.'

'You choose, then. He can stay with you, but you can all move as I suggested. Or, he can come with us and you can manage without him. What do you decide?'

His father did not answer, and looked to Tomasz for help.

The Hauptmann noticed and turned to Tomasz. 'Tomasz, do you not want to be German? Do you not want to help our fight?'

Suddenly, the other four soldiers appeared from outside as if a secret signal had been given to them. Each held a gun. Each pointed the gun at a person's head. One gun at his mother. One at his father. The soldier with Zofia had his pistol trained on the back of her shining, raven hair. Then Tomasz felt the metal at his own temple.

Tomasz looked at the fear in his mother's face, her shaking hands. His father's face had turned to stone, as though if he didn't move, they could not hurt him. But Tomasz could see that his long, thin legs were shaking.

Tomasz needed to answer. He looked to Zofia. A silent tear was now tracking its way down her face, her eyelashes wet, her lips dry. He needed her. He could not leave her. But the gun. *The gun, Tomasz,* his brain told him.

'Ah, I am getting bored,' Lieberenz said and stood, raising his arm in the air. Tomasz saw the soldier with Zofia ready his pistol to shoot.

'No!' Tomasz shouted, moving towards Zofia, to take her in his arms. 'I'll go,' he said quietly.

'Good, good! I knew you would see sense,' Lieberenz said.

Tomasz felt arms pull him away from Zofia, away from his family, taking him outside and pushing him into the back of a jeep. He heard the engine start.

This couldn't be happening.

The driver put the jeep in gear. *Zofia,* he thought. *I haven't said goodbye. I have to…* Then they were moving. The jeep was driving him away from his home – it was real. 'Zofia!' he shouted, turning to look at the house.

Tomasz had only cried a handful of times in his life. The worst time was when he fell out of the barn loft and hit his head on a piece of wood on his way down. The shock of the fall, the wind knocked out of him, the faint taste of metal on his lips, alerted him to the fact that he was hurt, and with this knowledge he cried. He was five years old then, and his mother had come running and clasped him to her bosom, encased in its usual white apron. He cried into the apron, as his mother shushed him with a stroke on the head and soothing words that only mothers know.

Now, in the back of the jeep, watching the farm disappear into the distance, he felt the familiar knot in his stomach and hot tears ran down his cheeks; and although he had not fallen, he felt as though the wind had been knocked out of him again.

The sun had dipped behind thick grey clouds as they drove away, and it seemed to Tomasz that all the colours had disappeared. The green grass of the fields was now muted; the roses in what was once Widow Reiter's garden were droopy and monochrome.

They reached the crossroads into town; a statue of the Virgin Mary stood watching them, her sad eyes turned to the baby in her arms. The crossroad was meant to be a special place where wayfarers would be under the protection of saints, but Tomasz wasn't sure anyone was watching out for them anymore. He couldn't pray, not when he knew he would never see her again.

The driver argued with Lieberenz over which way would be the quickest, and stopped the jeep. Tomasz looked back towards his home and saw a blue dot in the distance, far down the track. The dot became bigger and bigger until he saw Zofia, the skirts of her blue dress flying around her as she ran towards him.

Just then, the driver made up his mind and turned left. Zofia stopped running and stood on the dirt track, a blue haze amongst all the grey.

CHAPTER FOURTEEN

Summer 1941

Tomasz wrote quickly as the candle burned low. His fingers were numb from holding the pen so tightly, but he continued to write, the nib scratching at the paper until suddenly the flame of the candle was extinguished with the hiss of wick in melted wax.

He tucked the letter into the waistband of his trousers and lay on his makeshift bed on the floor of the barn.

After a few minutes, Tomasz turned onto his side. He could hear his friend Jan snoring next to him. He closed his eyes and tried to fall asleep. He could feel the letter in his waistband and thought of everything he was trying to say – everything he had seen.

It had been over a year, over a year since being taken away from home, since being sent to war.

His mind raced over the months of training, followed by deployment. There was Kraków, the day he witnessed the murders of a group of academics who had been lined up against the walls of the library and shot; their bodies slumped forward into the dirt, blood quickly covering the ground. In Lublin, he saw a Polish journalist hanging from a lamp post; his crime had been daring to sing the Polish national anthem. He could still smell the bread from the bakery, hear the sound of cars, the footsteps of pedestrians and the chatter of the soldiers as they marched past the hanging body, as if it wasn't there at all.

He had not fought yet. Had not met an enemy besides the odd peasant who, with their rusted shotgun, fired at them as they marched past.

He had trained. Trained and then marched. He had worked in a factory on base in Kraków, storing, packing, sending supplies to the men on the front, the big strong German soldiers who were pasted onto posters around the city. Tomasz, Jan, Eryk, the men he had met in training, they were not these men. They were Polish and not what the Führer wanted on the front line when the enemy first caught sight of the invincible Germany.

He opened his eyes and lay on his back – it was pointless. These night-time images had become normality for him: the faces of the dead swarming around him; the journalist's face, full of blood, his neck elongated from the stretch of the rope, looking down at him whilst women, with their children held tightly in their arms, looked at Tomasz with still, dead eyes. No matter what he did, they would not disappear. As the night wore on their faces would become distorted and replaced with features of those that he knew: Zofia, Andrzej, his mother and father.

He shifted again; the straw was making him itch. He heard someone moan, then shout, fearing something in their dreams. Someone else coughed and rustled about, making themselves comfortable.

Tomasz thought of the beginning of all this – that day on his father's farm when Hauptmann Lieberenz took him away from Zofia, from his home.

He turned again, trying not to think, trying to make his mind a black space, hoping his thoughts would tumble into it like a hole and he would fall asleep.

'You all right?' Jan asked.

'No,' he answered.

He heard Jan shuffling around. 'Cigarette?' he whispered.

Tomasz nodded, even though Jan would not be able to see him, grabbed his shoes and followed his friend outside.

Although it was late, the sky was not black but seemed bruised to Tomasz, streaked with grey and purple, heavy with the promise of a summer storm. They picked their way across the farm courtyard and sat underneath the willow tree that grew on the edge of a slope, the spread of the Ukrainian countryside below them.

'Here,' Jan said, handing him a cigarette.

They smoked in silence for a while, listening to the sound of the wind in the trees and the gentle snoring of thirty of their fellow soldiers coming from the barn.

'How much further do you think we have to go?' Tomasz asked Jan.

'Who knows,' Jan answered.

'Do you think we'll get to Russia?'

'Probably. At least, we will if we are not killed.'

'That's not funny, Jan,' Tomasz said, punching his friend in the arm.

'Lighten up. What can you do?' Jan ground the stub of his cigarette under his boot and immediately lit another. 'You still dream of them, don't you? You still see their faces?' Jan asked.

Tomasz nodded. 'Do you?' Tomasz asked him. 'Do you dream about what you have seen?'

'Sometimes. Most of the time my head is empty, and I don't remember anything.'

'You're lucky.'

'I think I would rather dream, though. Sometimes, it feels as though I am dead – just blackness.'

'I'd swap with you,' Tomasz said.

'Ah, now. Come on, Tomasz, enough of this. Let's think of happier things. Tell me again about Zofia.'

Tomasz smiled. He liked this game. He would tell Jan about how they met, the fair, Kapaldi. He would tell him about their dreams for the future.

'You think you will ever see her again?' Jan asked.

'I hope so. I only got two letters from her when we were training and both were censored, so it didn't feel like her, like it was really her talking to me. You know what I mean?'

'I know.'

'I think I will see her again. If I just keep my head down, try to get through it. The war can't last forever.'

'So that's your plan? Stay in this hell of an army that has taken your home from you?'

'What choice do we have, Jan?' Tomasz turned to look at his friend. 'What choice? You don't do what they say, and they kill you.'

'I'm only doing what they say for now. But not for long. I'll get out, you'll see.'

'And where will you go?'

'I'll join my brothers in the fight. Join the partisans.'

'And you think it will be easy just to leave?'

'No idea. But worth a try.'

Tomasz shook his head.

'You could leave too.'

'I can't. Zofia and my parents are safe because I am here.'

'What? You think they will be in danger? No one will care if a few Poles leave. Think about it.' Jan tapped the side of his head. 'I need some sleep. You coming?'

'Not yet.'

He felt Jan squeeze his shoulder and heard the crunch of his footsteps as he walked away.

For the rest of the night Tomasz sat looking out at this foreign country that reminded him so much of home, thinking about what Jan had said. Would no one really care? He imagined himself running away, hiding on a train perhaps – but he could never imagine reaching home. Instead, it was the image of Zofia and his parents at gunpoint that sprang into his mind. He tried to shake the thoughts from his head, and headed wearily to the barn to get some rest.

The next morning the battalion moved out, and instead of marching north towards the train station were given orders to march east towards a hamlet where some partisans had killed a small group of German soldiers that had tried to take it a week before.

They were joined by a gunner and two jeeps filled with extra ammunition. 'How many of them are there? They said it was a hamlet,' Tomasz whispered to Jan.

'Not many. They just want to teach them a lesson.'

Tomasz sweated in his uniform, which scratched his skin raw under his armpits and between his thighs. He looked to the sky, wishing for the storm to break, for the clouds to part and allow the rain to fall.

Soon they reached the crest of a small hill. The hamlet was in the valley beneath, a loop of dense woodland above and around it, seemingly protecting it.

Before they even had full sight of the houses, the sound of bullets ripped through the hot thick air. Tomasz, Jan and Eryk took cover behind an old oak tree whilst officers roared orders to move forward, behind the safety of the jeeps and the gunner whose constant machine fire lit up the air with quick cracks.

Tomasz held his rifle, felt the trigger under his finger. He crouched behind the jeep, getting ever closer to the whitewashed houses. Suddenly there was a flash, and he threw himself behind a tree as a grenade exploded, taking the front of the jeep and the driver with it.

He felt something at his shoulder and looked to see Jan's dirty face streaked with sweat. 'Seems they've got some weapons there!' he shouted at Tomasz above the rattle and crack of the exchange of gunfire.

Another explosion, then another, and Jan grabbed Tomasz's arm and pulled him through some thick undergrowth. Tomasz tripped, fell flat on his face, and remembered being in the woods at home, running from the Germans. He didn't miss the irony that he was now one of them.

He got up, checked his rifle and chased after Jan, hoping he would lead him away, lead him out of this. Jan stopped in front of him, and he saw that there were others; Eryk, and three other German soldiers from training.

As Tomasz reached them, they turned, put a finger to their lips, and motioned for him to sit back on his haunches. He did. Then they pointed. There, just twenty metres down a grassy slope, was the hamlet.

'We can take it,' a German soldier called Andreas said.

'Are you mad? You saw what they have. It's a trap.' Eryk shook his head.

'You would say that, Pole. Stay here then and do nothing, see what happens. You'll be court martialled.'

Tomasz looked to Jan to see if he should stand with the others and charge with them. Jan dug around in his pocket and brought out some cigarettes which he offered to Tomasz and then to Eryk. Andreas and the two others sneered at them and ran down the slope towards the first house.

'They may be right,' Eryk told Jan. 'If we don't do something, then they will court martial us.'

'They'll never make it out alive, you'll see. We're better off here.'

Within minutes, gunfire rattled through the houses. Then, Andreas was running back towards them, two partisans at the window, their sights trained on him.

With a quick pop-pop, Andreas went down, his legs coming away from underneath him, causing him to droop over like a wilting flower before hitting the ground, blood spurting from the holes in his chest and covering the green of the grass in a sickly crimson. Tomasz could see the men at the window look to the undergrowth where Jan, he and Eryk still sat.

'Move!' Eryk shouted at them. 'Get back!'

Jan scrambled away first, then Tomasz and Eryk at the rear. Branches scraped at Tomasz's face as he ran through, and he felt blood trickling down from a cut above his eye.

Before they could find a place to hide, they found that they had run through the woods and come out at the other end of the hamlet. A few metres in front were five men dressed in peasant clothes, holding back the ten or so soldiers who were inching themselves towards them behind the barrier of the last jeep.

'They can see us,' Jan said.

'They haven't looked our way yet.' Tomasz looked at the peasant men again, whose backs were to them.

'Not them – I mean our comrades over there. They can see us, and they want us to do something to help them.'

'So what do we do?'

'We do nothing. I told you, I am not fighting for them. I am doing nothing.'

'We can't just stand here – we'll be killed, Jan.'

'Fine. Look as if you are going to do something then. Just don't kill anyone. Shoot in the air, miss on purpose. Let them capture us, or let us escape. Either way, do nothing, Tomasz.'

Tomasz dug around in his pack for a grenade; Eryk saw him do it and readied his rifle. Jan did the same.

Tomasz dropped to the ground and inched forward, chest in the grass. He licked his lips. They were dry and cracked. He wanted to look behind him to Jan and Eryk, see if they were still there, but he could not. The peasant men were just like his father, like Kowalski. He knew men like this.

He could feel the sweat dripping down the nape of his neck. Why hadn't Eryk or Jan fired? What was he meant to do?

Suddenly, he heard gunfire smattering the ground in front of him, dirt blasting into the air and grinding into his eyes. Tomasz pulled the pin, waited, and then threw the grenade before scrambling back towards his friends.

He did not see the explosion and hoped that he had missed. But the sound told him that he had been on target. Someone screamed and wailed with a pitch Tomasz hadn't thought possible. He turned to see three of the men, still on the ground. Another was being dragged away; the skin that once covered his ribcage was now gone, burned away by the explosion to reveal the mangled bone and bloody insides where his organs tried to hold on.

Tomasz doubled over and vomited until there was nothing left but bile.

That night, the men camped not far from the hamlet, where the last of the executions had been conducted by the more bloodthirsty of the soldiers. The last partisan to die, Tomasz was told, was the one whose body had taken so much of the explosion from his grenade. 'He died calling for his mama,' a soldier called Albert told him.

'You shot him?' Tomasz asked.

'No. How could I? He deserved to feel that pain until the end. He was one of those that killed Andreas. Good work, Pole.' He slapped Tomasz on the back.

Tomasz sat with Eryk and Jan, who had found a good spot leaning against the rear tyre of the jeep. Someone had lit a fire and was cooking a rabbit they had shot, whilst another peeled potatoes they had found in the houses. Others were still down there, looting, laughing, and spending the night in a bed, they said. But it was someone else's bed, and Tomasz could not imagine sleeping in the bed of someone he had killed.

'You had no choice,' Jan said.

Tomasz smoked his cigarette and did not look at either of them. He had chosen. He had made his choice whilst they had done nothing, whilst they lay on their bellies doing nothing.

Eryk passed him a bottle. He looked at it, at the clear liquid inside. 'Vodka,' Eryk said. 'One of them has found a stash of it.'

'I don't want it,' Tomasz said. 'It isn't mine.'

'Drink it, Tomasz. You need to. After what happened. Drink.'

Reluctantly, Tomasz took the bottle and drank the vodka back, feeling it burn his throat.

'I used to have a dog,' Jan said suddenly, as if they were all somewhere else, sitting at a café, talking as friends do.

'Me too,' Eryk said. 'When I was a boy.'

'Did you? Did you have a dog when you were a boy, Tomasz?'

'Bruno,' he answered. 'We were going to plough the whole of Poland together in a tractor.' Tomasz noticed his speech was already a little slurred as he spoke. He took another sip of the vodka.

'I can't remember what my dog was called,' Jan said. 'That's terrible, isn't it? I can't remember his name.'

'We can't remember everything,' Eryk said.

Jan and Tomasz nodded.

Soon the alcohol took hold and he fell asleep with his head leaning on Jan's shoulder.

Before dawn broke, he was woken by an officer. 'Jasieński?'

'Yes, sir?'

'Get up. You're leaving.'

Tomasz stood and looked down at his two friends who slept in foetal positions, their rifles by their sides filled with unused bullets, the knapsacks still containing their grenades. He turned away from them and followed the officer to the top of the hill, where a jeep waited to take him away.

'The powers that be have heard about what you did. They have a reward for you,' the officer said. The engine quickly roared into life, taking him away from Jan, from Eryk and from the bodies of those dead by his own hand.

On the drive, he felt uncomfortable, scared even. It was not normal, was it, for a soldier, a private, to be rewarded for doing his job? Perhaps he would get a new rank, but why would he be moved? 'Where am I going?' he finally asked the driver.

'Train to Kraków.'

'Any idea why?'

The driver shrugged. 'Probably get some time off.'

'But I'll come back to this?'

'Probably. Who knows? I'm not really the right person to ask.'

He was awarded an actual seat on the train rather than travelling in a cattle car, as he had done before. It was second class – a wooden bench in a compartment with a middle-aged woman in a flowery summer dress that had once been fashionable but was now thin and stretched unflatteringly over her large bosom. An unshaven and sweating man sat next to her, and every few seconds he wiped his damp palms on his knees.

Tomasz sat across from them, saw that they looked at his uniform. He smiled at them and they looked out of the window. Would it always be this way? he wondered. Would anyone ever be able to see the real Tomasz again, the man who everyone knew to be kind and helpful? He had never noticed before how lucky he had been; he could smile at people, talk to them, and he had taken it for granted. Now, he was in a uniform he did not wish to be in and was ignored, spat on and shot at. He thought of the partisan he had killed with the grenade. He wanted to go back, go back and shout out to them that he was one of them, he was in the wrong uniform, that was all! But he couldn't. They would have killed him, or his fellow comrades would have had him court martialled. Either way, he would have been dead by now.

Jan and Eryk had not shot a single round; they had not even tried. They let Tomasz throw the grenade, take all the guilt, all of the responsibility. He didn't feel bad that he had not woken them when he left. He was being promoted, being taken away from this soldier's life, and he deserved it – not them. They had done nothing.

The train had picked up speed and Tomasz had not even noticed. The sweating man was rolling a cigarette and he noticed Tomasz watching him. The man looked to the woman, and then back at Tomasz. Once the cigarette was rolled, he handed it to Tomasz and said something, but Tomasz did not understand. He took the cigarette from him, smiled, and said thank you. The man nodded back and started to roll another cigarette for himself.

Tomasz decided to smoke alone and stood up to leave the compartment. As soon as he did, he heard the woman start to shout at the man. He turned to look, seeing her jab her finger at him whilst the sweating man ignored her and lit his cigarette.

At the end of the corridor, he stood next to the train door and pulled the window down to watch the countryside race by. Heads of corn bobbed in unison in the breeze, a golden carpet, looking innocent as if nothing had changed. For a second, he was angry that it all looked so serene – so *normal*. It should look different – the green of the grass should not be so bright, so eager; the sunflowers should not be turning towards the sun. Instead, they should be dipping their heads in acknowledgement of everything that was happening around them.

On a bend, the train slowed, and Tomasz saw a farmhouse in the distance and two large bay horses grazing in a field nearby. He thought of his own family, of his own farm. Would Tata be tending the cows? Would Mama be cooking as always in the kitchen, humming a tune as she worked? He doubted it, but he wished it to be true.

He blew out a thick plume of smoke that rushed out into the wind. And where was Zofia now? As soon as the thought entered his mind, he tried to ignore it, the pain of thinking of her too much. But thoughts of her assaulted him as he neared his own country. He let himself hope for a moment that he might see her again. He wondered what reward he would get. A week's break would give him chance to see her, even a day, two days. But then his imagination took over. Perhaps he could be reassigned, perhaps he could tell them he was good at fixing engines, and they would let him mend things, instead. Maybe he would be able to see Zofia at the weekend, still get married, and still have a life that they had planned.

Of course he regretted what he had done. Of course he felt sick at the thought of the man with his flesh burned away. But he had been freed now because of it. He was free.

CHAPTER FIFTEEN

The train slowed, its wheels squealing against the tracks as it pulled into Kraków station. As the train shuddered to a stop, the platform filled with steam. Tomasz looked out of the window but could only see vague shapes through the thick haze. As it cleared, he saw the pockmarked face of Gefreiter Drange – a familiar face from his days of training.

When Tomasz stepped out, he realised that the train had entered a large terminus and for a moment he looked around him at the sheer size of it. So far, he had seen small, provincial stations, with very little happening. This was different, though. All around him was noise – screeching and whistling from the trains, the rumble of porters pushing large carts filled with luggage, the hurried steps of commuters. Soldiers were everywhere, coming, going, laughing, marching. People sat on benches waiting for their train whilst others scattered towards the terminus exit. As Tomasz followed the exodus with Drange, he saw a little girl holding on to her father's leg. The father, in the darkest shade of SS black, picked up the girl and held her close, then kissed her cheek. The girl sobbed into her father's shoulder and held him tighter. As Tomasz passed them, he looked away.

Outside the station a jeep waited with its engine warming, a driver at the wheel. Tomasz climbed into the back and looked out of the window as they made their way through the city traffic towards his reward.

They reached a five-storey gothic building on Wehrmachtstrasse, a busy street with office workers coming and going, and trams tinkling their bells as they raced up and down the cobbled road. Tomasz caught a glimpse of trees on the corner – a park and then a café, a bookshop. For a moment, just the briefest of moments, Tomasz felt alive again, as if the world hadn't ended just yet. The names of streets had changed, but here – look here – this was still his Poland.

As Tomasz followed Gefreiter Drange up the stone steps to the heavy front door, he noticed that some of those who walked by kept their eyes cast down as they passed. The feeling, so fleeting, of being alive, of feeling some joy, was immediately gone. He was suddenly aware again of the uniform he wore, of who he now was.

Inside, Drange led him up two flights of stairs to the second storey and down a dark draughty corridor where their feet marched noisily on the shining wooden floor.

It was a large office; five floor-to-ceiling windows let the summer light in, illuminating the dust particles that danced in the air, and Tomasz saw yet another familiar figure sitting in a wingback sage-green chair.

'Come in, Tomasz. Please, sit.' It was Hauptmann Lieberenz – the man who had taken him away, the man who had threatened to kill him.

Tomasz's heart missed a beat. He was supposed to be rewarded – but this? Lieberenz was no reward.

Tomasz slowly walked across the thick Oriental rug that covered most of the floor and took his seat opposite Lieberenz. He waited for him to speak. But Lieberenz ignored him and for a few moments, he attempted to roll a perfect cigarette. When he seemed happy, he took a box of matches out of his pocket and scratched a flame, lighting the cigarette and inhaling deeply.

A small thread of tobacco had escaped, and Tomasz watched as he stuck the tip of his tongue out, the tobacco on the end, and with his fingers lifted the strand and then frowned with distaste. Lieberenz looked at the cigarette and stubbed it out. Then he started his process again; rolling the tobacco in thin white paper, his brow creased with concentration.

A piece of music was playing on a gramophone on the Hauptmann's desk, the music soft at first, soothing, but then growing louder and more fervent. Tomasz tried to listen to the music and closed his eyes, ignoring where he was, ignoring the Hauptmann and his cigarette routine. He had heard this piece of music before – old man Abkewicz had played music in his sweet shop, and this had been one of his favourites. Tomasz was suddenly assaulted with the memory of his past – the smells and sounds; the taste of the creamy toffee *krówki* on his tongue as Abkewicz regaled them of stories from his childhood. But then, Tomasz remembered that Abkewicz was gone. He opened his eyes and looked at the Hauptmann; he didn't like the music anymore.

Finally, a curl of smoke appeared over Lieberenz's head, and the Hauptmann nodded in appreciation and faced Tomasz.

'This tobacco is not great,' he said, speaking to him in German. 'I am always searching for the best. This is some I bought whilst in Hungary. It is not good. But it will do.' Lieberenz then closed his eyes and waved his free hand in the air as he smoked with the other, conducting an imaginary orchestra.

'It is beautiful, no?' he asked Tomasz, his eyes still closed, still lost in a dream of music.

Tomasz tried to answer but found that his mouth was completely dry, his tongue seemingly stuck to the roof of his mouth.

The Hauptmann opened one eye to look at him.

'There is water over in that jug,' he said, pointing to a small table with a jug and glasses next to it. He closed his eye again, and Tomasz stood and helped himself to a glass of water. He could hear the man humming along with the music.

He drank quickly, almost choking, then poured another and took it with him to his chair.

'It is Beethoven,' Lieberenz said.

Tomasz nodded.

'His ninth symphony. You know music?'

'No, not really,' Tomasz finally spoke.

The Hauptmann opened his eyes and watched Tomasz for a moment. 'Ah, as a farmer it is not necessary to listen to such music, I suppose? But soon, Tomasz, you will see, music like this will be in every household in the new Germany. You will have a gramophone like I have one here. Wouldn't you like that?'

Tomasz nodded.

'Are you scared, Tomasz?' Lieberenz suddenly switched languages, asking him the question in Polish.

He swallowed hard, then took a gulp of water, remembering what had happened at the farm, remembering the guns pointed at his family, at Zofia.

'It is all right if you are scared.'

'I'm not scared,' he finally said.

'You have done a brave and wonderful thing, my friend. Brave and wonderful!' The Hauptmann clapped his hands. 'As soon as I heard, I was congratulated on having recruited this Pole who felt so much loyalty to the party and to our cause! As such, we find that perhaps there are more just like you. Just as brave. Just as loyal.'

Tomasz watched as the Hauptmann came over to him and perched on the edge of his desk in front of him.

'In a moment, a photographer will arrive from our prestigious magazine, *Die Wehrmacht*, and do you know what, Tomasz?'

Tomasz shook his head in response.

'You and I are to be photographed together, photographed whilst I award you this!'

With a flourish, Lieberenz took a blue velvet box from his pocket, opened the lid, and showed Tomasz the treasure within.

'It's the Iron Cross, for your bravery, you see. The photographer will come, ask you some questions, and write a lovely article about how our Polish brothers are coming together in the fight. You are going to be famous, I wager!'

Tomasz felt his stomach turn. He didn't want to be famous for what he had done. He didn't want the medal. He wanted time off to see Zofia, to check that the world was still the same somewhere, waiting for him to return.

'You know, because of you, I have been promoted to Major. So, I have to thank you.' Lieberenz held out his hand, and Tomasz stared at it. 'Shake it.'

Tomasz took his hand, and the Major grasped it tightly.

'Thank you, my friend. Thank you.'

For a moment, Tomasz felt calm. The Major was truly thankful. The Major who had threatened him, threatened his family, had said thank you.

There were three quick raps on the door before it opened, revealing a small man with a large camera.

'Where shall we stand?' the Major asked him.

The photographer indicted the large bay windows. 'The light is good here; it will make the medal shine, I think – catches the sunlight.'

The Major nodded towards the window, and Tomasz stood and followed him.

First, the Major pinned the medal on his lapel and the small man clicked away at the camera. Then the medal was unpinned, and Tomasz held it in its velvet case for the world to see. Next, a shot was taken with the Major shaking Tomasz's hand. The camera clicked and clicked, and the room was hot, and Tomasz, tired and confused, felt the room spinning. He looked at the Oriental rug that seemed to dip and roll. Suddenly, he felt strong arms holding him up, sitting him in a chair.

'Drink this.' The Major handed Tomasz a heavy crystal glass filled with whiskey. 'All of this excitement! I see you are tired. Drink up. I think that is all for now,' he told the photographer, who left quietly.

After a few minutes, Tomasz felt the room had stopped moving. He sipped at the whiskey. It tasted woody with a hint of honey. The taste suddenly reminded him of home, of summer days and fresh honey smeared on thick pieces of homemade bread.

'You need to rest,' the Major said.

Tomasz nodded.

'I have secured a room for you in a boarding house. Your own room. You can rest, then come and see me tomorrow. I have a new job for you; a better job.'

Tomasz nodded once more and sipped again at the whiskey.

'You are to help recruit some more of your Polish brothers into this glorious army. Once they see you, and see the article, I am sure they will flock to join.'

Tomasz looked up. 'How?'

'How? Don't you remember how you were recruited? That is how. But if you are as persuasive as I know you could be, it can be much easier, much simpler.'

Tomasz drank down the rest of the whiskey and looked at Lieberenz. His face was animated, cheeks rosy and eyes bright. If he had met him before the war, he would have thought that he was a good man, a fine man, who spoke eloquently and who maybe would have been his friend. But Tomasz knew better than to trust the smiling face, the neat, styled hair and well-defined features. He knew better.

'Things are changing yet again,' Lieberenz continued. 'We have not yet defeated our Russian enemies and the Führer fears a winter war. We have lost many good German lives, so it is time to ask our Polish friends to assist us. Now we *make sure*

Polish men sign the Volksliste so that they can fight for their Germany.'

'I'm not going back?' Tomasz asked.

'Not for now. For now, I need you here. Downstairs, Gefreiter Drange is waiting to take you to your room. That is nice, is it not? No more sleeping with all those other men?'

Tomasz nodded.

'You see, I am good to you if you are good to me.' Lieberenz smiled, reminding Tomasz of the story of a wolf he was told as a child. 'Report here to me tomorrow morning.'

Tomasz stood slowly, trying to take in everything that had just happened, everything that was going to happen. He walked to the door and turned to salute him.

'Oh, and by the way,' Lieberenz suddenly said, stopping Tomasz. 'Your brother. He is back from the dead – a rat of Kraków, nonetheless – working in the underground. It seems miracles can happen.'

Tomasz's hand dropped to his side. It was all a game. Lieberenz was playing a game with him. He waited a moment for the Major to arrest him or hit him, something to show that the lies that had been told by his father were now uncovered and Tomasz was going to pay the price.

But nothing happened. Lieberenz said nothing.

Tomasz finally walked out, closing the door behind him.

The game continued as he was taken away from Lieberenz. He was sure they were taking him to prison, to a work camp or worse, but instead he was taken to a small house not far from Lieberenz's office where a thin German woman, with eyes that were too far apart, gave Tomasz brown trousers and a shirt and showed him to his room.

'Only officers stay here,' she told him as she handed him the bundle of clothes. 'But you're not an officer, are you?'

'No,' he replied simply.

'Not German either, are you?' she asked.

He shook his head.

She eyed him for a moment as if his face would give her some answer she craved. But admitting defeat, she lowered her eyes and handed him a bar of soap, which felt oddly heavy in his hands. 'You need to wash,' she said, then held her head high as she left him, as if disgusted with him and the smell of him.

Tomasz washed and changed, then sat on the single bed, wondering what to do. This was his reward, or part of some elaborate game – a small camp-size bed with a rough brown woollen blanket and a job recruiting his own into an army he hated. He felt foolish for thinking that he would see Zofia again, foolish for believing that he was out of the worst of this.

He heard footsteps on the stairs, coupled with deep voices. Then came laughter. He opened the door, and three men were heading downstairs; the last looked at Tomasz.

'*Abendessen*,' he told him.

Tomasz nodded. '*Danke.*'

'*Schnell.*'

The man continued his descent and waved for Tomasz to follow.

Tomasz reached the bottom of the stairs and made to follow the others into the small dining room, where they sat around a table covered in a crisp white cloth. But the woman from earlier, with the far-apart eyes and thin lips, appeared, blocking his entrance.

'*Polen sind nicht willkommen*,' she told him.

Tomasz saw the other men stop talking, and look to see who she was speaking to.

'Polish are not welcome,' she said again slowly. '*Bist du dumm?* Are you stupid?

Tomasz shook his head. 'Where do I eat then?' he asked, trying to get the German correct on his nervous tongue.

'You think I care? Go out. Find your own food. Curfew at ten. You're not back, I report you.'

'*Danke*,' he said, unsure of what else he could say.

As he walked, he checked over his shoulder, uneasy with his new freedom, scared that he was doing wrong. Was this a trap, perhaps? Had the woman sent him out knowing he would get in trouble? But no one was following him; no one seemed to care.

Yet uniforms were everywhere – black SS uniforms, grey soldiers' uniforms; batons and guns strapped to their belts. They did not bow their heads when they walked – they looked at everyone, and anyone who did not look back when they approached was met with questions: *Who are you? Where are your papers? Where do you live?*

Tomasz automatically checked the pocket of his trousers for his own identification papers and wished he could have stayed in his room.

He rounded a corner and came upon two men smoking, leaning against a chemist. As soon as they saw Tomasz approach, they stopped talking, turning their eyes away. A stray dog cocked its leg against a lamp post, then trotted past Tomasz, and oddly he wondered where it lived.

He turned down a small street, cobbled and quiet, then another and another until he was not sure where he was anymore.

A woman walked across the street, arm in arm with a man in an SS uniform. Her hair was shiny, her clothes new, and she laughed with the man. Another woman passed them wearing a grey skirt and brown cardigan, her head bent low.

Tomasz saw the SS guard notice the woman – notice how she kept her head down. He stopped walking with his date and turned.

He shouted at the woman, who stopped and very slowly turned around. The SS guard walked to her and asked her a question. She still did not look up.

Tomasz stopped walking and watched as the SS guard said something else to her, and she shook her head. He reached to his belt, reached for the baton, and the woman instinctively held her hand to head.

Tomasz, without thinking, ran across the street and was almost knocked down by a car that screeched on the road to avoid him. The squeal of the tyres stopped the SS guard, and he looked over to see what had happened. The woman, sensing her chance for escape, turned and ran.

The SS guard did not notice that the woman was gone; his eyes were on Tomasz. 'What the hell are you doing?' he asked Tomasz. 'You want to be killed?' Then the SS guard followed Tomasz's gaze to where the woman had been. He looked back at Tomasz. 'Papers. Now,' he commanded.

Tomasz handed them over, his hand shaking a little. He watched as the guard scrutinised the identification, shaking his head. 'Lucky,' he said as he handed them back. 'Very lucky.'

The woman in the nice clothes and shiny hair had stood back during the scene. Now she stepped forward, a smile plastered on her face along with the make-up. She nodded at Tomasz, then took her date's arm. 'Come,' she said. 'Let's go for that dinner.'

Tomasz heard her voice, heard the accent. She wasn't German, she was Polish. As she walked away, she turned her head and looked quickly at Tomasz, and he saw that the smile had gone.

Tomasz continued to walk, trying to shake off what had just happened. He wanted to go home, home to his parents where things would make sense again. He would be Tomasz, son of Piotr the farmer. He would have his girlfriend back, and they would get married. He would have babies with her and watch them grow up. He would walk the streets and not feel fear, out of place in his own country. Then, he would go to bed at night and sleep. He would sleep without nightmares.

Tomasz looked around him, trying to work out where his wandering had taken him. To his left, he saw the river and suddenly felt as though he were home. He walked to it – the Vistula, a river that tracked through Poland all the way to Warsaw. He wanted to sit, to put his feet in the water like he had when he was a child.

Behind him he heard shouting. He turned and two Gestapo were beating a man on the pavement. Even from this distance, Tomasz could make out the star stitched into the man's clothing.

One of the Gestapo noticed Tomasz and shouted something to him, but Tomasz pretended he hadn't heard and walked quickly away. A bridge was a few metres away, over the river. Tomasz walked over it, away from the Gestapo, away from the beaten man.

He wanted to stop, to find food, but his feet would not comply. They moved him down alleys, around shuttered houses, through empty parks as though they feared if they were still, they would not be able to start again, would not be able to force themselves to get back to the house with the officers and the thin-lipped woman – *Polen sind nicht willkommen.*

But then he did stop. The shock of what he saw stopped his feet, filling his shoes with lead, and he wished he had never crossed the bridge.

In front of him were two stone arches. A Star of David sat atop them, just like the one from the swimming pool that had been smashed by the soldiers in Poznań. Guards stood at the entry point, their guns ready – always ready.

A small man pulling a wooden cart came towards one of the guards from the inside of the arches. He was thin, so thin that Tomasz could not understand how he could pull the cart. The guard said something to the man, and pointed at a pile on the floor next to another guard who was smoking a cigarette.

Tomasz could see that the little man had the star on his clothes. Tomasz looked to the ghetto that the man had come from; he had heard of it, of course, but had never seen it.

The man went to the pile on the floor, bent down and dragged something towards the cart. A body – the man was dragging a body.

The guard laughed at the man, who was trying to lift the body into the cart as it repeatedly fell onto the cobbles. The more it fell, the more the guard laughed.

Tomasz could smell something now – a smell of death. It was a foul odour that he thought would stick to him forever. Then, strangely, he thought of the stray dog and wondered if he had managed to escape from here, or were animals allowed to be free but not the people?

The guard laughed again as the body hit the cobbles once more; this time the head smashed, and blood covered the stone.

Someone bumped into Tomasz, then another. He was standing in the middle of the pavement.

'*Ausweichen!*' A woman said angrily to him as she banged into him – get out of the way!

'*Przepraszam,*' he said. *No, wrong language.*

'Stupid Pole,' the woman spat back.

Polen sind nicht willkommen: Tomasz heard it again and again in his head. He looked at the arches, the man, his cart. *Polen sind nicht willkommen.* The SS guard and his date, the Gestapo beating the man. *Polen sind nicht willkommen. Juden sind nicht willkommen.*

He started to walk again.

He walked quickly now, away from the arches, away from the man and his cart and the bodies. He bumped into people as he strode along the pavements who looked at the soldier, wondering who he was. What was his rush? Where was he going?

He tried to retrace his steps, getting lost as he wandered down streets with strange names and past buildings he had never seen before. He wanted to run but knew he could not.

He tried to find the bridge, the river, but found himself in a small park, a rectangle of green grass bordered with sweet-smelling flowers and thick bushes. A bench was at one end and a small water fountain. No one was around. It was as though this place were separate from the whole of Kraków, and Tomasz wondered whether he was imagining it. What was it his father had said that people saw in the desert? A mirage? Yes, this was it, a mirage.

He sat down on the bench and felt the reassuring wood underneath him: could you feel wood in a mirage? He didn't think so.

The sky had darkened, and heavy black clouds hung menacingly low. He needed to get back. He had turned left then right, then left? No. Right then left?

He thought of the man and his cart again. The man could never go home. Neither could Tomasz. Suddenly, he heard the rumble of thunder. He stood and walked back to where he thought he had come from. Without realising his mistake, he turned left when he should have turned right and was back near the bench again.

In the distance he heard the clatter of footsteps over the pavement. Then the roar of thunder clashed overhead, and a flash of lightning lit up the sky. The storm was finally breaking.

He looked left and right, trying to think again which way to go, when from the side of a tree in the park, he saw a shadow emerge. A strike of lightning illuminated the figure, and Tomasz peered at it, straining to see who was there, almost unable to believe his own eyes as he made out the colourful scarf wrapped tightly around the man's neck. Tomasz walked towards him.

It was Kapaldi. 'You always said you were magic,' Tomasz whispered, allowing his friend to pull him into an embrace. 'I believe you now,' he told him.

Kapaldi held him close. Tomasz could smell the familiar scent of bonfire on his friend's clothes, the smell of Kowalski's field – of home.

'There isn't much time,' Kapaldi said, letting him go. 'It wasn't by magic that I found you, but by your brother.' He pulled an envelope out of his pocket and handed it to Tomasz. 'Take it. It's from Andrzej.'

Tomasz took it and looked at the familiar writing. 'You have seen Andrzej?'

'I have – he is well. I am working with him, have been for some time,' Kapaldi said, standing a little taller, proud to be helping the fight. 'Our friend Kowalski saved me and took me to him. He reminds me a little of you.'

'I am nothing like him,' Tomasz said. 'Nothing. He fights for Poland, and I am fighting against it. Take me to him, please. Take me with you.' Suddenly, Tomasz felt tears on his face; he wiped them away with the back of his hand. 'Please, Kapaldi, take me with you.'

Before he could say anything more, he was once again embraced by his friend who shushed him like a baby until the tears stopped.

Tomasz stood back. 'Please,' he asked again, exhausted.

'I cannot for now, Tomasz, but how dearly I wish I could,' he said. 'You need to be where you are for now – we need your help.'

'My help?' Tomasz wanted to laugh. 'What help can I be? They know Andrzej is alive, they know that Tata lied. It's all a game they are playing with me. They'll kill me, Kapaldi, I just know they will.'

'But you are not dead now. You are alive. You are breathing, well fed. Your family, Zofia, they are still alive. For now, you are fine. You are well. And we need you now.'

'I think you should tell Andrzej he is wrong. I cannot help.'

'You can, and you must. Read the letter from your brother. Be brave, Tomasz, think of the day that you saved me from those boys who were beating me. Think of how brave you were then.'

Tomasz shrugged, feeling less brave as an adult than he did at ten years old.

'You walk so quickly now,' Kapaldi said, a smile on his lips. 'I remember when you were young, you could hardly keep up with me. But now, now you stride like a man!'

Tomasz smiled a little as Kapaldi swung his arms and goose-stepped, grateful that his friend was trying to make him laugh and bring some measure of joy to him.

Suddenly, lightning illuminated the dark heavy clouds again, and a clap of thunder was overhead. Kapaldi stopped his imitation and looked at the sky. 'Still no rain,' he murmured.

'It will come,' Tomasz said.

'Maybe, maybe not.' Kapaldi shook his head wearily. 'The storm is here to rage for a while, I think.'

Tomasz looked up to the sky to watch the lightning, and then he counted, waiting for the thunder. When he dropped his head, his friend was gone.

CHAPTER SIXTEEN

By the time Tomasz found his way back to the boarding house, it was almost the curfew. He opened the front door and the landlady, her thin lips pursed, stood, watching the grandfather clock in the hallway as it ticked loudly towards the hour.

Tomasz nodded at her as he entered. She turned on her heel and stalked away.

He climbed the stairs to his room and shut the door, locking it, remembering the earlier stares from the German officers.

He sat on the edge of his bed and kicked off his shoes, then opened the letter from Andrzej.

Brother,

I hear you are back. There are ears everywhere – you'll soon see. Some of the ears have already heard why you are back and what you are to do. It seems that Major Lieberenz has made you one of his friends – one of his useful Poles. Yes, my brother, I know of him. Don't be so surprised. We all know of him. Know how he enjoys it when someone refuses to join the army – what he does to them.

He knows of us too, I am sure.

I need your help now, Tomasz. We all do. You have access to things, to areas and offices where we cannot go. There will come to you some requests, one by one. You won't recognise the faces, or the voices that tell you what they want, or the hands that deliver notes to you when you least expect it. But know they are your friends, my friends.

Brother, be careful. You are in a situation now that could easily fall apart.

Now, I need you to destroy this letter. Destroy all letters that come to you.

To give your mind some rest, know that Mama and Tata are all right and Zofia is fine.

Kowalski says hello. Said to remember the day on the tractor, how you almost mowed down those boys! You are braver than you think.

Your brother,
A.

Tomasz did not destroy the letter straight away. He read, then re-read it. Then he lit a cigarette. After a minute or two, he held the cigarette to the corner of the paper and watched as it slowly burned.

Early the next morning, Drange came to collect Tomasz and took him to the same building that held Lieberenz's office.

He was led to a different office this time, and given some papers to sign for his new role by a secretary whose ashtray overflowed with cigarette butts. Other secretaries sat at their desks, all of them smoking and chatting, the tip-tap of the typewriter keys hitting the creamy paper filling the office space until Tomasz wondered how they didn't go mad with the repetitive noise. Some of them smiled at Tomasz; one girl, who wore red lipstick, blew him a kiss, then giggled with her friend. Despite himself, Tomasz smiled.

He was taken to the rear of the building where jeeps and cars were parked. Two soldiers were kicking a ball of newspaper between them, laughing and trying to score against the other. Drange shoved Tomasz in front of them, stopping their game.

The soldier who had just scored had his jacket open, revealing a white vest underneath. He smoked a thinly wrapped cigarette that seemed to be stuck to his bottom lip. When he looked to see who had interrupted his game, he removed the cigarette and flicked it on the ground.

'Who is this?' he asked Drange.

'Tomasz Jasieński. Your translator.'

'Ah, *danke*,' he said. Tomasz saw that he had a large scar that ran from the left side of his cheek all the way to his ear. 'So, you're who the Major sent? He said you were the best. Better be.'

Tomasz heard Drange's footsteps retreating behind him.

'You'd better speak German, Pole. I am not speaking your language.'

'I speak German,' Tomasz said, his pronunciation too thick, too false.

The soldier with the scar laughed and the other, shorter soldier, joined in. 'He speaks German. You hear?'

The soldier started to button up his jacket. 'I'm Officer Bauer, and that there is Private Schröder. Same rank as you. You can just call him Schröder. Me, you call Officer. I earned it. See?' Bauer leaned towards Tomasz, running his finger down the scar. 'Some Pole did it at the start of all this. Right, Schröder, you drive. Jasieński in front; me, I get the back seat. You two are my chauffeurs.'

Schröder ran around the side of the jeep and climbed in. Tomasz made to open the door when he felt a kick towards the back of his knee, making him fall.

'Open mine first,' Bauer told him. 'Didn't your mother teach you manners?'

Tomasz opened Bauer's door, and Schröder laughed.

'Stupid Pole,' he said, as Tomasz climbed in beside him.

As the engine sputtered into life, Tomasz looked out of the window, swallowing the anger that was trying to find its way out of him.

They did not drive for long and pulled up outside a row of brick houses with a factory at the end of a cobbled street that churned out white smoke into the blue sky.

'What's the time?' Bauer asked.

'Almost ten,' Schröder said.

'Perfect.'

Tomasz climbed out of the jeep and opened the car door for Bauer, who stood staring at the factory. 'Another few minutes,' he said to no one in particular.

Schröder led the way to a house close to the factory and knocked on the door.

'When they answer, you tell them we're here for Kacper,' Schröder said.

Tomasz stood next to Schröder and waited. He could hear Bauer behind him, tapping his foot and whistling out of key.

'Knock again,' Bauer said.

Schröder knocked again. Harder this time. '*Öffnen!*' he shouted, hitting the door with the butt of his rifle.

Suddenly, the door was opened by a woman who was pale with fear.

'Go on! Tell her,' Schröder said.

'We are here for Kacper,' Tomasz said, as gently as he could.

The woman held rosary beads and ran them through her fingers. 'He's not here. I told them before. He's not here.'

'She says he is not here,' Tomasz told them.

Bauer stepped forward now, and with an open hand slapped the woman hard around her face.

She screamed but did not fall. 'He's not here, he's not here!' she repeated to Tomasz.

Bauer hit her again, and this time she fell, crumpled like litter onto the dusty floorboards. Instinctively, Tomasz moved to help her, offered her his hand to take.

'What are you doing?' Bauer asked him.

Tomasz looked at the woman, whose eyes were full of tears, and back to Bauer. 'Nothing,' he said.

'Ask her again. Tell her he has been seen. Tell her he is to go into the army, he will sign the list, he will go.'

Tomasz relayed what Bauer told him.

She looked at him in amazement. 'You are Polish,' she said. 'You are. Why are you helping them? My son is young. Why does he have to go and fight? He is not German.'

Before Tomasz could answer, footsteps were behind them, quick, fast across the cobbles – Kacper was escaping.

'Perfect,' Bauer said, smiling.

Schröder ran first; Bauer walked behind. Kacper was quick, and Schröder could not keep up.

Kacper was in front of the factory doors as twenty or so men exited, smoking cigarettes, eating bread rolls – break time.

Tomasz watched as Bauer stopped walking, pulled his gun from his holster and, with a quick shot that echoed off the brick walls and the cobbled ground, hit Kacper in the back, sending him flying. He landed in front of the men; his body sprawled on the floor whilst the chimneys above him from the factory puffed out white smoke.

'Perfect,' Bauer said again, turning to grin at Tomasz.

Behind him the woman was wailing, still on the floor, holding her stomach.

'That will teach them. They'll all see that. When it's their time, they won't try to run.' Bauer lit a cigarette and stood by the jeep, waiting for Tomasz to open the door.

'What next?' Schröder started up the jeep.

'Paperwork. Few things we haven't had chance to do. Jasieński can do them for us, can't you?' Bauer said.

Tomasz only nodded; his voice seemed to have disappeared.

His assigned desk was a small one, near to Schröder's. A door behind led into Bauer's office, which he kept closed and locked. Schröder was allowed in; Tomasz was not.

Tomasz was given files containing lists of names – men who had signed the Volksliste, men who hadn't signed and should be made to. It was now Tomasz's job to keep track of the names, find the men, and search out individuals like Kacper who were reluctant. Bauer liked these the best – it was just like hunting, he told Tomasz, but easier and with more satisfaction at the end.

Tomasz stared at the names – there was an Andrzej, a Jan, an Eryk. His own name jumped out at him too; all of them were just like him, and he was to find them and send them away – or worse.

He tried to concentrate, tried to file the papers in some order, but his mind could not settle after the events of that morning. Who would pick the body up? Would the men help or would Kacper's mother have to pick her own son's dead body off the road?

Schröder came out of Bauer's office, took some cigarettes from his desk, then went back inside, locking the door. Tomasz stared at the door for a while, thinking of where he was, and of Andrzej's letter. Then he turned to the papers and began to sort them: men who were free, men who were not, and finally, another pile – men who Andrzej may be able to help.

That first day he did not take any papers with him. Schröder came back to his desk around four and did not leave again.

But that night, in his room, Tomasz looked about, wondering where he could hide the papers even if he brought them back. Surely, Lieberenz mentioning Andrzej meant that he thought he would get in touch. Was this all part of his game? He couldn't do it, could he? Could he risk it?

He thought of the dead men that he had killed with his grenade, then he thought of the boy Kacper and how he had run to save his own life. Yes. He could take this risk. Be brave, like Kapaldi asked him to be.

He lit a cigarette, and with bare feet walked over the floorboards, seeing if any were loose. In the corner, next to a small wardrobe, a plank creaked as he put his weight on it. On all fours, he pulled at the board until it gave way from the thick, rusted nail that held it down. Underneath was less than an inch of space, dusty and dirty. He could fit some in there. Not too many, but a few at a time. He placed the plank back, edging the corner of the wardrobe onto it.

He sat on the floor, his back against the wardrobe, and lit another cigarette. He had to be brave, but he felt no courage – he had to try and find some. He looked at the cigarette and wondered if Zofia smoked now – everyone seemed to. His mind wandered to her again even though he didn't want it to. Suddenly, he was flooded with a memory of her when she was sixteen or so, and when a friend of hers at school was bullied for being Jewish. She had told him about it on their walk home from school; how the girl had been spat on, punched and kicked. Finally, the bullies had stolen her lunch and thrown it in the bin, so at lunch, she'd sat at a table on her own and stared at nothing.

'I didn't know what to do,' she had told him. 'What would you have done?'

'I'm not sure. I'd like to think I would have stopped it, but that's an easy thing to say, not to do. These are strange times.' Tomasz had remembered his earlier meeting a few weeks before with Kapaldi, when he'd seen the orange ring around the moon. 'Things are changing. I don't know what we are supposed to do anymore.'

'I think I should do something. You should have seen her, on her own. I felt my heart break for her a little.'

Tomasz had wrapped his arms around her shoulders and pulled her close. 'You are too nice. Too caring. If you do anything, you know they will target you too.'

'I'm not Jewish.'

'Doesn't matter. Everyone is picking sides – that's what Andrzej says.'

The rest of the walk home, Zofia had been unusually quiet. Normally, she would argue her point with him until he agreed that she was right. This time, she stared ahead of her, a little crease in her forehead, as if whatever she was thinking about, she couldn't share with him.

The following day, Tomasz waited outside Zofia's school. She didn't come out with the rest of her classmates and for over an hour, Tomasz stood and waited. Just as he thought he would go home – perhaps she had been taken ill – he saw her appear. She reached him. There was dried blood on her nose, a bruise already appearing near her eye; her hair was pulled out from its braid and her dress was torn. Yet she had a huge grin on her face, and kissed Tomasz on the lips before handing him her school bag for him to carry as normal.

'What happened?' he asked.

'I helped her,' she said, as she took his hand.

'But look at you. Why are you so happy?'

'Because I helped her.'

'Zofia! Stop!' He grabbed her arm and pulled her to a standstill. He looked at her, at her top lip which was beginning to swell. 'Look what has happened to you! Yes, you helped her, but look at you!'

Zofia's smile dropped. 'Tomasz, she needed someone to stand up for her, to be brave for her because she couldn't. It was all right for me to do it. They can try to bully me and hit me, but I can handle it. She cannot. I sat with her at lunch and shared my food with her because they had thrown it away again. She was so grateful, Tomasz, so grateful.'

'But it's not right, Zofia.' He stroked the side of her face.

'Was it right when they did it to her?'

'No, but this is you. I know you.'

She dropped his hand. 'So bad things can happen to people as long as you don't know them?'

The anger in her voice made Tomasz's stomach flip a little – he had never seen her like this before. 'That's not what I meant…' he started.

'But it's what you said. I thought I loved someone who was brave and who would always take care of everyone – as much as he could.'

'You do. That is me.'

'Is it?'

They started to walk once more. After a few minutes, Tomasz took her hand. 'You are brave. You are the most courageous creature I know. I will learn to be like you. Give me time.'

She did not look at him, but her thumb stroked his hand as he held it. He was forgiven – for now.

The memory of her bravery, of what she had said to him, resonated with him now, as he sat with his back to the wardrobe. He would prove it now – he was doing what she would have done; he just wished he could tell her so she would be proud of him. One day he would tell her. He stood up and made sure the wardrobe was flush against the wall. Then he lay down on his bed and fell into a dreamless sleep for the first time in months.

It was a week later when he finally got the chance to put his plan into action.

'Are you ready?' Bauer came out of his office, buttoning up his jacket.

Tomasz looked up from his desk and saw two of the secretaries walk into the office, the smell of their perfume cloying in the cramped space. One of them kissed Bauer on the cheek; the other looked at Schröder as he stacked his papers importantly on his desk, even though, Tomasz knew, he had not done any work that morning.

'We're going for lunch,' Bauer told Tomasz, as he walked past with his date who hung on to his arm.

Tomasz nodded.

'Stupid Pole,' Bauer said as he left. Schröder laughed. The women laughed. And Tomasz felt his face flame with anger.

As soon as they were gone, he pulled a file out from the top drawer in his desk. The file contained around forty men who lived in Kraków and nearby suburbs. He opened it, checked that it was the right one, and quickly took the papers out, folded them – once, twice –opened his jacket and put them into his shirt pocket.

As soon as he did, there was a knock on the door behind him, and Tomasz jumped in his seat.

'Officer Bauer in?'

Tomasz turned and saw the face of another secretary who was a little chubbier than the other girls and wore too much make-up.

'He's gone already. For lunch.'

The woman nodded at him, looked longingly at Bauer's door and then back at Tomasz. 'You all right?' she asked him.

'Yes. Why?'

'You just look…' She stopped, cocked her head to the side. 'I don't know. Sort of ill. A bit pale maybe. I don't know.'

'Would you like me to give him a message for you?'

She looked at the closed door again and gently shook her head. 'No.'

Tomasz smiled at her, wishing she would leave. Looking down, his jacket was still open, the papers in his pocket visible, and he quickly leaned forward to try to cover them.

'Where are you from?' she asked suddenly, and walked into the room. She sat on the edge of Schröder's desk.

'From here. Well, not here exactly. Poland. I'm Polish,' he spluttered.

'I thought so. Your German is pretty weak.'

'What about you?'

'Berlin. Jumped at the chance to travel, go somewhere new. But really, it's all the same. Same men, same people.' She waved her hand dismissively.

Tomasz nodded, unsure what he was meant to say. She was silent for a minute, tapped her long nails on the desk and looked at Bauer's door again. 'Do you have a girlfriend?' she asked.

'Yes,' he said.

'Shame.' She stood up and walked to the door. 'I'm Elsabeth.'

He smiled at her. 'Tomasz.'

She nodded at him and walked out, closing the door behind her.

As soon as she left, he buttoned his jacket quickly, his stomach turning, over and over. He tried to concentrate on his work but could not; the papers in his jacket felt like a weight pressing down onto his skin.

The afternoon dragged by and was made worse when Bauer and Schröder returned and asked to see some of the papers he had organised.

He stood, for the first time, in Bauer's office. Bauer sat behind his desk and looked at the names, where the men worked, their ages.

He looked disappointed at the names in front of him. Then he took one out. 'Give this one to Schröder. These are easy; they signed the list and live within the city. He can do them.'

Tomasz took the paper from him. 'Am I to go too?'

'No. Keep going through the names. It's easier if we can organise a big round-up. See if we can get a good bunch in some of the factories.'

Tomasz nodded, handed a paper to Schröder, and sat back at his desk.

The tick-tick of the clock made him itch with nerves, the small bundle of papers at his breast weighing him down.

The sky had just turned its late-summer dark blue by the time Tomasz left the office. He was glad to be away, glad that his mission had worked. Now all he had to do was get back to the boarding house and hide the papers. Birds trilled their evening song, and a warm breeze whispered through the elms that lined Wehrmachtstrasse. Tomasz listened to the birdsong and felt uncomfortable – it was as though they did not realise what was happening around them. People were being shot, rounded up, pushed into ghettos and worse. But the birds still sang in their trees, still flew in the blue sky.

He was almost back to his room, back to his silent landlady, who he had found out was called Frau Schneider, and the officers who looked at him with disgust, to eat a meal of bread and cheese in his room, when he felt a light tap on his shoulder.

'Don't turn around,' the voice behind him said. 'Keep walking.'

The figure then appeared at his side and overtook him, walking in front quickly so Tomasz still could not see their face.

He checked behind him and saw two women, both carrying shopping bags, chatting to each other. Then he looked in front of him, thinking he was to follow the person, but they were gone.

Confused, Tomasz stopped walking. He looked down the street, back behind him. The two women with their shopping passed him, laughing at something.

Then there was nothing, but the birds trilling their bedtime stories.

When Tomasz reached his room, he unbuttoned his jacket and took off his shoes and trousers. As he did so, a small square of paper fell to the floor. He picked it up.

Try the best chocolate in Kraków.
Visit Lewicki Pijalnia Czekolady. 10 Rynek Podgórski.

A.

CHAPTER SEVENTEEN

Later that evening, Tomasz dressed in a dark shirt and trousers, folding the note from Andrzej into a tiny square and placing it in his pocket. He took the papers from under the floorboard where they had been hidden for only an hour or so, folded them and placed them in the waistband of his trousers, pulling the shirt over the top.

He waited as late as he could to leave, until the heavy footfall of the officers was gone from the stairs. He knew he did not have long and could easily be caught. Frau Schneider locked the front door each night at 10 p.m. and did not open it again until morning.

Above him he heard the first door close, the first set of footsteps heading to bed. Then, the second and the third.

He breathed out heavily, steadying himself. He could do this. He could. He closed his eyes and thought of the man with the cart. He thought of the soldier laughing. He thought of Zofia being brave at just sixteen. He opened his eyes. He must do this.

Tomasz opened his bedroom door and looked down the stairs. He held his boots in his hand so his socked feet would be quiet on the stairs.

Slowly, he closed his door and winced as the latch clicked into place. Would the Frau hear this? He waited, counted: *One, two, three.* Then he looked at the door, at his hand holding the doorknob; he could not lock it, it was a risk. His brain told his hand to let go of the doorknob, and he watched as it slowly, gently, let go.

Tomasz crept down the stairs as quietly as he could, imagining that each noise meant death, as though he were treading on a mine.

He reached the bottom and stood waiting for a sound. He could hear that she was in the kitchen; pots and pans were being hauled about as she prepared for the officers' breakfast.

There were three steps to the front door – just three. He made each one as though he were treading on ice – steadily, quietly, lightly. Finally, he reached the door and turned the handle, praying it would open, praying she had not locked it early. With a neat click, the door unlatched, and gently, Tomasz opened it and crept out into the still-warm September night.

Tomasz walked quickly, avoiding the main square where there were too many eyes, too many people. Instead, he skirted around towards the river, towards the bridge that would lead to the chocolate shop. Every time a military vehicle drove past, he tried to hide in the shadows of doorways. Every part of him wanted to run, to get there as quickly as possible, but he knew it would make him stand out, make someone suspicious.

On the bridge there were two officers and two girls, and they were laughing. As he drew closer, one of the girls took the hat off the officer's head and put it on her own. The officer laughed and kissed the girl. Tomasz thought of Zofia, then looked away and crossed onto the other side.

Tomasz heard a clock chime out ten and he walked quicker. He got lost again and walked in circles, down alleyways once more, until by chance he found himself outside Lewicki Pijalnia Czekolady.

The shop was smothered in darkness. He was late – too late. He waited for a few minutes, but no one came; no colourful scarf, no Andrzej.

He gently knocked on the door, but no one answered, and he ran his hand through his hair wondering how he was going to get back into the boarding house now. His plan had been to wait until morning, now the house was locked. Tomasz was about to walk away when he heard footsteps inside. He knocked again, and the door creaked open to reveal the face of Andrzej. 'Tomasz, come inside,' he said, his voice barely a whisper.

Andrzej led Tomasz down some steep wooden cellar steps, entering a room to be met with the smiling faces of Kapaldi and Zygmunt.

He looked at his brother, who he had not seen since the night in the woods. He had not changed. Only his eyes told the story of the past year – heavy, dark rings underneath and a smattering of fine lines in the corners that had never been there before.

'You look well,' Andrzej said, taking him into a quick hug, then patting him on the shoulder like his father would do when he was pleased to see him.

'I don't feel it.'

'Better at a desk than in a ditch, though?'

He nodded. 'I have something for you.' Tomasz handed Andrzej the list of names. 'Maybe you can help them, you know. Stop them from being forced into it, like I was?'

Andrzej grinned. 'You did well, little brother.' He ruffled Tomasz's hair as if he were still ten years old.

Kapaldi wrapped his arm around Tomasz's shoulder. 'Of course he did well! He is brave. I knew he could do it.'

'You'd better get going.' Andrzej looked at his watch. 'It's time.'

'Are you ready?' Kapaldi asked.

'For what?' Tomasz said.

'To see what all this is about.' Kapaldi picked up a small sack that bulged with something inside, and moved a bookcase away from the wall. There, Tomasz saw a narrow tunnel. 'In you go.' Kapaldi pointed into the dark.

'What's in there?'

'You'll see. Go.'

Tomasz had never thought he was claustrophobic, but the tunnel seemed devoid of air. He could hear Kapaldi behind him, his breathing even.

'I can't see,' Tomasz complained.

'You don't need to see. Just crawl forward.'

Tomasz did as he was told. He could feel stones biting into his palms and his knees scraping against the rough-cut floor of the tunnel.

'All right. Stop,' he heard Kapaldi order.

There was nothing to see. It was still too dark to see his hand in front of his face. He concentrated on his breathing – in, out, in, out – trying to slow his racing heart.

He heard the sound of a wood pigeon, then he was blinded with light. He blinked a few times and looked up to where the light had come from, but could only see shapes. Again, he blinked and saw the smiling face of Kowalski above him.

Kowalski put his fingers to his lips and heaved Tomasz out of the tunnel. Tomasz found himself now in another basement so small that he had to duck his head lest it touch the clammy stone ceiling.

He watched as Kowalski helped Kapaldi out of the tunnel, the two men sharing a handshake. Kapaldi then reached back into the tunnel and pulled out the sack that he had been dragging behind him.

'It's time to go to work,' Kapaldi whispered, smiling at Tomasz, yet the smile did not reach his eyes as it always used to.

Kowalski blocked the tunnel with a metal grate. He then switched off the light in the room and flicked on a torch.

'Come, let's go.'

Together the three men climbed a narrow staircase out of the basement and up to the street above. Tomasz looked back to see where they had come from. The building above the basement was a pharmacy. The basement had a separate entrance, one that was hidden from view by weeds and fallen bricks.

He felt a tug on his arm and followed Kapaldi and Kowalski through the quiet streets. As they walked, Kowalski checked constantly around him, keeping to the shadows, and often ducking into doorways. It was only when they reached a row of buildings surrounded by barbed wire and lookout posts that Tomasz realised where he was.

Before they reached the fence, Kowalski turned quickly into a building. Tomasz and Kapaldi followed into a darkened hallway. A moment later, Kowalski stopped in front of an apartment door. He knocked lightly, and the door was opened by a little girl of no more than six years old. Kowalski bent down and picked up the child, then turned to Kapaldi and Tomasz and beckoned them to follow him into the room.

The room was dimly lit by two candles. Sheets hung from the windows to block out any light. Tomasz stood in the middle of the room, taking in the scene around him; a table was crammed into a corner, a few books on top. He was taken by the beauty of the table, the chestnut ornately carved, the legs of the table almost as alluring as a woman's – it did not sit properly in this modest room.

Two beds took up the rest of the space, and in one an old woman lay. Her cheeks were sunken and grey, and for a moment Tomasz thought she was dead.

'How are you, my princess?' Kowalski asked the little girl. He kissed the top of her nose and sat her down on the floor. From his pocket he produced a biscuit. The child grinned with delight and hungrily took the biscuit in her small hands.

'How is your mother? Shall we see?'

Kowalski and Kapaldi moved to the woman in the bed. Tomasz hesitated; he did not wish to see another dead body.

'It is fine.' Kapaldi looked at him. 'Come and see Hanna. She is not dead, just sick.'

Tomasz edged to the bed and saw that indeed the woman's chest was rising slowly. *Hanna* – the same name as his own mother.

'You said it is her mother…' Tomasz looked at the child.

'She looks a lot older, but she is my age,' Kapaldi said sadly. 'She is starving, Tomasz. She is starving and sick. Her son was beaten to death three weeks ago. They beat him with the butts of their rifles and left him on the street to die. It was not until morning that someone found him and told Hanna. They found a small piece of bread in his hands. They killed him for stealing to feed his mother.'

'Papa!' the little girl suddenly cried.

Tomasz turned to see a thin man walk into the room. He bent down to the child and hugged her.

'I am sorry that we have come too late,' Kowalski began.

Kapaldi handed the sack to the man. 'It is not much. But we will bring more.'

The man cried silently, holding his daughter, too weary to speak.

They did not stay long and left as quickly and quietly as they had come, back through the streets, into the tunnel, leaving Kowalski behind in the ghetto, and back to the chocolate shop. The entire way, neither Kapaldi nor Tomasz spoke.

When they returned, the basement of the shop was empty. Kapaldi scraped the bookcase back into place. 'You are all right to get back?' Kapaldi asked him.

'Where's Andrzej and the others?'

'Busy working.' Kapaldi rubbed at his face, then smiled, but Tomasz could see once more that the smile was false and refused to reach his eyes.

'What's wrong?' Tomasz asked him.

'What do you mean? I am fine.'

'You're not. You're different. I don't know how. But something has changed.'

Kapaldi looked at the bookcase as if he were looking through to the tunnel. 'I am tired. I am just tired of all of this. I just want to go back to those days on the riverbank, telling my stories to a little boy who thought I was full of magic.'

Tomasz felt warm at the memory. 'You are magical.'

'Perhaps. Perhaps not anymore. We have all changed, Tomasz. You too are different from that little boy.'

'I'm older.'

'It's not age. You are angry. You see the madness around us and see that you have no control. It is easy then to lose control yourself. But you must remember, my friend, that these times are so abnormal, so horrendous that you cannot rationalise them. You cannot judge the things your friends, your family are doing in order to survive.'

Tomasz nodded and thought of the man whose skin had ripped away from his body; the grenade that had torn it away and the hand that had thrown it to begin with.

'You cannot judge yourself either,' Kapaldi said, as if reading his mind.

Tomasz climbed the steps out of the basement and opened the door of the shop. It was then that he smelled the rich sweetness of the chocolates, the sweets, and his mouth started to water.

'Do you remember when I looked into the fire when you were a child?' Kapaldi asked him.

Tomasz nodded in the dark and despite himself could not think properly – all he could think of was that smell – that smell of chocolate.

'I told you then that I saw something else, but that it didn't matter then for you to know it. It matters now. You need to know what I saw.'

Tomasz suddenly snapped his attention back. He could see the fire again, see Kapaldi looking into it, telling him that he owed him a debt. 'What did you see?'

'All I can tell you, Tomasz, is that you must save your own life, no matter what. Do not risk it for me, for anyone.'

Kapaldi's eyes were wide, and for the first time, Tomasz saw real fear in them. He had always thought him to be truly invincible. Now in front of him was a man, a man who was just as frightened and confused as everyone else. Tomasz put his hand on his friend's shoulder and squeezed it gently.

Kapaldi took some papers from his pocket and handed them to Tomasz. 'My story,' Kapaldi told him. 'Mine and yours, of our days when you were a child. Just in case. And here, take a chocolate. We need something sweet now and again. Takes all this bitterness away.'

Tomasz nodded, folded the papers and put them in his pocket. He ate the chocolate, tasting the sweetness on his tongue for a moment before it disappeared for good.

Tomasz did not write in his diary again until November when the snow was falling thickly, freezing the city and its people.

And on a blank page he wrote just one line: *What have I done?*

CHAPTER EIGHTEEN

Isla

England, 2015

Spring had sprung when I returned to the park once more. Daffodils were in abundance, their bright happy heads bobbing in the breeze whilst beds of neatly planted red and purple tulips edged the pathways.

I sat on what I now considered to be my bench and looked at the lake where the trees had thickened out, their leaves brightening the grey sky above and their heavier branches drooping into the water. A grey squirrel darted quickly over one low branch and for a split second he was almost in the water, but then he scuttled up into the tree away from sight.

As I watched the water, the diaries and letters came into my thoughts once more. Those words – 'What have I done?' What had he done, and how could I find out? And ultimately, did I really want to?

There was no point in giving the diaries to my grandfather – they would upset and confuse him. There was no point in giving them to my grandmother either; what would it tell her? Her husband was forced into the German army; then he did something, something he was ashamed of which could never be explained. It would be cruel. Too cruel.

'Hello.'

I felt the bench slat move underneath me slightly as someone sat down next to me. I turned and saw an old man, his hair white as snow, but long, reaching his lapel. 'Hello,' I said and smiled.

'I like it here,' he said. 'It's nice and quiet.'

I nodded. 'I like it too.'

'You don't mind if I sit here a moment with you?' I could hear a faint accent in his voice.

'Not at all.'

'That's a colourful scarf,' he commented. 'Reminds me of a rainbow.'

'Yes. Me too,' I agreed.

'Colour is nice in your life. I always thought that. Too much black and grey in the world now.'

I wasn't sure what he was talking about, so I just nodded and smiled.

'The colour in my life went a while ago. My wife died.' The old man rustled around in his pocket and pulled out a paper bag, opened it, and offered me a sweet from inside.

'Thank you.'

He popped a sweet into his own mouth and for a few minutes we sat silently, each looking at the lake and eating our sweets.

'Why do you come here?' he asked.

'I'm not sure. To remember, I suppose. To think.'

'Who are you thinking of?'

'My grandfather. He has dementia. And there's other things.'

'I see.'

'I'm just not sure what to do.'

'About what?'

'About finding out the truth. I mean, I could just leave it alone, just forget about it, and it would be fine. But there's something that is stopping me. Sorry.' I suddenly realised how odd I sounded. 'Sorry. I'm rambling.'

'I'm not sure what you really mean,' he began. 'But I think you have already decided what you are going to do. You are maybe just scared to take the next step. Sometimes, finding the truth can be painful. But then, it can be liberating too.'

I nodded. 'Perhaps.'

'Well. If I were you, I would get on. Don't sit mulling on a park bench with an old man. It is spring, after all; time for new things, time to get moving. Time to find some colour in your life.'

'Thank you,' I said.

He offered me another sweet. I took it, popped it into my mouth and walked away. When I looked back to wave at him, he was already gone.

And then, I knew what I had to do.

CHAPTER NINETEEN

'He's not here,' the receptionist told me. The rain beat down on the roof and the pavement outside, sounding like bullets. The drips of water that fell from my raincoat made a messy puddle on the marble floor, and I couldn't think how this could get any worse.

'He's not here,' she said again, and looked distastefully at the mess I had made. 'You should have called.'

Yes. I should have. Rather than getting on a plane to Poland, trekking once more to the retirement home, I should have called. I just assumed that a ninety-something-year-old man wouldn't go anywhere. 'Where is he?' I asked, shifting the bag that contained the diaries to my other shoulder.

'Visiting family.'

'Where?'

She shrugged.

'I'm sorry for not calling, but I have come from England. I'm his niece, his great-niece.'

She looked at me and raised an eyebrow. 'He's visiting his cousin. Agnieszka. In Poznań. I cannot tell you the address – it would not be right.'

I nodded my thanks and called my dad.

'Yes?' he answered on the third ring.

'Dad, it's me. I'm in Poland.'

'Poland? Ha! Why's that then? Taking a holiday? You should have told me, I could've come. Early retirement isn't as fun as advertised – no sailing and golfing for me. Nope. Grocery shopping, taking Dad to the doctor's, taking Mum shopping for shoes, picking your mum up from work. I'm a taxi driver now.'

'Dad!' I interrupted.

'Sorry. Right. You're in Poland.'

'Yes. Do you remember Grandad having a cousin called Agnieszka? You talked about her a few times – so did Grandad. She lives in Poznań, I think. I need her address.'

'Oh! I'm not sure. Let me think. You could ask Gran?'

'No. I don't want her to know. It's a surprise, for Grandad's birthday,' I lied.

'Ah, yes! Wonderful. Good job. Well, let me have a look. There are some addresses and such in your Gran's address book. I was going to head over there now to see them; I'll pop round and take a sneaky look-see.'

'Can you be quick?' I asked, watching the rain pelt the driveway outside, the sky turning a night-time blue.

'As quick as a flash!' he answered, excited at the prospect of the stealthy adventure.

The receptionist allowed me to dry off in one of the bathrooms and warmed to me enough to offer me a coffee and a biscuit whilst I waited.

As soon as Dad called back, almost breathless with the news that he had the address, the receptionist was already on the phone, ordering me a taxi to the station, a relieved smile on her face that she had finally got rid of me.

The two women who sat across from me on the train wore matching hooped earrings and red lipstick. I watched them chat in rapid Polish to each other, wondering whether I would ever learn to speak Polish fluently.

I gazed out of the window, at the fields that rushed by in a streak of green under the ever-darkening sky, and thought about whether my grandfather had seen these same fields when he had travelled through the war. There wasn't much mention of his journeys in his diaries. He had skirted over them as though they were an irritation. But then, I suppose, they were the moments when he had had time to think, to feel – too much time. And for a young man, full of fear, in the wrong army, he would not have wanted to think or feel too much. He would have wanted to ignore the pain, the longing for his previous life, for his love of Zofia.

When I imagined him, young, in love, I could not see it. It was as though the Tomasz of his youth and the grandfather I had were two separate people. Their lives did not seem to overlap – one was in love with a girl called Zofia and fought for Germany; the other was in love with a woman called Helen and fought for Poland. How did he get from being one Tomasz to the next?

I rested my head on the glass and closed my eyes, feeling the gentle rock of the carriage underneath me. Soon I fell asleep and dreamed that the receptionist from the retirement home was Agnieszka and had hidden Andrzej in a chocolate shop.

The train slowed as it edged into Poznań station and then shuddered to a stop.

I disembarked and checked the time – 1 a.m. I shook my head as if I could shake the tiredness away. I couldn't go to her house now; I needed a hotel, a bed, a shower. I stood on the platform, the smell of diesel filling my nostrils, and looked for the sign to the exit. It was foolish, all of this. I wanted to go home.

Above me, the train shed was made of glass that stretched towards the main terminus. Ultra-modern, clean and sleek, it put London stations to shame.

I saw the two women who had sat across from me on our journey walk down the platform, their lips still bright red, as if they had reapplied their lipstick every hour of our seven-hour journey. They walked towards the exit sign and I stood staring after them, my eyes feeling as though grains of sand were scratching the lenses. I wanted to go home, but I couldn't; I had come this far after all. Instead, I followed the women out towards the exit, and as I walked, I found a hotel online – Pensjonat Gabowicz in the old town square that would take a five-minute taxi ride. That would do perfectly.

Although it was late at night, when I arrived at the hotel, Mrs Gabowicz herself was bent over a newspaper at the front desk, her name badge displayed prominently on her large bosom. Her eyes were creased in concentration as she read, and wisps of grey hair escaped from the rough bun on the top of her head so that a strange halo seemed to emanate around her.

I stood for a few minutes and coughed quietly, hoping she would look up. She didn't. I pulled my small Polish phrasebook from my pocket and attempted a few words. '*Dzień dobry.*'

Nothing.

'Erm… *jak się masz?*' I tried feebly.

She sighed and raised her head to look at me. 'It's terrible, isn't it?' she asked.

'I'm sorry?'

'This.' She stabbed a thick finger at the newspaper and frowned. 'News. It's terrible.'

'Yes,' I said. 'Terrible.' I could feel my face flushing.

'Is all bad. War. No food. Murder.' She folded the newspaper roughly and grabbed a key from the multitude hanging behind her.

'I'm Isla,' I said. 'Isla Jasieński.'

'You Polish?'

'No. My grandfather.'

'He is here now?'

'No. England. I just need a room, for one night.'

'Is terrible.' She shook her head. 'Here, take key.' She handed me a key and walked from behind the desk to a door at the side. When I didn't follow, she looked at me and frowned again. 'Come!'

My face was burning now, and I followed quickly, wondering how I had upset her.

She took me up a carpeted flight of narrow stairs which opened onto a long landing. I couldn't believe how many rooms jutted off from the hallway; from the outside, the *pensjonat* looked as if it would hold ten rooms maximum. It seemed like some sort of illusion. 'It's bigger than I thought,' I said.

She stopped walking and looked at me quizzically.

'You know,' I continued, 'from the outside. I thought it was small.'

'Of course, is big! Lots of rooms. You want small hotel, you go somewhere else. This is family hotel. My family. We look after lots of people.'

With that said, she turned quickly and walked to the end of the hallway. She took the key she had given me and opened the mahogany door to a large room which had not changed since the 1950s; a four-poster bed dominated most of the room, and heavy wooden furniture that was chipped and scratched filled the rest.

'See. Family hotel. All my things.' Mrs Gabowicz stroked the wood of the chest of drawers.

There were four large balcony doors that would thankfully let in a lot of light, and dilute the heavy greens and reds of the carpet and bedspread. I placed my bag on the floor and walked towards the window to look at the view of the square.

'You go out here' – she pointed to the balcony – 'but be careful. Don't fall. Many people fall before.' She shook her head. 'Is terrible.'

She went to the en suite and turned on the light, all the while keeping up with her preferred adjective of 'terrible' to describe the too-hot water and the burns it could potentially inflict, and the toilet that did not like toilet paper being flushed down it too often. The people who didn't listen to her instructions about this were, of course, 'terrible'.

Once she had satisfied herself that I was not going to be a terrible guest, she nodded her approval and patted my arm in her first friendly gesture.

'Here, you are all right,' she said to me before she left. 'Here, now you are with family.' She smiled at me.

'Thank you,' I replied, smiling back.

She closed the door, and I lay down on the bed and went straight to sleep.

The following morning, I wanted an early start and did not linger in the hotel, nor did I take in the square or the tourist attractions. Instead, I bade goodbye to Mrs Gabowicz, who was telling an Australian couple that Australia was terrible for being so far away, and climbed into a taxi, relaying the address to the driver.

'It's far,' the driver said.

'How far?'

'Hour, maybe?' He shrugged.

'I thought it was in Poznań?'

'No. In country!' He laughed. Seeing the look on my face, he stopped. 'You want go?'

I nodded.

'Don't worry. Not much money. Is OK. I give you special price, OK?'

I smiled. 'Special price' – how many times, in how many countries, did taxi drivers say that exact same thing?

We were soon winding our way out of the city, passing first a river then a large cathedral, its green dome almost touching the blue sky above.

'You come here before?' the driver asked.

'No. First time.'

'Come back the city again. Look at square. Is beautiful.'

I agreed; the square that morning had looked beautiful. Buildings painted pale pink, green, blue and yellow stood next to each other, bright in the day's sunlight. Stalls selling flowers, tourist trinkets, paintings, and smoked ham and sausages which dangled from thin ropes were dotted about the square, whilst tourists photographed the quaint shops, cafés and the fountain of Proserpina which stood near the town hall.

'I'll come back,' I said. 'I'm just visiting.'

'Who?'

'Family.'

'You Polish?' The driver was excited.

'Yes. I suppose. My grandfather is. So, I am a little.'

'No! You Polish!' He smiled into the rear-view mirror. 'Not little bit. You Polish, OK?'

'OK.' I smiled back.

'OK. Now we listen Polish music, and you tell me if good, OK?'

He switched on the radio, and it blared so loudly with a mixture of folk, classical and Polish pop that my brain was overwhelmed with it. Coupled with his commentary of each singer and song, my journey of a couple of hours quickly passed.

Soon, the road underneath us became nothing more than a rutted track, which he did not slow down for. The car bounced its way along, as fields full of dairy cows on the edge of the road followed the car with their large brown eyes.

Rounding the bend, a small orchard appeared, and as we drove, I saw it suddenly spread before my eyes. Rows upon rows of apple trees reached down all the way to the silvery snake of a river at the bottom. I knew the place. I had never been, yet I knew it.

'The orchards,' I said. 'I've read about these orchards!'

'Apples!' The driver was excited too. 'Soon you see them. They still growing but soon – so many.'

It seemed magical to me. Of course I had seen orchards before, but these trees beginning to show the first signs of bearing fruit, their leaves the brightest of green under the clear blue sky, were different though I couldn't say how.

Soon the driver slowed the car and stopped at the front door of a stone farmhouse, the red slate tiles haphazard on its slanting roof and the wooden doors peeling what was once red paint. 'OK. We are here. Price is good.' He wrote down some numbers – zlotys – and handed it to me. I didn't try to figure out the exchange rate and handed him the notes he asked for, plus a bit more.

'Thank you! You need me again, here, take my card, you call me. My name on there. My name Tomasz. OK?'

I nodded, smiled, took his card, and climbed out of the car. Tomasz. I couldn't get away from him.

I waited until Tomasz had pulled away and then knocked on the door. No one came. I knocked again and again. Finally, I heard footsteps.

A woman, grey-haired, tall and willowy, opened the door. 'Agnieszka?'

She nodded, pulling her yellow cardigan around her.

'I'm Isla. I'm Tomasz Jasieński's granddaughter. I'm looking for Andrzej.'

For a moment, she did not move, just stared at me, her bony hands grasping her cardigan. Then she moved forward, her arms wide, pulling me into an embrace.

'Welcome! Oh, welcome. Please come in. Come in! Andrzej! Andrzej! Come see who is here.'

Seconds later, the tip-tap of the cane on the tiled floor announced Andrzej's arrival. 'Isla,' he said. He did not smile, yet he did not look surprised to see me.

'I went to find you,' I said.

'I'm not there.'

'I know. I found you here.'

'So, it seems.' He walked away, as rude as ever.

'Don't you worry about him, come in, come in. He's an old goat. Really old. All bent out of shape.'

Her English was sharp and precise, her accent barely noticeable. 'Your English is wonderful,' I told her as I followed her into the house.

'Ah yes, it should be. I tried very hard with my languages. I speak six, you know. English, Polish, German, Russian, Ukrainian and Czech.' She counted each one off on her fingers. 'A good mix. My French and Italian are good also, although not perfect.'

'Impressive,' I said. 'I barely remember the French I learned in senior school. How do you know so many?'

'Andrzej didn't tell you? He told me you visited him. No, I doubt he did tell you about me. Not the most talkative of men. Never was. Always brooding about this and that. I helped him, you know, him and the others. I was a quick student. Quick to learn languages, quick to learn people's routines. I used to travel the trains mostly, smuggling people, things, food. You know?' She waved her hand in the air as if it was an everyday job – people smuggling.

'He never said.'

'What *did* he tell you?' She turned to face me, stopping me at the entrance to the kitchen.

'Nothing much at all. He gave me some diaries and letters that were my grandfather's. I read them – well, had them translated. I've brought them back.' I nodded at the bag that dangled off my arm.

'Just brought them back?' she asked.

'I may have a question or two,' I admitted. 'The story seemed to end, and I wondered if Andrzej could tell me the rest.'

She grinned. 'Good. I'm glad you came. Questions are good. We'll get him talking, don't you worry.'

CHAPTER TWENTY

I followed Agnieszka through her hallway into the kitchen, noticing not one, but three depictions of the Sacred Heart of Christ, and a painting of Mary and the Baby Jesus. The kitchen was not without its artwork either, with a gold cross hanging above the fireplace and a smaller version above the old Aga. Grandad had one of those crosses and the Bleeding Heart picture in his dining room. Although they were meant to be comforting, I always felt a shudder when I looked at them, seeing the dripping blood from the heart and the thorns that pierced it.

Agnieszka sat me at the kitchen table across from Andrzej, who pretended I did not exist and hid behind a newspaper, every so often rustling and straightening it with a slight cough.

'I'll make you some coffee. Have you eaten?' she asked.

I nodded.

'I'll bring you some pastries just in case.'

'This place was Kowalski's, right?'

At the mention of the name, Andrzej looked over the top of his newspaper.

'It was, yes,' Agnieszka said, placing a cup of hot smoky coffee in front of me.

'When did you buy it from him?'

'I didn't. It was mine – well, ours. He was my husband.'

She looked at my face, which must have showed what I was thinking.

'Yes. Yes, he was a lot older,' she said. 'I met him when I was eighteen and he would have been forty then. We married after the war. I was twenty-one and he was forty-three.'

'What was his first name?' I asked. 'In all the diaries and letters, he is only referred to as Kowalski.'

'Borys,' she said, laughing.

'Borys?'

'Yes, like your English, Boris. He hated the name. His mother named him after her favourite cat. For some reason, he always felt like he was that damned cat – fickle, fat and lazy! So, he referred to himself as Kowalski. Only Kowalski. It did not take long for people to agree with him that that should be his name. Not many people liked to disagree with him!'

'Why, was he violent?'

'No! Not at all! His entire life, I only once saw him raise his voice and arm in anger. People just assumed it – he was a quiet man, he kept himself to himself and did not gossip. He drank like a man, worked hard, yet had the softest heart in anyone I have ever met.'

I tried to imagine the Kowalski that Agnieszka knew, and realised it was not hard. He had helped smuggle food into the ghetto, he had taken care of my grandad and Andrzej. Then a thought occurred to me. I had read something about Kapaldi – he had told my grandfather the story of how he came to be in the field, of who his family was.

'Kapaldi and Kowalski?'

'Yes,' she said. 'Brothers – well, half-brothers, of course.'

I took a moment to take it in, realising that the stories my grandfather had told me of his childhood were not embellished. He had remembered them with care, remembered Kapaldi's story, so that it could be told again and again.

'You should take a walk, have a look around.' Agnieszka's soft voice broke through my thoughts.

'How long are you staying?' Andrzej asked from behind the newspaper.

'Andrzej! How rude. She's just arrived. She can stay as long as she likes.'

I took a bite of the pastry, which was glazed with sugar and a sticky jam. I didn't want to stay long; he needn't have worried. I took another bite, then another, and washed it down with some coffee. 'I brought the diaries back.'

'You didn't need to,' he said.

'I did.'

'They're not mine.'

'I know. But Grandad wouldn't understand them anymore.'

He put the newspaper down and looked at me. 'Why are you here?'

I took the diaries out of my bag and placed them on the table. He didn't make a move to take them, so I pushed them gently towards him. 'They were helpful.'

'Good.'

'Are there more of them?'

He shrugged.

Although he was belligerent, I quite liked the game we were playing. Childishly, I enjoyed asking questions that I knew would annoy him, and I wondered whether he had been like this with Grandad when they were children.

Agnieszka stood all the while looking at Andrzej and me, watching the stand-off as if at any moment one of us would pull out a weapon and commence an actual duel.

'He stopped writing,' I said, breaking the silence. He had won this round.

'People do. What more do you want?'

'The last words in the diary are "What have I done?" What did he do? What did he do that made him stop writing and ask that?'

'I'm going to leave you two. I will go to the market and get something for dinner.' Agnieszka picked up her bag. 'You'll be here for dinner?'

I nodded.

'Good. Andrzej?'

'What?'

'Be nice.' She closed the door behind her.

The line ran deep in his forehead and it deepened the longer we sat across from each other in silence. He would not look at me and instead stared at the diaries, blinking behind his thick-rimmed glasses.

Finally, I said, 'Tell me, please, or else I won't leave – ever.' It was childish and a loose threat, but it seemed to work.

He looked up with a brief smile, his eyes watery with age, not with sadness or fear. 'You don't need to know.'

'I do.'

'Why?' he asked.

'What did he do to you that made you forget him for so long?' I countered. 'You said he made a mistake, one that you found hard to forgive. So, why did you forget about him?'

'Why do you say that?' he snapped, his hand hitting the table so hard that his coffee cup jumped slightly.

'What other reason is there for you to disappear from his life? Why else would he ask what he had done?'

Andrzej shook his head. 'I wish I still smoked.'

'Me too.'

He looked at me, and despite himself, he smiled. 'You want to know – really?'

I nodded.

'Even if it changes things – changes what you think of him?'

I took a moment, looked at the diaries and nodded again.

'OK,' he said, leaning back in his chair. 'Your grandfather was a traitor. Sold out his friends, his family. Killed innocent men.

All for a woman, or so he claimed. And it was for that reason I could not forgive him. I sent him that newspaper article; you know, when he was in England. I sent it to remind him of who he had been – what he had done.'

'But—' I began.

Andrzej held up a hand to silence me. 'I know it was cruel. It was wrong of me to do that. But I was angry. Not about the medal or any of that. For the choice he made afterwards, for deciding to give up his own brother for a woman.'

'Which woman? Zofia?'

He nodded.

'And from that day on you never spoke to him again. What did he do?'

'I never said that. I never said I didn't speak to him again. What I am telling you is what he did, the choice he made that day. And on that day, he was a traitor – he chose wrong.'

'Tell me,' I challenged him, not taking my eyes off his.

He looked at me for a few seconds, then closed his eyes. 'Oh, I wish I still smoked.'

I could hear the ticking of the clock and counted out sixty seconds, then another, and another. He still sat, his eyes closed, picturing it all once more as if a film were playing out on his eyelids. His hands twitched now and again; his foot tapped every ten seconds. Five, six minutes; then before I started counting the seventh, he opened his eyes: 'Come. Let's take a walk.'

At the bottom of the orchards was a field and in it a dilapidated wooden caravan, its paint peeling. In the corner was a rusting tractor. The scene I knew well – all that was missing was a fair-haired young boy, a horse and a gypsy.

We sat on the bank. Andrzej took off his shoes and socks, revealing veiny, bony feet, the toes bent with thick yellow toenails. He put his feet into the river and let out a satisfied, 'Ahhhh,' as the cool water enveloped them.

I followed suit, and although the water was too cold, I forced myself to keep them in so together we could move our feet gently in the water, watching the ripples, enjoying the silence.

'He wrote me a letter,' he began. 'I have it still. I will find it and give it to you. I remember though what he wrote – how he explained what he had done. I read it many times – too many. He was sorry. Of course he was. But I was still angry. All those years lost because of anger.

'He was good at first – brave, I think. He brought lists of men – Polish brothers who we could help, could recruit for our cause. But then, for a month, perhaps more, there were problems. We lost three men who were found in the ghetto, and it was getting dangerous, too dangerous for him to see us anymore and to help us. I told him to keep his head down, work, sleep, eat. I told him not to contact us. He did what he was told…' Andrzej stopped and shook his head slowly.

I didn't speak in the minute or so of silence that followed. I let him breathe, let him think.

'It was winter. Snowing, cold, freezing. It was harder and harder to get food to the ghetto. Harder to help men who were being rounded up. I heard that Tomasz was working well, being a good German – he had them fooled, you see. Had them all fooled.'

'He never wrote about those months,' I said, trying to remember his story.

'Would you? Would you write that you had forced men and boys that wanted freedom for your homeland into the army that had forced you? Would you write that those men probably swore at you, spat at you, called you a Nazi pig, and that each night when you went back to your room, you would lie down and feel a weight, something so heavy pressing down on your chest, struggling to breathe, wondering when this would all end?'

He was right. I couldn't imagine writing down the worst of me, the things I wished I had never done and never seen.

'He had them fooled. Completely. But then there was one time, one time he did not listen and tried to make it all better,' Andrzej continued. He took his feet out of the water and dried them on the grass.

I copied him and crossed my legs, ready, waiting for the rest of the story. Andrzej shuffled himself backwards towards the trunk of a tree so he could lean against it as he spoke. 'He did it to make himself feel better, I think, about what he had been doing. He did it to make him feel like he was on our side again. But it was the wrong time. I told you it was winter, cold, icy. At night it was hard to work because we were so cold too – not as cold as those in the ghetto, but cold enough. One night, I think perhaps a Tuesday, but I don't know, Tomasz came to the basement. He was thinner than he should have been; he had always been well fed, well looked after by the Germans, so I was worried when I saw him, but he shook it off and gave me a list of names, of dates; the movements of trucks filled with troops – more than he should have.

'"How did you get these?" I asked him.

'"I stole them. I stole them from an office – a secretary, Elsabeth. I think that was her name. I took them."

'He was sweating, his eyes red and dark circles underneath them as if he was in a fever. It was the fear, the fear of what he had done and what he was doing.

'I took them from him and told him to go home, to sleep and rest and not try to do this again. It was too dangerous – eyes were watching us everywhere, and who knew if anyone had followed him.

'It was too late, though. Too late. He had been seen leaving his lodgings. He was tired and sloppy and forgot to look behind him.'

Andrzej stopped, took a handkerchief from his pocket and blew his nose. 'I tell you his letter now. I tell you what happened next.' He leaned forward and took out a battered old wallet from his back pocket, opening it up and pulling out grubby, folded pieces of paper, so worn and creased that when he opened it and separated the pages it seemed they could fall to pieces at the slightest breeze…

CHAPTER TWENTY-ONE

January 1942

Beloved Brother,

Months have now passed since we have seen each other, and I wonder when we will see each other again. I am no longer in Poland. I have been sent away, towards Russia, to fight in a battalion known for their ruthlessness.

The soldiers I am with are no friends of mine. Strangely, I think fondly of the days of training with Jan, of our active duty, which although only a year and a half ago, seems to me to be a lifetime away.

These men are different. Cold, hard. They are true soldiers ready for battle. I am not them, and this they know and speak of in hushed and not so hushed tones. I make nothing of their talk, so they pretend that they do not understand me and I them. Just let them say what they want against me, let them condemn me. I did not ask to be in this army.

I thought that perhaps I would be lucky and see Jan and Eryk once more. So far, I have not. There are many men, and we all blend into one – we are like a storm cloud, dirty, unwashed and heavy with the weight we carry.

We arrived here in the Ukraine, using jeep convoys and trucks to reach the front. Yet many became stuck in the snow or the engines froze with the cold, so we had to march. During those first few days, the marching quickly deteriorated and became a stagger. The bravado of these strong, serious soldiers has diminished upon feeling the cold that seeps into every part of us and will not leave, no matter what we do.

I live now a warrior's life. Muddy, I cannot wash or shave. It is cold. Colder than you can imagine. And as we inch our way through the thick snow, I can feel every part of me freezing slowly.

It feels as though we never stop, never sleep. I am sure I do though, I just don't remember it. There is constant noise here, constant; nothing like I have experienced before. The rattle of guns, the boom of the tanks as they fire, the shout of the men, the cry and scream of the planes that are overhead. It is too much. I just wish for quiet.

I shot a Russian today. It was the second time that I have had to engage with the enemy. It was odd really, the whole experience. I was sitting in a ditch with two others and for once there was quiet. We should have wondered at the silence, should have questioned it. We did not. We were digging in towards the enemy's camp, laying lines where we could later use explosives, when suddenly I felt a tap on my shoulder. I turned around and in front of me was the face of a Russian. I don't know why, but I was shocked at his appearance – shocked because he looked so much like you or me.

He had sneaked in, probably out on patrol, and was feeling lucky at seeing three Germans together. He didn't know I was Polish. But then, he probably wouldn't have cared; it would have meant the same to him. I jumped forward and saw he had a bayonet and was going to stab me. But I was first. I will say it as it was. I shot him. I had to.

Only now, as I sit here and write to you, do my hands start to tremble with the memory of what they have done. Only now does my mind realise that this is something I will have to do again.

I suppose, though, you do not care for this. What you care to know is why I did what I did.

It was late when they came for me, perhaps early morning a few nights after I had seen you last in the basement, when I had given you those lists and documents and you had chastised me, telling me I had taken too much of a risk. You were right. Of course you were. They dragged me from my bed, out into the snow with no shoes on my feet, and the iciness burned the soles of my feet.

They took me to see Officer Bauer, but they did not take me inside – instead, I stood outside on the pavement, the coldness burning and burning my feet.

He smoked and the air seemed thick with the smoke.

'You've been busy,' he said. 'Elsabeth says you took something from her?'

I denied it. Of course I did. I denied it when they beat me; I denied it when they held my head so long in the snow that I had a headache so bad I thought I was going to die.

But then, I looked up. And in a window, I thought I saw her – saw Zofia. Just a second, just a moment. I thought he had her – Lieberenz. I thought he had taken her.

Bauer asked me what I had done with the papers.

I couldn't answer. I remember my lip was swollen and there was blood in my mouth and then someone kicked me in the stomach, and I felt as though my insides were being forced from my mouth – crimson upon crimson splattered the snow.

I remember crying out that I did not know, I did not know. Then I don't know what happened – I truly don't. Perhaps it was the pain, perhaps it was thinking that they had Zofia, I don't know, but I told them about you all, I told them where you were.

But no harm came to any of you, did it? I knew that you would be out at that time – out in the ghetto. I knew that the eyes you place around the shop would see what was happening, would warn you. Bauer was mad that no one was there and placed some men to sit and wait. They found nothing. I knew it would be a fruitless task. I knew you were all too clever for him.

But, of course, I did not really know, did I? Instead, I hoped. I hoped that it would be all right and thankfully I was correct. It was a chance, and I took it, and it was dangerous.

I am sorry. Those words mean little – too little, yet I don't know what else I can say.

Bauer sent me away, sent me to be part of the infantry once more. I had no time to ask for Lieberenz's help – he needed me just as I needed him, and I like to think he would have helped me if he had known.

I am staying in a small village in an old woman's house. When we arrived, she would not meet my eye, and I saw the fear she had for me.

We are near the border now, I think. Near Russia. I think it is Kharkov we aim for. Do you know where that is? I don't. I was never good at geography. You were, though. You always had an instinct of where to go and what to do, and I blindly followed you, trusting you because you are my brother.

Around an hour ago I stepped over the sleeping bodies in this back room, and very quietly I made my way out into the night. No one woke when I left – nor would they. They are tired and sleeping like the dead, as I should be. Yet, I cannot.

Outside, the moon was half obscured by cloud but shed enough light for me to walk around the quiet village. My boots crunched into the frozen snow, and it was the only sound until I heard a bang as someone closed a front door. I felt as though I were a ghost – each house was cloaked in darkness, and I felt oddly at peace.

Then, through the quiet came something. It was a scratch of a bow on a violin, playing music I did not know. I stood with my eyes closed, listening to the musician, the sound of loss, of longing flowing out into the cold night. Then I thought of Zofia, of what it would be like to dance with her in the snow, her eyes blue, as blue as her dress, the flakes falling softly on her dark lashes as I spun her around, her laughter filling the dead air.

The violin abruptly stopped, and I opened my eyes. For a moment, I thought I heard the crunch of footsteps. I stopped and listened, but hearing nothing I began to walk again, blowing warm air into my gloved hands.

I walked until my feet felt numb with the cold. Only then did I give in and sneak back into the house where all those men slept soundly.

I must sleep now. I must. Goodnight, my brother, wherever you are.

Your brother,
Tomasz

I woke this morning, filled with a dream I had. I had to tell you. I write quickly now; we are making ready to leave, and I must persuade the woman of the house to send this to you, and hope one day your hands will find it at our parents'.

It was a strange dream as dreams often are. Zofia came to me, came to see me. We were in the cold snowfields, and I looked down and saw she wasn't wearing any shoes.

'You need shoes,' I told her.

'I don't. I don't feel anything anymore.'

'Are you dead?' I asked.

'No. Not dead. How can I be dead if I am here?'

Suddenly, behind her came Bruno our dog, who had died years ago.

'Bruno!' I cried out to him and patted him. 'See, if Bruno's here, and he is dead, you must be dead.'

'Then you are dead too,' she said.

I stood up from patting Bruno, but she was gone. Then I looked down and Bruno was gone too.

Then I saw two arches and a star – like the entrance to the ghetto in Kraków, but the star was bright and hanging in the sky. The man was there with his cart, and he was trying to load bodies onto it, but the people were still alive and moved around.

I ran through the snow. 'They're not dead! Wait!'

The man did not turn around, and I reached the cart and saw someone I knew, but now I cannot remember who it was.

I tried to grab the body, but it was pinned under the other bodies and would not move. I pulled and pulled, and the cart started to move away under the arches, and the guard was laughing at me. Then suddenly, I was awake.

What do you think it means? Mama always said that dreams have meaning. I wish I could ask her what this means. It seemed so real. It scares me.

Ask Kapaldi. He will know. Ask him what it means.

Tomasz

Folding the pages and tucking them back into his wallet, Andrzej let out a heavy sigh and wiped his forehead with his handkerchief. Then he slowly rose to his feet and held out his hand. 'I am old. Help me back to the house.'

He leaned heavily on me as we walked, as if the telling of the story had exhausted him. I felt heavier too and wanted sleep. Every part of me had started to ache and my head spun.

'No one was killed, though, so it was OK,' I said. 'He made a mistake, but everyone was fine.'

Andrzej shook his head. He stopped walking and looked over my head at the rows of apple trees. 'Two men died. Two of our best. They found the hole; they went into the ghetto. After that we had to leave, and quickly.'

'But he didn't mean to do it.' I defended Grandad, feeling almost tearful that his own brother could have been so angry at him for so long.

'I know.' Andrzej's tone was quieter, gentler. 'I know that now, Isla. But I was angry because we were helping people, you see, and then it was taken away from us. That's why I keep his letter with me now. I keep it and read it and remind myself not to be angry.'

Suddenly, I remembered something from the diaries. 'That little girl, the one whose mother was sick. Did you manage to save her?'

'No. No, I did not.'

My heart felt even more weighted down with that news. A part of me had always known that would be the end of that girl's story, and why shouldn't it be? Millions of others awaited the same fate. But because I had read that my grandfather and his friends had seen her, had promised to help, I had hoped that somehow, the ending of her story would be different.

CHAPTER TWENTY-TWO

Our conversation that evening was dominated by Agnieszka's endless questioning about my life. She seemed less interested in my mission to find out my grandfather's story and far more interested in making some sort of connection to me.

'You must stay a few days,' she said.

'She's got everything she came for,' Andrzej said. He took the last piece of bread to mop up the sauce from his plate.

'Well, I know what happened, I suppose. But how did he get to England? He was in the Polish army there; I remember Gran saying so.'

'He gave himself up, probably. Sent to England. There's nothing more to know.'

As soon as he said that, Agnieszka tilted her head to the side, questioning him. When she noticed I was looking at her, she began to clear the plates.

'You'll stay a few days, have a holiday at least,' she said. 'There's lots to do and see.'

I hadn't booked a return ticket, so I acquiesced; I still had some holiday to take from work. Somehow, I knew that there was something both of them were not telling me. I had the strangest feeling I couldn't leave until I had found out what it was.

They retired to bed early, and I sat outside on the porch and watched the purple storm clouds roll in over the orchards. I closed my eyes and breathed in that cool, fresh scent that comes with the beginning of a rainstorm, and imagined my grandfather and Kapaldi doing the same. I pictured them in the field, trying to make it rain, trying to make a rainbow appear.

It was strange to think of them. I had heard the stories, the memories, yet it was still so hard to believe it all actually happened.

There was this whole part of my family's lives that I wasn't a part of, and could never be, yet I wanted to know it all, to keep their stories alive and recount them in the years to follow.

I heard a noise behind me and turned to see Agnieszka, wrapped in her pink dressing gown. 'Ah, you're here. I thought you would have gone to bed by now.'

'Not yet. I'm just thinking.'

'I have something that will help calm your thoughts.' She walked inside and returned with a bottle of red wine and two glasses.

We drank in companionable silence, both of us staring out at the silhouette of the orchards against the darkening sky, both of us lost in the stories of this place.

'Why are you here, Isla?' Agnieszka suddenly asked.

'I'm not sure,' I said honestly. 'At first it was all about my grandfather; I needed to reconcile who I thought he was with what that photograph said about him. But I'm not sure why any of us really make a decision to do things – it's almost imperceptible, like something going on in our subconscious, and before we know it, we are doing something that we never thought we would.'

'That's not normal for you, is it?'

'No,' I said. 'It's not. When I'm at work, I know why I think something: it's because the facts tell me to. But in this case, it was different. The fact is, he was in the Wehrmacht, but my feeling was that I couldn't believe he had committed any crimes. When I found out that he'd been forced into it, I should have stopped – really there was no need to delve further.'

'But you did.'

'Yes. I did.'

'And has what Andrzej told you answered all your questions? You are satisfied now?'

'I think so. I mean, there are other things I'd like answers to – like, how did he get to England and what happened to Zofia? He seemed to have loved her so much, and yet it appears he never came back for her. But the answers won't really change anything else. I know who he is. He is still the man I always thought he was – brave, courageous and loving.'

'Yes,' she said. 'He is.' She patted my arm and stood. 'Now, to bed. Let's see what tomorrow brings.'

I stood, gave her a brief hug and went to my room, where thankfully no bleeding hearts adorned the walls.

That night I slept deeply despite everything I had heard. My dreams were thick like mud, and I could not pull myself out of them. They changed constantly, and I was one moment standing in the snow with cold feet and then running through a wood, dogs barking, a scarf around my neck.

When I woke, I found myself tangled in my sheets, sweating and unable to fully understand where I was for a moment. I lay still for a minute or so and stared at the spider cracks in the whitewashed ceiling until I remembered – Poznań, Andrzej and Agnieszka.

My limbs still ached, and my head was fuzzy. It was a few more minutes before I realised – I was ill.

Bit by bit, I managed to heave myself from the bed. Coughing, with a nose bunged up, I dressed and found my way into the kitchen, and poured a glass of orange juice.

It was early still, before six, and no one was up. The sun was rising over the orchards, and I let myself out into the garden to watch, letting the cool air rush over my fevered skin.

In the distance I could see the darkened fuzzy tops of trees silhouetted against the still lightening sky. A dense mass – the woods, perhaps, which he ran through as a boy? I turned a little this way and that, trying to see another building, trying to find my grandfather's childhood home.

'Hello there.'

I screamed and spilled orange juice all over my top. In front of me stood a tall, dark-haired man, wearing jeans and a grubby T-shirt.

'I'm sorry!' He took a step forward. 'I'm Stefan.'

He said it as if I would know who he was. I shook my head.

'I work for Agnieszka. In the orchards.'

'Oh, right, I see.' I tried to pull my sodden T-shirt away from my body.

'And you are Isla,' he said. 'Agnieszka filled me in yesterday. She said I would get to meet you.'

I sneezed once, twice and then rubbed at the bridge of my nose. 'Sorry, I think I have a cold.'

'You might want to change that then?' he suggested, nodding towards my now orange T-shirt.

'Good idea,' I agreed, and made my way back inside to change.

When I came down to the kitchen, Stefan was sitting at the table with fresh coffee, Agnieszka at his side. 'Here,' he said, as he handed a mug to me.

'Thanks.' I sat down across from them.

'Stefan says you're not feeling well?' Agnieszka reached over and placed her hand on my forehead.

'I'm all right, just a cold.'

'We'll go to town, to the chemist, get you some things?'

I nodded, already feeling better at the thought of Lemsip.

'I'd better get to work.' Stefan stood. 'Nice to meet you, Isla.'

I smiled, then sneezed.

'Get better soon.' He patted my shoulder as he passed.

As he did, I noticed he had a slight scar on his cheek as if scratched recently, maybe by a branch in the orchard? He smiled with his eyes too – not many people did that. *Green eyes.*

'I'll tell Andrzej we're going to town,' Agnieszka interrupted my thoughts. 'He'll want to come. Likes to wander.'

CHAPTER TWENTY-THREE

When Agnieszka said 'town', what she meant to say was 'city' – we ended up in Poznań.

'May as well see some sights,' she said, parking near the Old Town, not far from Mrs Gabowicz's *pensjonat*.

'Meet you back here in an hour.' Andrzej was already out of the car and hobbling away across the cobbles.

'He's in a rush,' I said.

'Pah! Ignore him. Always up to something. Usually nothing. I expect he's gone straight to Pijalnia Czekolady – a chocolate shop. When you feel better, I'll take you – best hot chocolate in the world.'

We walked around the square, with its buildings each painted a different colour, the cobbled pavement, the busker with his violin, the market stalls selling trinkets, cheeses, sausages. It all seemed too quaint, too picturesque. But then, I had read my grandfather's diaries; I had heard what had happened here and had let it taint my view. Now it was a tourist attraction, a beautiful one at that. I tried to look through the eyes of a tourist and see this Poznań as something new, rather than something masking its past.

At the chemist I bought cold and flu capsules, Lemsip and some cough medicine. On the stroll back to the car I noticed a familiar face. Andrzej sat at a café with another man, talking animatedly, laughing, and slapping his hand down on the table at something his friend said. It was an Andrzej I hadn't seen before.

As soon as Agnieszka and I approached, they stopped speaking and looked up, almost guiltily. 'Coffee?' Andrzej offered, sweeping his hands to indicate the two extra chairs as if he had been waiting for us all along.

We sat.

'This is Zygmunt. A friend. A very old friend.'

'I've read about you,' I blurted.

Zygmunt looked at me, then at Andrzej.

'It's a different person,' Andrzej said. 'Not the same.'

I nodded and silence descended on the table until the drinks arrived. We drank lattes. Agnieszka took sugar, two; I took none.

'You need some sweetness in your life,' she commented.

'I have some.'

'I saw you talking to Stefan in the garden this morning,' she said.

I licked the foam from the top of my lip.

'He likes you. You like him. It's sweet.'

Andrzej and Zygmunt looked at me, leaning forward as if eager to hear what I had to say.

'I don't know him,' I said.

'You should get to know him. He's a good boy – well, man. He came back from Germany where he worked as a curator in a museum to look after his mother and father, who are quite old. And of course, I offered him a job. He's such a good boy…' She smiled as if he were an angel from heaven sent to help them all.

'Ha! As if that's the only reason.' Andrzej laughed. 'You forgot to mention he lost his job and *had* to come home. Always making up fairy tales, this one.'

'That doesn't matter.' She waved his comment away as if swatting an irritating fly. 'He's lovely. Isla should get to know him.'

'He lives here, anyway,' I said. 'And I live in London.'

'Pah!' Andrzej hit the table and laughed.

'What?' I asked.

'Distance is the problem? Think, Isla, think!' He tapped the side of his head and then signalled to the waiter for an espresso.

Trying to change the subject, I turned to Andrzej's friend. 'Zygmunt, I'm Isla.' I proffered my hand.

'He doesn't speak English,' Andrzej answered for him.

Zygmunt took my hand in his and shook it so lightly that I could have imagined his touch.

He wore a hat, dark blue, wide-brimmed and worn in places, and when he stood to say goodbye, he tipped it towards me, then clicked his heels together and did a little bow. Suddenly, I started to laugh. 'Grandad does that too!'

Zygmunt looked at me and was about to smile, as if he had understood what I had said. Then he shook his head, ever so slightly, and spoke rapidly to Andrzej.

'He says to say goodbye and nice to meet you,' Andrzej said for him.

'It was nice to meet him too.'

Andrzej translated and Zygmunt walked slowly over the cobbles, disappearing into an alleyway, its shadows enveloping him.

'Right, we go home now. You get that cold sorted.' Andrzej stood and threw some notes onto the table. 'We're old, you know. We get your cold, and it could kill us.'

'Ignore him.' Agnieszka took my arm.

We reached the car and Andrzej climbed into the front seat. As soon as Agnieszka got behind the wheel, she unleashed a torrent of Polish, so quick, so harsh, that I could understand the shock on Andrzej's face. It took him a few seconds to compose himself before he hit back with words of his own, none of which I knew.

Finally, Agnieszka slapped the steering wheel hard. 'Well, what's the point in it all then?' she shouted at him in English.

Andrzej looked over his shoulder at me and then back at Agnieszka, who said crossly, 'We're old, Andrzej. Old. And here she is, wanting to know our stories, and you are playing silly games with her.'

My ears pricked. 'What games?'

'Zygmunt is Zygmunt. The one you know. The one you read about.' She turned to look at me now. 'Zofia's brother.'

'Why did you lie?' I asked Andrzej.

He shrugged. 'Maybe he wouldn't want to be pestered with your questions.'

'Does he have something to tell me?'

'No.' 'Yes!' Andrzej and Agnieszka said at the same time.

'What?' The cold was making it hard for me to hear and to concentrate. I tried to think of what I wanted to know – what did I want? The story had ended, hadn't it? He fell out with his brother; he was sent back to the front. What else was there?

'He knows something.' Agnieszka reached out and stroked the scarf around my neck – Grandad's scarf, Kapaldi's scarf. She let it drop. 'Something that happened to your grandfather that changed him, perhaps made him keep this secret for so long.'

She turned back to face the steering wheel and said something to Andrzej, quietly this time, gently.

A few minutes passed in silence. Then Agnieszka made to turn the key in the ignition, but Andrzej reached out and stopped her. He nodded and climbed out of the car.

'What's going on?'

'We're to wait a few minutes, then we can go and see Zygmunt. Give him a minute to speak to him, to see if he wants to talk.'

CHAPTER TWENTY-FOUR

Zygmunt's apartment was on the top floor of a five-storey block with a café underneath. There was no lift, just a tiled staircase with a wrought-iron railing.

'You all right getting up there?' I asked Agnieszka.

'I can't believe you asked me that! Of course I am.'

Although she was slow, she did make it to the top, less out of breath than I was. She knocked on Zygmunt's door, which opened quickly, Andrzej on the other side.

He let us into the apartment, into a small living room. A large bookcase dominated the main wall, stuffed full, bits of papers falling out of it. A small TV was in the corner, and a faded green recliner and couch were set up so they looked directly at it. The saving grace of the room was the double glass balcony doors, which had the most magnificent view of the town square.

'Same old place, Zyg. Nothing has changed!' Agnieszka smiled brightly, and for a second, I could imagine her as the risk-taking teenager, laughing and joking, keeping everyone in good spirits.

She hugged Zygmunt, who let her, and then he pulled away.

'Andrzej said you wouldn't stop. Say I may as well tell you.' Zygmunt's English was thick and unusual on his tongue. I noticed his wide-brimmed hat from earlier had been replaced with a soft beret.

He saw me look at his head and self-consciously rearranged the hat. 'Sit. Please.' He indicated the couch and took the chair for himself. All the while Andrzej sat in the little open-plan kitchen, pretending to read the newspaper that was open on a small Formica table, though I noticed that he never once turned a page.

Zygmunt sat back in his chair and knitted his fingers together. Then slowly, like a radio being switched on, the volume being turned up little by little, Zygmunt started to talk.

'It's been a long time since I think of your grandfather and those days. It is not something you think about normally. Andrzej is right, though. It is an important story, and we should tell it before we are all forgotten.'

I looked back to Andrzej who had still not moved, knowing his ears were pricked and ready, surprised that he had advocated for me, for the story to be told in its entirety.

'It was 1942. In July, I think, when it all started. I was on mission to bomb an SS headquarters in Warsaw, dressed as an officer, when the bomb exploded quickly, too quickly and everything fell down, including me. I was trapped under the rubble, and I didn't remember anything until I woke in a Nazi hospital – they thought I was real officer, you see; I even had a tattoo done to match theirs. It funny now to think that they tried to save me, but I was the one who was trying to kill them all the time.

'For a long time, I sleep, then wake, then sleep, then wake. But then soon, I am awake a little more and soon I am feeling better. Not perfect – but better.' He took off his beret and swept his hand over a puckered scar that ran across his skull.

I stared at it for too long, so he placed his hat back on his head.

'I'm good at hats now. Very good. With this head you have to be good at hats.'

I nodded and blushed a little.

'The nurses, they got mad at me and told me I must be still, not move, be quiet,' he continued. 'But I was bored. Always at night I was bored. All the other patients, they moan and scream for their parents and their wives, and I could not listen to it. So, I am sneaky – but I have been good at being sneaky all my life, and I crept out of the bed and I walk the halls, careful that no one see me.

'One night, I walk far from bed, and I went down a hallway that was so quiet you cannot believe. Here there was no crying and no screaming for family. Everything quiet and it smells to me like lemons or oranges – so fresh and clean. In my own bed, in that ward, it smells like death all the time. Is a strong smell, death, so strong. I cannot explain it, but when you smell it, you know.

'Anyway, there were rooms, special, private rooms in this hallway, and I am jealous that they get own rooms.

'So, I read some files that were outside on doors. Soon I see this is where people come when they have shocks – like you know…' He tapped the side of his head and then said something to Agnieszka in Polish.

'A breakdown, when your mind goes away,' she explained for him.

'Anyway,' he said. 'I open file and there I see it – Tomasz Jasieński. I look down the hallway, left, right, and no one is there. So, I pushed door gently open and walked in. The room white; everything – the sheets, walls, even the light from ceiling, I felt like it made me blind.

'I close door. I walk to bed, and he is there, looking at white ceiling above him. "Tomasz?" I ask him.

'He turns his head, and his eyes looks at my face, but he no sees me properly, so I say to him, "It's Zygmunt."

'He turns back to look at white above him on ceiling. I sat by bed for long time, waiting for him to talk to me, but he did not. Soon, the pain in my head came back, and I had to leave him.

'Each night for a week I returned like ghost to that white room. Each night I sat whilst Tomasz stared at the ceiling. Sometimes, I speak to him, told him things that had happened to me.

'"I heard," I said to him one evening. "Just bits of things. But I heard."

'Tomasz blinked, then turned his head to look at me.

'"I'm sorry," I said.

'"I couldn't save him," Tomasz said. His voice was dry, and I picked up water glass and put it to his lips. He lifted his head and drank, then fell back down.

'"I couldn't save him," he said to me again.

'"Shhh. You don't have to explain. It not your fault," I tell him.

'Tomasz just look at ceiling. He did not speak again that night, so I left him and went to my bed.

'I am not sure exactly what had happened in Warsaw to Tomasz. People told it to me in whispers, guessing what had happened, but no one really knew but Tomasz. It was when I was in the building and the bombing goes wrong which brought me to Tomasz.

'I did not see him again for a few days because I am trying to get well, because I am not German, I know soon they will find out and I must leave quickly. Maybe one week later I think to myself that I can leave now, and I wait until night-time, and I get dressed and go towards exit.

'But you see, Tomasz was friend of mine and he loved my sister and I think, I must say to him goodbye because if I do not, I will always wonder.

'So, I go to his room and he was sitting in bed, some paper on his lap and a pen in his hand.

'"You feeling better," I said.

'"I need to write it," he says to me.

'I look at what he writes – something about Kharkov where he was, and a man called Rolf. "Be careful who sees it."

'"My eyes are in pain. And my head. I can't see what I write."

'"You need to rest," I tell him, then look at the door because I really need to leave quickly.

'"Will you help me?" He gives me paper.

'"I don't know the story. Only what other people are telling me."

'"Write what they say to you. And then I tell you if you are right or wrong."

'I shook my head. "I am leaving now."

'He nodded and took the paper and pen back.

'I rubbed my hand over scar on my head. We had all seen things. We had all done things. "All right," I said. "All right. We do this quickly."

'Tomasz smiled at me and gave me pen again, and this time, I take it and I start to write just what I know and just what he says.'

Zygmunt picked up a book from the side table and handed it to Agnieszka, who opened it to reveal neat lines of writing.

'I kept it for him. He asked me to. He said it was important in case he forgets, and he cannot forget this, always must remember. But here, you get Agnieszka to read. Her English better than mine. And you write better for me too. Show everything. You think how it was, Isla, and you write it. Make it clear for everyone. Because for us, it is lost.'

CHAPTER TWENTY-FIVE

Tomasz

Ukraine, February 1942

Kharkov was colourless. The grey, muted buildings, half demolished, lay among the frozen, churned-up dirty snow.

Tomasz had grown up with the cold. He was used to smashing the ice off the pigs' and cows' water buckets each morning; he was used to seeing the river slow, then stop as the freeze took hold. But the cold here was different. It seeped through his thin overcoat until he had relented and joined the others, taking the clothes of their dead comrades, wearing multiple jackets of differing sizes, smelling of different men. Yet, no matter how many layers he wore, the cold still found its way through, stinging his skin.

He grew a beard. Not by choice; by necessity and by default at the same time. The first time he had seen his reflection, he had recoiled, his heart pounding, wondering who was looking at him through the glass of the abandoned bakery. He had stopped and walked closer to the glass, watching the hairy, skinny man do the same. He had stroked the beard, the reflection copied.

Men died daily; some from battle wounds, most from the cold and the hacking pneumonic coughs that rattled their chests, until finally they lay back in the snow, silent. It did not upset Tomasz anymore, but strangely, the bodies of the horses disturbed him still. They died emaciated, whinnying for help, for food, for

warmth, and it made Tomasz want to weep for them. Some of
the soldiers killed the horses so that they did not suffer as the
men had to, and so that they could cook and eat whatever meat
was left on them.

Sometimes, when their sergeant allowed, they would take
turns to sleep underneath the trucks and jeeps, lying close to the
exhausts to feel some heat. And on those nights Tomasz would
dream that he was at home, safe, warm in his small single bed,
the sound of his father rocking in his chair, the crackle of the
logs burning on the fire, the smell of his mother's cooking filling
his dreams.

At night they would sometimes build a fire, if it was safe. On
those nights, the men would sit together, warming themselves in
front of the meagre flames, talking and sharing songs from their
childhood. On those nights, Tomasz forgot that they were German,
and he was Polish – on those nights they were all the same.

One day, a soldier called Werner went mad.

Tomasz was sitting in the trench on an upturned metal bucket
that had a hole in the side. He was concentrating on keeping
warm, and not succumbing to the thought of undressing and
just letting the cold get him, kill him. He heard Werner before
he saw him. It was a cry like a child that was hysterical, followed
by shouting that he wanted to go home, he wanted to go home.

Then Tomasz saw him. He half ran through the trench, slipping
in the shit and stink whilst the rest of the ground was frozen solid.

No one stopped Werner. Everyone watched, blowing warm
air into their hands, but no one stood.

Tomasz stood up too late. Werner was already on the ladder,
pulling himself up, his face covered with snot and tears – he was
going home. As soon as his head reached the top, it snapped back,
and for a second, or perhaps less, it was as though he realised that

he had been shot between the eyes and his left hand let go of the ladder as if to check his head, check the bloody hole.

He fell backwards after that second. His heavy weight hit the solid ground of the trench.

Tomasz shivered. He looked to the other men whose eyes were on Werner, lying still, his large trench coat open, showing his round belly. Tomasz moved quickly. He rolled Werner out of the coat and dressed himself in it, wrapping the excess material around him, smelling the sweat of Werner.

His tin bucket had fallen onto its side, and Tomasz put it straight again and sat down. He turned his back to the men, turned away from their jealous stares, and hid his hands in the long sleeves, thinking only of keeping warm.

'You did well,' a private called Rolf said.

'Thank you.'

'I'll get it next, if you go before me.'

'All right.'

'Cigarette?' Rolf offered.

Tomasz took it and let Rolf talk, let him tell him about his life, let him be his friend.

The whump of snow hitting the ground from a nearby tree woke Tomasz. He was on watch duty and, despite the cold, had fallen asleep, his head resting on Rolf in front of him. He had dreamed of those men, singing around the fire, and was confused when he woke and looked about for the missing warmth.

He moved his toes in his boots and his fingers in their thin, useless gloves. Rolf turned around and Tomasz looked at him. His beard had frozen white, though a small patch was thawing where a cigarette stuck out between his lips. 'You sleep well?' Rolf joked. He turned around now to face Tomasz in the small dugout in a field covered with white cotton snow.

'Cigarette?' Rolf asked, already rolling one for him.

'Did I sleep long?'

'An hour maybe. Nothing has moved since you fell asleep. I thought at one point that maybe we are all dead and no one has bothered to tell us.'

Tomasz smiled and took the cigarette from Rolf, wincing as his cracked, cold lips split again, opening up new stinging slits. 'How long until this thaws, you think?' Tomasz asked Rolf.

'Spring isn't far off. Another month maybe.'

Tomasz shifted where he sat and pulled Werner's trench coat around him.

'You know, I'd like to be a carpenter one day,' Rolf said.

'Ha! Can you even make anything?' Tomasz asked.

Rolf shrugged. 'I'd make tables and chairs mostly. And I'd have a shop where women would come with their large backsides and sit on my chairs. I'd like that.'

Tomasz laughed and inhaled deeply on his cigarette. He looked at the sky, which had now changed from pale grey to a darker shade, the night drawing in although it was only mid-afternoon.

'You have a girl already, though, don't you? No need for me to keep a woman to the side for you?'

'Yes, I have a girl.'

'What is her name again?'

'Zofia.'

'You don't speak much about her. It's strange. You hear all the other men always talking about their girlfriends. Why don't you?'

'It's hard to think of her.' Tomasz shrugged. 'As soon as I do, I try to forget. I don't know if I will ever see her again, so it seems pointless to try and remember.'

'You should remember her. I need some distraction. Tell me about when you met her.'

'I don't want to.' Tomasz ground out his cigarette in the snow.

'Come on. We'll be here for ages. May as well talk about something. Please?' Rolf looked at Tomasz and held his hands as if in prayer, begging him. Tomasz laughed and nodded.

'I met her at a fair when we were very young,' Tomasz relented. 'But it wasn't until years later, perhaps I was thirteen or so, that I met her again, and from that moment on, we were always together.

'It was a cold winter that year – like they all are, I suppose, but maybe not as cold as this. The school had closed because the snow was so deep; there was no way we could all get there.

'I was happy once the school closed as that meant I could spend time with my friends and play in the snow. Back then, my best friend was Wojtek, and we liked to sled on the hills around us. One day we decided to go to the largest hill in the village, which everyone played on – well, those brave enough anyway.

'"You scared?" Wojtek had asked me.

'"No."

'"Is your brother there?"

'"Probably," I said. Andrzej would definitely be there, but I knew he wouldn't be sledding or playing games. He was seventeen, perhaps, then, and he would be sitting with his friends, smoking and acting older than they were.

'"They say if you go on this hill, you are risking your life!" Wojtek walked ahead of me, pulling the sled eagerly.

'"Ha! You believe anything. It's just a hill," I told him.

'"Yes, but have you seen it? It's huge!"

'It was not long until we reached it. I could see my brother at the top of the hill with his friends who were talking to a group of girls. The sledders came down the hill at speed, just as Wojtek had said they would. They moved so fast that some of them fell down and tumbled, leaving their sled behind them.

'"You want to go first?" Wojtek asked me.

'I shook my head.

'"Come to the top with me," Wojtek said.

'I followed Wojtek, my breath coming quickly as the incline became steeper. I was almost at the top when I tripped and landed face down in the frozen snow.

'Deep laughter came from the summit, and as I made to get up, a hand reached down to help me. I looked up to see someone I had not seen for some time – the girl from the fair, the girl with the blue dress and blue eyes – Zofia.

'"Are you all right?" she asked me.

'I nodded, forgetting my words for a moment, and took her hand.

'"Hey! I know you," she said. "I knew I would see you again."

'"I'm Tomasz," I said, feeling stupid.

'"Yes, I know. I remember. You gave me your heart at the fair. How could I forget?" she laughed.

'I remember smiling at her and feeling like I would never stop smiling again. I watched as she ran the few metres to the summit to her friends, her dark hair streaming behind her.

'I followed her to the peak where Wojtek was preparing himself to sled down.

'"You not going, brother?" Andrzej yelled at me.

'The group of girls stopped giggling and chatting and turned to look at me, and despite the cold air, I could feel my face begin to flame.

'"In a minute," I answered.

'"You should go now, show us all how it is done!" Andrzej yelled.

'"Wojtek wants to go first," I said.

'"Ah, still so little, brother. Still a chicken!"

'The boys laughed and a few of the girls resumed their giggling, and I wished I was at home so I could punch Andrzej in the arm – hard – tell him he was a pig, and fight with him until Father broke us up.

'I saw that Zofia was not laughing. She looked at me and smiled gently – she felt sorry for me.

'"All right then," I said. I walked to Wojtek, who stood up and let me take his place on the sled.

'"Give it a proper push!" Andrzej yelled.

'Wojtek held on to my shoulders, and I gripped the thin rope at the front of the sled as he rocked me back and forth over the lip of the hill.

'I remember I felt sick. The hill, now I was at the top, was a lot higher than I had realised, and my sled was homemade and rickety, the wooden slats nailed roughly together – it would never get me to the bottom safely.

'"One!" I heard them all shout, counting me down.

'"Two!"

'"Three!"

'I held my breath, shut my eyes, and suddenly felt the wind rush at my face as I flew over the snow. At first, I thought it was going to be all right; I was moving in a straight line. I opened my eyes and smiled. I was going to make it. The fields rushed past, blurry on either side of me – I was almost there, almost at the bottom. Then, the sled hit a rock that was covered lightly by the snow, and I veered left. I tried to hold on for as long as I could, but I soon lost my grip and felt the sled come from underneath me, and suddenly I was tumbling, rolling, the snow in my eyes, my ears, stinging my face with its cold.

'Once I stopped rolling, I lay on my back in the snow, looking up at the purple-blue sky, heavy snow clouds weighing down on me, and I wondered if I was actually dead.

'I heard the sound of someone running in the snow towards me. "Are you all right? Are you hurt?" I heard Zofia's voice shout as she reached me.

'Suddenly her face was above mine, blocking the sky from my vision, and I found my smile from before.

'"You're smiling," she said. "Are you all right then?"

'"Perfectly," I answered.

"'I think you should go home and rest. Just in case."

"'Will you come with me?" I asked her, not believing I had said those words to her.

'She smiled down at me. "I'll have to, won't I?" She laughed. "Make sure you don't get into any more trouble. I'll have to keep my eye on you, Tomasz."

'Then, from her pocket, I watched as she pulled out the small wooden heart from the fair, holding it in her palm until I took her hand in mine.'

The sudden roar of planes above them stopped Tomasz from continuing his story, and he looked to Rolf whose face was suddenly full of fear. Within seconds, there was a crash, a boom so loud that all Tomasz remembered was being thrown into the air, his ears ringing, his mind still on Zofia and the day she gave him her heart.

When Tomasz woke, he was warm. He knew he must be dead. If he was alive, he would feel the cold, he'd be unable to move his toes. Yes, he was most certainly dead.

He could hear voices and screams, crying, wailing – the other dead. He opened, then closed his eyes. He was surprised that he had eyes and ears when he was dead. He had always thought he would be a light floating spirit, or perhaps submerged in total blackness.

'You're awake,' he heard a male voice say. German.

He opened his eyes again. A medic stood over him, wrapped up in as many clothes as Tomasz had been in.

'You're warm?' the medic asked him.

Tomasz nodded. He looked down; blankets, coats, uniforms covered his body.

Tomasz watched as the medic took a vial of something from underneath his armpit.

'It's morphine,' the medic said, following Tomasz's gaze. 'Stays here with me so it doesn't freeze.' The medic pricked at Tomasz's arm and injected the liquid.

'Where am I?' Tomasz finally found his words.

'Kharkov. You are lucky, you know. A millimetre further and the shrapnel would've hit your femoral artery. Your friend didn't make it. Rolf.'

Tomasz nodded and closed his eyes, letting the morphine take hold, letting it take him into blissful black oblivion.

CHAPTER TWENTY-SIX

Over the coming days, Tomasz shifted in and out of consciousness. Sometimes, he woke to the cries of men; sometimes, he woke because it was too quiet.

Some men left, carried on stretchers, their eyes bandaged; legs, hands, feet too. 'Where are they going?' he asked the medic.

'Taken to Berlin or elsewhere. Rehabilitation and whatnot.'

'Will I go?' Tomasz reached under the layers of clothing covering him and felt the raised ridge of puckered sewn skin on his leg.

'Doubt it. You may get a few days' rest out of it, though.'

Tomasz lay back in his bed, wondering why the shrapnel had not gone that millimetre further.

After a week, he was given leave to rest in a small village a few miles east of where Rolf had died in the snow fields.

His lodgings were with a husband, wife and their teenage daughter, who eyed their guest with suspicion. Tomasz did not care. His head, still foggy from the pain medication, made him long for a bed, for warmth, for sleep. Thankfully, the family obliged, and he was given a small room under the sloping eaves of the house. A modest fire burned in the grate and he had a bed with fresh sheets, a bowl with warm water and a clean cloth.

When he arrived, he leaned on the door frame, looked at this room and wanted to weep.

'Is not good enough?' the woman asked him, the German as foreign to her as it was to Tomasz.

'No. It's perfect,' he said. '*Danke.*'

She nodded, and he could see how she was confused at the odd soldier, with his strange German accent and his emotion upon seeing a clean bed.

He was given two weeks. At first it sounded like a long time to him, but after the first four days spent sleeping, eating and sitting by the fire, he soon realised he would be back a lot sooner.

He asked the wife, Marta, if she had any paper and a pencil or pen. She nodded towards her daughter, a young girl of fifteen with wide eager eyes, who sat by the fireplace.

'Mama says you want something?' the girl asked. Her German was more measured than her mother's; her posture showed too much confidence for a girl so young.

'Yes, I have filled my diary.'

'I'll see if I can bring some extra from school. There's nowhere else here.'

'Thank you.' He smiled at her. 'I'm Tomasz.'

'Klara,' she responded, then looked away.

He stood awkwardly in their small living room and soon turned away and climbed the stairs to his room.

It was two days later when there was a faint knock on his door. He opened it, but no one was there. On the floor was a small, bound notebook and a fountain pen. He picked them up and saw that there was a name inscribed on the pen – Klara. He smiled.

He wrote then, without stopping to think, for hours. He wrote what had happened to Rolf, he wrote letters to Zofia, to his parents. Finally, the ink ran out and, spent, he lay back on his bed and slept for fourteen hours.

Another two days passed, and Klara brought him some more ink. 'Mama said you had used it all.'

He nodded, sat up on his bed, and she walked towards him, placing the ink in his hands.

'What are you writing?' She nodded towards the almost full notebook.

He shrugged. 'Silly thoughts… And letters, to my parents. If I ever get to send them.'

She nodded. 'I hope that can last you now. I don't think I can get any more.'

'Thank you,' he said. 'I appreciate it.'

She turned to leave, then looked back. 'Tomasz. That's not German, is it?'

He shook his head. 'Polish.'

She walked out of his room and closed the door.

Tomasz turned to the last blank sheet in his notebook and, slowly this time, he began to write.

To my darling Zofia,

When did I write last? I do not remember anymore. In my mind I have written you hundreds of letters, but I don't think I have sent them all, and I doubt that the ones I did send have ever reached you.

Do you think of me still? It has been years now. Years have passed and I am still not home.

I thought I saw you once. In Kraków, at a window. I realise now I imagined it, imagined you, perhaps because I was afraid and seeing you would make me help myself – you would've told me to save myself.

These past few days I have been away from the battle, from the death and screams of men and noise of bullets, and my mind has nothing else to think about but you. And I wonder where you are and if I will ever hear from you again or if I will ever see you again?

Do you remember that night when we sneaked out of our houses and met in Tata's barn, just because we missed each other? It had only been a few days, I think. Now it has been years. And the missing of you has become almost normal. Do not think that I am not in pain when I think of you not being with me, I am. But it's as if the pain is a part of me now – just as my arm or leg is. I do wonder though, what it will be like once the pain stops. Will that be happiness again?

I wonder if we will ever get to have a life together. I used to think it was certain – nothing could stop us. But now, everything is different. There is so much death, so much. It is as though it is following me wherever I go and one day it will find me, lonely, in a corner, in a hole, a ditch where all the light is gone, and it is quiet. Then, I won't be able to fight it.

At Christmas we made a bonfire. We sat around it and the men said they wished they had mistletoe. My friend Rolf, he said what was the point, when there was no one to kiss. I thought of you.

I wonder what you did for Christmas. I hope you were home with your family. I hope you ate and slept without worry.

We made plans for our Christmases together. Do you remember those? We would have children and a dog, and there would be a fire burning and it would be snowing outside.

I wonder if Andrzej has seen you. Or Kapaldi. I wonder if you are with your parents still living the life you always had – just without me.

It is snowing here. Is it snowing there? Are you in a ghetto? Are you cold? Are you with Hanna and her little daughter? These thoughts, whilst they scare me, I realise they could be real too. I realise now that you are not safe, just as I am not. None of us have a choice, none of us can determine our future anymore.

I cannot write more, my love. I cannot. I must go now. I must go and make my thoughts get away from this. I cannot think of this anymore. Of you.

I love you.
Tomasz

CHAPTER TWENTY-SEVEN

After writing the letter, Tomasz did not leave his room again except to use the bathroom. All day, he lay on his bed, trying to make his thoughts change, trying to see something other than the ghost of Zofia at the window of Lieberenz's office, or in the snow, in the ghetto.

On his last day, Klara came to the door to see him off. Her mother stood in the background, watching the exchange.

'Give me the letters,' she said. 'Give them to me and I will send them for you.'

Tomasz looked at the young girl, at the eager eyes that begged him to trust her. He quickly ripped out some pages and gave them to her after hurriedly writing the addresses on them.

She took them and folded them carefully. Then she closed the door.

Back on duty, Tomasz opened up the notebook. He read and re-read the letter he had written to Zofia. He hadn't given Klara that one, couldn't bear letting it go. What if Zofia never got it? What if it sat there, alone in a post office? What if he received a reply, a reply to tell him that she was gone, and couldn't be found?

He closed the notebook and put it into his pack. She would stay with him a little longer yet.

Within a week of being back on the front, the spring thaw was more than underway. Practically overnight the once solid ground had turned into a thick mire, and Tomasz found that he now missed the cold. The cold meant that during the day the mud would be solid. Now, it was up to his knees; even the cars and tanks would get bogged, making the daily grind of battle slow to an almost dreamlike state, as men walked sluggishly through the swampy earth.

The men had started to thaw too. In the depths of winter, Tomasz had not been able to smell his own body odour. It was as though the freeze had suspended the smell of urine, the sweat of unwashed bodies and faeces that clung to their underwear. Now though, the air was ripe with it.

He missed Rolf. He missed having someone to talk to, someone who would let him lean against him. Although, Tomasz thought wryly, Rolf would not let him lean against him now with this smell.

The gravediggers took the broken bodies out of the mud that had been stuck there during the winter, and Tomasz watched as they were dragged onto carts and taken away from the battlefields forever. He was envious of them.

The spring also brought the rain; a cold, ugly rain that turned the mud into a dirty river. Tomasz's boots had holes in them, so his feet were wet every day, making the soles so soft that blisters and cuts formed easily.

Since Rolf had died, he had made no other friends, and he found that his brain was becoming confused. He no longer had any distraction, a friendly voice, someone to remind him of the day, the month, the year. Now he looked about him, tiredness in his eyes like grains of sand, trying to remember how he'd got here, trying to remember his own name.

He amused himself by watching the planes that flew overhead, trying to guess how many seconds it would take from spotting the plane to its bomb hitting the ground. He was right most of the time – five to ten seconds; they didn't waste time.

He began to imagine himself having conversations with Kapaldi. Perhaps he would know what to do to stop the rain. This type of rain would not result in a rainbow when it stopped. The sun did not shine here, and Tomasz imagined that it had never shone here. It was either freezing or grey and wet. That was it.

If Kapaldi were here, he would tell Tomasz to do the rain dance regardless. He would believe that no matter what, something beautiful could be made. Tomasz smiled, closed his eyes and tapped his foot in the mud, imagining himself twirling round, arms open wide in front of the battalion. They'd shoot him, he knew. He opened his eyes and grew still. Kapaldi was not here. Rainbows would not appear.

It had been raining now for three weeks, the days creeping into June and warmth, but the rain would not stop. Tomasz sat in his dugout, the mud up to his shins, looking at the splatter as the raindrops hit the puddles. No planes flew overhead, none now for a few days. No distractions, no counting.

'You should move about,' a grenadier told him. 'Don't just sit in it, letting your feet sink.'

Tomasz looked up at the voice, feeling the rain on his face. He turned away to look at the ground so that the drops would instead fall on his helmet.

'Stupid Pole,' the man said and moved away.

The sound of the rain hitting the metal of his helmet was almost comforting to him. It reminded him of the old tin bath at home that his mother kept outside when it was not in use. The tin bath sat under Tomasz's window, and on rainy days he would wake to the musical drops that the water made as it landed.

He listened now to the sound on his helmet and imagined himself back at home once more, in his bed. Soon, his mother would wake him, and he would sit with her at the kitchen table eating fresh cooked eggs and bread, and drinking thick, hot coffee. Then, within minutes, there would be a knock at the door. His mother would open it, and Zofia would be there, drenched but smiling, her legs splattered with dirt after the run from her house.

'Jasieński?' A voice suddenly broke into his daydream.

Tomasz looked up to the face of his Unteroffizier.

'Get up.'

Tomasz stood, his boots sinking into the mud. He looked to the soldier who had called him stupid. He must have told the Unteroffizier. Could he get in trouble for allowing mud into his boots?

Tomasz followed him to his bunker and removed his helmet.

'You're being reassigned,' his Unteroffizier said.

'Where?' Tomasz asked.

'Warsaw. A new job. You've been requested by Major Lieberenz. You leave straight away.'

Tomasz stood, wondering which was worse, staying or leaving.

'Can you hear me?'

Tomasz nodded.

'Report to barracks.'

Tomasz nodded again and turned to walk out of the bunker.

'Stupid Pole,' the Unteroffizier said.

As soon as Tomasz reached barracks, he was stripped of his uniform and de-loused with a powder that stung the cuts on his skin. He shaved and was given a fresh uniform that was too big for him, so he had to keep hitching the sleeves away from his wrists.

Once dressed, a short, fat Obergefreiter called Richter escorted him to the train where he was seated with a man his own age, whose head was bandaged and was missing his left arm.

'You going home too?' the soldier asked Tomasz.

Tomasz shook his head. 'New post.'

'Unlucky,' he said.

Tomasz looked at the empty sleeve that hung from the man's left side. 'Yes,' he said, 'unlucky.'

*

As the train pulled out of the station, Tomasz turned to look out of the window. Bit by bit, the flat, muddy fields and grey sky became blurred as the train picked up pace, away from the guns, the lice, towards something else.

He picked at a piece of skin on the side of his ragged thumbnail and reasoned that whatever awaited him could not be worse than what he had been through. He thought of Lieberenz and was thankful that the Major was saving him from Bauer's punishment. Then he thought of the job he had done before – the rounding up of his Polish brothers – and what that had made him, and a part of him wished he wasn't leaving anymore.

The skin finally gave way from his thumb, and he watched as it bled a little. He put it in his mouth, and sucked on it as if he were a child again. Tomasz tried to scan the speeding scenery, but his tired eyes could not keep up. Resting his head against the rain-splattered glass, he closed his eyes and allowed the blackness of deep sleep to overcome his battered brain and body.

CHAPTER TWENTY-EIGHT

The sky had just turned to navy as Tomasz arrived in Warsaw, and Richter shepherded him to a military jeep where Gefreiter Drange was waiting for him.

'Any problems?' Drange asked Richter, then nodded towards Tomasz.

'None. Why?'

Drange shrugged. 'Just wondered.'

Tomasz felt Drange push him between his shoulder blades, making him stumble and almost fall into the back seat of the jeep.

Drange climbed into the other side, and Tomasz saw another soldier at the wheel. 'Your train was late,' Drange said, as the driver pulled away.

Warsaw was a city he had never visited, a city that was the heart of his country, its capital, and yet to Tomasz it looked as though it were sagging under the weight of its occupiers. The streets were busy with uniformed men who stood straight and tall, but its inhabitants bowed their heads to look at the pavement. The windows were shuttered, curtains pulled against the outside, the buildings scarred and pitted with bullet holes.

Soon the car turned into a wide, leafy street and slowed to stop at the kerb.

'Get out,' Drange said.

Tomasz opened the door, and Drange came round and grabbed him by the arm, pushing him towards the stone steps that led to a three-storey house from which music and laughter flowed.

Drange opened the door, and Tomasz followed him into the cool marbled hallway. A grand staircase curved its way upwards towards the chandelier that hung from the high ceiling. Tomasz saw that in a room to the right a large dining table was littered with gifts wrapped with elaborate bows, in pinks and pastels.

Drange pushed him towards two double doors that led into an office and told him to sit at the chair in front of the shining mahogany desk.

He heard the click of the doors as they closed behind Drange, then the sound of footsteps behind him.

Lieberenz sat down behind his desk and faced Tomasz. He roughly stubbed out his cigarette in the ashtray, but it continued to burn, smoke rising to the lofty heights of the ceiling.

Tomasz watched it curl upwards, seeing another chandelier hanging from above.

'It's nice, isn't it?'

Tomasz nodded.

'I heard what happened with Bauer.' The Major shook his head. 'Unfortunate.'

Tomasz nodded once more.

'But you gave him what he wanted, giving up your friends in that basement, and that gave him a promotion. Gave me some more money too. Naturally, I was not happy that Bauer had sent you away. You were an asset – that much was clear. He missed that detail, missed that you had made a mistake – just a mistake. A small one. But made up for it with something far larger?'

Tomasz heard the question mark at the end. He nodded.

Lieberenz walked around to the front of his desk. 'You know why I asked for you to be assigned to me once more, Tomasz, despite your mistake?'

'No, sir.'

'Because you remind me of myself. I was like you. It took me time to understand my loyalties. But once I did' – he clicked his fingers – 'everything fell into place. You made a mistake, giving papers to your brother. But I understand that too. He pressured you, made you think you could do some good? And when you finally realised that nothing could be done, you gave up your brother and his friends, and for that I see you finally made the right choice. You saw who was more powerful, who could help or hinder you. I believe you have been punished enough, out there in those frozen trenches.'

Tomasz looked at the Major who smiled at him. He thought of what Lieberenz had said, the story he had told himself. Did the Major really believe it?

'Now. You need some rest, some food. Drange will take you to your new rooms.'

As he walked to the front door, he looked at the presents again, wrapped delicately, as if for a woman. He looked at Drange who was smirking. Suddenly, Tomasz felt something – not fear but an uneasy shift. He felt taunted by the presents, as if he had been brought to a private party, as though he were part of a game once more, but no one had told him the rules.

Tomasz was taken by Drange to a dilapidated building that had been requisitioned by the Wehrmacht as a boarding house.

Drange opened the door to let Tomasz in and closed the door behind him. Tomasz could hear his quick steps as he made his way back to the car.

Tomasz waited. 'Hello?' he said into the quiet of the hallway.

A short woman, her legs in thick stockings, the rest of her blanketed in a plain brown dress, opened a door at the end of the hallway and walked towards him. She stopped in front of him and looked him up and down.

He looked at her and thought of Frau Schneider, of her thin lips and wide-spaced eyes. Would this woman treat him the same? *Polen sind nicht willkommen.*

'I'm Tomasz,' he said.

'You are Polish?' she asked him, her eyebrows raised.

'Yes.' Tomasz looked at her, waiting for her to swear, to tell him he was a traitor.

She stared at him. 'Come.'

He followed her up the creaky staircase to a room on the second floor – a single bed, a wooden chair, a washbasin, and a blanket.

'Thank you.'

She nodded, then stepped forward and placed her hand on his arm. 'I have three sons,' she said. 'One in England, one in the Luftwaffe, one in a work camp.'

'I'm sorry,' he said.

She squeezed his arm and left him alone in his new room.

He sat on the edge of the single bed. He took a packet of cigarettes that he had been given in Kharkov out of his pocket, shook one out and lit it.

He smoked the cigarette until there was nothing left. He lay back on the bed and closed his eyes, but his brain was awake. His feet twitched and jumped as though they had a mind of their own.

He swung his legs off the bed and lit another cigarette. He tried to massage the muscles in his thighs, tried to control the spasms. He couldn't – he snorted with laughter – he couldn't control his own legs.

As he smoked, he stared at the wall in front of him. Spider cracks ran over the plaster, interwoven almost like streets, like a map. He stood up, pulled the wooden chair close to the wall and sat down. With his fingers, he traced the lines. Here, just near this point near the window, was his house. And here, where there was a small hole, that was the woods. And next to it, where a deep groove ran in the plaster, that was the river. He mapped for over an hour. Kapaldi's caravan, the orchards, the farm. Finally, his fingers stopped. There, two dots. That was him and Zofia. Tomasz smiled. He was like God; he was looking down from above at his life. That dot – that was Zofia. He stroked the mark, imagining that he was sending her all his love.

Tomasz rubbed his hand over his face. He was tired, a tiredness he had never known existed. It hurt his body, his mind. It had broken him. When he tried to sleep, he saw, replayed for him, the scenes of war, of bodies half buried in the snow, of the fear in every man's eyes as soon as they woke.

He looked at the wall again; the dots, him and Zofia. Tomasz stood, his feet still restless; he needed to walk.

He made his way down the wooden stairs barefoot, his boots in his hand. He reached the last stair and looked about him. He stepped down into the hallway and followed it back towards where he had seen the old Polish woman come from. He pushed open the door and found himself in a small kitchen, where the woman was sitting at the table staring at a cup that she clutched in her hands.

'What's wrong?' she said as she looked up.

'Nothing,' he answered, and turned to walk away.

'You can't sleep?'

'No.'

Tomasz turned to face her. She pushed herself up from the table, pain registering on her face. 'My knees,' she said.

'Can I help you?'

She waved his offer away.

'Goodnight,' he said.

'Just in case there is an emergency… There is a key in that pot near the back door.' She shuffled past him. 'Just in case.'

Tomasz nodded.

'Goodnight.'

He waited until she had left the room and turned out the light, then he took the key and placed it into the lock. Before he turned it to hear that opening click, he paused. For a moment, he felt something strange, something in his stomach and then in his mind – fear? He could no longer recognise his own emotions. He shook the feeling away and opened the door.

He stood outside in the small grassy garden and smoked his cigarette. He could hear the shouts and laughter of men from a tavern a few doors down. Tomasz closed his eyes and thought of the last time he had laughed – a proper laugh full of joy that made him double over.

The only scene that flashed through his mind was when he had sat with Kapaldi one summer afternoon in his fifteenth year.

They had talked for hours; Kapaldi had travelled back to Italy for some time to see some old friends, then finally re-routed back towards Poland, back towards Poznań, to keep his promise to his young friend.

This time Kapaldi had a broken arm – broken by some drunken soldiers on his travels. Tomasz had looked at his friend, concerned.

'Don't worry about me,' Kapaldi had said. 'I have you.'

'Me?'

'Don't you remember stealing Kowalski's tractor? Trying to mow those poor boys down?' Kapaldi grinned at him.

'It wasn't funny,' Tomasz said. 'It was frightening.' Yet as he spoke, he could feel the corners of his lips turning upwards into a huge smile.

Kapaldi suddenly laughed. His voice roared, tears streamed down his face, and Tomasz joined in, holding his belly tight as the muscles spasmed with laughter.

Now, he opened his eyes and imagined his friend with him in this enclosed scrap of a garden. If he imagined hard enough, he could almost hear the chimes that hung from Kapaldi's caravan and the sound of his friend's voice.

'Tomasz,' Kapaldi said. 'I wondered when I would see you again.'

'How did you know I was here?'

'I know many things.' Kapaldi winked at him. 'How are you, my friend?'

Tomasz shrugged. 'Tired. Worried. I haven't seen you for such a long time. Zofia too. Andrzej.'

'She is well.'

'Is she safe? Have you seen her?'

'Of course she is safe,' Kapaldi said.

'You promise me?'

'I promise. You shouldn't have left your lodgings. Stay indoors. It's not safe.'

Suddenly, there were angry shouts coming from the tavern – a fight had started.

'You worry too much now. You have changed. You are not happy and colourful anymore.'

'I have no choice. I am not the same man I was. Neither are you.'

Tomasz wished he could pull his friend close. The imaginary conversation disappeared with each breath that hung for a few seconds in the air. He imagined the embrace, smelling the open fires, Kowalski's field. Then he heard his friend's voice in his mind once more: 'Ah, Tomasz, you are turning soft on me,' and Kapaldi's image disappeared.

Tomasz walked towards the gate that led into an alleyway, his feet taking him towards the shouts – more laughter now. The fight had ended, and Tomasz was thirsty.

Outside the tavern, a large soldier leaned against the doorway, smoking and talking to a woman in a short red dress. She smiled at Tomasz as he walked past them to open the door; the soldier noticed and pulled her roughly towards him. She laughed and took a cigarette from his packet.

Inside, the bar was a scattered affair; small tables and chairs were placed messily around the small room with ashtrays that overflowed amongst the empty glasses, and a few bar stools were pushed up against the rough wood of the bar. Most of the tables were taken by soldiers and their dates who sat on their laps and laughed at whatever the men said. There was a piano at the far end of the room and two SS were arguing over which song to play next. Tomasz chose a stool towards the end of the bar, away from the door and near to the piano.

He ordered a beer and drank it quickly – too quickly. Then he ordered a whiskey, which cost him almost the rest of the little money he had.

He hated the way it burned his throat and he hated the taste. Yet he enjoyed how quickly it made him feel warm and relaxed.

The money he had left would buy him a shot of local vodka. He ordered it and let it sit in front of him for some time, not wanting to drink it back, not wanting to return to his room.

Loud laughter made him look up. At the door three soldiers entered, joking and laughing at something one of them had said. Tomasz recognised one of them – Lieberenz.

'Ah, Tomasz!' Lieberenz staggered towards him. 'My friend. Now come. Sit with us. We are drinking and you will drink with us, with your comrades!'

Tomasz took in the Major's appearance; his eyes were blood-shot, the top two buttons of his shirt and jacket were open and his tie was gone, discarded before he'd arrived here.

The two others went to the piano and started a loud discussion with the SS over what song would be played. Lieberenz dragged a stool to sit next to Tomasz, stumbling a little as he tried to clamber on.

'Do you have a girlfriend, Tomasz?' the Major asked. He offered him a cigarette.

'No,' Tomasz said. Lieberenz lit the cigarette for him.

'What about that pretty thing you were with when I first met you?'

Suddenly, music filled the room. A German song, one which made all of the patrons turn their head to the pianist, slap their knees and begin to sing.

'You know this one?' Lieberenz asked.

'No.'

'Doesn't matter. Stupid song really, made for this lot. Makes them feel like they are home again, eating their mama's food!'

Tomasz smiled.

'So, that girl?'

'Zofia.'

'Yes! Zofia. How is she?'

'I don't know.' Tomasz drank the rest of his vodka and pushed himself away from the bar as if to leave.

'Come now! It can't be that bad. Bartender!' Lieberenz slapped the bar and got the barman's attention. 'Another vodka for my friend and one for me – no, make it two – two each. Here, drink. It can't be that bad?'

Despite himself, Tomasz drank. Then he drank the next. He hadn't eaten, he remembered now, as his stomach rebelled against the volume of alcohol he had poured into it. He was used to weak coffee and dirty water that looked and tasted like the ground he slept on.

'You all right?' Lieberenz patted Tomasz on the back. 'Go out back, clear it out.'

Tomasz stumbled to the back entrance and, leaning against a wall, allowed his stomach to empty its contents. When he had finished, he stood for a moment breathing in the cool air, but his head still felt fuzzy – he needed to go to bed.

As he went back inside the bar, he heard some arguing from the front entrance once more. For a second, he stopped and thought he heard a voice he recognised. Then Tomasz staggered through the door past the piano that now stood empty and silent, back to his stool.

'I have to go home,' Tomasz said to the Major, who was leaning heavily on the bar, a whiskey untouched in front of him.

'Me too. Me too, Tomasz.' He stood, wrapped his arm over Tomasz's shoulder and started to walk towards the door. 'I need to get home. Tonight, we had a party for my girlfriend – did I tell you I had a girlfriend? I do. She's beautiful. But she went to bed early – had enough of the party. But I was enjoying myself, so here I am.' Lieberenz stopped walking and with his other hand rubbed his forehead. 'We had a drink, didn't we? Yes, we did. I got you some vodka. See, I am good to you.'

Lieberenz then took his arm off Tomasz and walked almost sideways to the door. Tomasz followed and, as the door was opened, Tomasz heard the voice he thought he knew once more.

The two SS and Lieberenz's two friends were outside. They were laughing at something on the ground, large bundles of something. Lieberenz walked over to them. They said something, then a voice came from the bundle. Then another voice and another. Three voices. On the ground. Tomasz squinted to see. He knew one voice. Who were the others? Why were they there?

He took two steps forward and saw three men kneeling on the pavement, facing the wall in front of them, their hands on their heads.

Lieberenz asked them who they were, why they were here, and the voice Tomasz knew told him that they were simply walking by.

The Major didn't like the answer and kicked them each in their backs, making their heads hit the wall in front with a loud thunk.

Tomasz's mouth was dry, and he was trying to scramble his thoughts together. *I know that voice.* He stepped forward once more so he could see the men better in the weak light afforded by the street lamp. He couldn't see their faces, but then, he didn't need to. One man had a scarf wrapped around his neck, the colours dulled. *Kapaldi.*

Tomasz pulled in his breath, held it in his mouth, forgetting what he was meant to do next.

Before he could think, the SS pulled one of the men to the side – a short fat man who had tears streaming down his face – and began to beat him and kick him until his body rolled into the street.

Lieberenz's friends, along with the other SS, pulled at the skinny man next – two of them dragging him by his arms whilst the other began raining blows onto his prone body.

'This one's for us.' Lieberenz turned to face Tomasz, his alcohol-fumed breath foul, his eyes redder than before. 'These gypsies. Scourge of a nation. Useless people.'

'I…' Tomasz began.

Kapaldi turned, saw Tomasz and smiled. In that instant, Lieberenz drew his arm back and hit Kapaldi's head with such force that it snapped back, and Tomasz was sure he had broken his neck.

Kapaldi recovered though and straightened up, his head bleeding, his lip bleeding, as he looked straight at Lieberenz. 'I was simply taking a walk with my friends. I was walking. Just walking. It's how I see my friends.' He looked at Tomasz.

Tomasz swallowed. What could he do? Was he imagining this again, just like he had imagined Kapaldi in the garden? Was this real?

The two other men were lying unmoving on the ground, and the soldiers and SS, having lost interest as they refused to fight back, were now making their way back inside the tavern.

'Hurry up!' one of them said to Lieberenz.

'In a minute. Are they…?' He nodded his head towards the other men.

'Think so. Who cares? They will be.'

Lieberenz nodded. He turned back to Kapaldi and kicked him hard in the stomach, making him curl into a foetal position to protect himself.

Lieberenz raised his foot now, ready to stamp on his head, and Tomasz reached out and grabbed the Major's forearm. Lieberenz looked at Tomasz. In that moment, the rage on the Major's face made Tomasz understand what he was really capable of.

They stared at one another, neither one quite knowing what the other one was planning to do. At that moment, a truck pulled up. Two soldiers got out to head into the tavern, and Lieberenz finally turned away from Tomasz to the young privates. 'Here. Pick those two up. Take them away.'

The privates looked to the two bodies, perhaps dead, perhaps not. They saw the Major's uniform, saluted, and picked the bodies up, throwing them into the back of the truck like bags of garbage. They made to climb back in and drive away when Lieberenz shouted out – 'Wait! There'll be one more in a minute.'

Tomasz looked at Kapaldi who lay now on the floor, staring at the stars above him. His eyes flitted to Tomasz, and he smiled at him.

'Here. I can't have all the fun,' Lieberenz said.

Tomasz felt the cold metal in his hand, unsure of how it had come to be there. He looked down – Lieberenz's pistol.

'Hurry up,' Lieberenz slurred, the alcohol making him lean now against the wall. He took a packet of cigarettes from his pocket and shook one out which fell to the floor. He tried again and this time got one. Still using the wall to keep him upright, he lit the cigarette and blew the smoke out thickly. 'You! Wait!' he yelled to the private in the truck, who had turned the ignition. 'I said there'll be one more. You can take me home too. Quick now, Tomasz, I have to get back. I told you my lady is waiting.'

'I can't,' Tomasz said.

Lieberenz laughed. 'You can't? Of course you can. I told you – this man, this Roma, is nothing. Worse than a sewer rat. You are doing him a favour – putting him out of his misery.'

Tomasz's hand was shaking.

'Come now! Where's the soldier that earned that medal?
Where's the soldier I have done so much for? Come now! It's easy,
see?' Lieberenz took the gun from him, held it against Tomasz's
temple. 'See. Easy. Just a quick pull back and bang-bang, it's all
over. Now you do it. But pull the trigger obviously!' Lieberenz
handed the gun back and laughed. 'Quick now. My lady is waiting.
I told you we had a party, didn't I?'

Kapaldi coughed, making Tomasz look down at his friend once
more. Kapaldi's face did not move, not a twitch or a blink, but there
was something in the way he looked at Tomasz, as if his eyes were
burning through into Tomasz's brain, telling him it was all right.

Tomasz knew Lieberenz was looking – his breathing was
quieter – he was trying to understand, trying to assess this look
between the two men that had gone on for far too long. Were
they speaking? Had he gone deaf? No one's lips were moving,
but there was something...

Tomasz's heart had calmed; the world had stopped fighting,
stopped hating each other for a moment. Then, Kapaldi closed
his eyes.

Tomasz pulled the trigger, his eyes closed as he heard the crack
that echoed in the street, which made time start again, and made
his heart race with what he had done.

He opened his eyes. Lieberenz was already bending over the
body, dragging it by the scarf around Kapaldi's neck. His eyes
were still closed, a neat bullet hole in his forehead.

The two privates came to help the Major, and Lieberenz
climbed into the front of the truck whilst the privates threw
Kapaldi's body into the back.

'See you tomorrow!' Lieberenz shouted to Tomasz as the truck
roared into life. As it drove away, Tomasz saw that the scarf was
in the Major's hand, all the colours of the rainbow.

He looked to his own hand which still held the pistol. He
threw it to the ground where it fell into the pool of still-warm

blood and looked again at his hand, the hand that had pulled the trigger, and wished he could yank it off, throw it away too for being so weak, for betraying his friend.

A voice, a voice in the back of his mind that sounded so much like Zofia, asked him one question – *What choice did you have? He saved your life – it was what he wanted.*

He shook his head, shook away the voice. He went back inside the tavern and ordered a vodka even though he had no money to pay for it. The two SS were back at the piano as if nothing had happened; the two friends of the Major had found girls to talk to.

'You going to pay for that?' the bartender asked.

Tomasz, confused, looked to the vodka, and then patted his pocket. Suddenly, there was someone at his elbow.

'I'll get it,' said the woman from the doorway, the woman in the short red dress. 'You look like you need it.'

Tomasz nodded his thanks and knocked it back.

'You here alone?' she asked.

'Yes.'

'They not with you?' She gestured towards the others.

'No.'

'Then I'll keep you company.'

'I have no money.'

'I didn't ask you for any, did I? I have my own. I'll get you another drink.'

They sat together for a few minutes and drank, and Tomasz pretended nothing had happened – as though this were the start of the night.

Before he could think, before he could react, he was off his stool on the floor, his head pounding, not from alcohol but from the fist of the fat soldier who had just hit him.

'Steal my girl, would you? I go for a piss and you steal my girl?' he yelled.

Tomasz could not answer as punches rained down, then suddenly there were more faces – the SS, Lieberenz's friends – who were pulling at the fat soldier, hitting him, saving Tomasz. The last thing he saw was the girl in the red dress, picking up her handbag from the bar, leaving quietly into the night.

CHAPTER TWENTY-NINE

Tomasz did not know where he was. His eyes would not open properly, and there was a woman's voice above him that he did not recognise. There was another noise, the drip-drip of water, then a cooling cloth on his forehead. 'Zofia…' he managed to say.

'Hush now,' the woman's voice came back.

'Mama?'

'It's not your mama. You remember, don't you, you remember me? I look after you here in my home, your room, in Warsaw.'

Tomasz tried to shake his head.

'I never told you my name, did I? It's Lena. You remember now? My voice?'

Tomasz nodded a little. Yes, he remembered, a little.

'You were dumped on the doorstep a few nights ago. Bloody, battered.'

A few nights. Kapaldi. Tomasz managed to open his eyes and tried to sit up.

'Now, now, settle back down. No need to move. Just rest.'

'My friend,' Tomasz began.

'Yes. Your friend. They dropped a parcel here for you yesterday.'

Tomasz looked at Lena, her face soft as she tried to soothe her patient. 'No,' he said.

'Yes. A young man. Said it was important.'

'Was he tall?' Tomasz asked. 'Did he have long black hair?' Perhaps he had missed the shot, he thought, perhaps it had never happened.

Lena took the cloth from his forehead and place it back into the bowl of water. She got up from her chair and left the room, but came back within seconds.

'Here, I put it in my room. Just in case. There are eyes everywhere. I didn't want you to get into trouble, not in the state that you're in.'

She handed Tomasz a small parcel, wrapped in brown paper. There was no address label, not even his name.

Tomasz's pale fingers opened the parcel slowly, unwrapping each corner until the paper was flat, the contents spilling out. The scarf. Tomasz picked it up and began to cry, holding the scarf to his eyes to catch the tears.

That night, Tomasz developed a fever, producing a heat that seemed to consume his room, and he felt like he could not breathe. He lay on his bed naked, feeling sweat from his body soak into the sheet underneath him. He could not take it anymore. Carefully he got out of bed and, shuffling bit by bit, made his way out to the small garden at the rear of the house. He stood, feeling the cool air on his fevered skin, and looked up to the sky. Dark clouds hung low with the promise of rain.

Tomasz took the scarf that hung around his neck and held it upwards. He turned in slow circles, slow and painful, chanting a mantra he would never forget, only stopping when the soothing cool of the raindrops fell onto his skin.

CHAPTER THIRTY

Isla

Poland, 2015

Agnieszka finished translating. I looked to Zygmunt, tears running down his face. 'We all knew him, Kapaldi. He helped us all. And Tomasz, he loved him as if he was his father.'

Zygmunt wiped his face with a napkin and placed his beret back on his head, covering the scar.

'I'm sorry,' I said. The words felt useless.

He nodded. 'Don't judge him. You were not there, in that war. You can never understand the decisions we made. He did it to save himself, and Zofia. He loved her, so much.'

'Is she…?' I asked.

Agnieszka looked at Zygmunt, who shook his head slowly.

'I'm sorry,' I repeated, incapable of thinking of anything else to say. My head felt as though it was going to burst – there was so much to take in and to understand. My grandfather had killed Kapaldi, his friend. He had been through so much, seen so much pain and death. I tried to think of something to say, something that would make them feel better for telling me, that the story hadn't been told in vain. But I had nothing. I raised my hand as if to gesture some form of emotion – but I wasn't even sure what I felt, I couldn't get it all straight in my head.

Andrzej walked into the room; he knew what to say. 'We should leave.'

I looked to him, glad that he was taking charge, stood up and kissed Zygmunt's cheek. 'Thank you,' I whispered to him, to which he responded with a desolate nod.

We drove home in silence. They had already known this memory of Zygmunt's, of course, but they were now reliving it, and I knew that couldn't be easy.

I closed my eyes and tried to picture everything Zygmunt had told us, imagining myself as my grandfather, young, afraid; the terror he must have felt in seeing Kapaldi; the weight of the gun in his hand; the horror of knowing that he had no choice.

Suddenly, the car hit a pothole with a loud smack, and I quickly opened my eyes. Now and then I stared out of the window and something was different – something was colder, greyer than before. The cathedral was not as impressive, its dome dull, the green of the fields washed away to a darker hue.

I had never thought that losing one's memory would be a good thing, but the more my brain refused to let go of the scene of my grandfather shooting his best friend, the more I came to realise that it might be a blessing for him. It was hard to think that he had been able to live a life after what he had been through. I felt proud of him for being so brave, so sweet and caring, even with all that he had to remember each day. I doubted I could have carried on if I had experienced what he had. My life suddenly felt so easy, so free. I could remember my days without fear, regret, guilt or shame. I could replay happy memories without horrific ones battering to be let in too. How had he done it all those years – how had he lived a life with all those memories?

I felt a tear track its way down my cheek, and I wiped it away with my sleeve, then blew my nose.

'Are you all right?' Andrzej asked, his voice, for a change, laced with concern.

'I'm all right,' I said, my voice choked. 'I'll be all right.'

Back at the farmhouse I sat in the kitchen cradling a hot tea, watching through the large windows as the sun set over the orchards. I imagined my grandad seeing this once more – looking at the countryside where he had been so happy as a child.

'How are you feeling?' Agnieszka sat next to me.

I shrugged. 'I honestly don't know what to do about it, if anything. Telling Gran or Dad would do nothing but cause hurt.'

'But at least you know. You know what happened in his life, why perhaps he didn't want to tell you.'

'Zygmunt said he found him in hospital – after a nervous breakdown.'

Agnieszka nodded.

'Was that when he was sent to England?'

'I'm not sure,' she said. There was something in the set of her shoulders now, the way she leaned forward, that suggested she did know more, but that it was upsetting for her. She was old, very old, and I kept forgetting that my line of questioning, my quest, must be very draining and probably unfair on her – and Andrzej and Zygmunt.

'I'll look at flights tomorrow,' I said. 'It's probably time I go.'

She raised her eyebrows. 'Really? Already?' she sounded sad at the prospect. 'We've barely had chance to get to know one another. It's Wednesday today. Why not stay until the weekend? Get your cold all better?'

I placed the mug on the table. 'I'm not sure.'

'It'll be good for you.' She stood and patted my arm.

I ran my hand over my forehead, which was still warm to the touch. I couldn't think of a reason not to stay for a few more days. 'All right,' I agreed.

'Good,' she said. 'Get yourself to bed now. Get some rest. We'll talk more tomorrow.'

The next morning, I woke to an empty house and the sound of rain, tap dancing on the roof. I made coffee and padded about the house looking for life, a note – some indication of where they had disappeared to. I sat by the French windows and watched the rain fall whilst I waited for their return from wherever they had gone. A rumble of thunder rolled overhead, and a sudden wind whipped the trees outside into a frenzy.

There was a bang as the front door blew open, letting in the storm and a windswept Stefan. 'Awful day,' he said by way of greeting.

'So I see,' I said, and blew my nose.

'Still feeling poorly?'

'Getting a bit better, I think.'

'It's meant to calm down soon.' He placed his bag on the kitchen counter. 'I've a fair bit to get done in the orchards today, so I really hope the weatherman is right. You have a nice day yesterday?'

I nodded, but my face gave me away.

'What's wrong?' he asked.

'I don't really know where to start,' I said, shaking my head. 'It's all a bit much to get my head around still.'

He dragged a chair out and sat down. 'Start from the beginning. Maybe telling it all to me will help?'

'I don't know,' I said.

He reached a hand across the table and placed it on top of mine for a moment. 'I know what it's like to have a lot going on in your head and in your life and have no one to talk to about it. Please, if I can help, let me.'

His gesture and frankness took me by surprise. I barely knew him, but he was so genuine and full of concern that I felt relaxed around him. I knew I could trust him.

I started with the stories from my grandfather's childhood, the diaries, his time in the army and finally how he ended up in hospital.

Stefan listened attentively, his fingers entwined, his shoulders hunched forward. Every now and then he would lean back in his chair and look outside, as if trying to figure something out.

When I finished, he didn't speak for a moment. 'Are you shocked?' I asked. Another moment. He looked at the trees, which had now settled to a gentle sway as the rain and wind had ceased.

Finally, he spoke. 'How did he get to England?'

'I don't know. I assume he was somehow sent there?' He was silent again.

All I could hear in the silence was my own raggedy breathing and sniffing, which was beginning to annoy me. I blew my nose a little too loudly and Stefan looked up. 'Do you feel up to taking a little walk, perhaps?' he asked. 'It's calm out there now.'

I followed Stefan through the orchards to the field next to the river where the caravan sat.

He skirted past the field, and we followed the river for a while. I was already coming to see that Stefan was someone who only spoke when he had measured out what it was he wanted to say, and I was not one for general chit-chat, so we walked in silence, yet companionably so.

He turned right into a dense crop of trees. 'The Czarownica woods,' he said as we delved deeper into the thick brush. Twigs cracked under my feet, and bare branches scraped my hands and arms as I tried to move them out of the way.

'Where are we going?' I asked, after a particularly nasty scrape to the cheek left me with a warm trickle of blood.

'Almost there,' he said. A few more steps and we were in a clearing of sorts. Three large trees dominated the forest floor, meaning nothing else had space to grow around them. It was peaceful here. 'Look up,' he said.

I did, and above me I could see a circle of clear sky, now blue, as if in the whole of this darkened wood, this was the one place that allowed light to seep through. 'It's beautiful,' I said.

'Now look.' He pointed to the trunk of one of the trees.

I bent down and there, carved into the wood, were a few words of Polish along with two names I knew – Tomasz and Kapaldi.

'It says, "To my friend, Kapaldi, I am sorry. I pray that rainbows appear wherever you are. Your friend, Tomasz."'

I traced the rough words with my fingers. 'He came here and did this.'

'Yes. That's why I wondered what happened after he left hospital. He must have come back here first.'

I sniffed, then took a tissue from my pocket. 'I don't know. I mean, Zygmunt, the others – they never said.'

Stefan held out his hand to help me to my feet. I dusted the dirt and leaves from my jeans, then looked once more upwards at the circle of light above me. 'You would be able to see a rainbow here if one appeared, I suppose.'

'I suppose you could,' he agreed.

'Do you want to carry on? We can do a loop back?'

'Sure, why not.'

This time, Stefan did not want silence. 'I found the tree when I first came back from Germany. My parents have a dog, and it ran into the woods here. I chased him and found him in the clearing. I always felt it was magical, you know – that circle of light. But then, when you explained about Kapaldi and who he was… it all makes sense to me now.'

'He wasn't really magical. Just a young boy's perception of a strange man.'

'Wasn't he?' Stefan looked surprised and almost hurt by the suggestion.

We were coming to the edge of the wood now. Light illuminated our path more clearly, and I was glad to be out of the darkness.

'Czarownica woods,' Stefan said again. 'You know that means witches' woods? That's why it feels awful in there. Until you reach that clearing, and then everything feels OK again.'

Despite myself and the silliness of his explanation, I shuddered.

In front of us now was a low stone wall, falling away into the overgrown grass. Beyond the wall were the ruins of a stone house, some outbuildings, and an old wooden cart with only one wheel.

'This was his house!' I said. 'He ran through the woods to his home. This must've been it.' Without waiting for Stefan, I hurdled the low wall and walked quickly through the grass up to the house. The roof was gone, and two walls had crumbled.

As I walked inside, I could hear the rustle of the house's inhabitants; mice, a pigeon in the broken eaves, a crow that cawed from its nest on top of the chimney, which jutted out into the open sky.

'Looks like there's been a fire or something,' Stefan said. He was crouched down, foraging amongst the debris, where charred black marks stretched along the floor and crept up what was once a whitewashed wall.

It wasn't easy to navigate as we walked around exploring what might once have been the living room, the bedrooms and kitchen. It was too ruined, too lifeless to imagine how my grandfather's home once was.

'Who owns this now?' I asked.

Stefan shrugged.

'It was his house. It was his father's. Perhaps Andrzej?'

'It would have belonged to the Reich. Then perhaps the Soviets when they came. After that, I don't know. You'd have to ask,' he said.

A sudden coughing fit overcame me, and after a minute or so, I felt Stefan wrap his arm around my shoulders, guiding me out of the ruin and towards home. He didn't speak, and I could feel his breath on my hair as he held me close. I had expected him to let me go after a few seconds, but he didn't, and I didn't wonder why. I was simply glad to be held.

CHAPTER THIRTY-ONE

Back at the farm, Agnieszka and Andrzej had returned and were sitting at the kitchen table discussing something. As soon as we opened the door, they looked up sharply.

'Where have you been?' Agnieszka asked as we stepped in, a little wet from the light rain that had begun on our trek back.

'Stefan showed me where you used to live,' I said, nodding towards Andrzej. 'Anyway, where have you been?'

'Oh, visiting a friend. Dropped some things round,' Agnieszka said. 'Lunch?'

I sat down, and Stefan grabbed his bag from the counter. 'I'll leave you to it,' he said.

'No. Stay for some lunch,' Agnieszka insisted.

'No, really, thank you. I've got enough to do.'

He smiled at me as he left, and Agnieszka saw. 'He likes you,' she said, as she placed a loaf of bread on the table along with some slices of ham and tomatoes.

'Who owns the house now, your old house?' I asked Andrzej, ignoring her.

He chewed thoughtfully on a piece of bread for a moment, then said, 'Me and your grandfather. Unless my father sold it after the fire. I never really wanted to know; it wasn't my home anymore.'

'What happened?'

'I don't know a lot of the details. But he was getting poorer and poorer. The Germans upped the quota for farmers, so they had nothing to eat themselves. His cattle died from starvation. He said the fire was an accident, but I always wondered whether he did it himself to stop the Germans from taking it – from some other family living in his home. It makes sense considering that he had moved out all the family valuables before the house burned down – who did you think saved Tomasz's journals from when he was young? Our parents moved to Poznań, to a little apartment, and my mother got a job as a secretary. He never worked again.'

'Why don't you find out if it is yours still?'

'Why? And do what with it?'

'Sell it. Build on it?' I was about to ask him whether he had children who would want it when the phone rang, and he used it as an excuse to leave the conversation.

When he returned, he said something to Agnieszka in Polish, and the two of them then looked at me.

'Eat up,' she told me. 'We've somewhere to take you.'

'Where?'

'Eat up.' She pushed the plate of ham towards me. 'Then you'll find out.'

Later that afternoon I sat once more in the back of Agnieszka's car, the rain pelting the windows so hard that her windscreen wipers could not clear the water away quickly enough. She slowed round bends to a snail's pace and then sped up on the straights, making Andrzej hold on to his seatbelt with both hands, his knuckles white with fear.

It wasn't long until Agnieszka turned left down a rutted track. Fields stretched out for miles with broken, rotting fences half lying in the long grass. Soon, Agnieszka stopped in front of a small, whitewashed cottage with the same red tiled roof as the farmhouse. The front door was painted a bright blue, and window boxes full of pastel-coloured flowers sat upon each windowsill. Even in the rain it was welcoming.

I stared out of the window, and through the droplets of water that obscured most of my view, I could see the blue door had opened and someone stood in the doorway. Once I got out of the car, I saw that the figure was Zygmunt, his hat in his hand as he used it to wave us over.

I ran from the car, the rain not missing me, whilst Andrzej held a large umbrella over Agnieszka's head, and they walked solemnly to the front door. I kissed Zygmunt on the cheek and stepped inside the dark hallway.

'What's going on?' I asked, once we were all inside. That was when I heard footsteps behind me and saw them all look over my head to whoever stood there.

I turned and in front of me was a short, old woman dressed head to toe in black. She looked me up and down and her brow creased a little, as if I were lacking something.

Zygmunt stepped forward and placed his hand on her back, as if encouraging her to move towards me. 'This, Isla, is Zofia. Zofia, this is Tomasz's granddaughter.'

'Zofia?' I asked, my head spinning – *But she's dead, isn't she?*

She nodded, then turned from me and walked into the living room.

'Come, come. She is fine.' Zygmunt's smile was strained.

We piled into the cluttered living room and stood on thick colourful rugs that covered the uneven floorboards. Deep mahogany furniture dominated the room and porcelain figurines clamoured for space on every available surface. There were no Catholic depictions of Christ or the Virgin here though, like at Agnieszka's – not even a dull, tiny cross. It was as though faith had no place in this small home.

'Sit,' she suddenly said, her English sharp, then she turned and walked into the adjacent room.

I sat as instructed between Zygmunt and Agnieszka, whilst Andrzej stood ramrod-straight against the bookcase, as if awaiting his sentence.

'Perhaps she doesn't want me here,' I whispered to Zygmunt.

He shook his head. 'She does. She's just not used to guests.'

Zofia returned with a tray filled with cups of coffee and slices of cake. She placed it on the low table in front of us, then sat in her rocking chair, which creaked slowly as she rocked, staring at me with eyes the most incredible sky blue.

I sipped at my coffee, unsure what to say, or whether to wait for her to speak. Eventually, she said, 'You come here to listen to my stories?' Her eyes flickered across my face, taking in every feature – lingering on Kapaldi's scarf which hung around my neck, before looking away, down at the pink rose-patterned china cup in her hand. She heaved herself up out of her chair, pain creasing her face as she stood. Zygmunt got up to help her.

'Sit,' she commanded.

Zygmunt sat.

She shuffled to her bookcase and moved Andrzej aside with a prod to the ribs from her elbow. Everyone seemed frightened of her, and I did too, but I wasn't sure why. She was an old woman, and yet when she spoke, it was if an army captain were ordering me about. I watched as she ran her bony finger along the spines of the abandoned dusty titles. Then her finger stopped. Slowly, she pulled out a large envelope, faded and smudged, and made her way back to her chair.

'You must know his story – he would have wanted this,' she said quietly. 'This, he gave me.' She pulled a bundle of letters out of the envelope. 'His thoughts, his love for me. I kept it safe for him.'

There were a few moments of silence before I felt a nudge in my side. 'Ask her your questions,' Zygmunt said.

'No. No questions,' Zofia said, silencing Zygmunt once more. 'I tell you now my story, and then I tell you from here his story' – she held the letters aloft – 'from his thoughts he wrote down. Then you have no need for questions anymore.'

CHAPTER THIRTY-TWO

Zofia

Poland, 1941

The puppy was light brown with a white belly and sat on my doorstep, crying. I picked it up; there was no note, no one about.

My mama said that God had sent it, to comfort me after Tomasz had been forced into the army, and I wanted to believe that it was true. I called the puppy Aniela, which means angel.

She was a spaniel-mongrel mix, and didn't grow very big. She kept me company on the long days and months without Tomasz, and I was grateful for the distraction. I hoped that Tomasz had somehow sent her to me, knowing how much I was going to miss him.

But it was over a year until I found out who had bought me the puppy. He arrived, just as the animal had done, without warning, on the doorstep at the beginning of winter.

'Nice to see you again,' he said.

It was the officer, Lieberenz, from outside the swimming pool. I didn't know what to say. I stared at him, his cheeks almost juicy red from the cold of the month. The snow fell behind him like icing sugar from Mama's sieve. Aniela licked my hand.

'Ah, you got my gift?'

I nodded.

'Can I come in?'

Mama appeared behind me and opened the door wide. 'Of course,' she said, her voice unnaturally high. 'Please, come in.'

I stepped aside as he stalked into our home. Just before the door closed, I looked out into the icy day and wished I could go outside with Aniela and not come back. The door closed; the latch clicked into place.

I turned to look at him. He seemed to fill our house, which up until now I had always thought was quite large. Now though, it had shrunk. He blew air into his gloved hands and looked about him as if he were upset at something, then settled himself into the pale green, sagging sofa.

'You have a lovely home,' he said.

My mother smiled, but her hands fussed with the apron that was tied around her waist – smoothing, bunching, then smoothing again. I wanted her to stop. 'Would you like a drink?' she asked.

'No, no, I won't be staying long. I've come for your daughter.'

I saw my mother's smile fall; her hands became still.

'Nothing to worry about. Just some business that only she can help with.'

I looked at Mama. 'Tata is not home,' I said, hoping that would mean something.

'No matter. I am sure he will understand that the Führer comes first.'

'Yes, of course,' my mother said.

I saw her eyes roaming about quickly, as though there were some secret answer in the room that would save me.

'Are you ready?' he asked me.

'I need to pack,' I answered hurriedly, looking at Mama, looking at the door.

He waved the comment away. 'Not necessary.'

I looked to Mama, who was trying not to cry. Aniela licked my hand.

'You can bring the dog,' he said, smiling, almost kindly. 'It was a gift from me to you.'

I needed to go to the toilet, but I was scared to say so. Mama hugged me, gave me her thickest coat, a scarf, mittens. I looked to her face for some reassurance, but her eyes were filled with tears and she blinked quickly – once, twice – finally letting them escape and track their way down her cheeks.

I couldn't think straight. I wasn't scared; I was numb. So many had been taken from their homes, and now it was my turn. That was all; it was my turn. I held Aniela close, wrapping her in my coat, soothing her and kissing her head.

He took me to Kraków, a city I had never visited before, to an office where he made me sit on a sofa and wait. He did not talk to me, which made me fear the worst. But I still didn't feel scared for myself. I only felt fear for Aniela – who would take care of her when I was gone?

I tried to recall the journey – a train, then a car. But my memory was fuzzy around the edges as though the whole thing were a dream and any moment I would wake, curled up on our green sofa, and Mama would tell me dinner was ready.

Aniela yawned and put her little head under my armpit to fall asleep. Then I heard footsteps, felt his breath near my ear, the smell of stale tobacco. 'Come to the window,' he said.

I stood up, and there was another man in the room in a uniform with a scar on his face. I walked to the window and looked out. It was snowing. I watched it fall, and as I did my eyes travelled down to the pavement. It was then that I saw him – Tomasz.

I put Aniela on the floor and my hands on the glass, and I wanted to run down to him. I watched as a soldier hit him in the legs, or kicked him, I don't know, but Tomasz was on the cold ground.

I was pulled away quickly from the window. I don't know whether he saw me or not – I think he didn't; I was there for just a second or two. I sat back in the chair, and Lieberenz left with the other soldier.

Aniela had gone to the toilet in the middle of the floor. I picked her up and sat with her by the window. My legs shook, but I wasn't cold, and I had strange stomach cramps. I tried to lick my lips, I tried to breathe slower and to stop crying, but I felt as though I was going to pass out. I watched the snow fall outside, so slowly, so lightly, trying to calm myself. He was there, and then he was gone. Where was he? Why was I here? It all felt like some strange game. But it was as though a light had been switched off in my head; the stress, the fear, took over to a point where my brain could not cope, and I blacked out.

When I woke, it was daylight. I blinked once or twice, trying to remember where I was.

'Morning,' Officer Lieberenz's voice came from behind his desk. 'Or rather, afternoon. You slept all day.'

'Where is he?' I asked.

Lieberenz stood up and walked towards me, a glass of water in his hand.

'Here, drink. I'll get some food for you too.' He smiled at me.

I wished I could refuse the water, but I was so thirsty that I drank it back in one go. 'Where is he?' I asked again, handing the empty glass back to Lieberenz.

'Gone back to work.'

'I don't understand.'

'He's a soldier, so he's gone to be a soldier. On the way to Russia, I believe.' Lieberenz sat down opposite me and relaxed in the chair.

It was then that I realised Aniela was gone. I stood up, looked around the room. 'She's been taken for a walk, don't worry,' he said.

I sat down; I needed her back. My legs shook again.

'She'll be back any minute now,' he said and leaned over, placing his hand on my lap to stop the trembling. 'I can take care of him if you like?'

'I don't understand,' I said, watching his hand as it left my lap and reached up to gently tuck a piece of hair behind my ear.

'I can take care of Tomasz. Make sure no harm comes to him whilst he is away. I can take care of you too, if you let me?'

'I want to go home,' I said.

His smile disappeared, and he snatched his hands away. He took a packet of cigarettes from his pocket and lit one. 'Do you?'

I nodded.

The door to the office opened, and a woman walked in with Aniela on a lead, a plate of biscuits in her other hand.

'Such a lovely dog!' She handed Aniela to me, placed the biscuits on a table. 'Shall I bring coffee now?' she asked Lieberenz.

'Not yet.' He waved her away.

She nodded. 'Such a lovely dog,' she said again as she left.

I went to pick Aniela up from the floor, but Lieberenz grabbed her first. 'She is a lovely dog,' he said. 'You love her, don't you?'

'Yes,' I said, my voice shaking, uncontrolled. I wanted her back. I didn't like him holding her, petting her.

'You love him too, Tomasz? And your parents?'

'Yes.'

Lieberenz handed Aniela back to me, and as his warm, slightly damp fingers touched my hand, I felt my skin goose-pimple. He leaned in, ever so lightly, and I could smell his stale breath on my face. I wanted to turn away, but I couldn't. Finally, he released Aniela, and his fingers let go of my skin. He sat up straight and smiled at me, a different smile, with his lips together as though satisfied.

I held Aniela close. 'Thank you, Herr Lieberenz,' I said, because I knew I must.

'Call me Franz. We are friends now, are we not?'

I licked my lips, blinked away the tears. 'Of course. Thank you, Franz.'

CHAPTER THIRTY-THREE

By the start of the New Year, I had been settled into an apartment in Kraków, and my sole job became to be ready and available for him. I slept with him, just as a man and wife would. But there is no need for me to remember this, no need for me to tell you what it was like; how sad and empty I felt afterwards, how I cried. It is gone now. I am grateful for that.

The only thought I had to get me through this was that Tomasz was fighting, and I had to fight too – both of us had to be brave.

But it isn't easy, being brave like that.

I remember when I was young, there was a girl in my school who was being bullied because she was Jewish. When I had told Tomasz about her on our way home from school, he asked me not to do anything about it as he worried I would get bullied too. That night, after our walk home from school, I thought about that girl – her name was Sara. She was a year younger than me, but she was clever, oh so clever, and she had been put into my class. She was beautiful – with long dark hair and deep green eyes. But she was quiet and didn't speak to anyone, and I hate to admit it, but she was so quiet that I forgot she was there.

One day, some girls told her she was a disgusting Jew and she shouldn't be allowed in our school. The teacher did nothing. He allowed the girls to tease and taunt her. Eventually, it led to violence. The girls hit her, pulled clumps of her hair and scratched her face. They took her lunch, put it in the bin and told her to eat it out of there. This whole time, Sara did nothing. She said nothing, did not cry or shout back. She calmly rearranged her hair, her clothes, and sat quietly once more in the back of the classroom. This seemed to make the girls angrier, and I could see that they would never stop.

I could not sleep for thinking about her, and soon I got up and sat in our living room, listening to the clock tick away the minutes.

As dawn broke, I knew what I was going to do.

That day at school, I waited until the bunch of girls took away Sara's lunch once more, then I stood up and told them to give it back to her. They, of course, laughed and would not.

So I went to sit next to Sara, which confused them more, and I gave her some of my lunch.

'You can't do that,' one of the girls said. I think she was called Ingrid. She was fat, this girl, but short. I wasn't scared of her.

'I can. I have.'

Sara looked at me and then at the food and would not eat it.

'Eat it, it's all right,' I told her.

'So, you're a Jew lover then? Bet you love gypsies too,' Ingrid said.

I immediately thought of Kapaldi. 'Yes,' I replied. 'I suppose I do.'

It was a bold and brave – or perhaps stupid – thing to say at the time, but I knew I could not sit by, day after day, and do nothing.

The first few strikes from the group of five girls were nothing more than slaps. So I hit back harder than I ever had before. I remember screaming like a wild animal, and this frightened them, so I screamed louder and louder and punched harder and harder until they backed away.

I had blood on my nose, and they had ripped my skirt, but I smiled at them and sat next to Sara once more.

'You're crazy!' Ingrid shouted at me.

'I am,' I said, and gave her the biggest smile I had.

This unnerved them, I think. So much so that they never touched Sara again.

Sara and I remained friends for some time until she was told she could not go to our school anymore, and I never saw her again.

As I sat in that apartment in Kraków, I would remind myself of Sara over and over again. I thought that she was now probably dead. I told myself to be brave, and that while I had to be with Franz, I was being brave for me, for Tomasz, for my family, and I would just have to keep trying until one day, it would all stop. The bullies would go away – they would finally see I was never going to give up.

I sat one evening in front of the fire, waiting for Franz to arrive. I sipped at a whiskey he had given me as a gift, in a thick crystal glass that had another person's initials etched into the bottom. I hated the taste, hated the muggy head that it gave me the next day, but the alcohol blurred the edges of it all so I could just about get through it.

I checked the time on my slim gold watch – he was late. He was always late, always showing who was in charge.

I stood and looked at my reflection in the hallway mirror; I didn't recognise the person that looked back at me. Gone was the long dark hair that once streamed down my back untamed. Now it was pulled back tight, pinned into an elaborate chignon that gave me a constant headache. My face looked pinched and pale, the make-up reminding me of the clowns from the fair when I was a child.

I smiled at my reflection, trying to make the girl in the mirror happy. But she didn't want to be; the smile did not travel up from the rouged lips to the eyes, to show real warmth, real love. I tried again. Still, she was stubborn and would not comply. I pulled out a lipstick from my handbag and slicked more on, ignoring the look from my reflection, ignoring the pain in the eyes. I sat back once more by the fire and waited. He'd be here soon enough. I drank the whiskey in one go.

I saw Kapaldi one afternoon when I was shopping. It was like a dream at first. One minute I was looking at a dress and the next, when I looked up, he was there.

I cannot tell you how happy I was to see him. I thought he had come to rescue me, but before I could say something, before I could hug him, he vanished out of the shop, his long legs taking him away from the uniformed men who had entered with their girlfriends.

It was only when I reached the apartment that I found a note in my bag.

My dearest Zofia. Do not lose heart. I am watching out for you. It will all be well soon. Be strong. I will see you soon.

I remember that first note. Some of the others I have forgotten; I burned them all quickly, so Franz could never find them. But that first one, I remember. I cried when I read it. Cried and cried until I could barely breathe. I was crying because I was happy in a way. Happy that someone knew what was going on, happy that things would be all right again.

When I had read it over and over again, I got a candle and lit it. I slowly lowered the note over the flame and watched as it licked across the paper.

It was going to be all right. If Kapaldi said so, then it would surely come true.

*

Franz was always a gentleman. He was always smiling at me, kissing me, holding my hand. One evening he said he would take me to the theatre because I told him I had never been. I didn't want to be excited, but I was. When he picked me up, I walked from the house to the car and when I got in, I saw that there was something wrong. He looked at my dress, a light blue.

'What are you wearing that for?' he asked.

I smoothed it down. 'I thought it was nice.'

'You thought? You shouldn't think. We are meeting colleagues of mine this evening. Important men and their wives, and you turn up looking like a stupid little Polish girl in her childish dress.'

'I thought we were going to the theatre?' I felt as though I was going to cry. I wanted to see people dance, sing, and pretend that everything was all right.

Suddenly, there was a pain in my ribs. I looked down to where Franz's fist was just moving away from me. 'Get changed,' he demanded.

I got out of the car, stunned. And then I felt ashamed of my own stupidity. Why wouldn't he hit me? Did I really believe he would take care of me? I was his toy – no more than a mouse for a cat to play with.

I went back inside and got changed, looking down as I undressed at the red mark that was spreading across my ribcage. I gently touched it. Nothing broken, just bruised. I changed into a dark green dress, pulled my hair tightly back and added extra lipstick.

When I got into the car, he looked at me once more. 'Good evening!' he said, as if it was the first time he had seen me that night. 'You look wonderful, my darling.' He kissed me on the cheek and told the driver we were ready.

I sat in the back of the car as it wound its way through the streets and felt so incredibly alone that, for the first time, I wished I was dead.

*

We did not stay in Kraków for long; Franz was moved to Warsaw and that meant I was to go with him. He received a promotion and he celebrated this by getting us a three-storey house to live in. 'Do you like it?' he asked me when we arrived, and kissed me on the cheek.

I looked up to where a chandelier hung from the high ceiling in the foyer.

'Come, look around.' He took me by the arm, Aniela following at my heels.

Each room was already furnished with heavy wooden book-cases, tables and thick spongy sofas. I picked up a silver hairbrush that sat on the dressing table in my bedroom, an elaborate L.M. carved into the handle, the same on the hand mirror, the same on the matching comb. I thought of the whiskey glasses in Kraków; everything, it seemed, belonged to someone else. Everything had been stolen in Poland.

I opened one of the drawers in the dresser and placed the brush set and mirror inside. I would not use them; I would try not to use much of anything – it was not mine.

That evening we sat in the living room, drinking whiskey silently whilst a record of an orchestra played on the gramophone.

'It's your birthday soon,' Franz said, breaking the thick quiet.

'End of June,' I said.

'Then you shall have a party. A large one, here. We can invite my colleagues, their wives, show them the house.'

'I don't want a party,' I told him. 'I don't need one.'

'But look at where we live!' he cried. He stood up and spread his arms wide. I looked at him. He was dishevelled, and his glass was half-full of whiskey.

'I don't know anyone here, though,' I said, trying out a new boldness with him.

He dropped his arms to his sides, and the whiskey spilled out of the glass. He placed the glass on the table beside his chair and walked towards me. His face was so close to mine that I could see the spider veins of red in the whites of his eyes.

'You'll have the party,' he hissed.

He moved his face away from me, and I exhaled. Then, he hit me. The force of it was not much, but the shock of it sent my head reeling back. I held on to my cheek, which stung from the slap of his palm, and looked at Aniela who stared up at me.

I heard him walk away, his footsteps echoing on the tiles of the foyer, then the slam of his office door.

Aniela walked up to me, and I picked her up and held her to me. I didn't cry. My tears had stopped long ago.

The next day, Franz brought me a gift: a woman and her teenage son who were to help run the house. Her name was Marika, her son was called Witold.

'I'm going away for a while,' he said. 'I'll be back for your birthday party. I will get a surprise for you. Something you have wanted for a long time.' He kissed me on my cheek. 'Marika and Witold will take care of you until I am back.'

'Thank you, darling,' I said, and forced myself to kiss him. I felt a weight lifted from my shoulders knowing that he would not be around for a few weeks. I didn't care what his surprise would be, only that he was gone. I looked to Marika and Witold – finally someone to talk to.

But neither spoke to me at first. Marika would cook and clean; her son helped in the garden, fetched shopping, and did any odd jobs that were required.

Every time I tried to talk to her or her son, they avoided my gaze, told me they had things to do, so I was left staring at the walls of a house that was not mine.

*

One day, I sat in the living room reading a book, Aniela on my lap, when Marika came in with tea and a cake she had made. She placed it onto the table, and I closed the book.

'Please, won't you sit with me?' I asked, my voice strange, begging.

She looked at me and cocked her head to the side like an inquisitive robin, then lowered herself slowly onto the couch opposite me.

'I'm Zofia,' I said.

She nodded.

'It's all right, you can talk to me.'

She did not look at me.

'Where are you from?' I asked her.

'Here, Warsaw.'

'Are you married?'

She nodded.

I cut a slice of cake and handed it to her.

'He's in the army,' she said.

'Which one?'

'The only one that matters, I suppose.'

'So, you are German then?'

'My husband had family that were. So, yes, I suppose we are.'

She bit into the cake, but her eyes still avoided mine.

'Does your son like dogs?' I asked her.

'I suppose.'

'Tell him he can play with Aniela whenever he likes.'

'Thank you.' She stood up and walked back to the kitchen.

The following day I saw Witold playing with Aniela on the lawn, then again the next day and the next. Bit by bit, I joined in their games, talking to Witold, telling him stories from my childhood, telling him about magic and rainbows and fairies.

'I'm twelve,' he said. 'Almost thirteen. I don't believe in magic.'

'Ah, you should!' I exclaimed. 'You need to believe in something.'

I watched him stroke Aniela. His eyes narrowed as he thought about what I had said.

'You love her, don't you?' I asked him.

He smiled at me. 'Yes, I do.'

'Can you make me a promise?'

'All right,' he said.

'Can you promise me that one day if I ask you to, you will take care of Aniela?'

'So, she will be mine?' he asked, his face full of joy.

I laughed, startling myself with the sound.

'What's wrong?' he asked when I suddenly stopped.

'Nothing. I just haven't laughed in such a long time.'

'You should laugh. It's good for you, Mama said.'

'Your mama is very clever. So, we have a deal?' I held out my hand.

He considered it for a moment, then took my hand in his and shook it. 'I promise to look after her,' he said. 'I'll love her just like you do.'

I smiled, feeling a sting in my eyes.

CHAPTER THIRTY-FOUR

A few days later, I walked Aniela in the park alone. Spring was at an end and the summer gardens were blooming. I stood looking at the rows of beautiful flowers, wondering how they could exist in a world like this. Then I saw another colour, the flash of a rainbow. A man walked behind me, whistling a song. Kapaldi. I watched him walk by me and stop near a tree. He seemed to marvel at the trunk and bent down to take a better look. Then, he straightened up and was gone.

I waited a minute, then went to the tree. There was a small knot in the trunk where he had been looking, and inside a tiny, folded piece of paper.

> If you ever need me, I am here. We had to leave Kraków. If you need anything, come to the address below. Ask for Herr Fischer. Tell them what you need. They will find me. Yours, Kapaldi.

I took the note, memorised the address, and vowed to burn it when I got home. As I walked with Aniela, I thought of the first time I had met Kapaldi, the night of the fair. He had been doing card tricks for all the children. Each of us paid a coin and we had to find the Queen of Hearts. It was funny really, as every child won something. I didn't think about it then, but how did he ever make any money if he always gave prizes away?

When I got back to the house, I searched in my belongings for the one thing that went everywhere with me. It was a heart, carved from wood, and Tomasz had won it for me at the fair.

I think that night I sat in my room for hours, just holding that heart, remembering Tomasz, remembering us. Finally, I got up and hid it once more. Burning the note, I told myself to be strong – things would soon change.

The night of my birthday, I sat in front of the mirror in my dressing room and tied a blue ribbon around my chignon to match the blue dress Franz had bought for me, when there was a light knock on the door.

Franz walked in. 'Can I come in?'

I turned and smiled at him, the smile from the reflection of the woman in Kraków.

'I just wanted to make amends – make sure we are still friends?'

'Of course.' I stood, walked to him, kissed him.

'You look nice in the dress,' he said.

'Thank you. It's lovely. It was a wonderful surprise – exactly what I wanted.'

'Here, let me escort you to your party.'

I took his arm and let him guide me along the hallway to the top of the stairs. 'You do look beautiful,' he said as we walked down the hallway.

Looking back, I cannot remember much of the beginning of that evening. There were drinks, food, gifts. People spoke to me; Franz laughed, drank.

Then, he disappeared.

'Have you seen Franz?' I asked an officer. He was tall, athletic; he was holding on to his fiancée, a petite woman who seemed far too small for him.

He shook his head. 'Went that way.' He pointed towards Franz's office.

Marika asked me if she should bring the cake out; someone else heard her and started to gather people around. I knew Franz would be mad if he missed it, if it hadn't gone to plan.

My eyes searched the room – he still wasn't back.

I smiled. 'I'll just fetch Franz,' I told the happy, drunken faces in front of me. 'He'd hate to miss it.'

My footsteps were light over the tiles of the foyer, and I was about to knock on the door when I heard his voice – Tomasz's.

I jumped back from the door as if it had scalded me. More voices; Franz saying something to Drange, his pockmarked helper. An address, a boarding house.

I ran away from the door, back to the dining room, picked up a glass of champagne and drank it down.

'Shall I bring the cake now?' Marika was at my side.

I nodded. 'Bring Witold to me too. I need to ask him to do something for me.'

An hour later, I feigned tiredness and a migraine and retreated to my room, leaving the party in full swing downstairs. Franz hadn't cared when I had left – the party was his anyway, not mine.

Witold came to my room, knocked gently on the door.

'I need you to take this letter to someone for me,' I said. 'You have to be quick and don't let anyone see you.'

Witold nodded.

I handed him the letter and the address that Kapaldi had given me, and some money. 'Be quick,' I said. 'And tell Kapaldi he must hurry.'

Witold nodded and left quickly, quietly.

It was risky, I knew this. But compared to the risks that Andrzej, my brother Zygmunt and Kapaldi took on a daily basis, I thought I could handle this. Tomasz was here. I could not get to him, but Kapaldi could.

*

I did not sleep that night. Witold came back late and told me he had delivered the letter to Kapaldi, who had gone to find Tomasz immediately. I thanked him again and gave him some more money.

I lay on my bed, expecting Franz to join me, but he did not. Instead, I heard him leave with some others – their laughter and voices singing in the street as they made their way to a bar to carry on the festivities.

I thought of the party. Why had he brought Tomasz to the house? He knew that we could have seen each other. Or was that his plan all along, to torture me?

I must have fallen asleep, as in the early hours I awoke to the sound of music, the clamour of banging.

I walked carefully, slowly down the stairs. Franz's office door was closed. I could hear him singing inside. Next to the front door he had dumped his coat and shoes – he was drunk. I turned to walk back upstairs when something caught my eye – a flash of colour underneath the heavy dark green coat.

I bent down to look. Something red, some yellow too. I gently moved the jacket aside, revealing a scarf all the colours of the rainbow. I picked it up. I knew this scarf, just as I knew the man who wore it, and the man I had sent to find Tomasz.

I knew what Franz was like. I knew he hated Jews, gypsies, Poles. I knew what he and his friends did for sport when they drank. He would sometimes gloat to me that he had killed more men in the city than soldiers had on the front.

I took the scarf and ran back to my room. I called for Marika and asked her to bring Witold to me.

'Take this scarf to this address. It's a boarding house,' I told him.

'Now?' he asked.

'No, tomorrow. It is too dangerous now.'

'What do I say?'

'Wrap it now in brown paper. Do not write a label on it. Knock on the door, tell them a friend has brought Tomasz a gift. Then leave. Run away.'

Witold looked at his mama who nodded at him. She turned to me and smiled.

The next morning, I did not leave my room. A sickness of sorts had overcome me, and I felt that every bone, every joint was in pain. Marika tended to me and Franz kept away, scared to get sick too. I didn't have a fever though, no symptoms other than pain. I slept a lot. Slept too much, I think, and each time I had terrible nightmares that reminded me it was I who had sent Kapaldi out to find Tomasz, yet Franz and his friends had found Kapaldi instead.

Later, Marika came to my room with her son. 'He's come to walk Aniela,' she said to me.

I nodded.

As he picked up Aniela, he looked at me. 'I delivered it,' he said. 'I did it.'

'Good boy!' I said. 'You are brave.'

'My brother, he is in Switzerland and has sent for me and Witold,' Marika said.

I was not surprised by this – I wanted her to leave, to keep Witold safe, and was happy that they could be free.

'I'll be sad to see you go,' I said. Then I looked at Aniela and felt my heart stop for a moment before thudding its way back into life. My Aniela. Her large eyes fixed on mine, and I wanted to hold her for a moment, but I knew if I did, I wouldn't be able to let her go. It was right for her – she had to go with them.

'It is very green there, he says. Lots of fields,' Marika said.

'I'm sure you'll be very happy there,' I replied, tears now erupting. 'It would be perfect for Aniela.'

Witold grinned at me, happy that he could fulfil his promise to take care of her.

'Are you sure? We don't have to take her, if you don't want us to?' Witold held her out to me, allowing me to take her back if I wanted.

'No.' I wiped my tears away and plastered on a smile for the boy. 'It's better for her. She'll have you to play with.'

Marika bent down and kissed me on the forehead, and Witold smiled sadly at me. I watched them leave my room, wishing them well, hoping that Aniela would enjoy those green fields, but also wishing that I could go with them.

Two weeks later, I was finally well enough to dress myself, leave my room.

I walked downstairs and entered the living room. Franz sat smoking. He turned to look at me and smiled. 'I was wondering when you would come back to me,' he said.

He stood and walked to me, kissing me and holding me close as if I had been on holiday and not upstairs, alone, recovering. 'Come, sit with me,' he said. 'I've missed you.'

I sat across from him.

'Now, let me get you a drink. I have some news.'

I watched as he poured a thick measure of whiskey into two glasses and handed one to me. He gently tapped his glass against mine. 'Cheers,' he said.

'Cheers.' I sipped the whiskey.

'So, we are to take a little trip, you and I.'

'Where?'

'Paris.' He smiled.

'Why?'

'I have to go for work, and you shall come with me. Isn't that exciting? Paris. So beautiful, so romantic. We can dine in little restaurants together, drink French wine!'

I felt my stomach tumble. I would be away from Poland, away from my brother, Andrzej, Tomasz, wherever he was. I smiled, though. I smiled and stood up and let him take me in his arms and dance me around the living room, as if we were going on our honeymoon.

The following day I took a walk in the park as I had done when I had Aniela. It was funny, but Franz had not commented on the whereabouts of my constant companion and I wondered, as I walked, if he knew what I had done. He had not cared that Marika had not turned up for work either – 'Plenty of them out there to work for us,' he had said.

'Zofia!' I heard my name.

I turned and saw a uniform, SS. I kept walking.

'Zofia, it's me, Zyg,' the voice said.

I slowed my walking and let my brother fall in step with me. Zygmunt, my brother. My brother who I hadn't heard from in years. I literally pinched my arm to check whether it was a dream or not.

'You're here,' I said, sounding stupid.

'You didn't think you could get rid of me that easily?' He grinned at me.

'But where have you been?'

'No time to get into details. I'm alive. That's all that matters.'

'But why are you dressed like that?' I asked, confused, worried and happy all at the same time.

'Ah, you know me. Always up to something.'

I saw him wince, then rub his hand under his cap – the skin was puckered and red. 'What's wrong?'

'Little injury. Nothing big. Listen, I saw Tomasz. In hospital. He's not doing so well.'

'What's wrong with him? Has he been shot?' I felt nausea rising. He was sick, dying; I needed to get to him. 'Where is he?' I half shouted.

'Keep your voice down,' Zygmunt commanded, looking at the others in the park, checking to see if they had heard. 'He's just unwell.'

'What do you mean "unwell", Zygmunt?'

'You don't know what happened?'

'No. What?' Frustration seeped into my voice. I wanted to punch my brother in the arm to make him get to the point, and quickly.

'Kapaldi is dead.'

I think I gasped. I think I did. But I wasn't shocked, of course I wasn't – I had known. The scarf and Franz, of course I had known, but I had tried to pretend that it wasn't real. 'But why is Tomasz sick?' Then I thought of my own malaise – the pain, the sleeping – and I understood. 'You'll take me to him.'

'No, Zofia, it's too dangerous.'

'I don't care, Zygmunt, I don't care!' My voice had risen, and two women sitting on a bench turned to look at me.

'Shush. Fine. I'll take you. It has to be at night. Can you get out?'

'I'd have to wait for Franz to be away for work.'

'Fine. Fine. I'll pass by your house, once a day. Put a vase on your windowsill. The day it has a flower in it, I will know that Franz has gone, and you can go that evening. Sound doable?'

'Perfect,' I said. It took all my energy not to kiss my brother on the cheek. Instead, I stood and watched him walk away, every now and then slipping his hand under his hat to rub at the raw skin underneath.

CHAPTER THIRTY-FIVE

Tomasz

Poland, Summer 1942

He thought that he had imagined her when he first saw her – surely she was a dream? But then she had bent down and kissed him. And he had come to life, for the first time in years, his arms reaching for her, his body moving towards her as he pulled her down onto the bed beside him and embraced her, kissing her, his tongue searching her mouth, tasting her, his hands pulling at the uniform, needing her, wanting to feel all of her, wanting to know that she was real.

It was a risk that they shouldn't have taken. But the corridors at night were like a ghost town. White quietness abounded in this part of the hospital – 'Keeps them calm,' he'd heard the nurses say once.

The next morning, he thought he had imagined her visiting him. Surely, he had – it could not have been her. He had already been going mad in this white room – imagining people and things that could not possibly be there, seeing Kapaldi in the room with him, every night. Now, he wondered if he was imagining Zofia too.

His doctor had told him that this was normal. Tomasz had told him his friend had died – not that he had any part in it. Just that he had died.

'Sometimes, when someone close to us dies, we don't let go of them and our brains recreate them in front of our eyes. You have to remember that this is not real. So, when you see your friend sitting in your room, close your eyes, and remember he is not really there. Then, when you open them once more, the vision will be gone.'

Tomasz had nodded at the doctor, unconvinced. 'I'll try that.'

For the next three nights and days, whenever he saw Kapaldi sitting in the chair in the corner, looking at him, he would close his eyes and tell himself that he was dead, he was not real. But every time Tomasz opened his eyes, his friend was still sitting in the chair, waiting patiently.

By the fourth day, Tomasz couldn't take it anymore. 'What do you want?' he yelled at him. 'Why are you here?'

'I'm just here to see my friend,' he replied.

'I'm not your friend! I killed you – don't you remember that? Don't you remember that night when I had to shoot you or die myself? I chose to live. I'm a coward – no friend of yours.'

'You're still my friend, Tomasz. You saved my life when you were a child, and I told you that one day I would repay that debt.'

Tomasz shook his head, then looked at his hand in his lap, remembering how it had held the gun, how his finger had pulled the trigger. 'It's not the same.'

'It is.'

'It isn't. It isn't. Because I took your life. Me.'

There was no reply, and Tomasz looked up. Kapaldi was gone.

He did not return for two weeks, and the doctor thought Tomasz was getting well. 'See. The treatment is working. Soon you will be able to go back to your life.'

His life. His life was what exactly? There was no way of knowing what awaited him when he left here. He thought of Lieberenz and felt the nausea rise, and the thump of his quickly beating heart against his ribs.

He couldn't go back to serve that man. He'd rather die.

'Don't be so pessimistic,' a voice said.

Tomasz looked up and saw Kapaldi in the chair once more. 'I thought you were gone forever.'

'I'll never be gone forever. You'll always remember me. So, I'll always be.'

'I can't go back out there,' Tomasz said.

'You can. You can. Be brave. What have I always taught you?'

'How to make it rain.' Tomasz smiled. 'That's not really going to help me now.'

'No. That's not what I taught you. I taught you that something good can come from bad. I taught you that you should always believe in something. I taught you to have hope and to be patient and wait for the day when that rainbow appears.'

Tomasz felt tears sliding down his face now, and he wanted to get off the bed, take his friend and hold him tight, but he was scared that if he did, Kapaldi would disappear, and he didn't want him to go just yet.

'You will leave here. You will.'

Tomasz wiped his face. 'I will.'

'And you'll remember me always.'

'And I'll remember you always,' he repeated.

Kapaldi walked over to him, and Tomasz saw him place something round his neck. Tomasz looked down and saw the scarf, all the colours of the rainbow.

'I'm sorry,' Tomasz said. He looked up. Kapaldi was gone.

The following days came easier to Tomasz now. He slept less; he wrote more in his diary and tried to imagine a future with Zofia. He entertained himself with thoughts of returning home to the farm, buying a house, raising children. He was sure that she, at least, had been real. He had been able to smell her scent on the sheets for days afterwards, and he knew that he could not have conjured what had happened between them.

It was towards the end of August, over a month later, when Zofia appeared once more. This time it was late – almost 3 a.m. – when she woke him.

'I thought you would never come back,' he said, pulling her close to him.

'We need to go,' she said. 'Quickly.'

She pulled away from him, and he sat up, rubbing at his eyes.

'What are you doing?' he asked, as she took a uniform from her bag – a captain's uniform.

'Here.' She handed it to him. 'Put it on.'

'What's going on?'

'Shhh, just put it on, Tomasz, quickly.'

He got out of the bed and pulled her up from where she was crouched on the floor, getting shoes out of the bag.

'Please, Tomasz,' she whispered.

'Zofia, I cannot walk out. Is that what you are thinking? That I put this on and just walk away? Where would I go?' His voice was low, but he still thought it was too loud in the quiet of the early morning. He looked at the door.

'You can. You must! Please, Tomasz, please. Put the clothes on. Trust me.'

There were footsteps clicking down the corridor. Zofia fell to the floor, rolled under the bed. Tomasz grabbed the uniform, threw it under the sheet and climbed back into bed.

A nurse entered the room. Tomasz pretended he was asleep, hoped she wouldn't turn on the light. He snored gently, turned on his side, and then heard the click of the door as it closed again.

He waited, counted to sixty – once, twice, three times. Then: 'Zofia,' he whispered.

She stood and placed her finger to his lips. 'Please, Tomasz. Please do this for me. We don't have long. I can get us out. Please.'

He looked at her – the blue of her eyes.

'Please,' she said again.

He held her face in his hands, pulled her to him and kissed her. She soon pulled away.

'You'll do it?' she asked.

'I love you,' he said.

It was easier than he thought it would be, to leave the hospital. There were no guards, no nurses at their desks – they were on their break, Zofia told him.

He wasn't sure who she was anymore, Zofia. He watched her as they walked out, her eyes scanning, her body alert for danger, as though she had done this before.

He walked out into the misty early morning and stood breathing in the air, feeling it fill his lungs.

'Get in,' Zofia told him.

He looked; she was holding open the door of a car. He bent over and peered at the driver – Zygmunt – and in the passenger seat, his cousin, Agnieszka.

Tomasz climbed into the back seat and the car pulled away before he had even closed the door.

'You look better,' Zygmunt said.

'You look older,' Agnieszka chimed in.

'What are you doing here?' he asked his cousin.

'I work with the resistance. Didn't she tell you?' She nodded towards Zofia.

He shook his head. 'It's not safe. You're too young.'

'Nineteen, thank you very much. I speak several languages, and they are coming in handy.'

'Any problems?' Zygmunt asked.

'None,' Zofia said.

Tomasz remembered the nurse that had come into his room but did not say anything.

'The train leaves in ten minutes,' Zygmunt said.

'Will we make it?' Tomasz asked.

'Left it late on purpose, so less time for you to wait. You go onto the platform, and get on. Agnieszka has all the documents.'

Tomasz shifted in his seat. The uniform itched his skin; he preferred the gown and pyjamas he had worn in hospital. He didn't like it.

'It'll be fine.' Zofia placed her hand over his. 'It'll all be fine.'

'Tomasz.' Agnieszka turned around so she could see him. 'Here are your documents. You are now Captain Frederick Weber, from Hamburg, who is being transferred to a desk job in Paris, after an explosion left you with injuries. Zofia will be your nurse – she speaks German better than you, so let her talk and you just look sick. I am now officially working as a clerk for a rubber manufacturer who has offices in Warsaw and Paris. I will travel near you and Zofia but not with you. Three of us would not work. All of the transfer cells en route have been warned that we are travelling. So, if we are separated, if anything happens, you have some addresses stitched into the inside of your jacket and some money. Go to the addresses. You must say, "I'm here to see Uncle Alfred." It is your code word, understood? And there is this too.' She handed him a thin gold pen. 'In it is microfilm, we are all carrying it. It needs to get to England.'

'We're going to England?' Tomasz looked at Zofia.

'Of course, where else would we be going?' Agnieszka answered, and Tomasz saw that Zofia smiled at her.

He felt the weight of it in his hand. 'What's on the film?'

'The ghetto mainly. The deaths, beatings. We managed to get someone into some of the camps too,' Agnieszka said.

Tomasz looked at the pen and thought of Kapaldi.

'You need to tell them what happened to you too. Tell them about the army, what you saw.'

'And what I did,' he added.

They all fell silent.

He tucked the pen securely inside his jacket.

Soon the car slowed, then stopped. Zygmunt turned around. 'Good luck,' he said.

Zofia kissed her brother on the cheek and climbed out of the car.

Before they split up, Agnieszka warned them to avoid speaking to too many people. 'If you don't speak, they'll be suspicious; if you talk too much, you'll slip up. Tomasz, remember not to talk at all. Look sick. Look as though you have lost your mind.'

He nodded. That part would be easy.

CHAPTER THIRTY-SIX

The station was busy even at this early hour; it seemed that the whole of Warsaw was packed in, spilling out onto platforms where trains streaming smoke waited like dragons.

It was as though everyone was leaving, and no one was arriving. Men in the dark uniforms of the SS held guns slung over shoulders and heavy polished pistols in their belts.

Tomasz tried not to look at the guns. He tried to walk confidently – he had the papers, he was now Frederick from Hamburg, he didn't need to fear the men in dark uniforms. Yet, his hand still went to his belt where his own service revolver was. His fingers brushed over the cool metal. It would be all right. He was Frederick from Hamburg. He had his own gun.

Zofia walked in front of him, taking quick steps towards the ticket office. He watched the money being replaced by tickets into her hand while a guard stood nearby and looked at Zofia, but she didn't seem to notice.

Agnieszka had disappeared into the throng of travellers, all of them laden with cases. It was then that Tomasz realised they didn't have any luggage. He placed his hand on Zofia's shoulder so she would turn to look at him. He wanted to tell her – the luggage, no luggage made them suspicious. But the guard was still looking at her, and now he turned to look at Tomasz.

Tomasz took his hand off her shoulder, letting it hang loosely by his side. Zofia turned, smiled at the guard.

'Come, Hauptmann Weber, let's get you on that train and settled.'

The guard smiled at her; the caring nurse. Tomasz felt himself relax a little. He allowed Zofia to take his arm as if guiding him. He gave a brief nod to the guard and leaned on his nurse as they walked towards the waiting train.

The train was busy, and Tomasz and Zofia struggled to find a compartment where they could sit together. Finally, they did, and they sat across from a young couple who barely looked up from their argument when Tomasz and Zofia sat down.

Tomasz wanted to hold Zofia's hand, to talk to her, but he could not. All he could do was sit, trying to look confident, feeling the pen inside his jacket pressing into his skin.

The train did not pull away from the station for five minutes and, as each second ticked by, Tomasz was convinced that they would never get away. The couple in front of him unwrapped some meat from greaseproof paper and took out some bread from a bag near their feet.

'Aren't you hungry?' the woman asked the man who picked at the meat, the bread.

'Not really,' the man replied.

His voice showed his irritation, Tomasz thought, and he wondered what they had been arguing about before they arrived.

'Don't eat it then,' the woman said. 'Waste it. See if I care.'

Tomasz watched the man bite into the bread, tearing a chunk out of it and chewing it slowly, all the while glaring at the woman, who stared out of the window.

Tomasz looked at her, and then realised that they were moving – the train had pulled away and now the city was becoming a blur through the window.

He settled back in his seat and exhaled. Then he put his hand in his pocket and felt the soft material of Kapaldi's scarf. He rubbed it between his thumb and forefinger, like a child taking comfort from a stuffed bear, and soon he started to fall asleep.

'Wake up.' He heard her voice, but it seemed to be coming from far away. 'Wake up,' she said again. And then he felt a nudge in his ribs. She was talking in German. Why was she doing this?

He opened one eye, then the other. The couple were still across from him; the woman staring out of the window, the man reading a newspaper.

'We are crossing into the Reich in a moment,' Zofia said. 'I thought you would want to see as we arrive.'

Her voice was merry, as if he really were Hauptmann Weber from Hamburg. 'We have just left Kutno station,' she continued as his nurse, his carer, his tour guide. 'I have shown our tickets whilst you were sleeping, but our documents have not yet been checked.'

He understood now why she had woken him. They were crossing borders; imaginary ones, as technically they were still in what Tomasz thought of as Poland, but it had been swallowed whole by the Reich.

'Soon,' she said, 'we go through Posen. You have been there, I think, once before, with your battalion. You remember, I think?'

Tomasz looked at her, nodded.

She smiled at him. 'It's lovely, Posen. Perhaps you will see it once more when you are completely better.'

He nodded again, wishing that he could take her hand in his. But he did not, and sat with his back straight against the thin stuffing of the carriage bench, waiting for their documents to be checked.

He did not have to wait long. A border official – short, pale and pudgy – arrived, seeming so stuffed into his uniform that the buttons threatened to pop off his jacket as he slid open the carriage door to the compartment. Behind him stood a tall, silent, dark-suited Gestapo officer.

'*Ausweis,*' the official said.

The man across from Tomasz stood up to hand over his documents and his wife's.

The fat official looked at the couple, then at their identification. Nodding, he handed them back.

Zofia went next, handing over her documents.

'*Und Ihre?*' he asked, looking at Tomasz.

'*Ich kümmere mich um den Hauptmann. Er ist immer noch schockiert nach der Explosion. Hier sind seine Dokumente.*'

Zofia spoke quickly; her German was certainly better than his. *I am taking care of the Captain. He is still in shock after the explosion. Here are his documents.*

The Gestapo officer now stepped forward to take a better look at the cards that the border official held in his pudgy hands.

'Where are you going?' the Gestapo asked.

'Berlin. And then on to Paris.'

'Why?'

'The Hauptmann has been reassigned,' Zofia said.

'I thought you said he was in shock?'

'He is. But he has been assigned a job for as soon as he is well.'

Tomasz tried not to speak, to add to what Zofia was saying. He tried to arrange his features so he would look ill. He gazed to the floor, allowed his shoulders to sag a little. The couple stared at him.

'Fine,' the Gestapo told the podgy official, who gave Zofia the documents and left the compartment.

Zofia sat down and put the documents into her handbag. She looked at Tomasz and smiled. 'Now, shall we look out of the window together as we go through Posen? There is a beautiful river there. A cathedral too. Lots of lovely orchards in the countryside. Perhaps we will both be able to spot them?'

He looked at her, then stood. He wanted to see it once more, once more for himself.

'You feel like a walk?' she asked.

He nodded, and they walked along the corridor, stopping at the door. As the train slowed, he saw the sign for Posen come into view.

Agnieszka was suddenly next to them, her eyebrow raised in concern. But she did not speak and pretended that this was the stop she was always meant to get off at.

The train juddered, then stopped with a sigh. 'We shouldn't,' Zofia said, quickly, quietly. 'It's not part of the plan.'

'We'll be quick. We'll get the next train. Please. Let me say goodbye to my parents,' he said. 'To my home.'

Zofia opened the door for them both, helped Tomasz off the train, still playing the role of nurse, and out to waiting taxis. Agnieszka did not follow. Instead, she waited at the station, buying tickets, and looking like this was the most normal day in the world.

They paid for a taxi to take them as far as the rutted track that led to the farm, and asked the driver to wait for them.

Hand in hand, Tomasz and Zofia walked towards the farm, and as they rounded the bend, they saw the charred ruin of his home.

Tomasz sprinted towards it as if it were still ablaze and he could stop its destruction. Zofia ran after him, yelling for him to stop, to wait for her, but he could not hear her anymore.

He ran inside the house, tripping on the broken, burned debris, searching for his parents. Finally, he stopped and looked around him. His father's rocking chair was still by the fireplace and somehow had miraculously escaped the blaze.

He walked towards it and brushed the ash and soot off the seat. He sat down, just as his father had done each evening, and creaked the chair backwards and forwards.

'Tomasz!' Zofia was out of breath.

'Are they dead?' he asked.

'I don't know. No one said anything to me about this.'

'Not even Zygmunt? Andrzej would know. He knows every-thing.'

'No one has said anything to me. I promise.' She looked around her, at the house she had visited, and he saw her wipe a tear away from her face.

'We should go.' He stood slowly and took her hand.

They both stepped outside and did not look back again at the charred house.

'Wait, one minute more,' Tomasz said quickly, as they began to walk down the track to the waiting taxi.

'Why?' she asked, but he did not answer her, and was already running away – running towards the woods as fast as his legs could go.

He was back minutes later.

'What did you do?' she asked.

'Something for Kapaldi. Just something I had to leave behind.'

She nodded and took his hand. 'We should go.'

By 3 p.m. the train pulled into Berlin, and Zofia's heavy sleeping head was weighting Tomasz's shoulder. He nudged her awake.

'I slept,' she said, surprised.

They left the train quickly, trying to navigate a way through the platforms full of people; bodies squashed together, chatter, soldiers, Gestapo, guns, families with cases, a child carrying a teddy bear with one eye. Pigeons flew upwards to the metal eves of the terminus roof, scattering feathers as they disappeared.

'Here,' Zofia said. 'Platform three.'

He did not have time to think, to worry about the eyes that watched everything around them. The guards were everywhere; they moved in between the flow of people, stood at exits and entrances. It was funny, they were less menacing here in Berlin. Perhaps because they were expected to be here. When Tomasz thought of them in their dark uniforms, walking through his hometown, their shiny boots pulled up past their calves, their heavy steps across the cobbles, he feared them. There they were misplaced, foreign and unpredictable.

The clamour of the station gave Tomasz the opportunity to talk to Zofia. 'I haven't seen Agnieszka,' he said, close to her ear.

'She'll be here somewhere,' Zofia said. 'Speak in German now, Tomasz, even to me.'

Tomasz nodded, swallowed his words, his voice, and boarded the next train behind his nurse.

This train was not as crowded as the other, and Tomasz and Zofia began their journey in a carriage to themselves. They were able to talk quietly, hold hands secretly, and for a very brief moment, he was able to kiss her.

But after a stop in Leipzig, they were disturbed by a heavily pregnant woman who looked at them both, and only entered the compartment after Zofia had smiled at her.

Tomasz reverted to being silent, but Zofia, who had seemed tired and pale most of the journey, now became animated with the arrival of the pregnant woman.

She asked her when she was due, where was she from, where was she going. Tomasz saw that the woman didn't really want to answer, but Zofia was oblivious.

'Do you want a boy or a girl?' Zofia asked her.

'I'd like a girl, I think. But I don't mind really; as long as they are healthy, it doesn't really matter.'

'I've always wanted two of each.' Zofia's face was almost dreamlike, and she placed a hand on her own stomach, imagining her future children.

The woman smiled at Zofia. 'I'll pray that you get what you want.'

Zofia was about to speak once more, when the woman placed her coat on the bench and tucked her legs up. She placed her head on her coat and closed her eyes.

Zofia sat watching the woman sleep, a smile on her face that Tomasz had never seen before, one he did not understand.

It was late into the night, perhaps just before midnight, when the train left the Reich and entered into France. A new country, another border crossed.

Zofia woke and went to use the toilet, leaving Tomasz and the pregnant woman in the compartment. Tomasz shook a cigarette from his packet and went out into the corridor to smoke it. He walked towards the rear of the carriage, seeing a window open near the door, and stood next to it, watching the smoke he exhaled travel out into the night.

He did not see the Gestapo officer, or the border official. He did not hear their footsteps along the corridor, or see them enter into the compartment. He did not know what the woman said to them or what they said to her. All he heard was a gunshot and the sound of a woman screaming. Then, silence.

He looked down the train corridor and saw the Gestapo officer talking to the border official.

A few heads peered out of their compartments to see what had happened and, upon seeing the Gestapo, quickly ducked their heads back inside, swiftly closing their doors.

Tomasz did not know what to do – he needed Agnieszka, Zofia.

Suddenly, the Gestapo shouted at the official who was shaking his head. Then, the pair turned from Tomasz and walked away quickly into the next carriage, towards the front of the train.

Zofia appeared by his side, her face pale. 'Is she…?' she asked. 'I think so.'

Zofia walked towards the compartment. Tomasz said, 'No! Zofia, no, you cannot go back in there.'

'My bag, Tomasz. My bag with our documents…'

'I'll go,' he told her. 'Stay here.'

Tomasz walked to the compartment, knowing what he would see, and he tried to ignore it, tried to step over the body that lay on the floor, face down, blood spilling out onto the slatted wooden flooring.

He picked up Zofia's bag and turned to leave, when he heard the woman moan.

'She's still alive,' Zofia said. Tomasz looked to the door where Zofia stood, her face paler still, her blue eyes too bright.

Zofia bent down, felt her neck.

'We need to leave, now,' a voice said. Agnieszka stood in the doorway, her eyes darting to the scene, then down the corridor. 'She had fake papers. They think she works for the underground; they'll search all of us, be sure of that now. Especially you. You two were with her.'

Tomasz shook his head; this couldn't be happening. More death. More. Would it never stop? He pulled Zofia up by her arm.

'We can't leave her.' Zofia was hysterical. Her voice was too high, too loud, and she spoke in Polish. 'She's pregnant. We can't leave her here.'

'Hush, Zofia!' Agnieszka warned. 'You want us killed?'

'I can't! The baby!'

Tomasz grabbed Zofia's arm roughly, pulled her to look at him. 'If we stay, we will end up like her too.'

'But…' Zofia pleaded, her face wet with tears.

Agnieszka checked the corridor. 'Come, quick!'

Tomasz had to drag Zofia out of the carriage, down the corridor, following his cousin. They reached the end, and Agnieszka opened a door into the luggage compartment.

Inside, cases and boxes were haphazardly stacked. Tomasz and Agnieszka scrabbled about, moving cases, boxes, until they could get to the other side where a slide door could be opened out onto the tracks.

'We'll need to jump.' Tomasz came back, took Zofia by the hand.

She shook her head. 'It's going too fast.'

'Ag, when is the next stop?'

'Soon, I think.' She checked her watch. 'Five or ten minutes, we should be stopping at Strasbourg. They'll get us all searched there. We'd still have to jump before the station.'

'I know, but it would be slower then, wouldn't it?' Tomasz asked.

Agnieszka nodded, her face pale – she hadn't done it this way before.

Suddenly, a noise of gunfire rang out.

'They're coming!' Zofia cried.

Tomasz looked at Agnieszka, the door; they were still going too fast.

'She's dead, isn't she?' Zofia was hysterical now, her voice high. 'She's dead, and the baby, the baby in her stomach!'

'Shhhh, shush now, my love.' Tomasz held her close, burying her face in his chest. 'Please, my love, you need to be quiet.'

'Tomasz, that box, there.' Agnieszka grabbed his arm.

Tomasz turned. Four large crates were stacked along one side of the carriage and Agnieszka was already opening them.

'They have clothes in them,' she said. 'Just clothes. We can hide in them.'

Tomasz opened a crate, got Zofia to lie inside. He helped Agnieszka into hers. Then he opened his own and closed the lid just as the door to the carriage was opened.

Tomasz was scrunched into a foetal position, his eyes looking through the gaps in the slats. He felt at his belt for his heavy pistol. Slowly, he took it from its holster, held it near his chest.

The clothes underneath him smelled of other people – used clothes. He could see some lace, some cotton, a dress perhaps – women's clothing. Tomasz could hear his own breathing and tried to calm it. In and out through the nose.

He heard footsteps and within seconds saw the uniform of the Gestapo. Tomasz held his breath.

The officer kicked at some cases, began to hum a tune, then walked towards the crates. Suddenly, there was the whistle of the train, deafening in the rickety carriage. They were nearing the station. The train whistled again, starting to slow.

The guard was at the crates now, humming again. Tomasz was cold all over. He needed to exhale. He tried to, slowly, quietly.

The Gestapo stopped humming. He was close enough now that Tomasz could smell him – musty sweat, cigarette smoke.

Then, there was a tap-tap on top of his crate, on top of the others. The Gestapo started to bang at the crates, louder, quicker, like a drum. Tomasz's heart beat as fast as they did. The train underneath him was slowing; the whistle sounded again. There was no time – he had to act now.

Suddenly, the tapping stopped. The officer bent low, his eye at one of the slats looking directly at Tomasz. Tomasz held his pistol against the slat and, as the train whistled once more, he pulled the trigger, the shot travelling straight through the Gestapo's eye into the back of his head. Tomasz pushed the lid off the crate and climbed out, his ears ringing from the sound of the gun. He opened the other crates, helping Zofia whilst Agnieszka jumped over the body and opened the sliding door to the tracks.

Tomasz turned and helped Agnieszka move the body whilst Zofia stood, silent and stunned.

'Quick,' Agnieszka said. 'The crate.'

Together they lifted the guard's body and hauled him into the crate, lowering the lid. Then, grabbing Zofia's hand, Tomasz took her to the edge of the doorway, looking out at the tracks running past, still at some speed.

'We have to,' Agnieszka shouted against the wind.

Tomasz nodded. Suddenly, Agnieszka was gone – out she jumped, into the grass on the side of the tracks, rolling in the dirt.

'I can't!' Zofia yelled.

'We have to. We can't get off at the station, and they will find that body. We have no choice!'

Tomasz looked at Zofia, her hair blowing out into the night. He pulled her to him, held her head in one hand, the other against the small of her back, and together he launched them from the train so that they rolled together down the embankment, finally coming to rest in the dust.

CHAPTER THIRTY-SEVEN

Zofia was gone. Tomasz felt about for her in the dark, finally finding her hand.

'Zofia?' he cried.

His hands felt around for her face, and he leaned down, his ear against her lips, listening for her breath.

'Is she...?' Agnieszka appeared beside him.

'She's breathing.' Tomasz sat back, held Zofia's hand to his chest. 'She's breathing.'

'We need to move, quickly. They'll be searching for us within minutes.'

'Zofia.' Tomasz shook her gently. 'Wake up. Zofia?'

'I'm awake.' Her voice was quiet.

'We need to move,' Tomasz said. 'Can you walk? Are you in pain?'

'I can walk,' she said. Slowly she pushed herself off the ground.

Tomasz held her close, hugged her, rained kisses onto her face.

'We need to go!' Agnieszka shouted at them.

Tomasz let Zofia go, held out his hand for her to take, and made to follow Agnieszka who had run towards the thicket of trees. But then he felt himself pulled back; Zofia was not moving.

'We let her die. We let that baby inside her die,' Zofia said.

'You need to run with me, you need to fight, just a bit more. Please, Zofia.'

There was silence. Just their breath curling into the sky.

'Please,' he said once more.

This time, Zofia began to move.

By dawn, they were still walking and were becoming more visible. Agnieszka was quick on her feet, although her face was blood-spattered with cuts from her jump, her tights were ripped and her knees bloodied, and kept them darting down streets, side alleys, gardens, so that it felt to Tomasz as if they were going round in circles.

'Where are we going?' Tomasz asked his cousin, who did not answer. Instead, she started to run away from them, sprinting towards the top of a hill.

At the crest Agnieszka looked back and waved to them to follow, to be quick. Tomasz tried to run, but Zofia could not, and he half dragged her towards his cousin.

'There,' she said. 'I knew I'd find it eventually.' Below them was a street of neat houses that bordered the embankment of a river. 'Never had to find it after jumping from a train. Usually, I'd get off at the station,' Agnieszka joked.

Tomasz smiled and looked at Zofia, who did not.

Agnieszka led them to the third house along and knocked on the door.

'Who is it?' a voice from inside asked.

'I've come to see Uncle Alfred,' Agnieszka said.

The door was opened by a slim woman in her forties, her hair pulled away from her face in a rough bun, her eyes keen and alert.

The woman did not introduce herself and did not ask any of them to tell her their names.

'Third room on the left for you two,' she said to Agnieszka and Zofia. 'Clothes and a washbasin.'

'Thank you,' Agnieszka said, and took Zofia by the hand and led her up the stairs.

'You' – the woman looked Tomasz up and down – 'second room. I don't know what will fit you. Choose the plainest clothes, I advise. No uniform. You're a peasant now.'

Tomasz nodded. 'Thank you,' he said, as the woman turned away from him and walked into the kitchen.

He washed his face, which was covered with dirt and small cuts. His hands were scraped and, when he undressed, he saw that his back had taken much of the impact of the fall and was red and tender to touch.

He found a plain green shirt that fitted him and a pair of brown trousers. He carefully unpicked the money and contacts that were stitched into his uniform and, pulling Kapaldi's scarf out, bundled them up in it and crammed it into his pocket.

There was a bed in the room and Tomasz wanted to lie in it, but he was scared to sleep. Instead, he sat on the edge and lit a cigarette. His brain was tired, and he could not arrange his thoughts properly. One moment he thought of Kapaldi, then the hospital, then the pregnant woman, her baby's blood on the floor of that carriage. Then he thought of the Gestapo officer, bleeding in that crate onto the used clothes.

Strangely, he started to think of the clothes. Why was there a crate full of used clothes? Who did they belong to? Where had they come from? If he could, he would have taken them, given them to the people in the ghetto.

There was a knock at the door. Tomasz tapped the ash off his cigarette onto the rug and with his foot brushed it into the weave.

'Come in,' he said.

Agnieszka came into the room and sat beside him.

'Where's Zofia?' he asked.

'Lying down. She's not doing too well.'

'Is she badly hurt?'

'No. But she's tired. And that woman, I think… what happened to her. She can't cope with that.'

'I should never have agreed to this,' he said, rubbing a hand across his face as if he could wipe away the tiredness.

'It's too late to go back now. No point thinking about that.'

'So, what now?'

'I've spoken with my contact downstairs. She's gone to send a telegram to the transfer cell in Paris. We can't go there now.'

'So, where do we go?'

'There's one other way we can try.'

'And Zofia?' he asked. 'Will she be all right, you think?'

'It'll be fine.'

Tomasz's cigarette had burned out; a small pile of ash was now on the rug. He looked in the packet – two left. He took one out and lit it, offering the other to Agnieszka.

'No, thank you,' she said.

'You don't smoke?'

'No. Can't stand it.'

'I used to hate it.'

'And now?'

Tomasz shrugged.

'I'll go and see if I can find us some food,' she said.

Tomasz nodded and dragged on his cigarette, then went to find Zofia.

She was asleep on her bed. He lay down next to her, pulled her body close into his and rested his head on her shoulder. Together, they slept until Agnieszka woke them hours later.

'We've got some transport, to Saint-Estèphe.'

Tomasz rolled onto his side and pushed himself up to sit and look at his cousin. The sleep had made him feel worse, and his body groaned with bruised bones and aching muscles from the jump off the train. He looked at Zofia, who had opened her eyes but lay on her side, staring at the blank wall.

'Why?' he asked.

'Why what?' Agnieszka said.

'Why Saint-Estèphe?'

'A contact has made the journey from there to England before. He's taking two other couriers tomorrow evening.'

Tomasz nodded. 'I'm thirsty,' he said.

'Get your things. There's coffee and some bread downstairs.'

Zofia still did not move, did not react.

'Zofia,' Agnieszka said gently. She walked over to her, placed her hand on her shoulder. 'You need to eat.'

'I'm not hungry,' she said.

'I know. But you need to. You know you do.'

He watched his cousin as she spoke to Zofia – there was something there, a familiarity that Tomasz hadn't known existed between the two.

Zofia finally started to get up, slowly pushing herself from the bed. Tomasz stood and placed his arm around her waist, holding her, taking her weight and guiding her downstairs.

The transport that Agnieszka had arranged was a small truck that held cows.

'You want us to sit with them? With the animals?' Tomasz felt as though he was going to laugh.

His cousin, though, was already climbing into the back, pushing cows out of the way – they responded with deep cries of annoyance. 'No one will look here, all the way at the back. Come on.'

Tomasz helped Zofia up, and made a path through towards Agnieszka who sat on a bale of straw at the back, with three cows' faces all looking inquisitively at their new guest. 'They're all right,' she said. 'They're used to this.'

Tomasz helped Zofia sit down and sat next to her. Then, there was the sound of metal on metal and darkness as the door was closed.

On the sides of the truck, small slats let in air and fragments of light. 'I can't stand the smell,' Zofia said. Then, she vomited onto the floor. She rested her head against Tomasz's shoulder, and he kissed the top of her head.

'It'll be fine,' Agnieszka said. But her voice was tired.

CHAPTER THIRTY-EIGHT

Almost a day later, the truck stopped. The three of them had slept for most of the way, their exhausted and beaten bodies grateful for the moment of quiet, of feeling relatively safe.

When they climbed out of the truck, the stench from the cows clung on to their clothes; even though Tomasz was standing by the sea, he could not smell the freshness, the salt of the waves. All he could smell was dung.

The truck drove away almost immediately, and Agnieszka led them through the dark to a small, pebbled beach. The air around them was still, and they stood for a moment, listening to the pull and push, the lap of the waves onto the shore.

'What time is it?' Zofia asked.

'I can't see my watch.'

'They'll be here soon, won't they?'

'You think we will be all right?' he asked, not looking at her.

'Yes,' she said, but Tomasz noticed something different in her voice. 'Are you wearing the scarf?' Zofia asked. 'I can't see.'

'No,' he said.

'You should wear it. It will bring you luck. Where is it?' she asked.

'My pocket.' He felt her pull at the pocket of his trousers, extracting the scarf.

'Now, look at me,' she commanded.

He turned to look at her and could just make out her features in the dark; the shape of her face, her long hair.

'I love you,' she said.

'I know. I love you too.'

'Good,' she said, and he felt her place the scarf around his neck.

She pulled the ends of the scarf so that his face came close to hers, and she kissed him.

'I love you,' she said again.

Tomasz was ready to answer, but at that moment, he heard the hum of an engine in the distance, then silence.

'They're here,' Agnieszka said.

Tomasz looked out towards the inky sea and saw the outline of a boat not far from the shore.

'You'll need to wade out,' Agnieszka said.

'And you too.'

'I'm not going,' Agnieszka answered. 'Here, take this pen. You have the one I already gave you? Take them. Tell them you are here to see Uncle Alfred, like I told you. Then, they'll ask you where I am. Tell them eyes were in Paris. More to follow.'

Agnieszka handed him the pen. He took it and hugged his cousin.

He took off his shoes and socks, put the pens inside and held them high above his head. Zofia did the same.

Together they waded out towards the boat. Now and again, he looked behind him to check that Zofia was all right. He could see her smiling at him in the darkness, holding her shoes high.

He checked once, twice. Then, just as he was within arm's reach of the boat, he checked again.

She was gone.

'Zofia!' he cried, turning.

Voices from the boat told him to shut up, but he didn't care.

'Zofia!' he screamed again.

His eyes roamed about, trying to see her.

'She's all right, she's all right!' voices said. Rough hands under his armpits pulled him into the boat.

'Zofia!' he screamed, dropping his shoes into the boat, scrambling to get to the side, back into the water.

'Here! She's safe! Look.'

Someone grabbed his arm, turned him to look, shone a torch that gave a weak beam towards the shore. There, the light picked out Zofia who was making her way to the beach. Agnieszka walked towards her, helped her out of the water.

The engine spurted into life, and the boat began to bob out to the sea, over the waves.

'No! Wait! Stop! Zofia!' Tomasz screamed, but his voice was drowned out by the motor.

He jumped over the edge of the boat, into the water. He could feel it in his nostrils, stinging his eyes. He stupidly opened his mouth to scream, and the saltiness swept in, making him gag, cough.

'Zofia!' he screamed. More water in his mouth. He went under a wave and swam upwards to get air. He gulped it in, took the air into his lungs, struggled to stay afloat, and tried to remember how to swim. His arms moved, his legs, but he wasn't getting any closer to shore, just like in a nightmare. He tried to swim back; he tried to get to her.

He heard the boat near him, the shouts of the men.

'Zofia!' he screamed again.

He could not see her; he could not see the shore. He tried to turn. Disorientated, he could not find the land.

Then, he went under. This time he could not figure out which way was up; it was as though his brain was filled with water too.

For a moment, he panicked. But just for a moment. Then, he stopped moving his arms, stopped fighting, and let the water pull him down. Just as the edges of his brain became fuzzy, his lungs burning as though they were going to explode, he was suddenly hurtling upwards out of the water. Then, he felt wood underneath him.

He coughed, spluttered, saltwater spilling from his mouth. Someone rolled him onto his side, put a blanket over him.

He heard the engine.

He did not look to the shore. He stayed on the floor of the boat, shivering. He felt another blanket placed over him, and another. Someone asked him something – was it in French? Where was he?

He was cold. He needed the scarf, Kapaldi's scarf. He checked his pocket, forgetting that it was already round his neck where Zofia had placed it. Instead in his pocket he felt something hard, the size of a chestnut and the same texture. He fingered its smooth edges, its shape. A heart – his heart. And Zofia had given it back to him.

CHAPTER THIRTY-NINE

Isla

Poland, 2015

Zofia sat back in her chair and looked over my head towards the window, where the world outside was obscured by a heavy net curtain.

'Now,' Zofia finally spoke, heaving herself from the chair, flashes of pain registering on her face. 'I go make dinner. Then you stay here tonight. Go walk outside and come back in a while.'

Agnieszka headed to the kitchen with Zofia. Andrzej sat on the couch, took the bundle of letters and the diary, and started to read.

Zygmunt and I obeyed Zofia and left the cottage. Although night was drawing in, it was light enough to take in the surroundings. Neat beds of vegetables and flowers sat in her back garden, which sloped down over a grassy hill to a stream that ran under three weeping willows.

'Shall we sit?' Zygmunt indicated the bench under the trees.

I followed him and watched the stream ripple over the stones.

'She was here all the time. Everyone knew,' I said, almost to myself.

'Yes, everyone knew.'

'Did Grandad?'

Zygmunt shook his head.

A wood pigeon flew overhead, then settled itself in the branches above us, cooing to its mate. 'Ah, I know that sound,' Zygmunt said and smiled.

I watched as he cupped his hands together around his mouth and called back to the bird.

'Our secret call,' he said. 'Andrzej was good at this, but your grandfather was the one who taught it to us. He was the best.'

I smiled. 'He probably still is.'

'Does he not remember anything anymore? All the memories are gone now?'

'I'm not sure. I think sometimes he has good days when he remembers everything – I hope so, but I can't say for sure. But then there are times when he forgets what day it is or who I am or where he lives. But I think the memories are still there – somewhere.'

'It will happen to us all.' Zygmunt seemed more hunched over, older than before, as if the stories, the memories, had taken their toll on him. 'But now you know it all. Now you can understand who your grandfather was. Who he is.'

'I can. Will you come and see him?'

'Me? I'm too old to travel far. And perhaps seeing me will upset him – if his memories are broken, it might upset him.'

I nodded. He was right.

'Dinner!' Zofia's voice rang out, disturbing the pigeon, which flew away, leaving a fluttering of feathers falling from the sky in its wake.

That night, I could not sleep. I shifted and turned in the small single bed in Zofia's cottage, getting more and more irritable as the night wore on. I felt guilty too, for lying in a bed that belonged to the woman who my grandfather had been in love with.

Sleep was not going to come, and my mouth was dry, so I sneaked out of the room to the kitchen and got myself a glass of water. It was only when I walked back to my room that I saw a figure sitting in the living room, motionless.

'Zofia?' I whispered.

Nothing.

'Zofia?' I ventured closer to her and placed my hand on her shoulder.

'I am awake,' she said, making me jump.

'Sorry,' I said, embarrassed.

'No – sit. I am thinking of you.'

I sat across from her, and suddenly light filled the room as she leaned over and switched on a fringed lamp.

'You look like him, you know,' she said.

'I know. I have his nose. It's too big.'

'No. It's perfect. Like your grandfather. Perfect.'

I smiled at her.

'I left him because of the baby,' she suddenly said.

'What baby?' I leaned towards her. 'A baby?' I questioned again.

'Mine. I was pregnant. Agnieszka knew. So did Zygmunt and Andrzej. Just your grandfather. He did not know. I could not tell him.'

'Why? He would have taken care of you.'

She shook her head. 'I wasn't sure it was his. I thought it was maybe to be Franz's. And would he really want to take care of me then? But I wasn't sure. Tomasz and I, when he was in hospital…' She trailed off. 'I missed him; we had missed each other.' She looked down at her hands so that I could not see her expression. Then, she raised a hand and wiped it over her face, wiping away the silent tears that were now falling. I stood and wrapped my arms carefully around her, feeling how delicate she really was.

Soon, she pulled away. 'Sit,' she said. 'Sit.'

I sat down. I watched her shift in her seat. 'I am so old,' she said, as she placed another cushion behind her. Finally, she was comfortable. 'I looked at the baby when he was born. He lay in my arms, and I looked to see if he is like Franz or Tomasz, but it looked like a baby.'

'Boy or girl?' I asked.

'Boy,' she said, smiling.

'A beautiful baby boy. But I could not love him properly – he could be Franz's baby. Then, what if one day he is like Franz? What if he is mean, dangerous and violent like him?'

'When did you know?'

'After about five years, when he was a little boy, he became more like his father. But by then it was too late, and he thought I was dead, and that is that.'

She heaved herself from her chair and walked unsteadily towards a cupboard. From it she pulled a framed picture and came back, handing it to me.

I looked down, seeing a man – a man who looked just like my father. A man who looked just like Grandad.

'I have a piece of him, you see. Always, a piece of him,' she whispered, smiling.

I sat holding the photograph, looking at my uncle.

'You never told Grandad?' I asked her.

She shook her head. 'It was too late,' she said. 'Too late.'

'What's his name?' I asked, already knowing the answer.

'Tomasz,' she said.

I stood and took Zofia in a strong embrace, feeling her body relax against mine. When I pulled away, we were both crying. She kissed me on the cheek and made her way to bed, leaving me alone in her living room.

I wiped away the tears from my face with a tissue and blew my nose. I took a notepad from my bag and started to take notes of what she had said, what everyone had said, recording my grandfather's history through memories, letters and stories. There were gaps – there always would be – and perhaps one day I could fill them. For now, though, I looked at the rough notes, the dates, the people now in my life, and wondered how much of this I could really trust.

It seemed to me then that our history wasn't just fact. Our history was much richer. It was handed down through stories, it was documented by witnesses, it was a memory – sometimes our own and sometimes others'. All of it was interwoven, with no distinct start or end. I thought of my own history. So far it wasn't a rich tapestry. It was based on careful decisions, on trusting fact. This trip had been the most exciting thing to happen in my life, and I realised that I couldn't go back to my sterile existence of work, gym and a gin in the evenings alone. I wanted my history to be more than that. I wanted what my grandfather had – people to create memories with, people who would always remember me.

I closed my notepad and climbed the stairs to bed, feeling more hopeful and freer than I had in years.

CHAPTER FORTY

The following day, I left Zofia behind and returned to the farm. I booked my flight home for the following afternoon – I needed to go, I needed to think about what I knew and what, if anything, I was going to do with it.

Agnieszka wanted a last hoorah before I went and organised a dinner party that evening, inviting Stefan, Zygmunt, Zofia and Andrzej.

We sat around the table, eating the *bigos* stew, knuckled ham and vegetables that Agnieszka had made. Stefan had brought a *babka* cake filled with chocolate and cinnamon, and Zofia had brought *paczki*, Polish doughnuts with orange and strawberry jam fillings.

The air was filled with Polish, the language swarming over me, and although I didn't understand any of it, I liked that it was a part of me – that all these people I had never known were all a part of my existence. Their decisions, their journeys, their lives had all culminated in my grandfather being in England, staying there and marrying Gran, raising a family. It was incredible to think how many people had such influence on so many lives.

'You're quiet,' Stefan said. 'All this too much? I can make them speak English.'

'No, no, it's fine. They're all catching up with each other, it's like a reunion for them. Look at them.'

Stefan looked: Andrzej, for the first time since I'd met him, was laughing at something Zygmunt was saying. Zofia seemed animated now she had Agnieszka by her side, and now and again the two of them would fall silent and squeeze each other's hands.

'Fancy a walk?' Stefan asked. 'Last look at the orchards?'

'Sure,' I said. 'Why not.'

Outside the moon was full, and we walked down to the edge of the orchards towards the river.

'What will you do when you go home?' he asked.

'I don't know yet. Get back to normal, I suppose.'

'And what is normal?' he asked.

I shrugged. 'It's weird to think that I have an uncle,' I said, changing the subject.

'Are you going to tell your grandad about him?'

'I don't know. I don't know whether it would do more harm than good. I mean, he can't remember, so why tell him he had this whole life happening without him?'

'Do you think it's your decision to make?'

'I don't know that either.'

'Maybe tell your gran first and your parents. See what they say. Ask Zygmunt and Zofia too, perhaps. It's their story too.'

I nodded. 'You've been great, you know. You've really been a help with it all. Maybe if you visit London some time, I can repay the favour?'

'Sounds like a plan,' he said.

'I'll miss this,' I said. 'It's so quiet. So peaceful.'

'I'm sure it will miss you too.'

I felt Stefan's hand graze mine as he said it.

'Time to go back?' I asked.

'Sure,' he said. 'Time to go back.'

Agnieszka and the others were in the living room when we returned, all of them drinking a nightcap of vodka.

'Join us,' Agnieszka said, moving up on the couch so I could sit next to her and Zofia. 'I'm sorry that we were talking so much earlier – it must have been so boring for you.'

'It was nice,' I said, accepting a glass from Zygmunt who poured me a hefty measure.

'You'll be glad I'm leaving, I'm sure,' I joked to Andrzej.

'Not glad,' he said. 'At peace, though.'

Suddenly, I remembered something. 'The diaries,' I said to him. 'How did you get them? The ones from when he was in the army. Your father couldn't have had them. They were Grandad's.'

'He gave them to me,' he said, and poured himself more vodka.

'Why though?'

He shrugged. 'He sent me them after he got married to your grandmother. Said he wanted to think of the future now.'

'And you kept them,' I said.

'Of course. Why wouldn't I? He's my brother.' He nodded, his speech slurring a little now.

Andrzej was a mystery to me. On the one hand, he was belligerent and seemed to care little for family, then, on the other, he had looked after his brother, his friends and his parents.

Seizing on his drunk state, I decided to ask a few personal questions. 'Were you ever married?' I asked.

'Of course,' he said.

'And?' I tried to get him to elaborate.

'And what? I was married. We had children. She died. My children are busy working. Now I am old, and you come here and bother me.'

I smiled at him. 'Such a lovely story,' I joked.

Zygmunt laughed and slapped his knee. 'He was always a romantic man!' He laughed again.

'Ignore him,' Agnieszka said. 'He's always been that way.'

Zofia reached into her handbag and passed me some letters – the letters she had read from, the letters from my grandfather.

'You take these. It's only right that you have his memories now.'

I kissed her on her cheek, the skin soft and paper-thin.

*

The following day, as I loaded my bag into Agnieszka's tiny car, Stefan arrived for work.

He gave me his hand to shake and said he would keep in touch and maybe visit London one day. I leaned towards him and kissed his cheek, smelling the light, fresh deodorant he wore, and the smell of him that could not be bottled. We wouldn't see each other again, and for the first time in my life I felt so utterly sad about it. It all seemed too bleak, so fleeting, so – pointless.

'See you,' he said and smiled.

'Yes. See you.' I climbed into the car and did not look back.

CHAPTER FORTY-ONE

England was just as I had left it. If anything, it seemed a bit greyer after the countryside of Poland. Arriving home, I switched on the kitchen light and dumped my bags on the floor. It was cold in the flat and smelled musty, even though I had been away just a week.

I flicked on the kettle and turned the heating up. Once tea was made, I sat on my couch and wondered what I was meant to do now. Could I really change my life?

The phone rang before I could think about the answer. It was Dad.

'Isla?'

'Yes.'

'It's Dad!'

'I know. It says so when you call.'

'You're back!'

'I am indeed. I messaged yesterday to say I would be, though.'

'Well, that was yesterday, and this is today, and I want to hear everything!'

I pinched the bridge of my nose, which was still painful from my cold. 'What about tomorrow?' I suggested.

'Tomorrow? No, that won't do at all. I told your gran you had gone to Poland, you know, and she wants to hear about it too.'

'Why? I told you it was a secret.'

'Well, you know me, can't keep things in for too long. Anyway, I won't take no for an answer. Be there to pick you up in forty. Well, depends on the traffic. If we go the way your mum wants to go, then it will be an hour. Yes, it will!' he shouted to my mother, who mumbled something in the background. 'Then, we'll go to see Gran for dinner. All right?'

I shook my head and said 'Yes' into the receiver, my brain working as quickly as it could, trying to pick out what I should and shouldn't tell them.

'Well, look what the cat's dragged in!' Gran walked towards me and held me in a strong embrace.

She made tea, and we sat together in the living room. All of them leaned forward, waiting for me to start.

'Where's Grandad?' I asked.

'He's already in bed. Couldn't keep his eyes open any longer. Goes to bed whenever now. Sometimes, he's up till the crack of dawn, sometimes, he goes in the afternoon.'

'OK.'

'So, you saw Andrzej, your dad told me. What did he have to say for himself?' Gran asked.

'He told me about Grandad and the war a little bit…' I ventured, still unsure of what I should tell them.

'And?'

'And, I'm not sure what to say. It's such a long story.'

'Isla, I'm old, I can't wait forever. I can see on your face that something is wrong, that you know something that is upsetting you. So, spit it out, for goodness' sake.'

I was going to tell them about who I had met, about how Grandad had come to England on a little boat, and leave the rest out. But my mouth had other ideas, and before I could stop myself, I was telling them about the newspaper article, the first visit to Andrzej and then the second – and as I told the story I found that it was as though it were falling into place. I could see it all now – see it as a whole.

It was past midnight by the time I had finished.

'I have a brother?' Dad asked – again.

I nodded. 'His name is Tomasz,' I said.

'I knew about Zofia,' Gran said, almost to herself, 'but a baby?'

'You knew?' I asked.

'Of course. Your grandad told me she was the first love in his life. We have no secrets from each other.'

'You knew about her leaving him?'

'Not a clue. I never asked him. That was the past, and we were excited about our future. No need to know any more.'

'I have a brother,' my dad said again.

I wasn't sure whether Dad's reaction was good or bad, and I felt guilty that I had spilled out all of Zofia's story without even asking her if it was OK to do so. 'You all right, Dad? Should I not have said anything?'

'Don't worry, sweetheart,' Mum said. 'He's had a shock. Needs time to get used to it. Come on, Graham, let's get you home to bed.'

'You'll stay though, won't you, Isla?' Gran asked me.

'Yes,' I said, worried that perhaps knowing Grandad had another child had upset her more than she was letting on.

Dad stood up and Gran gave him a hug goodbye. Then, turning to me, she gave me a quick kiss on the cheek. 'Get some sleep, Isla, we'll talk more in the morning,' she said. 'And I'm fine, I'm not upset,' she added, as if reading my mind.

The problem was, I couldn't sleep. I tried not to think about Grandad's story, and found that all I could think about was Stefan – the awkward kiss on the cheek, that little flip in my stomach when I remembered the way he smelled. I turned over again.

'Isla.' I heard a whisper and sat up in bed.

'Who's there?'

'Grandad. Turn the light on.'

I switched the light on, and he came over and sat on the edge of my bed in his green paisley pyjamas. In his hands he held Kapaldi's scarf. His face was animated, his eyes wide and bright.

'I see this downstairs when I go for water. I see this and poof! Like magic I remember whose it was. I showed it to your gran, and she tells me that you went to Poland…'

I nodded and felt a lump in my throat. I climbed out of bed and wrapped my arms around him, feeling his head rest on my shoulder and his hand pat my back.

'Now, now. You sit. You sit now and you tell me. What you do in Poland, what you know now about this scarf?'

'I found a picture,' I began, 'something Andrzej had sent you years ago when he was mad at you. It was you with another soldier—'

'I wasn't a Nazi,' he interrupted. 'I wasn't.' He felt around in his breast pocket and pulled out a dull piece of metal. 'I got this. Your gran, she hid it from me. I should have got rid of this, should have buried it. But I kept it, to remind me to be a good man. A good husband. Never to be what this medal means.' He handed it to me – the German Iron Cross for bravery.

'I know, Grandad, I know.'

'But I was in their army. And I killed my friend. You know. This scarf…' His fingers stroked the material.

I wrapped it around his neck. 'I know, Grandad, it's all right.'

He placed his hand on my cheek and looked at my face, as if trying to memorise every detail. 'You're a good girl, Isla. A good girl.'

I kissed his forehead.

'You know everything?' he asked. 'You know all my memories?'

'Almost,' I said. 'I know Zofia left you on the beach.' Then I remembered something she told me: *When he was a little boy, he became more like his father. But by then it was too late, and he thought I was dead, and that is that.* Why would Grandad think she was dead? And then there were the letters, describing my grandfather leaving. How had she got them if she'd left him on a beach? I handed him the letters, told him what she had told me.

'I sent her letters,' he said. 'Many, many letters, after she left me.'

I nodded.

'I saw her again too,' he said, his watery eyes scanning the faded ink on the paper.

'You saw her?'

He nodded. 'It's funny how I remember things now. I am sure in the past things were different, but now they are so blurry around edges. When I think to my childhood, I can remember some places – pieces of memories, but not the whole…'

CHAPTER FORTY-TWO

Tomasz

England, 2015

It's funny how I remember things now.

I have moments when I remember everything and it is so clear, Isla, I want to cry out, tell the world that I am back, but I get scared to move in case the memories disappear. So, I sit and close my eyes, watching them like a film playing out on my eyelids, until they become blurry again and I wonder where I am, and why I am sitting in my pyjamas when the sun is up.

Tonight though, I remembered – not everything, but some things – and instead of watching those scenes for myself, I decided to be brave and tell you, Isla, what I know, what I can see, before it all goes away from me again.

I can't see all of the war, the early years, but I can see some of the pieces, so the whole must be true. I can feel it all. I can feel the fear, the tiredness.

I remember Kapaldi, his death. I remember being in a white room and a nurse taking me away. You tell me that the room was a hospital and that the nurse was Zofia, and this makes sense to me. I remember funny things about that. I remember another nurse coming into my room, and I hid under a blanket. I remember being in a car, and Zygmunt drove, and I wore a uniform that was not mine.

The train journey I remember too. Pieces of it. The bad pieces, but I wonder if that is all of them; perhaps there are no good pieces from that journey?

The Gestapo officer I shot and hid in the crate, jumping from the train. The fear. I feel that again. I feel it all the time, even though I cannot remember the memory that created the fear.

When I think of Zofia, I think of a colour – blue. She is and always will be the lightest yet deepest of blues at the same time. Can you understand that? If I close my eyes, that's what I see – light blue, and yet I fall into its depths too.

It is the blue that I remember now.

It was night. I flapped about in the freezing sea, trying to get back to the colour of blue, Zofia, who was walking away from the shore, becoming smaller and smaller. I was dragged from the water, dragged up and out until I lay back on the floor of the motorboat, feeling the engine vibrate underneath me and the sting of salt in my eyes and throat.

I don't know how long I lay on the floor of the boat. I know I began to shiver. My teeth rattled against each other, and I felt as though they were louder than the engine. Someone put a blanket over me... then, something in my hand. I can see it now; opening my hand, seeing that wooden heart, Zofia's heart. I wrapped my hand around it, holding it tight, feeling it against my skin until it hurt.

Perhaps I fell asleep, but I remember a call, a shout. 'Land!' someone said.

Then the other two start to sing a silly song about drinking and women and someone laughs. They are happy: they are free now perhaps. But I am not.

But I get up, sit up and watch the land appear, a pebbly beach, grey skies, and drizzle. I can see some green behind, but that is all. This is England then, I thought.

The other men all lit cigarettes and one was given to me. I took it and smoked it quickly, watching as the beach came into view and three men stood on it, all of them holding black umbrellas.

I heard something above me – a cry. I looked up at a swarm of white and grey birds. I know now that they are called seagulls, but then, I hadn't ever seen them before. I didn't like them with their screech. I didn't like the look of the men with umbrellas, and I didn't like all that grey.

The boat stopped a few metres from the shore so that we had to climb out and our feet got wet. The seagulls above me cried louder now that the dawn had broken, and I wanted to climb back in the boat, go back to Zofia. I felt inside my breast pocket and the pen was there, so I started to walk towards the beach.

'I'm here to see Uncle Alfred,' I said to the short fat man in the middle of the other two – his umbrella was bigger than the others. My English was not good, and I could see I had made a mistake.

'Alfred,' I said again. Then I repeated it again in Polish.

The man nodded. 'We've been expecting you,' he said. His Polish was perfect.

'You're Polish,' I said.

The man laughed. 'Of course I am.'

I felt like I should know who the man was, and I felt foolish for not knowing that a Polish man would be there to meet me.

The men turned and beckoned me to follow them to a black car parked just off the beach. I followed them.

Now I am in an office.

It is warm in the office. I am sure I must have got in that car near the beach, but I do not remember the journey, and I do not know where that office was. Perhaps London. Yes, London, it must have been.

The man who had the bigger umbrella sat behind a desk, and he told me his name was Pavel.

Pavel had red cheeks as if he'd been outside in the cold for too long, or perhaps in the warm. He smiled a lot, Pavel. He reminded me of Andrzej for some reason, and I remember wondering why, Andrzej was never one to smile.

I liked the office. It had a carpet and colourful wallpaper, and an English lady brought me cups of tea and some cake. She told me, slowly so that I could understand her English, that she had made the cake herself. I liked the cake, full of sugar and butter, these things I had not tasted for such a long time.

I ate the cake quickly, licking my fingers. She brought me some more, and fresh hot tea. Yes, I liked that office.

But then Pavel started to ask me some questions, and I wanted to leave.

'So, your brother, that's Andrzej?' Pavel asked me.

I nodded. I didn't understand why he was asking about Andrzej.

'And the code word you were given, the pen, that came from one of our couriers, a girl?'

I nodded again and almost said Agnieszka's name but wasn't sure whether I was supposed to.

'But you are not a courier?'

'No,' I said.

'You were in the Wehrmacht.'

'Yes.'

'Tell me what happened. Tell me how you came to fight for the Germans and then end up here, with a pen and a code word you shouldn't really know.'

I swallowed the cake that had been in my mouth while he questioned me.

I told him the story as best I could, and he wrote it down and told me it was all going to be fine as long as I told the truth.

When I had finished talking, I felt sick, and I asked Pavel if I could go to the toilet, my stomach was not used to the sugar.

Now I cannot remember anything else after that. Strange what my mind chooses to remember and what it leaves out. I told you, didn't I, that my mind is going, that I lose my thread? You are writing this down? Ah yes, I see that, so you don't forget, Isla. Very clever!

Where was I? In England, on a toilet! That is funny!

Yes, wait a minute, let me close my eyes and think for another minute. All right, yes, OK, I see now.

I am on a train.

This train is nice. There are no German guards, just English people. I sat with Pavel. He said he is taking me to Scotland.

The seats were green like peas, like the peas your grandmother makes – very green. There was a hole in the seat next to me and some fluff was sticking out, and I kept poking my finger in it and pulling more out.

I was thinking of Zofia on that journey. I was thinking about how she left me and why. But my head was swirling round and round, and I could not come up with an answer. Perhaps she was too afraid, perhaps she thought I would be safer without her. But Agnieszka was helping to walk her away from the beach. Then I began to think maybe Agnieszka made her go away from me, and then I started to pick at the fluff again on the green seat.

You ask me if I was sad? Yes, of course sad. But I was tired, Isla. It was a tiredness I had never known before. All I had seen; all I had done. My friend Kapaldi. You know about this? I did this, I shot him. That woman, a woman on the train and the blood and losing Zofia – all of this made me so tired and so confused I could not think. All I wanted to do was lie down and not wake up until it was all better, just like a child. But I could not.

'You feeling better now?' Pavel asked me, and he was rubbing his fat belly.

'A little,' I said to him.

'You need to watch what you eat for a few months. Take it easy. No rich things.'

I nodded at him, then closed my eyes. I didn't want to talk, I wanted to sleep.

'You need to learn some English too. I got you this.' Pavel gave me a book.

I opened my eyes and looked at it and turned some pages, then closed it again.

'Don't worry, you'll soon pick it up,' Pavel said.

I closed my eyes again.

Who was Pavel, you ask me, Isla? Pavel worked for the Polish government in exile. He was, an in-between, you know, an in-between the couriers and the British intelligence. A liaison, yes, a liaison. He had to question me, you see, because of the pen and what was in it, and because I was in the German army. He wanted to see if I really had been forced into it and if I had learned anything. I told him everything: Lieberenz, what was happening in ghettos what was happening to Polish men – being forced into the army. Pavel said that a lot of soldiers had come to England already, leaving the German army behind them. I wasn't the only one you see.

Now, my thread is gone. No, don't apologise, it is not you, it is my head.

Yes, a train, I was on a train and going to Scotland.

Scotland was raining. Sorry, Scotland was rainy. That is correct English. I was getting cross about the rain now; everyday, all day grey and rain.

Pavel took me to a rich house, a fancy one, your gran would say. It was like a castle with little things on the top – turrets? Yes them, it had turrets on the top. It had lots and lots of windows. I thought maybe we were at the Queen's house, but I didn't want to ask this to Pavel.

'Requisitioned by the Parachute Brigade. Largo House, a stately home,' Pavel told me as we walked into the hallway.

'Parachute?' I asked him. I had never jumped in a parachute before. Why had he brought me here?

'Yes. I told you I had the perfect posting for you. You're here to train. You're now part of the First Independent Polish Parachute Brigade. No longer a German now, Tomasz. You're back to being Polish.'

'But I have never done this,' I told him.

'Be brave, Tomasz, you will learn.'

I was a little bit scared, but then I remember I feel something I had not felt for a long time – I was excited.

When I had been a little boy, Andrzej and me would take our sleds in the winter to the top of big hills and race down. Whenever we went to the top of a hill, I had the same feeling – scared and excited. That day in that big house in Scotland with the rain, and the grey, and no Zofia, I felt something from my past, of who I used to be, and it made me happy a little.

I was given a room with some men and the room was clean and quiet and they said to sleep for a while and eat and get strong again. I don't know how long I did this. I remember they gave me a uniform, a Polish one now, and it was too big for me – I had gotten so thin. And they said keep the big one because you will get bigger and it will soon fit you.

I wrote letters all the time to Zofia when I am not sleeping; I tell her what I am doing, what I did before. I tell her about how, in the hospital I imagine I am seeing Kapaldi and we talk and he forgives me, and I tell her that I dream of him still and sometimes I still think he is with me. I ask her if she thinks I am crazy as I can't tell anyone else. I write to Agnieszka too and ask her what happened. I need to understand it. I send letters to my parents' house, her parents, Agnieszka's – I send them anywhere I can think. For weeks I get nothing back. Nothing from anyone.

But, I could not sleep forever and think about Zofia – I was now in the Polish army and they wanted me to train and I wanted to show everyone I was Polish, not German and if I could, I could go back to Poland and find Zofia.

How do I know she is in Poland? I don't know. Maybe she is in France. But why would she stay in France? She would go home. She didn't know anyone in France. Doesn't matter to me anyway, I just need to leave England, be closer to where she might be or where I may see someone who can help me.

I make new friends in Scotland. Aleksander who is from Gdańsk and Jakub from Kraków. Jakub was like me, was forced into German army, and his brother who refused to join was sent to Auschwitz. Aleksander, he was different. At beginning of war, he came to England and joined straight away Polish army. He was my sergeant and he trained me, but he was like rest of us – all joking and smoking together, all happy to be speaking Polish and to feel Polish again.

You know, they were the first friends of mine since Jan and Eryk – and yes Rolf. You know, Jan, he died maybe two months after I left him. He shot himself. Eryk, he disappeared. Just gone, poof, into the air. Maybe he is caught by Russians and taken away, but me, I like to think he got away too. Got free.

They were correct about the uniform, it soon fit me like two gloves. You laughing? Ah, yes, like a glove, not two gloves? But there are always two gloves. Anyway, it fit me just nice now.

I still write to Zofia. First almost every day. Then, just a few times a week, then, soon, I am writing once a month and I am now in Scotland for one year! Can you believe it?

One year.

Every day we go to a place called the Monkey Grove – it is where we climb a big tower and practise jumps down. I liked jumping.

Every time I was scared, but then at the bottom, I was excited and wanted to do it again. It was the only time my brain was quiet, and I did not think about Zofia or my family. I just think about the jump, and being good at it.

Then, we go up in planes to practise. I don't remember if this is my first time I think of now, but I remember going up and the engines so loud and there is a door that is open for us to jump. I look through the door and see below me some clouds and I wonder what it will feel like to go through them – will it be soft? Cold?

Under the clouds I could see green trees and fields. Aleksander tells us where we are to jump and where we must aim.

I think it was Jakub who went before me and I sat and watched him disappear.

The engines are still loud now, the air is rushing in and Aleksander is shouting at me to get ready and I feel my heart beating; beating, so quick and so angry against my chest and then suddenly I am flying. Oh Isla, it is wonderful. My mouth is dry and my heart beating so fast and I am thinking about when I must pull the cord. But then, for a moment, is just nothing. Just falling. Flying like a bird. I go through clouds and they are not spongy and soft but that is all right. Then under the clouds, then the ground coming closer, closer. *I must pull it now*, I think, but I almost don't want to; I want to keep flying.

But I pull it. The parachute sends me upwards again, away from the ground, and it pulls underneath my armpits.

I have to think now, pull left, right so that I get the correct field. I see everything below me, trees and fields, and little roads. Then lower, some cows, cars moving on the roads. Then finally the grass, the green is rushing towards me so fast that I don't have time to think and then, thud, just like that, with a thud, I am on the ground.

Jakub is there and he claps for me, says well done, you are now proper parachute soldier.

When was this? The jump? In springtime, I think. Or maybe later. I don't know. It was the next year from when I arrive, so what year is that do you think? 1943. Yes, that is probably right.

One day, maybe near the jump, I don't know, but Jakub comes to me when I am in my room and I am polishing my boots. He says, 'You have a letter.'

I was shocked. Almost one year and no one had sent me anything and now I have a letter.

He gives it to me, and I look at the handwriting on the envelope and I do not know it. I stopped polishing my boots and I decided to go outside to the garden to sit and read it.

I remember now the smell. I stand on the stone steps and they go all the way down into the garden and someone that day has cut the grass. I breathe in that smell and breathe out. There was a bench near a small lake in the garden and I went to sit on it. I opened the letter, quickly, so I wouldn't think too much about what could be inside.

I did not read it straight away, instead I read to the bottom where I could see who it was from and it was from Zygmunt.

Then, I read from the top. He tells me he went home, to see his parents and he saw the letters I send to Zofia. He says to me, I am sorry Tomasz, but Zofia never came home – neither did Agnieszka. There were some bombing raids and they think that perhaps they were caught in them.

As I am reading the words, over and over again, some rain starts to fall, and it makes all the words become blurry. I quickly fold the letter and put it into my pocket. As I do, I feel the heart, Zofia's heart. I took it out and looked at it – my heart from when I was a boy.

Soon, I felt water on my face. *The rain*, I think. But no, it was my tears, falling from my face just like the rain. I wiped them away with the back of my hand and suddenly, I feel empty, all of me, empty. I cannot explain it. My stomach, all my insides are gone, just a body left.

In anger or because I am in pain, I threw the heart away from me, into the lake, watching it sink to the bottom and disappear. She is gone. Zofia is gone.

We must stop a minute now. Just a minute, Isla. Let me catch my breath, my thoughts. So many things racing around now in my head about Zofia, about my feelings. It is too much. No. I don't want to stop. Just give me a minute. Let me rest my eyes. Let me see what comes next.

When I close my eyes, I try to see it, like a film. But I told you, it is blurry and there are big gaps, black, and no matter how I try to see it in colour, the memory remains black.

I went to my room after reading the letter, then it is as though things speed past me: more jumps, parachuting, drinking with Jakub, singing songs, but inside I am still empty. Then a train. I am still in England, I think. I go somewhere else to train, but I am now the teacher. I am showing British men how to do what I do.

It is near the end, almost the end of the war, when I am sent away. I was surprised, because it has taken so long, I thought I would never go back to war. I would just teach.

It was just after a summer. When is France free, Isla? Check the history. I cannot remember. 1944? Really? Are you sure? That means I was here in England for two years before I saw war again. It does not feel that way to me.

It was after summer, and I remember this because there was an Englishman called John and it was his son's birthday soon, and he was angry that we were going so close to it. September maybe? I was with the Polish Parachute Brigade part of First British Airborne Division – see you can see on my medals.

It was a night-time when we were to go. But the fog was in and we could not. All the men were twitching their feet and smoking and could not rest. You see, when you must jump, you get lots and lots of energy. Then, when they said we could not take off, we were sat on our bunks with all this energy and nothing to do with it.

We all smoked a lot. I played cards with Jakub and with John who got angrier and angrier. He wanted to be at home you see, with his family. He was from Yorkshire. A big strong man. He remind me of Eryk.

But, maybe the next day or the next, I don't know, we were finally on the plane and they said we were going. As the plane started to pick up speed, I felt sick. It was actually happening.

'Going to Driel,' John said, looking at the map that was being handed round.

Driel was not where we were supposed to go. We had a different landing site, but I cannot remember where. All I know is that we were scared now. We hadn't studied the maps, hadn't looked at the landing sites, nothing.

Me and Jakub looked at the map John gave us for as long as we could. Each of us promising that we would look out for the other.

Suddenly, it sounded like there was a hailstorm. Ping, ping, ping, on the metal.

'Bullets,' John says.

The hatch at the back of the plane was opening.

'We have to jump now?' Jakub shouts. He is scared. There are bullets.

I said to Jakub I will go in front of him and I did. I edged out, like the others, one at a time until there were all these men falling from the sky, while a gunner on the ground tried to shoot us like some ducks he wanted for his dinner.

I was not scared this time. I don't know why because I should have been. I was worried more about the landing and what to do when I reached the ground. I knew I would get there – dead or alive.

Maybe a minute later, I was there and there were two men lying on the grass, and they were bleeding. I turned to see that one of them was Jakub. I checked his pulse, but he was dead. The other man – I did not know his name – he was dead too.

I was so angry with myself. I had promised to look out for Jakub, and he was dead. I know it was not my fault, but it felt like it was.

There were some more shots, more. So loud too. I couldn't think.

I remember I ran. What else could I do? All these German and guns and there was me and I could not see the rest of the brigade. Maybe they were all dead?

I found some trees. There were apples on the ground and for a second I thought maybe this was all a dream and I was at home in Kowalski's orchards.

But then a voice – John. 'Get digging,' he says to me.

We start to dig foxholes to protect us, and some more men come, and more. We all dig then settle into the dirt; our guns balanced on the edge.

Then, I looked at John and saw a little teddy bear in his top pocket.

'My son gave it to me,' he said. 'His favourite. It will keep me safe.'

I nodded. I understood. I had Kapaldi's scarf in my own pocket. We had funny thoughts, didn't we? A scarf and a bear to keep us safe from those machine guns!

'See that one over there?' John asks me.

I took the binoculars from him and I could see a German helmet. Suddenly he starts to fire and John begins to fire too.

I feel in my bag and my hand goes around a grenade and I pull out and throw.

Then I fire and I keep firing until all bullets are gone. When I fire, I am thinking about the woman in the house in Kraków. The woman who say to me, *Polen sind nicht willkommen.* I cannot not stop thinking these words. Over and over. I put more bullets in the gun, start firing again and I see man go down, then another, and there is something in me now, I feel I am crazy and I keep wanting them all to go down – *Polen sind nicht willkommen, Polen sind nicht willkommen.*

'Grenade!' John shouts and I think he means for me to throw one, then suddenly I was in the air, twisting and turning. There was dirt everywhere, and I could not see John. I see now there was an explosion – someone had thrown a grenade in our foxhole – but then, I didn't know what was happening.

I hit something hard. So hard. There was a ringing in my ears, and my mouth was full of blood. I tried to find John, but my head was so full of pain I closed my eyes and let myself go away.

CHAPTER FORTY-THREE

When I woke, it was dark. The ringing in my ears had stopped a little and I could hear the guns still, but they were further away now.

Next to me was a fallen tree and under it was John. John's hands were on my legs, as if he had been trying to pull himself out from underneath it. I put my hand on his hand and squeezed it. I knew he was dead.

I needed to move. I tested my legs and arms and they all working. I checked in my pocket for the scarf – it was still there.

Slowly, I moved around in the dirt, feeling for a gun. Instead, my hand found the bear, John's bear. I took out Kapaldi's scarf and wrapped the bear in it – I would give it back to his son.

Every time I tried to stand up, I seemed to walk sideways, and my legs were like that jelly you would have at your birthday parties. I had to sit down instead. I was trying to think of what I was supposed to do now, but my brain was so slow.

Then, I see two men, and I think that they are German, and I wave my hands in the air to surrender. 'Polish,' I say to them. And then I fell into the dirt and in my head was blackness.

No, no more breaks, Isla. I am all right. I am getting tired, so if I stop now, I will sleep and then tomorrow it will all be gone.

Now, I am in hospital.

There are lots of lights and voices. Someone is asking me if I am awake and I could not answer.

It was an English voice. Was it John? I tried to turn my head so I could see who it was.

The voice said: 'You're all right, mate. Took a bad beating to the head.'

'Who is that?' I managed to ask.

'Willie. My name's Willie.'

'Where are you?' I asked him. I couldn't move my head properly. There was white above me.

'To your side. In the bed next to you. A good thing you can't turn your head – I look like shit!' He laughed.

'Where am I?'

'Hospital. Field hospital. You're still in the Netherlands, mate. Not home just yet.'

Then I don't know. More blackness. Then a new voice was asking me if I was awake.

'Where am I?' I asked the voice. Maybe, I thought, I was dead this time?

'It's Pavel. You're in hospital. You hit your head. Do you remember?'

I opened my eyes and looked at him. Why was he here?

'Don't try and move or speak. Just rest. I wouldn't have woken you, but I have to leave. Warsaw calls. Things are happening very fast now. But I heard you were here, and I heard something else too, something that may interest you.'

'What?' I asked. I was cross that he was here. I wanted to be asleep.

'Lieberenz,' Pavel said. 'And Zofia.'

I didn't understand what he meant. 'Zofia is dead,' I told him.

'Since when?'

'I had a letter. She never went back home. She and Agnieszka disappeared.'

'Not sure why anyone would tell you that. Agnieszka is still a courier. Zofia is in Paris.'

'Help me sit up,' I commanded him. As I sat my head swam and the room was moving a bit and I had to really concentrate to keep my eyes in some focus.

'Lieberenz, it seems, was in Paris when it was liberated last month by the Americans and British. He was there with a woman who has been identified as Zofia.'

'Are you sure?'

'Sure, as I can be.'

I couldn't understand. Why had she gone to Paris? Why was she with Lieberenz?

'I have to see her,' I said to Pavel.

'I'm not sure you can,' he said.

A nurse came, told Pavel he had to leave.

'Please!' I shouted to him as he walked away. 'Please!'

The next few days I tried not to sleep too much. I tried to stay awake and eat and I wrote to my brother, to Zygmunt, to everyone about what Pavel had said.

Next I remember a new voice. 'You awake?' An English voice but had funny accent sound.

I opened my eyes and there was a man stood next to my bed.

'Tomasz?' he asked me.

'Yes.'

'Get dressed.'

The man handed me my uniform, did not tell me his name, why he was there, all he said was, Zofia.

I changed as quickly as I could, and the man led me from the hospital, and I was put into a car and the car sped away towards her.

Isla, get me some tea? And a biscuit. I need that. Do we have whiskey? Your gran hid it, see if you can find it. You won't get in trouble with her. I'll sort her out. Yes, whiskey now, no tea, no biscuit, the whiskey will do.

Do you not want some? Ah yes, you young ones these days drink those colourful drinks, don't you? You're not eighteen anymore? Are you sure? I'm getting confused, Isla. What was I saying?

Paris? Oh yes. I was telling you about Paris. About Zofia. Wait, let me have some whiskey. Let me try and remember it all.

I am in Paris.

It is hot here and I don't know why. It is not summer anymore – or maybe it is – just it is stretching and stretching on forever. The streets are dusty and busy and there are soldiers everywhere – Americans and British.

The man who brought me here, a courier, I think he must have been. He said he would help me find her, and then I had to go back to England. He would take me, he said.

In the street I saw a boy hit his friend with a stick, then he laughed and hit him again. It made me angry that he did that and I wanted to shout at the boy. I didn't shout though; I didn't say anything to anyone.

The courier took me to a bar. He said that she had been seen here. We sat in the bar, then at one of the tables on the pavement and he bought me a drink and gave me some cigarettes.

I smoke for some time and then there is some noise in the street, and it is like singing but shouting. Chanting, yes, chanting something in French and I don't know what it means.

The courier says that it is the partisans and they are shaming any collaborators with the Germans. I asked him what he means, and he says we will go and see.

We walk towards the chanters and there are lots of people now watching something that is happening in the middle of it all. I push forward to see. People are clapping and shouting and are happy that someone is being punished.

I keep pushing forward because I cannot see, and then I do.

I must take a breath now. I wish I hadn't remembered this. This is something no one should see.

There are some women. They are kneeling on the floor. And someone next to me throws some rotten fruit at them and a man who is smoking a pipe, he takes the pipe from his mouth and he spits at them – brown, tobacco spit – and it hits one of the women and she wipes it away with her hand and she does not look up to see who has done it.

I look at the women, each one, kneeling in the dirt. They have no shoes. Then I look across the women, the third, fourth and then the fifth, and then I realise that this woman is having her hair cut off. All of it. It is falling around her, and a wind comes and takes some of the hair up into the air and it floats away, and it lands on the kerb nearby.

The woman is not looking up. And I turn to the courier and I ask him why they are doing this. I say these are women and this is not right. But he will not answer me, he just stares at the woman with her hair being cut, and now she is nearly bald.

Then, the woman looks up. She has a dirty face and it is streaked from where tears have gone all the way down and then I see her eyes. Her blue eyes. It is Zofia. The man who is cutting her hair has now stopped and everyone is crying out and shouting these French things I don't understand, and the heat is making them all crazy I think, and the dust and dirt is everywhere. I cannot think. It cannot be real and first I turn away from it and then force myself to look again.

It is real. It is real and I think I must have tried go forward to free her from those men, but the courier man stopped me. He grabbed my arm and pulled me back. There was more shouting now, from the man above Zofia and I do not know what was said – he said things to them in French and they were angry at him, at me. And Zofia, who had been looking at me, was still looking, and there was something in her face, something I cannot understand.

I shout out that I love her in Polish and she smiles, then she hangs her head again and one of the men grabs her arm and drag her away and the courier is talking quickly in French now, so quickly, waving his arms and hands and I want to just get a gun and shoot the man who has Zofia, but there are so many people, so many of them angry with the heat and I can see they want blood and I must be clever.

The courier pulls me aside, says that Zofia is the fiancée of a German Colonel. And they say they want the colonel, and I say to the courier, I know who he is; tell them we will find him and bring him here and they must give me Zofia, and the man, the partisan who has a big moustache, says all right. Bring the Colonel and you can have Zofia.

When we walk away, the courier tells me I am stupid, how are we going to find Lieberenz? I have no idea, but I say to him that he, the courier, is clever, has lots of contacts, and I am sure we can find something out.

We stay in a small hotel that night and the courier goes out and tells me to stay in the room and he will come back. He is mad at me because I am making him take more risks to find Lieberenz. He knows he can do it. He just does not want to take the risk, I think.

I sat on the edge of the bed and I tried not to think about my Zofia and Lieberenz. But then, I started to understand it all you see. All of it – she was doing it to save me. Think Isla – she helped me out of hospital, I was brought back from a battleground to work in Warsaw, and she sent me away to England because she knew Lieberenz would keep using me for what he wanted. He was an evil man, Isla. Evil man. There was just black in his heart, like tar. And he wanted nothing but suffering.

I sat on that bed and I smoked cigarettes and I got angrier and angrier and I wanted to kill him. It is first time in my life I ever wanted to kill someone. So much anger, Isla. I pray you never feel it. It made my head hurt, and I didn't know how to make it stop.

The courier comes back though, and this stops me from going mad. Now, he tells me his name – Benoît, he said. Call me this, he says, as I have been calling him courier and he doesn't like it.

Benoît says that a transfer cell know where Lieberenz and some others are hiding, and they will tell the partisans. So Benoît says we sit and wait now, for the handover. But I don't want to wait. I want to see Lieberenz one last time, I want to see him taken away by those angry French men.

So Benoît agrees, but says if I get hurt, he will say that he was never involved, and I agree and that stops him from being so angry about me and what I am making him do.

We go to a building far out in the city. Benoît drives fast like he knows every street. When he smokes, he does it at the side of his mouth and I watch him, smoking on one side, blowing the smoke out the other. It is funny, but watching him makes me feel like everything will be all right.

The building we go to is strange. It has been bombed on one side but the other side you can still live in and then suddenly you would open a door and there would be no room on the other side, just the outside world.

We can hear noises inside and we go in and Lieberenz is there and three men, one of them is the man with the large moustache, and they are speaking to him and hitting him.

Then, he sees me and his face, Isla, his face is suddenly full of relief, for here I am his trusted friend. Here I am – that man he has used and taken his girl from him too. But it's all right for him to do this because he is German, and I am a stupid Pole and I am owing everything to him. I feel the anger again. It is rising and rising, and I can barely breathe, and then he says something which makes the anger worse:

'Ask him,' he says to the men. 'He knows me. I am no colonel. I am a soldier. Just a soldier, and I was forced into this army.'

Can you imagine! He is taking my story, taking the stories of all those men who he forced into the army and now he wants my help.

The moustache man looks at me and says, 'Well?'

I did not answer the moustache man. I spoke in Polish to Lieberenz.

'You let them take her,' I said to him. 'Why should I help you? You deserve this. You made this happen to yourself.'

'I don't understand?' he says to me and he is looking confused at me. 'Tomasz. My friend. What is wrong? I was worried when you disappeared, but I didn't let anyone search for you. I let you go. I was good to you. I knew you needed to go. You had been through so much…'

'Stop!' I shouted at him. 'Stop this! You did not help me. You used me. You took Zofia for your own. You used her!'

He was still acting confused Isla, still confused. 'But she loves me,' he says.

'Why did you leave her with these men?' I asked him.

'I had no choice! I had no choice, and she knew this, and she offered to protect me because she loves me.' He was almost crying now and for a moment I am starting to think maybe he is right. Maybe he is telling me the truth. Maybe Zofia never loved me and maybe he has been trying to protect me too?

But then he says something because he is panicking now, and he needs me: 'She is no good Tomasz! No good. Don't think of her. She is nothing but a whore. She used you and then she used me to get what she wanted. Can't you see that? I thought she loved me, and you thought she loved you. She used us. We are friends Tomasz you can't—'

Then, before I know what is happening, I am hitting him, quick hard fast punches in his face until it is covered with blood and he is now still.

Benoît stops me from killing him and pulls me away and I am breathing so quickly like I have run the whole of Europe. 'He is a colonel,' I tell the moustache man. 'He is everything you think he is. He murdered people – people like you, like me. He is who you say he is.'

He nods and says something to the other men, and they drag Lieberenz from the house and Benoît speaks to the moustache man.

'What will happen to him?' I ask, but I know the answer, I just want to hear it.

'We will kill him,' he says. Just like that. Simple. We will kill him.

I am sorry if that upsets you Isla. It must, I am sure. But it was a different time then, and I cannot say that I felt upset that he would be killed. He had killed my friends, he had made me kill Kapaldi, and he had stolen my Zofia from me – almost had her killed to save himself. I did not care. He had played a game with me, with my life, because he could use me, torture me and finally destroy me.

Benoît says to me that the moustache man tells us to go to our hotel and he will send Zofia there. One of his men will bring her, he says.

*

Benoît and me, we go back to the hotel, and I wash the blood of Lieberenz off my hands and Benoît goes and buys us some whiskey, and we sit and say cheers, because now, it is over. Zofia will come to me and then we will go.

We drink for some time and then soon there is a knock at the door. I am like I was when I learn to parachute, all jumpy, and my heart is beating fast again.

I get up and open the door and Benoît is smiling, happy for me. But, when I open it, there is no Zofia. Instead, there is a man.

'Tomasz?' he asks me.

I nod.

'Here,' he says and hands me a letter and then he is gone.

I go and sit down and Benoît leans forwards to look too and I open the envelope and I read a letter.

Wait, I stop here now. I give you the letter. I don't want to read it again. Once is enough. You ask someone to translate for you tomorrow and you add it to your story. But now. Leave it. All you must know is that Zofia is dead.

To my love, my Tomasz,

I want you to know that I love you and I always have. I write this quickly now. I saw you today and I wanted to cry I was so happy you had come for me, but I am tired, Tomasz. So tired. So much has happened, but know that I was not with him because I loved him. He forced me as he forced you, and I only stayed here to protect you, Tomasz. I wanted to protect you just as you tried to protect me.

They have him, I know. And they will kill him. They won't kill me, Tomasz, but I am already dying. I can feel it. I am so cold, so tired, and I cannot breathe. I am sick, Tomasz. I have been sick for some time.

They know I am unwell now. They know it is too late. They said I can write, and they will bring you this.

I must go now, my love. It is my time to go. Please do not think of me too much. Move forward in life and find someone else to love.

Remember only the good times, remember lying in the orchards, hand in hand, looking at the shapes the clouds made above us. And whenever you see a rainbow from now on, think of me. Think of me, and Kapaldi, who brought us together that day at the fair.

I love you.

There is nothing more to say.

Zofia

I remember after reading the letter I made a noise, like a wolf howling, or like a dog that had been hit by a car. I could not contain the pain inside, and I started to throw things around the room and scream and cry.

Benoît stood back and let me. He did not stop me. But soon the owner of the hotel knocked on the door and told us to stop and I sat on the floor with my head in my hands and I cried and cried until I was so exhausted I fell asleep, right there on that cold floor of the hotel, with all broken bit of furniture around me.

Wait. I need minute. Yes, I am crying. It is all right, though. It is good I tell you this. I see you are crying too. I wish I could have saved her. But the biggest thing that makes me so sad is that she died alone. Without me. I am glad now, for my memory being terrible. Because before, every day of my life, I remembered this. I remember that image of her, with no hair, and so thin and afraid, and I imagine her dying alone and I cannot forgive myself. But now, I do not remember mostly. And it makes me glad that tomorrow I will forget. I am all right, Isla. It is the end now. I am so tired.

What? What time is it? Did I fall asleep? Ah, look! Your grandmother is awake. You woke her, Isla, for me? Why? I am not upset. Ah, maybe I was. My memory is not good.

Come here, my love, come, and sit with me now. I am telling Isla the last bit, the bit where things got better. I am telling her when I met you.

I was in a hospital again in England. Still I was not right from that explosion in Driel, and I would not eat because I was so sad about Zofia and I wanted to die myself.

Every day, I lay in the bed with Kapaldi's scarf around my neck, and I wished that this was the day I would die.

Then, one morning, a new voice is near my bed.

'I like your scarf,' it says. 'Colourful.'

I turn around and there is a new nurse standing there.

'I'm Helen,' she says to me. 'They tell me you won't eat?'

'I'm not hungry,' I say to her. But I don't turn away from her because she has a nice smile and is so pretty and kind and she smells nice.

'I like colourful things. It's good, isn't it? Makes you feel all cheerful.' She came close to me and stroked the scarf. 'You know, the sun is out. We could take a little walk in the garden? Maybe after a walk you will be hungry?'

'It is raining,' I said to her. 'Has been raining all the time since I came back.'

'Sun's out now, though. Trust me.'

She holds out her hand and I take it and she leads me out to the garden and I am so weak I have to lean a little on her, but she is strong and she makes jokes to me and makes me smile. Soon, I am a little happier that I am walking in the garden and I think maybe I will eat a little something for my dinner.

Then, we decide to go back inside as she is worried that I will do too much, and just as we are about to go inside, I look up at the sky and you know what I see, Isla? I see a rainbow.

CHAPTER FORTY-FOUR

Isla

Poland, 2015

A strong breeze blew through the field; the long grass whispering to me as I walked, the heavy clouds above promising rain. I made my way to the caravan and sat on the front steps watching the river, snaking its way silently, listening to the late-autumn apples in the orchards make a soft thud as they hit the ground.

The others would be here soon, yet I still did not move from my position in that field. I had the scarf around my neck.

I closed my eyes and listened to the sounds around me, imagining my grandfather as a child, imagining Kapaldi as a child, making a small wooden cross for his mother who had conceived him here, and died here too.

This field, however bland to the outsider's eye, held so much life within it, and I felt oddly at peace – as if it was where I was meant to be all along.

Soon, my father and mother would walk to this field, helping my grandfather, grandmother and Zofia – a belated birthday party for Grandad.

I still felt so incredibly sad for both my grandfather and Zofia. She had left him in Paris, lying that she thought she was dying, thinking still that her child could be Franz's when all along it was Grandad's son. He had carried the pain of believing she was dead for years, and he would never now fully realise the truth – it was too late.

Tomasz, my uncle, would come too today, helping Agnieszka, Zygmunt, Andrzej, all of them coming together to remember Kapaldi and Kowalski, and all their friends and family who were now gone. And finally, Stefan. He would come here and help me and my family say goodbye to the past that my grandfather had lived through, and help him celebrate his birthday, a birthday that he would quickly forget, but one that we would all remember always.

For now, though, just for now, it was only me. From my other pocket I pulled out the diary entries I had copied from my grandfather's journals, and Kapaldi's scribblings which told of Kapaldi's life and how he came to learn how to make rainbows appear.

My Polish, whilst still sketchy, was good enough to make out the instructions.

I looked to the sky and could see that the sun, whilst weak, was strong enough to break through the cloud. Soon, there was a clap of thunder and the sky seemed to darken. The storm was beginning.

I stood up and began to dance in a circle, twirling my arms high above my head. I tried to chant, tried to make the kind of strange noise that I imagined Kapaldi, the Rainbow Man, would have done. Soon, a drop of rain fell onto my upturned face, and I stood still, feeling the water fall onto my body, soaking me to the skin.

It was almost time.

I waited again for the sun to reappear through the clouds, never doubting that it would. Slowly, I opened my eyes, and there above me, the rainbow appeared.

It was over now. It was the end.

I went back to the house, where my grandfather sat in Agnieszka's garden at a long table laden with food. His dementia had grown rapidly worse, and by the time we got here, he could not remember anything.

'Tomasz,' he had said to the man. 'The same name as me.' Then, he smiled.

Younger Tomasz, now in his seventies, had white-blond hair and the same blue eyes as Zofia. He was gentle with his father, pouring him a glass of wine and offering him food. He talked as if my grandfather knew who he was, and told him about his life and his family.

'I took my family skiing last year,' he told him. 'They really loved it. Perhaps you can meet them one day.'

'Skiing.' My grandfather suddenly looked up, clear-eyed. 'I can't ski – but you and me, Andrzej, we went sledding so much! You remember? We stole Tata's old barn door and made a sled, and he was so angry!'

'Pah!' Andrzej laughed and slapped his hand on the table. 'I remember!'

Zofia looked at my grandfather, and I wondered if she was waiting to see if he remembered the day he met her in the snow, sledding from the biggest hill in the village.

He looked at her and smiled, then turned to Tomasz, his son. 'What's your name again?' he asked.

I saw Zofia turn away, but then Gran took hold of Zofia's hand and gave it a squeeze. 'You're in there somewhere, don't you worry,' I heard her say softly.

In that moment, I felt as though my heart was going to burst with love and pride, for Gran and for all the family. I hoped I could live up to who they were and what they were able to accept in life, and not let them down.

Here they all were, back together once more, all the memories coming together one last time. I had hoped my grandfather would have a lucid moment on his visit – long enough to remember everyone and everything – just a moment so they could reminisce, laugh and tell each other about their lives. I realised, however, that it probably wouldn't happen, but perhaps it was for the best this way.

Grandad recognised Zygmunt and Agnieszka's names but had trouble joining the dots that they were the same friends from his past.

Suddenly, as Agnieszka brought out a roasted ham, Grandad turned to look at the orchards. 'Kapaldi,' he said.

Everyone quietened and watched him.

'Kapaldi,' he said again. Then, staring out into nothing, he said: '*Niedługo Cię odwiedzę. Przygotuj ognisko i wino to co ostatnio, pamiętasz? To czerwone. Przywiozę twoją apaszkę. Nie udało mi się sprowadzić deszczu. Idź już. Niedługo się zobaczymy.*'

Grandad turned back to look at us all. 'My friend,' he said. 'He came to see me. I told him I would see him soon.'

The silence around the table was too much, and I wasn't sure what was happening. Then Gran stood and kissed him on the cheek. 'Not just yet, my love,' she said. 'Now. Do you want some of that lovely ham?'

Grandad nodded and everyone started to talk again, but I could not take my eyes off where Grandad had been looking. I tried to figure out, with my limited Polish, what he had said.

I felt a nudge at my side, and Zygmunt whispered into my ear: 'He said, "I'll come see you soon. Get the fire ready. Get me some of that wine – you remember, the red one. I'll bring you back your scarf. I could never make it rain! Go now. I'll see you soon."'

I looked out beyond the tableau, at the orchards which spread down to the river, their leaves dancing in the evening air. The pigeons cooed to one another from the woods, readying their nests for their mate. I imagined I could hear the tinkle of chimes in the air coming from the too-far-away broken caravan, which sang a song that only a few would understand. Tears pricked my eyes, but I did not wipe them away.

Suddenly, I heard Stefan laughing loudly at something Andrzej said – a joke about selling him his childhood home, the burned carcass we had visited, for an extortionate price.

'It's not funny,' Andrzej admonished Stefan. 'I need the money. I may be here for a few more years yet, and I like the idea of a cruise.'

'You are ridiculous.' Zygmunt waved his spoon in the air. 'Ridiculous!' Then, he dropped the spoon on the stone paving.

'And you're drunk,' Andrzej retorted.

'I'll get you a new one,' I said, standing.

Zygmunt handed me the spoon he had picked up. 'Can you hear the chimes?' he asked.

For a second, I thought he meant the chimes from the caravan, but then I heard it, the ding-dong of the church bells alerting us to the time that had now passed. I smiled at him and walked inside.

'Hey,' Stefan said, following me. 'I've not had chance to talk to you yet.'

'I know. It's all been a little bit crazy. Getting Grandad here, after everything had come back to him so vividly, hoping he would remember still, and then he forgot again.'

'At least you did it for him. You found out his story. You gathered his lost memories.'

'I guess,' I said.

He picked up a carafe of wine and went to walk back outside.

'Wait,' I said. 'Wait.'

He turned.

'I thought about you when I got home.'

'You did?' He raised his eyebrow.

'Yes. I did. And I was wondering if perhaps we should go on a date or something?' I could feel my cheeks burning as I spoke.

He grinned at me. 'But you live in England and I live here.'

'Well, we can figure that out, can't we? I mean, there are no guns, no Nazis banging down our doors, no war raging outside. The only problem we have is distance – basically a flight. We can sort that, can't we?'

Stefan looked outside for a second – at my family, at his friends – then he turned to me and kissed me on the nose, just as my grandfather used to do to Zofia. 'All right. We can sort it.'

He started to walk outside again, then turned around. 'What are you going to do now?' he asked. 'Your mum said you had quit your job? Are you staying around here for a while?'

'Perhaps. I have something I was thinking of doing, and doing it here is as good a place as any.' I stood at the kitchen counter, tapping my fingers on the wood. My laptop was on the kitchen table, and I picked it up, along with a few diaries and some of the letters.

I sneaked away from the party on the terrace and walked through the orchards, hearing the whisperings of the leaves to one another. Finally, I reached the river.

I sat and opened my laptop. Then, I began to type.

This is Poland…

A LETTER FROM CARLY

Hello,

Firstly and most importantly, a huge thank you for reading *The Rainbow*. I hope you enjoyed reading it as much as I enjoyed writing it.

If you want to keep up to date with my latest releases, just sign up at the following link. I can promise that your email address will never be shared and you can unsubscribe at any time.

www.bookouture.com/carly-schabowski

The inspiration for *The Rainbow* was one born from my own family history – it portrays a little-known historical wartime experience of Polish men and boys who were forcibly conscripted into the Wehrmacht. Little has been written about the fate of Polish soldiers in the Wehrmacht, whether in historical fiction, in German or Polish academic works or biographies, while in the UK, the part played by Poland in the war more generally has often been sidelined. Whether through trauma or shame, it is not known why their stories were not recounted.

As a child, my grandfather would tell me the story of his journey to England from his home country of Poland; his memory, to me, seemed sharp and yet the facts were bland – he was a soldier in the Second World War, and he came to England

and trained with the Polish army in exile. When the war ended, he stayed and married my grandmother.

It was only years later that my grandmother revealed he had first been a soldier for the Wehrmacht, and only subsequently joined the Polish army upon arriving in the UK.

Upon questioning, my grandfather did not wish to speak of his experiences in the Wehrmacht – whether through shame, trauma or both, he never said. Yet, there are memories I have of him telling me a story about how he was captured as a boy; he hid in the woods, his brother was too young, and he alone went into the German army, forced at gunpoint. When I think of this memory, however, I cannot help but question whether he told me this himself or it was in fact my grandmother.

I asked my family what they knew and there were variations on the theme: he hid in the woods but was captured; he was in Poznań for ice cream and rounded up; his father made him go after he was threatened by Nazi soldiers. This, then, is the problem with memory for a writer of historical fiction; it is handed down through Chinese whispers with each person's memory playing tricks on them, and each of them filling in the blanks of the forgotten parts.

There were other fragmented memories that I recall being told about: a battle in France, a friend who died, someone in the family who went to Auschwitz – moments he suddenly recounted, yet even now I do not know whether he narrated these stories to me, or if it was a family member. It was these stories which embedded themselves into my mind and I could not let them lie; was my grandfather a Nazi or was he forced into it? Did it happen to others?

In *The Rainbow* I sought to reclaim this relatively unexplored story of a quarter of a million Polish boys forced into the German army. This is a story largely hidden from (or perhaps by) mainstream history; it is not the story of the victor or of the defeated; it is an in-between sort of story, more about people and less about politics, and one which has as yet been under-served by historical record.

It's always wonderful to hear from my readers – please feel free to get in touch directly on my Facebook page, or through Twitter, Goodreads or my website.

Thank you again,
Carly Schabowski

🐦 @carlyschab11

ACKNOWLEDGEMENTS

This novel has been seven years in the making; from a nugget of an idea in 2014 to being part of my research project for my PhD, it has consumed me in more ways than one!

A big thank you to Michal Rodzynski for his translations and help with the research for this book – his help was invaluable!

I would like to thank all the staff at Oxford Brookes University who provided ongoing support and encouragement, particularly James Hawes for his creative feedback on the novel.

I would also like to thank my friends and family for their support, including those of whom I sent endless drafts and begged for constructive criticism, including Alison Baxter, Benedicta Norell, Freya Alexander, and my agent, Jo Bell, who never gave up on this story and loved it as much as I did.

Also, a huge thanks to my editor Kathryn, who spots my mistakes and knows instinctively how to make sure the story comes alive in the best way possible.

Finally, I want to acknowledge my grandfather and all the men who were forced against their will into the German army. This story is for you.

BIBLIOGRAPHY

Books

Halbwachs, Maurice, *On Collective Memory*, ed. and translated by Lewis A. Coser (Chicago: University of Chicago Press, 1992).

Kochanski, Halik, *The Eagle Unbowed: Poland and the Poles in the Second World War* (London: Penguin Books, 2012).

Koskodan, Kenneth K., *No Greater Ally: The Untold Story of Poland's Forces in World War II* (Oxford: Osprey, 2009).

Kowalski, Stanley J. and Alexandra Kowalski Everist, *No Place to Go Home: A Polish Soldier's WWII Memories* (Baltimore: America Star Books, 2010).

Lucassen, Leo, David Feldman and Jochen Oltmer, 'Immigrant Integration in Western Europe, Then and Now' in *Paths of Integration, Migration in Western Europe* 1800–2004, ed. Lucassen et al (Amsterdam: Amsterdam University Press, 2006).

Pomykalski, Wanda E., *The Horror Trains: A Polish Woman Veteran's Memoir of World War II* (Pasadena: Minerva Center, 1999).

Schwartz, Lynne S., *The Emergence of Memory: Conversations with W. G. Sebald* (New York: Seven Stories Press, 2010).

Whitehead, Anne, *Trauma Fiction* (Edinburgh: Edinburgh University Press, 2004).

Williamson, David G., *The Polish Underground, 1939–1947* (Barnsley: Pen and Sword, 2012).

Zajac, Matthew, *The Tailor of Inverness* (Sandstone Press, 2013).

Online resources

1st Polish Independent Parachute Brigade: https://www.paradata.
org.uk/unit/1st-polish-independent-parachute-brigade

Dzieci Wehrmachtu Lektor PL (Documentary regarding Poles in
the Wehrmacht): youtu.be/aaLJfwCJhZc

Testimonies from Polish soldiers in the Wehrmacht: www.
wehrmacht-polacy.pl

Pomorzanie i inni Polacy w mundurach Wehrmachtu', *Czytaj
więcej*: (2010)

https://dziennikbaltycki.pl/pomorzanie-i-inni-polacy-w-mun-
durach-wehrmachtu/ar/320342

The Phenomenon of the Polish Underground State: https://
warsawinstitute.org/phenomenon-polish-underground-state

The Polish Institute and Sikorski Museum: http://www.sikors-
kimuseum.co.uk

Articles

Bitenc, Rebecca Anna, 'Representations of Dementia in Narrative
Fiction', *Knowledge and Pain*, 84 (2012), 305–329.

Mostafa, Dalia S., 'Literary Representations of Trauma, Memory,
and Identity in the Novels of Elias Khoury and Rabi Jabir',
Journal of Arabic Literature, 40:2 (2009), 208–236.

Parkinson, David, 'Night Will Fall: The story of file number
F3080', BFI (2018).

Paul, Marla, 'How Your Memory Rewrites the Past', *Northwestern
Now* (2014).

Taylor, Becky and Martyna Śliwa, 'Polish Migration: Moving
Beyond the Iron Curtain', *History Workshop Journal*, 71:1
(2011), 128–146.

Watson, Alexander, 'Fighting for Another Fatherland: The Polish Minority in the German Army, 1914–1918', *English Historical Review*, 126: 522 (2010), 1137–1169.

Documents from the National Archives, London

Letters, reports and memos regarding former Polish Wehrmacht soldiers arriving in the UK, including:

Captain Ludwick Kochanski Intelligence Report

Minutes taken from meeting regarding Polish prisoners and ex-Wehrmacht Polish soldiers: Prisoners of War Department, August 13, 1944

Uncensored Letters to the Wehrmacht: (W.P. 43) 358

War Cabinet Memoranda: (W.P. 43) 351 – (W.P. 43) 406, Vol. XL

Wolfgang Spirling Intelligence Report; 174/5A

Research undertaken in Poznań

Armoured Weaponry Museum
Military Museum of Wielkopolska
Muzeum Martyrologii Wielkopolan (Fort VII)
Muzeum Narodowe w Poznaniu (The National Museum)
Poznań Uprising Museum

Made in the USA
Las Vegas, NV
24 November 2021

35088855R00198